Y0-BCW-312

FLAMEOUT!

Too late. The missile, an AA-8 Aphid, slashed into the tail of Tomcat 233 and exploded. Beaver struggled to bring his aircraft under control, but the fight was clearly hopeless. While his own heat-seeker struck an enemy MiG, Batman screamed to his wingman. ''Punch out, man! Punch out!''

Beaver's Tomcat continued to fall, twisting in midair until it was upside down, pancaking toward the sea seventeen thousand feet below. An engine flared. Fuel ignited, and flame erupted like a bomb blast from the port engine. ''Beaver! Hard Ball! Eject! Eject!'' Two MiGs came in hard on Batman's own six o'clock. He lost sight of Beaver's stricken aircraft as he went ballistic, boosting hard, hot, and vertical. ''Beaver and Hard Ball are hit,'' Malibu called, as clouds rotated around the canopy of the climbing F-14. ''Beaver and Hard Ball are hit and going down. Negative chutes . . .''

Batman began jinking his Tomcat every way he knew how. But even as he maneuvered, he saw six new bandits breaking past the Viper One F-14s. The thin American line had been overwhelmed. The enemy was breaking through . . .

Also by Keith Douglass

THE CARRIER SERIES:
CARRIER
VIPER STRIKE
ARMAGEDDON MODE
FLAME-OUT
MAELSTROM
COUNTDOWN

THE SEAL TEAM SEVEN SERIES:
SEAL TEAM SEVEN
SPECTER

CARRIER

Book Five
MAELSTROM

Keith Douglass

JOVE BOOKS, NEW YORK

If you purchased this book without a cover, you should be aware that this book is stolen property. It was reported as "unsold and destroyed" to the publisher, and neither the author nor the publisher has received any payment for this "stripped book."

CARRIER 5: MAELSTROM

A Jove Book / published by arrangement with
the author

PRINTING HISTORY
Jove edition / April 1993

All rights reserved.
Copyright © 1993 by Jove Publications, Inc.
This book may not be reproduced in whole or in part,
by mimeograph or any other means, without permission.
For information address: The Berkley Publishing Group,
200 Madison Avenue, New York, New York 10016.

ISBN: 0-515-11080-9

Jove Books are published by The Berkley Publishing Group,
200 Madison Avenue, New York, New York 10016.
The name "JOVE" and the "J" logo
are trademarks belonging to Jove Publications, Inc.

PRINTED IN THE UNITED STATES OF AMERICA

10 9 8 7 6 5 4 3

PROLOGUE

Close-up camera angle of Soviet T-72 tanks rumbling in column along a highway, threading their way past heavy civilian traffic. Switch to shots of APCs and trucks, then of Soviet MiG-29s flying in formation low above city buildings.

"The continuing collapse of the Soviet Empire seems, ironically, to have brought the world closer to destruction than perhaps any time since the height of the Cold War. That, at least, is the private assessment of many military officials here at the Pentagon."

Shift to a slowly moving panorama of massed crowds gathered in a city square, then to shots of politicians addressing a gathering, of joyful people waving Czech and Hungarian and East German flags with the Soviet government crests cut from their centers, of scenes of young people clambering triumphantly atop the Berlin Wall as East German soldiers impassively look on.

"During the past eight to ten years we in the West have been witness to truly astonishing changes in the shape of world power. In 1989 we watched in amazement the so-called velvet revolutions, dramatic expressions of what came to be known as 'people power' toppling Communist regimes in Eastern European countries from the Baltic to the Black Sea. In 1991 we witnessed what appeared to be the ultimate triumph of people power within the Soviet Union itself, as old-guard Communist hard-liners attempted to wrest power from the liberal reformers of Soviet economic and political policy, and failed.''

More crowd scenes, these of enormous crowds gathered in Moscow and defending the Russian parliament building; of civilians surrounding and shouting angrily at confused-looking soldiers; of civilians clambering on tanks and APCs, waving Russian Federation flags; of massed demonstrators shaking their fists and chanting in unison; "Yeltsin! Yeltsin! Yeltsin!"

The scene shifts, then, to shots of empty grocery shelves, of weary-looking people standing in endless lines, and of an ominous-looking line of Soviet army marshals watching a military parade.

"Sadly, however, the sheer inertia of a nation as vast as the Soviet Union has always prevented any quick fix of the social and economic problems plaguing that country. With the reformers unable to reverse the collapse of the Soviet economy, unable even to guarantee bread on the grocers' shelves while half of the Russian harvest rotted in the fields, hard-liners within the military have reemerged as a significant power behind the scenes within the marble halls of the Kremlin. Where democratic forces sought to create a loose federation of sovereign states, the militarists pursued the reestablishment of a strong, central union. By late last year, it became clear that the militarists had won out, as tanks put down popular demonstrations in Georgia, the Ukraine, and within Russia itself.''

Rubble in a city street. People scattering in confusion and panic. Other people gathered in crowds, looks of horror on their faces. Fire engines playing streams of water on a demolished government building.

"Two weeks ago, a terrorist's bomb assassinated the latest of a string of reformist presidents of the Soviet Union as he attended a conference in the capital of Norway. Amid confused rumors of a Communist coup within that Scandinavian country and of possible civil war, Soviet military forces launched an invasion of Norway.''

More scenes of Russian soldiers, of an endless line of

tanks rolling down a country road as helpless civilians watch. File footage shows Norwegian soldiers deploying from APCs, firing machine guns, and patrolling on skis.

"Soviet government spokesmen insisted that the invasion was intended to restore order within Norway and that the incident was, quote, solely an internal matter concerning the sovereign peoples of the Soviet Socialist Republics, unquote. At the same time, however, Soviet forces also moved swiftly to secure the neighboring republic of Finland in order to provide a safe corridor through which they could outflank Norwegian border positions.

"In the first week of the invasion, large portions of northern Norway, from North Cape to Trondheim, as well as a pocket of territory in the far south around the capital of Oslo, were all overrun by Russian tank, ground, and airborne forces. Norwegian home defense forces have proven to be more stubborn than expected, however, and a large area in the south-central part of the country, centered around the city of Bergen, remains under the control of free Norwegian forces.

"President Connally's support of the Norwegian resistance immediately resulted in heightened tensions between the USSR and the United States. Moscow declared a military exclusion zone covering both the Norwegian and Barents Seas, and a warning was delivered by the Soviet ambassador to the President that the Soviet Union would tolerate no outside interference from any foreign power. The incident signaled a return to the Cold War days of military confrontation and brinkmanship. Worse, it presented the old NATO alliance with a challenge that, seemingly, it simply could no longer meet.

"Norway, you may recall, was a founding member of the North Atlantic Treaty Organization, which was founded on the basis of mutual cooperation against the Soviet threat. Since the dissolution of the Warsaw Pact in July of 1991, however, NATO's forces have been drastically scaled down, with member nations unable to agree on the charter's future course, let alone on a proper response to Soviet

aggression in Scandinavia. With Great Britain's withdrawal
from the organization two years ago, and the subsequent
loss of American bases in that country under the policies of
Britain's new Labor government, there seems to be little
will among remaining members to enforce the treaty's
provisions for mutual assistance.''

*File footage of an American aircraft carrier at sea, the
number 74 painted on her flight deck. Subsequent scenes
show American sailors on her deck, wearing helmets and
green or brown or yellow jerseys, readying an F-14 Tomcat
for launch; of jet-blast deflectors rising behind thundering
engines; of naval aircraft hurtling off the bow of the carrier
as steam boils from the catapult.*

''Despite considerable opposition from congressmen who
warned that the United States was involving itself in foreign
matters that were no longer in America's best interests and
that military posturing could lead to world war, President
Connally last week ordered an American aircraft carrier, the
U.S.S. *Thomas Jefferson,* accompanied by a number of
supporting vessels, to defy the Soviet exclusion zone as a
show of support for the embattled government of Norway.

''Early reports of actual combat between American and
Soviet forces, of aircraft shot down on both sides, and even
of American surface ships and Russian submarines being
sunk in a series of engagements from Iceland to the coast of
Norway, have not, at this time, been confirmed. A virtual
press blackout has settled over the Pentagon, indeed over
this entire city, though ACN has been able to confirm that
the President has ordered a DEFCON 2 alert. That means
that U.S. forces are mobilizing and are now at a state of
readiness only one step removed from all-out war.''

*The camera view finally switches to the ACN reporter, an
attractive young woman with blond hair and a direct,
professional manner, standing in the Pentagon press room,
speaking into a microphone.*

''Clearly, military confrontation has once again brought
the world to the brink of war. It is widely believed here in
the Pentagon that the marshals who now rule the Soviet

empire have gambled on a foreign adventure, the invasion of Norway and Finland and a military confrontation with the West, in order to distract their people at home from the continuing crisis of empty food shelves, widespread shortages, and a collapsing economy. By forcing a showdown with the West, one which they evidently feel they are strong enough to win, they may be able to secure at last their own power in the face of growing resentment at home, the ultimate threat of *people power* . . . and civil war.

"Only time will tell whether the deployment of a single U.S. carrier squadron—a token force by any standards— will buy the time America needs to marshal its diplomatic armies against this renewed Soviet threat.

"For ACN, this is Pamela Drake reporting live from the Pentagon."

CHAPTER 1
Wednesday, 18 June 1997

1420 hours Zulu (1520 hours Zone)
CIC, U.S.S. *Thomas Jefferson*
Viking Station, the Norwegian Sea

Cruising steadily through calm seas, the U.S.S. *Thomas Jefferson* followed the northward leg of the imaginary racetrack labeled Viking Station by the wits in her Combat Information Center. She was America's newest nuclear-powered supercarrier, a high-tech leviathan almost eleven hundred feet long, with the population of a small town crammed into the miles of passageways and living quarters and work spaces beneath the four and a half acres of her flight deck.

The seas were calm, but the atmosphere aboard mingled exhaustion with the electric crackle of tension. *Jefferson* was at war. No declarations had been made as yet, but the first battles had already been fought, the first casualties taken. After years of Cold War, of revolution, of wild shifts in world politics, military confrontation and miscalculation had brought the United States and the Soviet Union to the brink of war.

And *Jefferson* was on the firing line.

In the Air Ops suite of the carrier's CIC, a cold, blue-lit cavern of dungaree- and khaki-clad men hunched over consoles and the ghostly sweeps of radar screens, Commander Matthew "Tombstone" Magruder reached past the

7

arm of a second class radarman and snatched up a headset. "Skywatch Three-two," he snapped, pressing one earpiece against his ear and holding the throat mike to his lips. "This is Camelot One. What the *hell* do you mean, 'contact lost'?"

There was a long hesitation before the reply. Camelot was *Jefferson*'s current call sign, and Camelot One meant CAG, the commander of Air Wing 20. The men aboard the orbiting E-2C Hawkeye would be thinking carefully about how they answered.

"Ah . . . Camelot, we've got quite a bit of ECM going in that sector. And the Russkies are using the mountains for cover. They just dropped off the screen."

"Well, drop them back on the screen, damn it. Go to base plus twenty and find them!"

"Roger that, Camelot. Skywatch Three-two proceeding to base plus two-zero."

Communications with the Hawkeye were on tight beam and computer-scrambled, but against the possibility that the enemy was still able to listen in, explicit instructions were coded. The "base" for the day was twelve thousand feet. Magruder had just ordered the Hawkeye radar plane to climb from its current altitude of twenty-five thousand feet up to thirty-two, the better to peer down into the mountainous heart of Norway one hundred miles to the east.

Less than two hours earlier, a priority flash from Washington had warned the American carrier battle group of a sharp increase in air traffic over and near air bases up and down the Kola Peninsula, twelve hundred miles to the east. Less than twenty minutes ago, the circling Hawkeye had picked up ominous signs—radar images, now revealed, now obscured in a fog of intense electronic countermeasures—of aircraft moving west.

Aircraft, many of them, moving from bases within the fastnesses inside the reborn Soviet Union, across occupied Finland and into neutral Swedish airspace.

Tombstone shivered. The air-conditioning in CIC was always going full-blast to protect the complex, expensive, and temperature-sensitive electronics that filled the suite of rooms located just beneath the carrier's flight deck, or "roof."

But his shiver was not from the cold. Forty-eight hours earlier, aircraft from the *Jefferson* had dealt a brutal setback to the Soviet Union's invasion plans for Norway, sinking a number of amphibious-warfare ships and even getting in at least one hit against a Russian aircraft carrier. Now, the battle group's radar picket had reported multiple bogies coming west across the mountains of Jotunheim. While not particularly high as mountain ranges go, they were the highest in Norway, with some of the peaks reaching above eight thousand feet, and the bogies were using the mountains for cover. Worse, their electronic countermeasures were turning out to be too damned effective. The Hawkeye had lost the contact in the clutter.

Jotunheim, Tombstone thought, the abode of the ice giants in Norse myth. There were giants among those mountains, certainly enough. Sleek, high-tech giants that could fly . . . and that could deliver fiery death to the American carrier group if they were allowed to get within striking range.

Tombstone's eyes stayed on the radar screen, which repeated the display aboard the Hawkeye over one hundred miles to the northeast. The Jotunheimen were visible, hard, bright returns stretching from north to south, the sharp edges softened by the blurring hash of Soviet ECM. Somewhere in that mess was a flight of Russian planes. But how many . . . and what kind? When first picked up, those bogies had been 270 miles away, traveling toward the *Jefferson* at Mach .9. That speed would put them close enough to launch ship-killers at the *Jefferson* in fifteen minutes.

They *had* to find out what those bogies were, and damned fast.

Tombstone glanced at the young, sandy-haired man at his left. "What do you think, Paul?"

Lieutenant Commander Paul Aiken studied the hash on

the display for a moment, then shook his head. "Whatever they are, they don't give a damn about Swedish neutrality."

"Well, we knew that was coming. Cuts down on the flight time from the Kola Peninsula, doesn't it?"

"Amen to that. I wonder if Stockholm has surrendered. Or if the Russians are just bulling their way through."

Tombstone glanced back over his shoulder at the transparent flight board listing the names and aircraft numbers of *Jefferson*'s aviators now aloft. "Who's on BARCAP east?" he asked. With combat possible at any time, *Jefferson* was keeping at least two BARCAPs—BARrier Combat Air Patrols—in the air at all times, positioned to block any surprise Soviet thrust from north or east.

"Two-oh-one and Two-one-eight," an enlisted rating at the board replied. "Grant and Crandall. Call sign 'Icewall.'"

Commander Willis E. Grant, running name "Coyote." Lieutenant Commander Alex Crandall, "Scorpion." Tombstone didn't know Crandall well, but Coyote was one of Jefferson's best aviators, the skipper of *Jefferson*'s VP-95 Vipers.

And one of Tombstone's best friends.

Tombstone brought the microphone to his mouth again. "Skywatch Three-two, Camelot," he said. "Deploy Icewall for a closer look. Tell them to watch themselves. They have weapons clear."

"Roger, Camelot. Skywatch copies."

Tombstone continued to stare at the hash-streaked radar display, willing the interference to vanish and the target to appear. The contact *had* to be a flight of Russian aircraft. Norway had little air force left, and Swedish planes would not be overflying Norwegian airspace. That left the Russians. It was a sure bet that the Soviet high command had decided to send a strike force against the *Jefferson,* routing them straight across conquered Finland and neutral Sweden from bases in the Kola Peninsula. Battle stations had already been sounded aboard every ship in *Jefferson*'s battle group, but the sooner the American force knew what the enemy force's strength and composition were, the better.

He drew a deep breath. It was still a little surprising, standing here in *Jefferson's* cavernous, red-lit Combat Information Center, directing the eighty-plus aircraft of CVW-20 in a shooting war. CAG: Commander Air Group . . . though the Navy no longer had air groups and the title was a holdover from an earlier war. Officially, Tombstone was Acting CAG. He still didn't feel ready to take on the job. He'd come aboard days before as Deputy CAG, only to find himself stepping into the senior slot when Captain Joseph Stramaglia had died in a dogfight over Iceland.

Tombstone was no stranger to warfare. During his previous tour of sea duty, as CO of VF-95 aboard this same carrier, he'd seen more combat than most modern naval aviators saw in their entire careers. He'd made his first kill in the skies over Korea, then gone on to participate in air-to-air combat during a military coup in Thailand, and in the mercifully brief so-called "Indian War," a police action that had brought India and Pakistan to the negotiating table and—just possibly—stopped a nuclear war before it started.

Looking around the red-lit CIC, he knew that this, *this* was what he had trained for all his life . . . not a police action, not a brushfire war in some remote corner of Asia, but a major naval war, a war against the Soviet Union.

He would still have preferred to be with Coyote on BARCAP between the endless blues of sea and sky . . . but the events of the past few days had proven to Tombstone once and for all that his training and experience were put to their best use here. He still didn't like the new situation, but he was learning to live with it.

Where . . . *where* were those bogies?

"Do you think this is part of that shuttle we've been watching up here?" Lieutenant Commander Arthur Lee was Tombstone's CAG staff intelligence officer. He reached forward, almost touching the outline of the Norwegian coast on the screen with his forefinger. He pointed to a spot on the coast to the north, beyond Trondheim. "The shuttle" had been glimpsed earlier that morning and had reappeared intermittently throughout the day . . . fast-moving blips that were almost certainly Soviet fighter planes, weaving through the mountains beyond Trondheim toward the west. The Hawkeye had been deployed farther north than usual in an attempt to track the bogies, but without much success.

"Doubt it," Tombstone replied, his voice curt. "More likely that shuttle of yours is fresh birds for the Russian carrier."

Somewhere far to the north of *Jefferson* lay the scattered elements of a Soviet carrier task force. Intelligence reports were still sketchy, but it was at least possible that the Russian carrier had been hit at least once during the far-flung surface action two days before. Certainly it had lost a large fraction of its air wing, and the shuttle might be an attempt to make up those losses.

If so, *Jefferson* was not in a strong position. The American carrier had lost aircraft during the past week, too many of them, and replacements were hard to come by at the far end of a supply line that stretched clear back across the Atlantic to Norfolk.

"Reinforcements," Commander Aiken added, echoing Tombstone's thoughts. "Pray God we get reinforcements of our own before they get their shit together."

Reinforcements *were* on the way . . . but the big question was when they would arrive. *Eisenhower*'s battle group was already in the Atlantic, and there was talk that either the *Nimitz* or the *Kennedy* was to be redeployed from the Med. With two or three battle groups in the region, plus a Marine Expeditionary Unit en route from Virginia, the Russians would *have* to back down.

Unless they could kill or cripple the *Jefferson* first. For the next few days, the U.S.S. *Jefferson* was likely to be the only force blocking the Russians in the Norwegian Sea, and that fact made her a prime target.

Tombstone watched the luminous glow painting the blur of radar clutter to the east. If the Russians were overflying

Sweden in a bid to hit the *Jefferson,* they'd be popping into view any moment now. North on the screen, two solitary blips raced toward the southeast, toward the jagged indentations of the Norwegian coast. Data relayed from the Hawkeye tagged them as friendlies—Coyote and Scorpion heading for their intercept. The seconds dragged by, agonizingly slow.

"What's the status on our Alert Five?" he asked. As soon as the bogies had been spotted, *Jefferson*'s Alert Five aircraft, F-14 Tomcats already fueled, armed, and ready to launch on five minutes' notice, had been given the word to go.

"Four minutes, CAG," one of his assistants announced behind him.

"Damn! Pass the word to step on it up there. Our people need some backup!" Tombstone felt frustrated, mad, and not a little scared. *Jefferson* was sitting blind, and God knew what the Russians were sending at them. Right now, there was nothing between the enemy and *Jefferson*'s battle group but two F-14s and four vulnerable men.

My friends.

Damn! *Where* were those bogies?

1422 hours Zulu (1522 hours Zone)
Tomcat 201
Off the Norwegian coast

Commander Willis Grant—Coyote to his friends and fellow Vipers aboard the *Jefferson*—eased back gently on the stick of his F-14D Tomcat, feeling the thundering power of the combat aircraft's twin F110 GE-400 engines as he edged into a gentle climb. Below, half a mile beneath the Tomcat's belly, sunlight flashed and dazzled in myriad sparkles from the cold, azure blue of the Norwegian Sea. Ahead and to the left, still forty miles distant, a purple-gray blur topped by billowing cumulus clouds lay across the horizon, dividing blue sea from bluer sky.

"How about it, John-Boy?" he called over the Tomcat's intercom. "What's going down?"

In the seat directly behind his, Coyote's RIO, Lieutenant John Nichols, was still trying to pierce the clutter of mountains and Russian jamming. The target, whatever it was, was closer now than when it had first been tagged from the Hawkeye—much closer.

"Nothing yet, Coyote," John-Boy's voice replied over the ICS. "I dunno. We should be close enough to burn through this hash by now."

"The bastards probably dropped low," Coyote said. "Hiding in the mountains. Stay sharp. They'll be popping up any moment now."

He looked away from the coast and out to sea. His wingman was tucked in tight, less than twenty feet off his starboard wingtip. He could easily see the helmeted heads of Scorpion Crandall and his RIO, Juggler Tyson. Scorpion noticed him watching and touched one gloved hand to his helmet in a mock salute.

Coyote acknowledged with a wave, then turned his attention back to the coast. The two Tomcats were on a converging course with the coastline. He could see mono-lithic rocks standing in the sea, the bulk of glacier-scoured headlands, the crooked meander of a small fjord. The surf seemed motionless at this distance.

But the coastline rapidly grew closer. He glimpsed beaches and fir trees, and the blurred impression of a cottage with a steeply pitched roof. "Skywatch, Icewall," he called. "Feet dry at base minus ten. Still no joy on bogies, over."

"Copy, Icewall. Maintain heading. Be advised, if bogies maintained course and speed, they should be coming round the mountain any time now."

"Affirmative." But of course they would have cut their speed if they were threading their way through some icebound pass in the mountains. "Skywatch, Icewall is splitting up. Let's see if we can get them in stereo."

"Roger, Icewall."

"Two-one-eight. Two-oh-one. Scorpion, are you with me?"

"Right on your wing, Coyote," the other aviator replied. "It's getting lonely up here. Whatcha got?"

"Not a thing. How about breaking high and right and taking eyeball."

"Roger. You got it." Scorpion's Tomcat stood suddenly on its starboard wing, turning its belly toward Coyote's aircraft. He could see every detail of Scorpion's weapons load—four AIM-54C Phoenix long-range missiles, two AIM-7M Sparrows, and two AIM-9M Sidewinders—a standard interception load for a mission that might require sudden death at almost any range.

Then Scorpion's afterburners flared, and his Tomcat arrowed into the distance. By splitting up, the two Tomcats could get better radar coverage of the still-masked target. In combat, the winner was usually the guy who spotted the *other* guy first.

Mountains bulked ahead, ice-capped and forbidding. Coyote could clearly make out the timberline along the mountain flanks. The ground below was rugged and divided among patchwork fields, thick forest, and boulder-strewn slopes. "Skywatch, Icewall," he called. "Say, do you have any idea if we're over friendly territory?"

"Hard to tell," the Hawkeye operator's voice came back. "You ought to be well on the good guys' side of no-man's-land. Of course, if the Norwegians think you look like MiGs, they're as likely to shoot you as the Russians."

"My, but we are cheerful today," Coyote replied. He watched the rugged ground flashing past. The landscape seemed peaceful, even idyllic. There were no signs of war, no burned-out tanks or APCs, no military vehicles on the roads. "Negative ground activity. I think we must be clear of the lines."

"Roger that, Icewall. But keep your mark ones peeled. There's a war on over there, remember, and you're in the thick of it."

Mark ones . . . meaning his mark one eyeballs, the first

and best sensors an aviator carried with him aboard his aircraft. Even in modern, high-tech, long-range warfare, a man's own senses, coupled with reason, gut instinct, and years of training, were still the most important tools he carried.

"Coyote, Scorpion!" Scorpion's voice was shrill, harsh with excitement in Coyote's headset. "I got bogies! Bogies!"

"Slow down, Scorp," Coyote replied. "What's the bearing?"

"Multiple bogies at zero-eight-five, angels base minus four. Range fifteen miles. I've got five . . . six . . . make that eight bogies, repeat, eight bogies in two groups, now at zero-eight-six."

"Copy, Two-one-eight. We still need a positive ID."

"Maybe you want me to go up and introduce myself?"

"I've got them," John-Boy said from the back seat. "Coming out of the clutter."

"Okay, John-Boy," Coyote said. It was strange, he thought, how he sounded a lot calmer than he felt. His heart was pounding with the promise of action. Or was it fear? Briefly, just for an instant, his thoughts flashed to Julie. *I don't want to die!* "Relay to Camelot. Tell them we're closing with the bogies."

He pressed the throttles forward, feeling the surge of raw power thundering astern. The miles flashed past, one every six seconds.

"Coyote, this is Scorpion! They're breaking for me! I've got launch! That's multiple launch by two . . . make that *four* bandits! Repeat, four bandits . . ."

Bandits now, instead of bogies. No longer unknown aircraft, but hostiles.

"Hang on, Scorp. We're a mile behind you and coming up buster."

White vapor curled off his wing tips as he smashed through the sound barrier.

CHAPTER 2
Wednesday, 18 June

1424 hours Zulu (1524 hours Zone)
Tomcat 201
Near Grotli, Norway

Coyote pulled back hard on the Tomcat's stick as he throttled into Zone Five afterburner. Clouds whipped past his aircraft as he climbed.

A village flashed beneath the belly of his aircraft, a collection of huts and larger buildings, nestled in the green at the head of a meandering fjord. South sprawled the Jostedalsbre, vastest of mainland Europe's ice sheets, sixty miles long and covering hundreds of square miles between upthrust mountains. Sunlight flashed from ice fields and frozen rivers like fire-struck diamond, more intense, more dazzling than sun-dance on the sea, but Coyote ignored the vista, dividing his attention between the computer-generated images dancing across the Vertical Display Indicator on his console and Heads Up Display projected onto the inside surface of his windscreen.

The VDI showed Scorpion's aircraft, hard pressed by the four nearest bandits six thousand feet above Coyote's position and almost three miles away. A second group of four maintained their original heading as they burst from the mountains of Jotunheim twelve miles to the east, climbing hard, still thundering toward the *Jefferson* at Mach 1.

"Skywatch, Skywatch," John-Boy called over the ICS.

"Icewall, Two-oh-one. We have eight bandits, repeat, eight bandits in two groups, designated Alpha and Bravo. Two-one-eight has target confirmation on Group Alpha."

"Icewall, Camelot," a hard voice said over the radio, and Coyote recognized the voice of Tombstone Magruder, CAG. "We're patched in. Priority target is Group Bravo, Group Bravo. Do you copy?"

Coyote hesitated. His wingman was tangling with the four Russian MiGs of Alpha, but CIC was ordering him to close with the *other* four targets, Bravo, still unidentified and still holding a straight-line course aimed at the *Jefferson*.

"Two-oh-one copies," he said tersely. "Engaging."

The orders made sense, in a cold and calculating way. Alpha was probably a fighter escort for something bigger, a quartet of Backfires, possibly, lumbering aircraft like the ones that had plastered Keflavík with AS-4 air-to-surface missiles a few days before. Those planes could not be allowed anywhere close to *Jefferson*, not without risking a devastating air-to-surface missile strike against the floating airfield.

But chasing Bravo meant leaving Scorpion and Juggler in a one-on-four scrap for several crucial minutes . . . an eternity in air-to-air combat.

"Range to Bravo now ten miles," John-Boy said.

"We'll go for Phoenix kill," Coyote decided.

"Roger. Targeting."

The AIM-54 Phoenix was a long-range killer, able to radar-home on a target over one hundred miles away. Using the million-dollar missile against a target a scant ten miles distant seemed a waste . . . but that was extreme range for heat-seeking Sidewinders, and his AIM-7M Sparrows, though they had a range of sixty miles or better, were semiactive radar homers. That meant that he would have to hold the Tomcat steadily on course, painting the targets with radar as the SARH missiles homed for a kill . . . and right now his wingman was in trouble.

"I have target lock," John-Boy announced. "Bravo-one at ten miles."

"Punch it!"

"Fox three!" John-Boy gave the warning call for a Phoenix launch as he punched the firing button on his backseat console. The F-14 surged upward as the half-ton missile dropped from the wing. When its rocket engine ignited, the missile corkscrewed ahead of the Tomcat at the tip of a billowing white contrail, arrowing into the hard blue sky.

"Next target! Acquisition."

"Got it! Fox three!"

Coyote glanced at the crawling blips and symbols on his VDI again and saw that Scorpion was in trouble.

1425 hours Zulu (1525 hours Zone)
Tomcat 218
Near Grotli, Norway

"We got two on our six!" Juggler yelled. "Two missiles hot for our six!"

As Crandall brought the Tomcat into a hard right turn, he glanced back and saw the missiles on their tail, white contrails scratched across the blue a mile behind them.

"Hang onto your lunch, Jug! It's pedal to the metal!"

Scattering flares like a string of burning stars, the F-14 dipped briefly toward the rugged mountain peaks below, trading altitude for speed, then pitched up, blasting toward the aching blue of the zenith. As the flares fell, he cut the Tomcat's afterburners and throttled back. Sometimes it was possible to fool incoming heat-seekers by giving them brighter, hotter targets. Losing power, the Tomcat climbed for seconds on momentum alone, then fell into a vertical reverse, a low-speed maneuver that let Crandall pull an extremely tight turn.

Then they were plunging toward the mountains, the F-14 shuddering as it picked up speed. Behind them, one of the contrails angled wildly off to the left, decoyed by the flares. The second missile corkscrewed in, still homing on the Tomcat.

Lieutenant Commander Alex Crandall was a big, bluff man, a native of Mountain View, Missouri, who had begun flying a Piper Cub as a teenager . . . and ended up flying Tomcats for the Navy. He loved flying, loved the rush of cloud past the cockpit and the feeling of solitude hanging between earth and sky.

He wasn't enjoying the solitude now, though, as he glanced at the screen of his VDI, spotting Coyote's F-14 and the hurtling, pinpoint blips of a pair of Phoenix missiles. He'd heard the 201 bird's fox-three call a moment before, heard the orders from *Jefferson*'s CIC to concentrate on Group Bravo.

Fine, damn it, but it would be nice to have a little help out here. Scorpion Crandall was feeling just a bit naked, alone in the wide-open sky with four MiGs and a couple of AA-8 heat-seekers. Two MiGs were behind him; two more had circled around in front, boxing him in. Things were not looking good.

The mountains filled his windscreen beyond the flickering data and drifting computer symbols of his HUD. Less than a mile above those craggy peaks, Crandall boosted the throttles to full military power and brought the nose up.

Acceleration clamped down on his body, pressing him back into his seat, dragging at his face and eyes and brain. He grunted hard, deliberately flexing the muscles of his neck and arms, fighting the pressure, fighting the drain of blood from his head that threatened to make him black out. As the G readout on his HUD hit 9.2, a black tunnel closed in on his vision from all sides, narrowing his view.

Then the pressure was gone as the Tomcat leveled off. Crandall gulped air through his mask, turning from side to side in the cockpit as he tried to see all of the sky, in all directions. "Jug! Where's the missile? I don't see it!"

There was no answer from the backseat. The high-G pullout had put his RIO to sleep, a common enough event when the relative positions of pilot and RIO put slightly higher G-forces on the man in the backseat. Glancing back over his shoulder, Crandall still could not see the second Russian missile.

Good enough. They'd lost it. If they hadn't, they'd have been hit by now. On this new heading, two Russian planes were bearing in on him, almost head-to-head.

Deciding to go for a Sparrow kill, he brought his stick over, dragging the targeting diamond on his HUD across the symbol marking one of the MiGs. A second later, he was rewarded by the flash of the letters ACQ as the Tomcat acquired its target, and by the tone in his headset of a radar lock.

"Fox one," he called, announcing a radar-homer launch, and his finger closed on the firing trigger. The SARH air-to-air killer shooshed from beneath his right wing, arrowing toward the approaching target.

The two enemy aircraft held steady for a moment, then split, one to the north, one to the south. Crandall eased the stick to the left, holding on the southern bandit, keeping it centered in the invisible cone of radiation projected by the F-14's AWG-9 radar.

Seconds later, there was a flash in the distance, and a blip faded from his screen.

"Splash one MiG!" he called over the radio.

He caught the glint of sunlight on a canopy, high above him and to the rear. The two MiGs to his rear had closed the range and were dropping toward him now like hawks on a rabbit.

Damn . . . *where* was Coyote?

1426 hours Zulu (1526 hours Zone)
Tomcat 201
Near Grotli, Norway

"Miss!" Coyote called, as the lead Phoenix blip merged with one target . . . then separated, seeming to pass right through the contact. "*Shit!* We missed!"

"Ditto on the second bird," John-Boy added. "I think they foxed them."

"At a million dollars a pop, you'd think they'd build missiles that could *hit* something!" Coyote's gloved fist came down on his knee.

"This ECM shit is bad, really bad," John-Boy said. "I'm having trouble seeing through this garbage."

The radar clutter was like a snowstorm on Coyote's display. As far as he could make out, Bravo group was still on course, but someone out there was jamming hard. It was increasingly difficult to see through the fuzz of ECM and make out the targets.

"Two-one-eight, this is Two-oh-one. Scorpion! Where are you?"

"Boxed in, Coyote!" his wingman's voice replied. "One down, three to go. They're all over me!"

"Can you get clear? We're oh for four, and I want a closer look at these bandits."

"Work . . . ing . . . on . . . it . . ." Crandall's voice was distorted, forced from his lungs in a series of grunts as he battled the effects of a high-G turn.

Coyote felt an instant of anguished indecision. He was going to have to work his way in close to those bandits, close enough to make a try for them with Sidewinders, and that was going to take more time than he—or Scorpion—had.

Damn, he *couldn't* leave his wingman. The mysterious bandits of group Bravo would keep. Angrily, Coyote put his stick over, dropping into a screaming turn. Ahead, he could see the twisting wisps of vapor trails, the furball of a dogfight. "Hang on, Scorp!" he called. "Two-oh-one is engaging!"

1426 hours Zulu (1526 hours Zone)
The Romsdal Valley
Norway

Standing in the turret of his M109, Løytnant Harald Snorisson craned his head back, staring into the intense blue sky halfway between the southern horizon and the zenith. Aircraft contrails writhed and tangled there, jets clashing in air-to-air combat miles above the glistening ice of the Jostedalsbre.

He felt a pulse-pounding excitement. He was twenty-three years old, a very junior officer in Norway's small regular army. His fierce eagerness to come to grips with the enemy that had invaded his country threatened to over-whelm all else.

Normally, he would have been stationed with the rest of his unit, the Second Regiment of the First Mechanized Brigade, but accident and war had dropped him here, alone, on a road running northwest along the steep and rocky banks of the Romsdal. Standing doctrine called for his unit to be airlifted to the far north in the event of a Soviet invasion of Norway, but the Russian attack, coming as it had with almost complete surprise, had overwhelmed Brigade North in a bitter, running fight through Finnmark. Norwegian command and control had been shattered, first by Soviet air strikes on command centers and army head-quarters up and down the length of the country, then by the savage amphibious and air landings at Oslo, far to the south.

General Nils Lindstrom was still in the midst of trying to salvage the situation from his emergency headquarters near Bergen, but the army's interior communications had not been as effective as they'd been during NATO maneuvers in the past. Snorisson's brigade had been ordered to Bergen, then to Trondheim, then finally thrown into a thin, ragged line across the center of the country.

Since June 12, the brigade reportedly had fought a series of delaying actions down the coast, all the way from Tromsø to Rørvik, but in all that time, not once had Snorisson seen combat. Somehow, in the storm of orders and counterorders, his vehicle had missed a planned rendezvous, and now it was just him, three enlisted men, and their M109 Roland antiair vehicle, alone on a country road in the Romsdal Valley.

With a fine sense of irony, his sergeant had painted the name *Skynd Dem!*—''Hurry Up!''—across both sides of the turret just beneath the launch tubes. Snorisson wondered if it was the same in all armies—hurry up, hurry up . . . then wait.

He ached to come to grips with the invaders. At first he'd been terrified, especially as each report from the front had brought news of another disaster. But he'd been born and raised in the small and somewhat isolated fishing village of Leiranger, overlooking the vast sheltering of the mighty Vestfjorden. His wife and young son were there still . . . or *had* been.

His fists closed, his nails biting his palms. Word had reached him only five days before that Soviet naval infantry forces had pushed south from their initial perimeter at Narvik, that Norwegian Heimevernet forces—the home guard—had ambushed a Soviet column on the road near Narvik, that Soviet naval infantry were rounding up hundreds of civilians throughout the area and shooting them in brutal retaliation. Leiranger, he'd heard, had been put to the torch, one of a dozen villages along the Vestfjorden destroyed as punishment and warning.

Løytnant Snorisson wanted to strike back, and strike back hard. For five days, he'd thought of little else, as the fighting ground ever closer from the north.

And this might be his chance. *At last.*

He ducked his head through the circular hatch of the turret. The M109 was an American vehicle, designed originally as a self-propelled howitzer, but refitted as a mobile launcher for Roland 2 antiair missiles. The Roland was a joint French-German SAM, a radar-guided, short-ranged missile system that could track targets sixteen kilometers away but needed to be considerably closer—six kilometers or less—to kill them. Several times in the past weeks, his unit had tracked hostile aircraft in the skies above Norway, but this was the closest they'd been to the action yet.

"Gunnar!" he called. "Do you have a target?"

The grizzled *stabsersjant*—staff sergeant—blinked back at him from the dim interior of the turret with tired, pale eyes. "Many targets, *Løytnant*. Range ten kilometers, altitude sixteen thousand. All still well out of range."

Snorisson raised himself back into daylight. Someone was fighting up there . . . Soviets and the remnants of the Norwegian air force, it had to be. The Royal Norwegian Air Force had been conspicuous by its absence during the past few days. In the first week of the invasion, plane after plane had been shot from the sky or caught on the ground by the vicious, roving packs of Soviet airborne wolves.

But now, some of his countrymen had emerged to make a stand in the skies above the Jostedalsbre. And if any of the hated Russian invaders ventured within range of his SAMS, Løytnant Snorisson would make his stand with them!

1426 hours Zulu (1526 hours Zone)
Tomcat 218
Near Grotli, Norway

The MiGs closed with appalling speed, maneuvering onto Crandall's six, the favored spot for making a kill squarely on his tail. Over his shoulder, he had a glimpse of both aircraft flying almost wingtip to wingtip as he pulled into a hard right turn.

"They're still with us, Scorp!" Juggler called. The RIO had recovered consciousness seconds after losing it, but he still sounded groggy, his voice strained. Crandall held the turn, calculating his chances.

His opponents were MiG-29s, "Fulcrums" in the old NATO nomenclature, sleek and deadly-looking aircraft outwardly almost identical to the American F/A-18 Hornet, with twin stabilizers rising just outboard of the two powerful Tumanski R-33D turbofans, and the gaping maws of the squared-off air intake mounted beneath the root of each wing. Effortlessly, the pair stayed inside Crandall's turn as he pulled his Tomcat into a hard left turn. They were so close he could see the racks for six air-to-air missiles beneath the wings, the mottled gray and green camouflage pattern, and the red stars outlined in white painted on the stabilizers.

With a shock of recognition, Crandall realized that the Fulcrums were too close for a missile shot. They were going for a kill with their guns.

Each Fulcrum carried a single 30-mm high-speed cannon, laser-aimed and incredibly accurate. Crandall remembered a briefing he'd had on the Fulcrum's laser targeting system. In the early days of testing, an electrical fault had kept shutting off the gun after only five or six rounds . . . and yet the Fulcrum had continued to score kill after kill, hitting every target dead-on. One of the plane's designers had insisted that, had they known how deadly the MiG-29's targeting would be in practice, they would have halved the ammunition load in order to incorporate larger fuel tanks in the design.

With that kind of accuracy, the Russian pilots would not be worried about leading their target, not when they were assured a hit with their first rounds. The only way to stay out of their line of fire was to fool them before he was tagged, to pull a maneuver so sudden and unexpected that they would be forced to break off.

And that would give him his chance to wax their tails.

"Keep them in sight, Jug!" he called. "Let's see how they are at barnstorming!"

Crandall yanked the F-14's stick back to the left, breaking

into a sharp split-S that would leave the Fulcrums on the outside of his turn and heading the wrong way. Somehow, as he'd almost expected, the Russians stayed with his maneuver, switching into a port turn that rapidly drew them toward his tail once more.

Before they were fully in position, though, he cut his throttles to sixty percent, letting the Tomcat roll to the left until it was upside down . . . and falling. Again, the mountains and the harsh glint of an icefield rolled past the Tomcat's canopy, twisting around until they filled the view ahead through Crandall's HUD. Wings sliding back, the Tomcat punched through the sound barrier, hurtling toward the ground.

"That got 'em!" Juggler yelled over the ICS. "They flew right past like they didn't even see us!"

Crandall grinned behind his mask. By the time the Fulcrum duo had figured out what had happened, he would be on the deck and lining up his shot.

To the west, another air-to-air missile crawled through the sky. "Fox two!" sounded over the radio as Coyote loosed a Sidewinder at the third plane of the trio dogging Scorpion and Juggler. "Scorpion! Coyote is in!"

"Roger, Coyote!" He started pulling back on the stick, feeling the G-forces mounting on face and chest and stomach. He had to force each word past clenched teeth. "Good . . . to . . . have . . . you . . . aboard . . ."

He glanced at his compass bearing, projected on his HUD. Zero-three-five . . . roughly northeast. A valley sprawled across the landscape dead ahead, the gleaming twist of a river shining from its floor. The two MiGs were breaking toward the east, three miles ahead and a mile above. Drawing his pullout into a shallow climb, he brought the Tomcat's nose up until he could tag one of the Fulcrums with a heat-seeking Sidewinder.

Target lock . . . *fire* . . .

1427 hours Zulu (1527 hours Zone)
The Romsdal Valley
Norway

"Do you have a target?"

"Ja, Løytnant," the staff sergeant replied. "Target lock! In range! But we're picking up none of our fighters' IFF . . ."

Skynd Dem's turret swiveled left, the heavy tubes on either side of the massive, centrally mounted radar dish swinging up to meet the target. By chance, the battle had carried several of the jets directly toward Snorisson's position. He could see the nearest plane now, a sleek, twin-tailed speck growing rapidly larger. Fear thrilled in Snorisson's veins. The plane was plunging for an attack. . . .

In combat, aircraft generally broadcast a transponder signal. Called IFF for Identification Friend or Foe, it was the only way enemy could be separated from friendly aircraft when battles were raging at supersonic speeds across ranges of tens or hundreds of kilometers. The Roland system's computer would refuse a target lock on a target tagged by IFF as friendly. Briefly, Snorisson wondered whether the fact that there were no signals from the aircraft circling overhead meant the computer was down.

It was by pure mischance that Snorisson had missed the directive filtering down from the command staff in Bergen, warning that friendly American naval aircraft had been operating recently in Norwegian airspace . . . and that their IFF codes did not correspond to those used by Norwegian forces.

At that moment, there could be no doubt at all in Snorisson's tired and pain-ragged mind that the jet diving toward him from the contrail-streaked sky was hostile. He dropped through the turret opening, banging the hatch shut above him. "The target!" he yelled at his sergeant. Rage burned like fire. "To the southeast! Get him!"

"We're locked. Tracking . . ."

"Then *fire!*"

There was a shriek like escaping steam, and first one, then the other Roland missile burst into the sky. At almost the same moment, the target thundered past, less than a mile away and a thousand feet above the rocky ground. The missiles swerved sharply in midair as their target swept from southeast to north. Boosters dropped away and sustainer motors took over, accelerating the rockets to Mach 1.6.

CHAPTER 3
Wednesday, 18 June

"Missile lock!" Juggler called over the ICS. "SAM! SAM! SAM!"

"Oh, *shit!* . . ."

They must be over Russian lines! He could hear the thrum of a pulse-doppler lock over his headset. Funny. It was unfamiliar, unlike any of the radar tones he associated with Soviet SAMs. What the hell was it?

No time to wonder. Most of the speed he'd won from his dive had been lost positioning himself for the climb back toward the enemy. He saw the contrails, two of them, racing across the terrain. He kicked in the Tomcat's afterburners as Juggler pumped chaff to decoy the missile's radar. Sluggishly, sluggishly, the F-14 began to arc higher. If he could pull into a tight enough turn, the oncoming SAMs might overshoot, might even lock onto the chaff clouds and detonate harmlessly. . . .

The first Roland missed by thirty yards and failed to detonate. Its radar lock broken by Scorpion's maneuver, it plunged harmlessly toward the horizon.

The second Roland, too, missed . . . but passed close enough that its proximity fuse was triggered. The warhead detonated twenty feet from the Tomcat's belly, sending a

31

storm of shrapnel blasting through the thin metal of the fuselage. A dozen red lights flashed on across the warning console, and Crandall was screaming "Eject! Eject!" as he reached for the handle that would rocket them clear of the disintegrating aircraft.

But fuel gushing from ruptured lines splashed across hot metal and exploded into flame before he could complete the action. The fireball consumed the Tomcat in a series of explosions that ate their way forward from engine to wing tanks, each detonation more savage than the last.

Seconds later, the wreckage slammed into a mountain, and the smoke of its burning was a black pillar staining the sky.

1428 hours Zulu (1528 hours Zone)
Tomcat 201
Near Grotli, Norway

Coyote saw the smoke, and he'd heard Crandall's last, desperate cry over the radio. With growing dread, he banked his Tomcat toward the crash site, searching for parachutes, for some sign that Crandall and Tyson had managed to eject before their F-14 hit the rocky slope below.

"Camelot, Camelot," he called. "This is Icewall Two-zero-one. Icewall Two-one-eight is down, repeat, down, apparently from SAM fire. I see no chutes."

Two MiGs from Group Alpha were rock-hopping back toward the east. Two more had been downed in the brief, fierce engagement.

Coyote and John-Boy were alone now, three hundred miles from the *Jefferson.*

There was a long silence on the radio. Then Coyote heard Tombstone's voice, ragged with some hard-suppressed emotion. "Roger, Two-oh-one. Camelot copies. Request an update on target Bravo, over."

Target Bravo . . . the unknowns he'd been ordered to pursue. CAG was not-so-gently reminding him that he'd dropped the ball on that one. The mysterious bogies of group Bravo were still on course, crossing the line from land to sea now as they continued to home on the American carrier.

He was going to have to do some hard flying to make good on their mistake now.

"Hey, I don't think the man sounds too pleased with us, Coyote," John-Boy said. "Maybe we shouldn't have broken off, huh?"

"Can it," Coyote snapped savagely. He opened the radio link to the *Jefferson*. "Camelot, Icewall. Pursuing contact Bravo. Stand by."

"Roger, Icewall. Be advised that Alert Five aircraft, call sign Backstop, are airborne and on intercept course with Bravo."

Climbing on flaring afterburners, Coyote took the Tomcat higher, hurtling west. It was difficult to maintain a fix on the targets. Three of them appeared to be fairly solid returns, like fighters . . . but the fourth was different, difficult to interpret on his screen.

And *fast*. Those aircraft were really traveling, hitting Mach 2.1.

Coyote was worried about their velocity. He'd been assuming that his targets were Backfire bombers, big Tu-22Ms able to hit Mach 1.8 at this altitude.

He felt an unpleasant crawling sensation pricking at his spine and the back of his neck. This was something *new*. . . .

Burning fuel at a prodigious rate, Coyote climbed to twenty-eight thousand feet, pushing Mach 2.3. Fortunately, he was well south of the targets' line of flight, which meant that he wasn't in a stern chase. He was able to lead the enemy aircraft and rapidly close the gap. Dun mountains and green forest flashed astern of the Tomcat, replaced by the ragged white of surf, then by the impossibly intense azure of the sea.

"Feet wet," he called. "John-Boy! Can you get a lock yet?"

"I'm . . . I'm trying, Coyote. They don't read as being very large. Damn! I keep losing them. ECM . . ."

"ECM won't stop Sidewinders," Coyote growled. "Or a 20-mm cannon. Let's close to knife-fighting range with these bastards and see what they are."

The range narrowed, mile by mile, John-Boy ticking off the distance. Coyote strained his eyes, scanning the horizon ahead and below. They *ought* to be visible.

He saw them first on the television display of his Tomcat's TXX-1 Television Camera Set, a system tied into a telephoto lens mounted in a blister beneath the F-14's nose. By locking the TCS into the radar data, he could acquire the enemy aircraft visually before they were in eyeball range.

There were four of them, specks swelling steadily on the TV display. In seconds, he could see them with his naked eyes. As he'd suspected, three were fighters, Fulcrums already breaking away from their larger consort as they swung to face him.

But Coyote had eyes only for the aircraft that the Fulcrums were escorting.

It looked like nothing so much as an enormous, dull-gray arrowhead, sharp-nosed, sharp-tailed, with slender, back-swept wings. Comparing its size to the Fulcrums, Coyote estimated the aircraft's length at over one hundred fifty feet, its wingspan at better than a hundred feet, larger than an American B-1B bomber, which, in many ways, it closely resembled. The Russian plane had the same large, paired engines at the root of each wing, the same smooth and sleekly streamlined configuration designed to cut down on the aircraft's radar cross section.

Coyote *knew* that shape, had been seeing it in recognition manuals and charts for years, but never had he seen one live: the Tupolev long-range bomber and missile platform dubbed *Blackjack* by the West.

Blackjack was a direct Soviet response to the American B-1, though painfully little was known about the Russian bomber's capabilities even after ten years. Clearly, like the

B-1, it had some stealth characteristics, though these were not carried to the extremes of the American B-2 and stealth fighter. The smooth design of the fuselage, the absence of bulges or sharply radar-reflecting surfaces, gave it a radar profile far smaller than its actual size might have suggested. Its slender wings could swing in and out like the Tomcat's; at low speeds, when extra lift was necessary, those wings would extend almost straight out from the fuselage. Now, in supersonic flight, they were laid back along the bomber's flanks, transforming it into sleek and deadly beauty.

The Blackjack, Coyote realized, was the source of the ECM jamming. This was an aircraft designed nose to tail to penetrate enemy radar, and survive.

The most disquieting aspect of the bomber's appearance, however, was more political than technical. Everything Coyote had ever read about that enormous machine suggested that it was—like the B-1—a *strategic* weapon, one meant to carry heavy bomb loads or long-ranged cruise missiles, possibly with nuclear warheads. The Blackjack was designed to attack an enemy *country,* not a single ship.

"Camelot, Camelot," he called, urgency rushing his words. "I have contact Bravo in sight. Target is one Blackjack, repeat Blackjack, with three Fulcrums as escort, on course two-seven-five, angels base plus thirteen, speed Mach two point two."

1435 hours Zulu (1535 hours Zone)
CIC, U.S.S. *Thomas Jefferson*
Viking Station, the Norwegian Sea

Aboard the *Jefferson,* all personnel were at their battle stations as the carrier's far-flung electronic web of sensors followed the oncoming threat. In CIC, Tombstone listened to Coyote's voice over a speaker as the aviator described the Soviet flight.

A *Blackjack,* of all goddamned things. Hearing movement behind him, he glanced back over his shoulder.

Admiral Douglas F. Tarrant, commander of the carrier battle group, and Captain Jeremy Brandt, skipper of the *Jefferson,* stood behind him, along with several of their senior staff people. Tarrant was tall, slim, and distinguished, immaculate as always; Brandt seemed the admiral's opposite, bulldog-ugly, short, and stocky, with a stubble of blond hair shading to gray. His khakis looked like he'd slept in them . . . as indeed he probably had. Everyone in CBG-14 had been running minus on sleep for the past several days.

"Excuse me, Admiral, Captain," Tombstone said, stiffening. "I didn't hear you."

"Carry on, CAG," Tarrant said. "Don't mind us. What's the word?"

"One of our F-14s is down, Admiral."

"Damn!"

"The other one just ID'd the intruders. Blackjack with fighter escort."

"A Blackjack!" Brandt said. "Only one?"

"Apparently so, Captain. Coyote—ah, Two-oh-one—has the group in sight. One bomber, three fighters."

"I'd like that confirmed, Paul," Brandt said, turning to Aiken. "See what you can come up with."

"Aye, Captain."

"What's worrying me," Tarrant said, his brow creasing as he scratched his jaw and studied a large repeater screen hanging from the CIC overhead, "is the fact that Blackjack's supposed to be strictly strategic. What the hell is it doing here?"

"It could be a message," Tombstone pointed out. "A warning not to widen the war."

"Back off, or we'll switch to strategic bombing?" Tarrant pulled at his chin. "Maybe. That's going to be something for Washington to work out."

"How long till it gets here?" Brandt asked.

Tombstone studied the data on a computer display. Range now . . . one hundred eighty miles. Speed fourteen-seventy. "Make it seven and a half minutes. If they've got missiles, they'll launch earlier. How much earlier depends on their warload.''

From what he'd read of the new Soviet bomber, Tombstone knew Blackjacks were supposed to carry the new AS-15, a cruise missile similar in most respects to the American Tomahawk. It could carry a nuclear or chemical warhead, though any launch against U.S. ships at this point in the conflict would probably be with high explosives.

Even so, AS-15s packed a terrific wallop. That Blackjack posed a serious threat to the *Jefferson*.

Brandt evidently agreed. ''I want that bastard out of here,'' he snarled, his doleful features more like a bulldog's than ever. ''Shoot him down!''

It was a difficult decision, but the only one possible. There was no time to relay the question back to Washington. There were only the realities of the moment, the realities of tactics, defense, and survival.

Tarrant nodded. ''Agreed. What do we have up there available for intercept?''

Tombstone glanced at a clock on the wall. ''Backstop One and Two launched ten minutes ago, Admiral. They're almost in position now, but at the moment it's Coyote Grant who's running the show.''

''Right. Pass the word. Take the bastard down.''

''Yes, sir.'' Tombstone turned back to the console and picked up a microphone. ''Icewall, Icewall, this is Camelot. Over.''

''Camelot . . .'' The reply sounded strained, as though forced out against the stress of a high-G maneuver. ''Icewall! . . .''

''You are clear to take down the Blackjack. Repeat, kill the Blackjack.''

''Copy.'' To Tombstone's ear, it sounded as though Coyote was pulling eight Gs. He must be turning and burning with the Soviet escort. ''Icewall . . . copies.''

1432 hours Zulu (1532 hours Zone)
Tomcat 201
200 miles east of Viking Station

Coyote felt his Tomcat shudder as he held the impossibly
tight turn, fighting to prevent the aircraft from losing so
much speed that it stalled or flamed out, fighting to maintain
control. The Fulcrums had separated widely, two to the
north, one to the south, then had closed on him from either
side.

"Launch!" John-Boy called. "Missile launch, three
o'clock!"

Coyote saw the white contrail corkscrewing toward his
canopy, heard the radar-threat warning chirrup in his
headset. "Going down, John-Boy!" he warned, and then he
threw the right wing over, sending the inverted F-14
plummeting toward the sea.

"It's an Alamo," John-Boy called, identifying the approaching missile. "AA-10."

"Stand ready with the chaff! Steady . . ." As the
Tomcat picked up speed, the radar-homer nosed over,
plunging after them. "Hit it!"

Packets of chaff—clouds of hair-fine threads of aluminized mylar cut to the specific lengths that blocked the radar
frequencies used in homers like the Alamo—exploded
astern of the diving Tomcat, creating tempting decoys.
Seconds later, when Coyote was sure the Alamo was
committed to its dive, he pulled back on the stick and
hurtled skyward again. The missile continued its plunge
toward the sea.

"Suckered 'em!" John-Boy exulted. "God, that's
great!"

Coyote didn't answer. As he brought the F-14 into a half
roll to the left, the southern Fulcrum drifted across his HUD,
closely pursued by his targeting cursor. "Come to Papa,"
he murmured. The diamond touched the moving speck of

the MiG; the ACQ display blinked on. "AIM-9 lock!" he called, as the Sidewinder registered the heat of the other plane's engines. He stabbed the firing button. "Fox two!"

The Sidewinder hissed off the launch rail, its contrail knifing through the sky. Coyote held the twisting Fulcrum centered in his HUD as the missile closed . . . then struck the Russian plane in the port engine. There was a flash and a puff of smoke, and then the MiG was falling toward the sea. The pilot's chute blossomed a moment later, white, almost motionless against the dark blue of the sea.

"Splash one MiG," John-Boy announced. "I see a chute. Good chute."

With luck, the pilot might be picked up by an American or Norwegian ship.

But Coyote remembered the suddenness of Scorpion's and Juggler's flaming end in the mountains, the emptiness of the sky as he'd searched for their chutes.

The other Fulcrums were out of sight, still circling in an attempt to get into firing position. Ahead, less than two miles away, the enormous gray arrowhead, the Blackjack, continued on course. Coyote was out of Sidewinders, but he still had Phoenix and one Sparrow. The Phoenix warhead was larger. He would go for a Phoenix kill.

"We'll take him with a fox three," he told John-Boy. "Lock him in!"

"Working . . . got it!"

But something was happening to the Soviet bomber. From a pair of bays between massive engine nacelles, first one . . . then another, then four more long, torpedo shapes plunged toward the sea. As he watched, they seemed to steady in their flight, to pick up speed. He was too far away to see wings unfold, but he knew what was happening.

Cruise missiles, each carrying several hundred pounds of high explosive or—the unthinkable!—a small nuclear warhead.

"Fox three!" he yelled, and he felt the Tomcat's skyward lunge as John-Boy mashed the firing button and a Phoenix rocketed from beneath the aircraft's belly.

But it was already too late. Winged death was racing toward the *Jefferson* at several times the speed of sound.

1435 hours Zulu (1535 hours Zone)
CIC, U.S.S. *Thomas Jefferson*
Viking Station, the Norwegian Sea

"We have missile launch," the second class at the CIC console announced, his voice professionally calm. "Tracking six contacts, probably Soviet cruise missiles, bearing zero-eight-five true, range one-six-three nautical miles, and closing."

"God damn," Tarrant said quietly, almost reverently. He looked at Brandt and gave a pale smile. "I hope this boat's as good as you keep telling me it is, Jeremy."

"Damned well better be," Brandt replied. His eyes were glued to the radar screen that showed the small flotilla of missiles closing from the east.

1436 hours Zulu (1536 hours Zone)
Tomcat 201
Off the Norwegian coast

Coyote watched the large air-to-air missile smash into the side of the bomber, just above the root of the wing and the massive port-side engines. The range was a fraction of the hundred-miles-plus for which Phoenix was designed; there were three distinct blasts—the first as the missile's warhead detonated, the second as its largely unexpended core of solid fuel exploded, and the last as the Blackjack's stores of avgas ignited in a dazzling fireball that lit up the sky.

He lost sight of the bomber almost immediately as it was enveloped in the cloud of its own destruction. Seconds later, it reappeared from the cloud's far side, the thing of beauty transformed into a crumpled, falling mass of flaming metal, its skeleton starkly visible as the fire consumed it.

"Camelot! Camelot!" John-Boy was calling from the backseat, his voice betraying excitement and sheer joy. "Splash one Blackjack! I say again, splash—"

But the RIO never completed his report, for the Tomcat was shuddering violently, as someone played a jackhammer across the fuselage aft of the cockpit. Coyote's helmet slammed against the canopy as the aircraft yawed hard to starboard. Warning lights flared across his right-hand console. He was losing fuel, half a dozen electronics systems had failed . . . and *damn!* The engine fire-warning light was on!

The Tomcat was buffeted again as a pair of silver shapes flashed past, yards from his port wingtip. Fulcrums! The last two MiG-29s had closed in on his six, opening up with a deadly accurate volley of cannon fire.

"John-Boy!" he called . . . but the ICS was out. He couldn't tell if his RIO was alive or dead, but he could hear the high, thin whistle of air through a breach in the cockpit.

Coyote slapped the switch that killed his port engine. Deprived of fuel, the engine fire light went out . . . but the Tomcat was limping now on one engine, and those Fulcrums were already circling for another pass, this time from head-on.

He battled the controls, but there wasn't a thing he could do to fight back. It was all he could do to hold the F-14 in the air. His radar was gone, his VDI blank, his HUD gone. In that moment, Coyote knew he was going to die, and the shock overwhelmed everything else.

Again, Coyote Grant thought of Julie, his wife, as he watched the Fulcrums drop into position for a final pass.

CHAPTER 4
Wednesday, 18 June

Captain Brandt and the admiral had left CIC Air Ops, but
Tombstone had not even heard them go. He was mesmer-
ized by the chatter between aircraft as Backstop One and
Two rendezvoused with Icewall. The drama unfolding two
hundred miles to the east had managed to shut everything
else from his thoughts.

The large screen showing air radar contacts repeated from
the E-2C was a crawling mass of blips, most flagged by
identifying codes and information on altitude, course, and
speed. Time seemed to have stopped since the moment,
seconds ago, when Coyote had reported he was hit. Backstop was within twenty miles of his position and had just
reported Sparrow locks on the two Fulcrums as they closed
for the kill.

"Icewall, Icewall, this is Backstop One!" Tombstone
allowed himself a smile, a small one. The exuberant voice
was a familiar one, belonging to an old friend of his. "How
are you, Coyote, you old varmint?"

"About time you guys got here," Coyote's voice replied.
"I got troubles."

"Roger that. Just sit back and leave the driving to us.
Hold her steady, Loon. I'm moving into position."

"Loon" was Lieutenant Adam Baird, in Tomcat 205.

"Roger, Batman," Loon's voice replied. "Take your shot, man, take your shot!"

Batman. Lieutenant Commander Edward E. Wayne, a young aviator whom Tombstone had once chastised for being an irresponsible pilot, a "hotdog," and who'd gone on to become one of the best flyers in the wing. He was now the XO of VF-95.

"I got tone," Batman called. "Fox one!"

"Missile launch, CAG," the radarman said. Tombstone could see the rapidly moving pinpoint of the Sparrow. Backstop was using an eyeball-shooter formation, with Loon painting the target while Batman popped the missile. A second Sparrow sped toward the targets as he watched.

The Fulcrums had been closing steadily on Coyote's limping Tomcat, but they seemed to become aware of the approaching Backstop F-14s at that moment, probably when their own radar receivers detected the SARH lock. On the radar screen, they seemed to be drifting apart. The missiles followed, curving steadily to either side as they pursued their respective targets.

It had grown very quiet in Air Ops, as the duty personnel listened to the unfolding drama. The Russian MiGs were still close enough to Coyote that they could finish the job on his damaged Tomcat quite easily. But as second followed second, it became clear that they were leaving the field, plunging back toward the Norwegian coast at high speed, each pursued by a tiny, deadly hound.

"They're running!" Batman called. "Camelot, Camelot, this is Backstop. Bandits have decided to get out of Dodge!"

The Sparrows pursued. One, the missile guided by Loon, merged with the target, then kept on going, as the MiG jinked hard to the right. Evidently, the Russian had decoyed the Sparrow with chaff.

The second missile closed . . . merged . . . and then the blip marking the distant Fulcrum seemed to expand, then fade. Individual pieces flickered in and out of existence as their radar aspects changed. The wreckage was falling into the sea.

"Camelot, Backstop One. Splash one MiG!"

Cheers rang out in CIC, as sailors yelled, stabbed clenched fists in the air, or slapped each other's backs and hands.

"Belay that!" Tombstone snapped. "We're not out of this yet!" He picked up the microphone. "Icewall, Icewall, Camelot One. What is your condition, over?"

"Camelot, Icewall. I'm . . . okay. I think John-Boy might be hit, though. Can't raise him on the ICS. Losing fuel, but not too bad. Down to twelve hundred pounds on one engine. All in all, I'm doing okay, I guess. Damn, those bastards can shoot!"

"Roger. We read you in the clear. Backstop will bring you in. Do you copy?"

"Affirmative, Camelot. Copy. But I hope I've got a place to land this piece of junk when I get there. You've got six buzz bombs on the way."

"We see 'em, Icewall, and it's up to Surface Ops now." He kept his voice light. "You just get yourself down on the deck in one piece. That's an order."

"Affirmative, CAG. I'll see what I can do."

But Tombstone's eyes strayed to the rapidly moving cluster of dots closing on the carrier. Coyote's fears were real. If *Jefferson* and her escorts couldn't stop that deadly formation of supersonic death, he was going to have to find a friendly airfield in Norway on which to land.

Because *Jefferson* might very well not be available within another few minutes.

1437 hours Zulu (1537 hours Zone)
Bridge, U.S.S. *Esek Hopkins*
Viking Station, the Norwegian Sea

The *Esek Hopkins* was a frigate, one of the ubiquitous Oliver Hazard Perry–class FFGs that now played such a prominent role in U.S. Navy operations around the globe.

Smaller than a destroyer, but crammed with nearly a DDG's punch in weapons and advanced electronics, she carried a crew of two hundred. Designed for antisubmarine warfare, her effectiveness crippled, her critics insisted, by budget cuts before the first of her class had been launched, *Hopkins* and her sister FFGs still performed a wide variety of duties, from tanker escort to air screen, from ASW to show-the-flag.

Hopkins was currently serving as part of the ASW screen protecting the leviathan heart of CBG-14, the U.S.S. *Thomas Jefferson*. The carrier was visible now as a vast, gray shadow on the western horizon five miles off the frigate's port bow. The ship had been at battle stations for a tension-filled two hours already. When word of the enemy missile launch crackled over the bridge speaker from CIC, it was like releasing a powerfully wound spring.

"Bridge! CIC! We have missile launch! Multiple contacts! Multiple contacts, bearing zero-eight-five, range one-six-zero!"

"Thank you." Commander Don Strachan, captain of the *Hopkins,* kept his voice level, conscious of the effect it would have on the men. He was a tall, gangly man of thirty-nine, a native of Baltimore who'd begun his career as an enlisted man because he'd not yet acquired the college credits necessary for graduation. Strachan had gone on to get his degree, and an appointment to OCS.

Now he stood on the bridge of his first command. His mouth twitched as he remembered the wardroom discussions he'd had with some of his officers over the merits of Perry FFGs. He didn't like them, didn't like the nasty tendency they had to burn when hit by even one ship-killer. Well, now they were about to find out just how the little ship could stand up to modern combat. "Maneuvering, come left four-five. Make revolutions for thirty knots. Weps Control. Stand by with chaff, starboard battery. Crank up R2, automatic mode." Unnecessarily, he added, "This one's for real, people."

Hopkins's Close-in Weapons System——CIWS for short,

commonly pronounced "sea-whiz"—housed its own track-ing radar, six-barreled Phalanx Gatling gun, magazine, and control electronics inside a prominent, white-painted silo fifteen feet high. Hence its other popular nickname, "R2D2." The weapon was mounted aft on Perry-class frigates, atop their helicopter hangars and overlooking the fantail helo pad. By turning left slightly, Strachan was giving the CIWS a clear view of the targets.

The only problem was, Phalanx had been designed as a last-ditch, close-defense weapon, its effective range limited to about 2100 meters, less than a mile and a half.

A cruise missile could cover that distance in a handful of seconds.

Modern warfare, Strachan reflected, was less and less a matter of men fighting men, and more of machines versus machines. A battle consisted of preparation and endless waiting . . . followed by a few stark and terrifying sec-onds of activity, speeds, and responses too fast for human minds to comprehend.

There was a flash to the east, and a streak of white smoke arrowed into the sky.

"*Winslow* reports Sea Sparrow away," DuPont reported from CIC.

"Damn! Too soon!" The *John A. Winslow* was another member of CBG-14, a guided-missile destroyer cruising parallel to the *Hopkins,* some fifteen miles to the east. Sea Sparrow was a surface-to-air missile with a range of only about ten nautical miles. *Winslow* had just wasted an antiair missile.

"Hold it a minute. Wait one . . ." There was a mo-ment's pause. "Captain, *Winslow* reports a failure with their Mark 29. Accidental launch and the launcher's down. They're out of it."

Worse and worse. Sea Sparrow did not always work as advertised. More than once during his naval career, Strachan had joined in with the hoots and laughter when the bridge would announce a test launch, followed by a puff of smoke and an embarrassed silence.

There was no laughter now. The tension grew palpably.

The minutes dragged by, punctuated by reports from Lieutenant Commander DuPont, the TO in *Hopkins*'s Combat Information Center. During that time, *Hopkins* clawed her way northward at top speed, interposing herself between the missiles and their presumed target—the *Jefferson*.

"Lead missiles closing at one-eight miles," DuPont's voice announced. There was a pause. "*Jefferson* reports Sea Sparrows ready for launch. They're tracking, range two-three miles."

"Do we have a Standard lock yet?"

"Negative, sir. We . . . belay that! We've got it! Standard lock!"

"Sound the alarm." The missile alert bell clanged for ten seconds, a final warning to those on the forward deck to clear the area.

"Fire!"

Hopkins's bridge lit up as the missile mounted on her forward deck immediately below streaked into the sky on a column of flame and white smoke.

"Missile away," CIC reported. "Reloading . . ."

Seconds dragged past, the wait drawing on with agonizing suspense.

"Standard missed."

"Damn! Keep firing!"

Seconds later, another launch shooshed skyward from the forward deck, streaking toward the eastern horizon. Strachan found himself holding his breath.

"One-two miles." There was a far-off flash at the horizon, like the silent popping of a camera's flashbulb. "Hit!" someone on the bridge yelled. "We nailed the bastard!" Someone else cheered and was joined by two or three others.

"Belay that!" Strachan called. "As you were!"

"Standard hit!" The voice of CIC broke the silence. "Remaining incoming missiles now at one-zero miles."

"Heading now steady on two-six-five, Captain," the helmsman reported. That meant *Hopkins* was steaming at a sharp angle to the oncoming missiles, presenting her stern.

"Missiles still coming," CIC reported. "Five targets, range from nine miles to one-five miles. Speed steady."

"Are you tracking with the Mark 75?" *Hopkins* carried a single OTO Melera Mark 75 turret on her deck housing amidships.

"Yes, sir."

"Very well. Commence fire."

The banging of the Mark 75 began almost at once, a steady *boom*-pause-*boom*-pause-*boom* from aft that hurled fourteen-pound, sixty-two-caliber shells at the rate of seventy-five per minute. It was designed for use against shore targets, ships or aircraft, and its effectiveness against a fast-moving missile was questionable at best. The remote-controlled gun had a range of ten or eleven miles but did not have the Phalanx's self-aiming radar lock.

But at least the reassuring thump of gunfire would help the waiting.

"Range six miles . . ."

"Bridge, CIC! Firing Standard!" Raw noise filled the bridge.

"Confirm CIWS on auto!"

"Confirmed, Captain."

Two more pinpoints of light arrowed away from the *Hopkins,* and after a pause of several seconds, two from the *Jefferson.*

Sea Sparrows and Standards had a kill probability of less than fifty percent on small, fast targets like antiship missiles. How many would get through? "CIC, Captain," Strachan said. "Manual select on the CIWS. Protect the *Jefferson.*"

"Aye, aye, sir. Our range to *Jefferson* now fourteen thousand yards."

Eight miles. *Hopkins* was squarely between the oncoming missiles and the carrier she was trying to protect.

"Ready on the RBOC."

"Standing by, Captain."

"Seduction mode. Fire!"

"Firing chaff." There was a thump from aft, blending with the steady thud of the ship's turret gun. The Mark 34 was a twin-tube chaff launcher installed aboard small Navy ships. Called RBOC, for Rapid-Bloom Off-board Counter-measures, it fired chaff shells into the path of oncoming missiles. By firing before the ship-killers' on-board radars locked on, it might be possible to lure them off course with several well-placed clouds of aluminum-coated mylar thread.

"RBOC fired, Captain."

"Keep firing, damn it!" They might not be able to decoy all of the missiles, but the more chaff clouds they could plant out there, the better their chances.

One of *Jefferson*'s Sea Sparrows struck, the detonation a brilliant flash only a mile off *Hopkins*'s port side.

"Four missiles now," CIC reported. "One locking onto *Jefferson*. The others aren't spoken for yet."

Then things began happening with inhuman speed.

1444 hours Zulu (1544 hours Zone)
Soviet AS-15
Viking Station, the Norwegian Sea

As the cruise missiles reached their search zone their radar seekers snapped on. The search radius was small enough that only one target should appear within each zone, yet large enough that the target would not have been able to escape during the missile's flight time.

But three targets showed where there should have been one. The missiles' brains were too primitive to register anything like surprise at the appearance of an extra target. Following programming, they began locking on the largest, strongest target.

Normally, that would have been the carrier, but *Hopkins* was dispensing a steady stream of chaff into the air astern of the fast-moving frigate, chaff that was blooming into an enormous, radar-reflecting cloud.

One of the AS-15s was diverted by the chaff, locking onto a ghost echo and veering sharply south. The remaining three missiles still had to lock on, and at this range selection was controlled by Moving Target Indication circuitry, or MTI, a feature designed to eliminate ground clutter and provide the missiles with a clearer lock on surface targets.

Moving targets. At sea level, chaff quickly loses any momentum imparted by the launcher as it disperses into a cloud, then falls at a rate of one or two feet per second.

Hopkins was still steaming northwest at thirty knots as the radars of three AS-15s ignored the chaff cloud and the more distant *Jefferson,* and locked onto her.

1445 hours Zulu (1545 hours Zone)
Hangar, U.S.S. *Hopkins*
Viking Station, the Norwegian Sea

The first cruise missile came in from *Hopkins*'s starboard quarter, ten feet over the water, as *Hopkins*'s Mark 75 banged away, sending geysers of water soaring up in tight-bunched pillars around the hurtling missile. Above the frigate's hangar, the Phalanx tower slewed about sharply on its axis, the six-barreled cannon swinging into line as the target came into range. With a searing, buzzsaw shriek, the barrels spun, spewing depleted uranium rounds at the rate of fifty rounds per second.

Neither explosive nor radioactive, each bullet killed by throwing a lot of mass very quickly. They were heavy, two and a half times denser than steel, and they hurtled into the missile's path at one thousand feet per second. The Phalanx's J-band, pulse-doppler radar simultaneously tracked both incoming target and projectiles, correcting the aim for each brief burst.

The CIWS fired again . . . corrected, then fired once

more. There was a flash of light, a flat bang, and chunks of metal splattered into the sea.

Shifting aim to tag the second oncoming contact, the CIWS engaged the final contact, but there was no more time. Faster than the speed of sound, the AS-15 flashed past the still-expanding puff of smoke that marked the destroyed ship-killer, arrowing toward the *Hopkins*'s stern. The CIWS had time for a single burst; one round nicked a fin and tore it free, sending the missile tumbling.

An instant later—and before the Phalanx could correct its aim and fire again—the warhead slammed into the frigate's starboard quarter.

It failed to explode immediately but plunged through the hangar bulkheads, shredding the fuel pipelines that serviced the frigate's two helicopters. When the detonation came half a second later, gushing fuel and vapor mingled with the blast, ripping the hangar apart in a thundering crash and sending the R2D2 unit spinning into the sky atop a geysering fountain of orange flame.

The second cruise missile streaked in from starboard seconds later, striking the frigate in her boxy superstructure twenty-two feet above her waterline. Designed to explode after penetrating a ship's hull, the AS-15 punched through bulkheads like a bullet through foil, exploding squarely beneath the bridge.

In a searing bloom of pyrotechnics, the *Esek Hopkins* began to burn.

CHAPTER 5
Wednesday, 18 June

1445 hours Zulu (1545 hours Zone)
U.S.S. *Esek Hopkins*
Viking Station, the Norwegian Sea

Flames broke from the shattered superstructure forward of the ruin of the mast as Lieutenant Commander DuPont made it out onto the ship's deck, fumbling with the snaps on his life jacket. Acrid smoke, made harsh by burning plastics, propellants, and chemicals, hung thick in the air, making breathing difficult.

From the starboard railing amidships, he could look forward and see the gaping, jagged-edged hole in the superstructure where the first missile had entered the ship. Much of the upper half of *Hopkins*'s deckhouse forward of the SPS-49 mast was simply gone, including the fire-control director, the comm shack, and the bridge. Flames roared into the sky, wreathing between the shattered struts of radar masts and the peeled-back wreckage of the bridge deck. A second fire burned aft amid the ruin of the helicopter hangar.

Everywhere, the backlit silhouettes of sailors moved against the flames, men pulling comrades from the wreckage, uncoiling fire hoses, playing water and foam against the blaze, or helping one another stagger away from the fire. The ship was listing to starboard, and DuPont had to lean slightly to stand upright.

"Commander DuPont!" From aft, Chief Castellano, enlisted head of *Hopkins*'s damage-control department, moved toward him, clinging to the safety railing. "Commander! I can't raise the bridge! Who's in charge?"

DuPont glanced again at the crater where the bridge had once been. Both the Captain and the Exec had been up there when hell had come calling. "I guess I am, Chief. What's the word?"

Castellano pulled himself upright. There was a nasty burn on the right side of his face, and his khakis and life jacket were oil-soaked and wet. "Don't know about forward, sir. I was on my way up there to see. Aft . . ." He shrugged. "It's bad, sir. Major fires. We have fire parties on them. Mostly burning fuel from the helo inside the hangar. Turbines are shut down. We're taking some water. Sprung plates, probably. Watertight doors are sealed and the pumps are working. We have ten degrees of list now but we seem to be holding." He flashed a wry grin. "So far, anyway."

DuPont nodded. If the list became too great, *Hopkins* would roll over and sink beneath the waves. "Communications?"

"Just sound-powered phones and walkie-talkies, sir. Ship intercom is out." He nodded toward the distant gray shape of the carrier, visible through the roiling smoke. "We do have radio contact with the *Jefferson*."

DuPont rubbed his face, thinking hard. What to do? The smart move might be to abandon ship now, before the frigate became so water-heavy she turned turtle and sank . . . or before the flames raged out of control and fried them all.

But Frank DuPont was a stubborn sailor, son, grandson, and great-grandson of Massachusetts seafaring men. He'd served on Perry-class frigates before. More than once, he and Captain Strachan had argued the merits of the misbegotten little vessels. He'd agreed with Strachan on the ship's shortcomings, but he'd been convinced of their value as well.

Besides, this situation was familiar, too familiar for him to give up all hope right away.

On May 17, 1987, just ten years and one month before, DuPont had been a very junior lieutenant on board FFG-31, the U.S.S. *Stark,* on patrol in the Persian Gulf, when an Iraqi Mirage F-1 locked on and fired two Exocet missiles. Both had struck the starboard side between the bridge and the Mark 13 missile launcher forward, though only one of the missiles had actually detonated. Damage had been severe, especially to the bridge, and thirty-two men had died. There'd been considerable debate afterward about the ship's lack of defensive preparations . . . but only praise for the efforts of her damage-control team. *Stark* had made it out of the Gulf on her own and ultimately limped back to the States for repair.

A year later, one of DuPont's friends had been on another Perry FFG, the *Samuel B. Roberts,* when she'd hit an Iranian mine in the Gulf. The explosion had broken the frigate's back and come within an ace of sinking her . . . but she too had been saved by the damage-control training, determination, and skill of the Navy men on board her.

Strachan's criticisms of the Perrys might be well-founded, but the fact remained that the FFGs were damned hard to kill. Hell, they might save the *Hopkins* yet.

The thought of Captain Strachan stung. "Okay," DuPont said, deciding. He watched as two sailors dragged a third between them out of the superstructure and laid him on the tilting deck. "We'll see to taking off the wounded first. Can a LAMPS set down on our helo pad?"

"Wouldn't risk it, sir. The fire aft's still pretty hot, and the deck may be damaged. But they'll be able to hover as soon as we get the fire out."

"Okay. Concentrate on that fire so we can get our wounded aft to the pad. We'll start taking them off as soon as you have the fire under control, as many at a time as a helo can manage. Radio *Jefferson* and have them get some helos airborne. And tell them to stand by to take off the DC parties if we need to abandon ship."

"If . . ." The chief looked startled. "We're *not* abandoning, sir?"

"No way, Chief. I want to prove something to Captain Strachan. We're going to *save* this bitch!"

"Yes, *sir*!" The chief snapped a salute, then grinned. "I heard you were on the *Stark*. Maybe your luck'll rub off on us too!"

"Right, Chief. Let's just hope it's the right *kind* of luck!"

1515 hours Zulu (1615 hours Zone)
Tomcat 201
Viking Station, the Norwegian Sea

"Icewall One, you are clear. Casting off."

"Roger, Tex," Coyote replied. His voice grated; his throat was dry. He eased back on the stick, breaking contact between his F-14's refueling probe and the basket trailing astern of the KA-6D tanker looming above and in front of his cockpit. "Coming left. Thanks for the drink."

"Any time, Icewall. Good luck."

Coyote let out a ragged breath as controls continued to function, as instruments continued to give acceptable readings. *Good luck* . . .

He would need every erg of luck he could muster to get his wounded aircraft onto the deck in one piece. Looking toward the horizon, he could just make out the *Jefferson,* a toy on the endless, glittering blue of the ocean, twenty miles distant. Pri-Fly had ordered him to stay aloft until the carrier's traffic patterns could be cleared, and his rapidly falling fuel levels had required him to rendezvous with the tanker, a "Texaco" in Navy aviation parlance. Refueling complete, he made a gentle turn toward the huge, oval racecourse in the sky known as the Marshall Stack, a holding pattern where he could loiter until Pri-Fly called him in.

A sharp, thuttering vibration from behind made it feel as though the aircraft was shaking itself to pieces. The engine-fire light was out, however. If his turkey——Navy slang for Tomcats——would just stay in one piece a little longer . . .

"Hey, John-Boy?" he called. "John-Boy! Can you hear me?"

No answer . . . and still no way to tell whether the ICS was working. The complete lack of sound from the F-14's backseat had convinced him that his RIO was dead or unconscious. Earlier, Pri-Fly had asked if he wanted to eject, and it was John-Boy's silence that had convinced him to stay with the damaged aircraft.

Years before, during the air operations over North Korea after the capture of a U.S. intelligence ship off Wonsan, Tombstone Magruder had won the Navy Cross. Part of his citation had described how he elected to stick with his crippled Tomcat, riding it in to the carrier's flight deck because his RIO was wounded and would have died in an ejection. Coyote found himself in a similar dilemma now. Safest would be to eject now, and let the SH-3 helicopter dubbed "Angel One," hovering as it always did during launch and recovery operations a mile off *Jefferson*'s port side, pluck him from the sea.

But he couldn't make a decision like that without knowing John-Boy's condition. As long as Pri-Fly gave him clearance for a trap on *Jefferson*'s deck, that was what he would try for.

Radio chatter crackled and buzzed in his headset, spill-over from other channels intruding on the traffic-control frequency. He caught the distant words ". . . fire on the deck . . ." and knew he was listening in on a conversation between the stricken *Hopkins,* now many miles to the southeast, and *Jefferson*'s CIC. Word that the frigate had been hit by two air-to-surface cruise missiles had reached Coyote during his return to Viking Station.

Guilt gnawed at him like a raw wound. He'd not been able to reach Scorpion and Juggler in time to save them, and he'd reached the Russian Blackjack just too late to stop it from launching its ship-killers.

Navy aviators tended to be an arrogant lot, though it was arrogance well-placed. They were the best at what they did, masters of their professions, of their domains.

But it was hard to admit *failure*.

Coyote knew now that he should have stayed on the Blackjack. Scorp and Juggler would still have died, but he might have been able to take out the Soviet bomber.

Might, *might* . . .

Coyote shook his head. Damn it all, he'd made the best judgment call he could. If faced with the same situation again, the same decision again, he was certain that he would make the same choice.

Another Tomcat pulled alongside Coyote's aircraft on the right. The number on its nose was 110, and the device painted in muted, camouflage grays on the tail was a bird of prey, diving with extended talons. VF-97, the War Eagles, was the other Tomcat squadron stationed aboard the Jefferson.

"Viper Two-oh-one," a voice called over his headset. "This is Eagle One-one-oh on your starboard wing. How about a visual, over?"

"Roger that," Coyote replied. "But if I'm missing something like my tail section, don't tell me."

"No sweat, Viper. Looks like you have some scraps missing from your stabilizers, but they're still in one piece. Sit tight a mike while we inspect."

Gently, the other Tomcat circled Coyote's aircraft as its RIO eyeballed the damaged F-14 from every angle. He'd already been inspected once by the KA-6D just before linking up for refueling. This, he knew, would be the inspection that decided whether or not the Air Boss was going to let him try a recovery.

"Okay, Viper Two-oh-one," the voice said after a moment. "You've got a bunch of holes topside, just aft of the canopy. Looks like your forward fuselage fuel tanks and the starboard engine bay were holed big-time. That's the bad news. Good news is there's not much damage visible on your underside. Your tailhook appears undamaged. Same for your wheel-well doors."

"Eagle One-one-oh, can you get a visual on my RIO? What's his condition, over?"

''Rog, we see him. Head's down, no response that we can see. Looks like he's out.'' The voice left unspoken the possibility that John-Boy was dead. ''There's some damage to the canopy. Looks like a round or a fragment hit it, starboard side aft. Can't tell if your RIO was in the way or not.''

''Okay, One-one-oh. Thanks.''

''Anytime, Viper Two-oh-one. We'll see you on deck.''

And then he was alone once more.

The memory stole up on Coyote, sharp and unexpected, a scene from the last time he'd been home, of him standing hand in hand with Julie, his wife, on a huge and weathered boulder at Great Falls. The vista of boulders, woods, and spectacular, crag-leaping waterfalls on the Potomac a few miles northwest of Washington, D.C., had all the intensity of a waking dream. Almost, he could sense Julie's warmth and smell the fresh-grass scent of her hair as she pressed close to him, inside the circle of his arm. The yearning made him tremble.

Julie . . .

Suddenly, he wanted her very much. The memory was replaced by another: their last night together before he'd left for the *Jefferson*. He was *there*, in the bedroom of their home in the officers' housing at Norfolk, as she rode his hips in the half-light of the early, early morning, her sides slick with sweat as he held her, the air heavy with the mingled odors of their lovemaking.

He missed his wife so badly his breath caught in his throat. And their daughter, Julie Marie . . .

Angrily, he pulled his oxygen mask aside and swallowed several hard gulps of the cockpit's air. What would happen to them if he bought the farm in these next few moments? After years of Navy flying, suddenly nothing else seemed to matter but the knowledge that he loved his family with a depth and passion he'd never before been able to more than dimly sense. He tried to read his cockpit instruments. It was as though his helmet visor was fogged and obscuring his

view, though the visor was up. For some reason he couldn't
see, couldn't *focus* . . .

"Icewall One, this is the Boss." The voice of Commander Jack Monroe, *Jefferson*'s Air Boss, crackled in
Coyote's headset and snapped him back to the here and
now. The Air Boss was the god of Pri-Fly, or Primary Flight
Control as it was more usually called, the control tower of
a seagoing airport. The Boss was lord of an aerial domain
extending for twenty miles around the carrier.

Damn. Coyote's hands were shaking as he refastened his
mask across his face.

"Y-yeah, Boss." The dryness in his throat was worse.
"Icewall copies."

"Icewall, you are cleared for trap. We have erected the
barricade. Do you copy, over?"

"Roger that. Barricade up." The barricade was a net
stretched across the flight deck in front of the island,
designed to snag crippled aircraft that, for one reason or
another, could not use their arrestor gear. Coming down on
a flight deck with the barricade erected was, for Navy
aviators, an unnatural act. No pilot likes to see an obstacle
stretched across the runway in front of him, and the shock
of impact was worse than the sharp snatch-yank of an
arrested landing.

"Two-oh-one, charlie now."

That was the command to begin his approach. Gently,
Coyote brought the Tomcat into a turn, following a precisely
regulated path that led past and astern of the *Jefferson*.
Normally, he would have slowed the Tomcat until it spread
its variable-geometry wings to full spread, but Coyote had
already been deliberately keeping his airspeed under three
hundred knots and the wings spread. With one crippled
engine he needed all the additional lift he could get.
Aviators referred to the F-14's wings-extended position as
"goose mode" because of the ungainly appearance it gave
their aircraft as they made their approach, and they usually
overrode the plane's computers to keep the wings back.

At this point, Coyote didn't give a damn for appearances. He just wanted to get down on the deck.

The shudder from astern increased in intensity, kicking and bucking as he fought the controls. Coyote clung to the control stick, his breath rasping inside the rubbery gag of his oxygen mask, sweat making his face slick and pooling where mask and helmet dimpled his skin.

Two hundred thirty knots. He dropped the flaps, praying that they would work. The bucking increased . . . then steadied as the Tomcat's nose came up. "Hang on, John-Boy," he said. "Damn it, hang on! . . ."

He pulled out of a twenty-two-degree angle of bank, dropping toward the ocean now at six hundred feet per minute. *Jefferson* was a toy on the water, ridiculously tiny, three quarters of a mile ahead.

The Tomcat's Instrument Landing System was out, dead. Dead too was the laser sight, a relatively new system that would have read laser light from the carrier and helped him stay in the proper glide path and attitude.

He was going to have to pull this one off the old-fashioned way. At least when he lowered the landing gear, that worked. He could feel the reassuring whine-thump as the wheels locked into position, more reassuring than the gear-down light on his console.

"Two-oh-one," he heard over his headset. That was the voice of the LSO, the Landing Signal Officer, who was watching Coyote's approach from his vantage point along the port side of the flight deck. "Call the ball."

Coyote's eyes sought the ball, the green bull's-eye on the Fresnel landing system tower that showed him, by seeming to drift above or below a pair of horizontal dashes, whether he was above or below the desired glide path. "Uh . . . Tomcat Two-oh-one, five-point-oh, ball."

That told the LSO that he had the meatball in sight, confirmed that his aircraft was a Tomcat so that the arrestor cables could be properly adjusted for the hurtling weight of the aircraft, and that his fuel was reading five thousand pounds. He'd not taken on a full load of fuel from the

KA-6D; if he crashed into the *Jefferson*'s roundoff, the less JP-5 aboard, the better.

Savagely, he shook the stark image—of his F-14 hurtling into *Jefferson*'s stern and exploding into a boiling fireball— from his mind.

If only his hands would stop shaking.

"Roger ball," the LSO said, confirming his call. "Remember your hook."

Shit! He'd forgotten to lower his arrestor gear, and the LSO had caught that through binoculars. He snapped the control, praying for the hook to swing down.

Thank you, God, it did.

Landing an aircraft on the tiny, pitching runway, the flight deck of a carrier under way at sea, was never easy. During Vietnam, aviators had been wired for heart-beat, respiration, blood pressure, and the like and their physiological responses recorded during a variety of typical flight activities. Trapping aboard a carrier—especially at night—made men's hearts race and their sweat flow more than any other single operation, including getting shot at by enemy triple-A or SAMs.

I am not going to crash, I am not going to bolter. I'm going to bring this bitch down lightly as a feather, snag the three-wire, just like a walk in the park. . . .

Other times, visualizing a perfect trap had steadied him in this, the one maneuver that Naval aviators never entirely looked forward to. This time it didn't help. His breathing was one adrenaline-tinged gasp after another, so loud in his own ears that he almost didn't hear the LSO's next words.

"Steady, Two-oh-one. Deck going down. Power down."

The LSO was telling him that the carrier's stern was dropping, that he needed to ease back on his power a bit to compensate. Gingerly, he brought the throttle forward, feeling more than hearing the engine's dwindling pitch.

The deck looked like it was rising, rushing up to meet him, accelerating now as he swept in toward the roundoff. These were the critical few seconds when a bad call by him or the LSO could screw everything. He took a last gulp of air, then held his breath. Details of the dark gray deck, of sailors standing to either side of the white guidelines burned themselves into his consciousness. He could see the barricade stretched like a tennis net across the deck forward, could see the gangling, Tinkertoy shape of the Tilly, the wheeled crane, and the crash crews standing ready in case he came down hard. . . .

"You're low," the LSO warned in his headset. "Power up. *Power up!* . . ."

Jefferson's stern seemed to rise in front of his cockpit like a gray steel cliff—an illusion, he knew, but terrifying nonetheless. He pushed the throttle forward, pulling the stick back at the same time, pulling the nose up . . .

And then he was out of time. The Tomcat swept in toward the roundoff, but too low . . . too low . . .

"Wave-off! Wave-off!" the LSO was screaming in his ear. Then, *"Eject! Eject! Eject!"*

He felt the savage jolt as his main wheels struck the rim of the steel cliff and snapped off. The full weight of the Tomcat came down on the nose wheel, which broke away under the impact, slamming the F-14's nose to the deck.

In the same instant, his vision blurred and shot through with dazzling sparks, Coyote grabbed the brightly striped eject handle and yanked it, hard.

Nothing happened. Coyote's scream was lost in the shriek of steel scraping steel as the Tomcat careened across the deck.

CHAPTER 6
Wednesday, 18 June

1532 hours Zulu (1632 hours Zone)
Vulture's Row, U.S.S. *Thomas Jefferson*
Viking Station, the Norwegian Sea

Tombstone had come up to the steel-railed walkway set atop the carrier's island, just beneath the clutter of her radio and radar masts and antennas. Vulture's Row, as the eyrie was called, was a favorite retreat of his. From here, he had an unobstructed view of the carrier's flight deck both fore and aft.

Moments after the word had been passed to stand down from General Quarters, Tombstone had come here to watch Coyote's recovery. The PLAT monitors in CIC were displaying the scene, of course, but he wanted to be *here,* willing his old friend to bring himself and his RIO and his aircraft down to the safety of *Jefferson*'s flight deck. He held his breath as he watched the damaged Tomcat make its approach, growing from a tiny speck in the sky astern of the carrier, to a Tomcat coming in nose-high, wings wobbling as Coyote battled the controls. Then the F-14's undercarriage slammed into the roundoff, the nose wheel strut snapped, and the twenty-ton aircraft was sliding wildly down the deck toward the barricade. Crewmen on the deck scrambled for safety as the F-14, its left wing dragging on steel, spun broadside, snapping the arrestor cables one after another as it hurtled toward a row of A-6 Intruders just abaft of the island.

Tombstone willed Coyote to punch out, but the Tomcat
continued its slide across the deck, sparks showering from
its undercarriage. It narrowly missed the Intruders, then
slammed into the barricade stretched across its path. The
carrier's 5-MC, the loudspeaker system on the flight deck,
was blaring an alarm klaxon, as a voice bellowed, "Fire on
the deck! Fire on the flight deck!"

And fire *was* licking from the root of the F-14's wing. As
jet fuel dribbled from ruptured tanks and pooled on the
deck, each second threatened to turn the Tomcat, trapped
now in the barricade net like an insect in a spider's web, into
a roaring inferno.

Tombstone watched, transfixed, as the flight deck fire
party, identified by their red jerseys, closed in on the
burning aircraft. Fire extinguishers shooshed and roared,
spraying clouds of CO_2 across hot metal, damping the
flames licking now about the cockpit. The Tilly closed in,
ungainly, swaying with its own uneven movements as it
edged a basket close to the Tomcat's cockpit. A man in a
silver flamesuit wielded his fire extinguisher, as hospital
corpsmen clambered onto the wing with a pair of wire-
frame Stokes stretchers. Other crewmen were already at
work on the canopy with pry bars.

"Come on," Tombstone murmured, half aloud. Then
louder, "Come on, damn it! Get them out of there! . . ."

1533 hours Zulu (1633 hours Zone)
Tomcat 201, flight deck, U.S.S. *Thomas Jefferson*
Viking Station, the Norwegian Sea

Coyote regained consciousness aware of a dozen anxious
faces pressed around his canopy. The Tomcat was at rest
and it wasn't burning, thank God. He fumbled with his
oxygen mask and pulled it from his face, gulping down huge
gasps of welcome air.

The barricade was made of interwoven canvas straps.
Those straps now pressed over his canopy, keeping it from

opening. Coyote's initial relief was engulfed by a new fear. If the aircraft caught fire now, he was trapped inside, unable to escape.

That thought led to another. Damn it, he had yanked the ejection seat handle, but nothing had happened. His surprise at that fact was almost the last thought he'd had as his aircraft had slammed into the deck. The powerful rockets in the bases of his and John-Boy's seats should have triggered, firing them both clear of the aircraft, allowing them to come down on parachutes into the sea.

There'd been a malfunction, obviously. But suppose the seats were to fire now, with the canopy firmly clamped in place by the barricade straps?

One of the enlisted men outside brought the blade of a power saw close to the plexiglass. There was a shriek, deafening and high-pitched, as the saw sliced through the canopy. In seconds, large sections had been broken away, and the barricade was being peeled back over the Tomcat's nose. Coyote was assaulted by the babble of voices of the men around him.

"Easy, sir! We'll have you out in no time!"

"Quick! Safe those seats. Damn it, I don't want those cooking off in our faces . . ."

"Shit, Chief! They're already safed. Both of 'em! The pins were never pulled!"

"Christ. No wonder they didn't fire. Hey, get a doc up here. Let 'im through."

"Make a hole there. Make a hole!"

"Hey, Doc! How's the RIO? Jeez, look at the blood! . . ."

"He's a goner. Lemme see the other one."

"C'mon, get them out of there. Gently! Gently, damn you!"

Hands reaching into the cockpit unfastened Coyote's safety harness, removed his helmet, hauled him out, and strapped him into a Stokes stretcher.

John-Boy was dead? It had all been for nothing, then.

Only slowly, as men hustled him in the stretcher across

the deck and down toward sick bay, did Coyote's initial surge of raw emotion return. He was alive. *Alive!*

1915 hours Zulu (2015 hours Zone)
CAG's office, U.S.S. *Thomas Jefferson*
Viking Station, the Norwegian Sea

Tombstone leaned back in his swivel chair behind his gray steel desk, a coffee mug with the striking-snake logo of VF-95 in his hands. He could feel the gentle roll of the boat—aviators always referred to an aircraft carrier as a *boat* rather than a *ship,* in defiance of the traditions of "the real Navy." The seas were picking up.

The CAG office was a small one, as most personal work spaces were within the small city that was the U.S.S. *Jefferson*. There was barely room for a couple of chairs and a desk with built-in typing stand, a battered IBM Selectric, a filing cabinet, and a small set of bookshelves hung from brackets on the bulkhead. His desk was buried in the usual clutter of work. CAG paperwork, he'd learned, was by definition never done.

Rising above the pile of forms and reports next to the desk lamp was a portrait, a photograph of a lovely blond woman. "To my favorite tomcat," the inscription read. "I love you—Pam."

Pamela Drake. Damn, why did he keep her picture around? She'd sent it to him during his last cruise aboard the *Jefferson,* two years back. Just before he'd returned Stateside from that rather eventful deployment.

Just before he'd told her that he wasn't about to give up his career for her.

He'd met her during the Thailand affair. She'd been a hotshot TV news personality for ACN; he'd been skipper of VF-95, and the unwilling subject of a human-interest story she'd been filming for her weekly news show. They'd fallen in love . . . or he'd thought they had. Perhaps their brush with hostage-takers in the Communist-inspired coup had made their feelings seem more intense than they really were.

In any case, she'd gone back to the World and her newscaster career, while *Jefferson* had continued her deployment. The crisis in India a few months later had added to strains. Pamela had once had a brother, a young Marine who had died in the 1983 truck bombing of his barracks in Beirut. Apparently she'd been afraid of losing another loved one to the military, and had been pulling all kinds of strings Stateside to find Tombstone a career, a *safe* career, driving jets for a civilian airline.

But India had convinced Tombstone once and for all of the necessity of what he was doing. Not that some other young Navy aviator couldn't do the job as well, but he knew that if he turned his back on Navy aviation, he would always feel, deep down, that he'd somehow faced the ultimate challenge of manhood and character . . . and failed.

And Tombstone hated the idea of failure.

So when he'd returned to the States, he'd told Pamela that he'd made up his mind. If she married him, she would be marrying a Naval aviator, not a pilot for United.

Bad tactics, he'd decided later. She'd turned him down cold. He'd seen her a time or two after that while he'd been stationed in Washington, but the spark, the promise had been gone. Since then . . . nothing.

So why did he continue to keep the damned picture on his desk? Angrily he picked it up and tossed it into a drawer. Just thinking about those striking eyes of hers, the way she could look into his soul . . .

There was a knock on his door. "Enter."

The door opened and Coyote walked in. He was wearing khakis, his commander's oak leaf insignia gleaming silver at his collar in the overhead lights. "Commander Grant reporting as ordered, CAG."

"Pull up a chair, Coyote," Tombstone said, gesturing to the only other chair in the compartment. Coyote looked terrible, worn and drawn. "How are you feeling, guy?"

"Dr. Wainwright certified me fit for duty, CAG."

"I know. I saw his recommendation. But how are *you*?"

Coyote drew a deep breath, let it go. "Okay. A bit shaky, but okay."

"That was quite a landing."

He smiled weakly. "I think I got a cut on that one." The LSO graded every trap aboard a carrier. The possible scores, recorded for all to see on the squadron's greenie board, were "okay" and "fair" for acceptable approaches, "no grade" for a pass that could have endangered the pilot or his aircraft, and "cut," which meant the trap could have ended in disaster.

"Well, you know what they say about any landing you can walk away from."

"But I didn't walk. I was carried." Coyote's face fell. "And John-Boy—"

"They say he was killed by one of those Fulcrums," Tombstone said. "Piece of a thirty em-em went through his seat and cut his aorta, just below his heart. The doc says he bled to death internally in a few seconds. There was nothing you could've done."

"Yeah." Coyote's expression was dark. "Maybe so. Sir."

Tombstone studied the man a moment. Coyote was wearing a suit of armor, armor so thick he couldn't read him. Once the two of them had been best friends, stationed together in California, dating the same girl . . . hell, he'd been best man at Coyote's wedding. Tombstone had always been able to tell what Coyote was thinking.

No more. Somehow, their friendship had never been the same since Tombstone had returned to the *Jeff* as Deputy CAG. There was a distance now, as though Coyote resented him.

It was true what they said, that there was a loneliness that came with command. Maybe, Tombstone thought, a CAG couldn't afford to get too familiar with the men he commanded. His orders that afternoon had sent three men to their deaths and had very nearly killed Coyote as well. Hell, that bad touchdown on the flight deck this afternoon had come *that* close to killing a dozen men and badly damaging the *Jefferson* herself. It had been God's own luck that no one on the flight deck had been injured, or that the 201 bird hadn't slid into the parked Intruders in a spectacular fireball, or that the damage to the deck hadn't been a lot more serious. As it was, the only damage had been the snapped arrestor cables, easily replaced.

But it could have been a lot worse. And apparently it was Coyote's disobedience that had caused all the problems in the first place.

Tombstone sighed, swinging his feet off the desk and setting the coffee cup aside. Best to confront the problem head-on.

"All right, Coyote. Let's hear it."

"Hear what, sir?"

Damn the man. He seemed determined not to make this easy.

"An explanation. You were clearly ordered to pursue and ID Contact Bravo and bring it down. You popped two Phoenix missiles at the target, then broke off. Why?"

"My wingman was in trouble, sir. The MiGs were all over him. I . . . after the Phoenix launch, we realized that it would take too much time to close with Bravo. In my judgment, Scorpion and Juggler didn't have the time, not at four-to-one odds. I thought that I would still have time enough for both of us to go after Bravo together. Sir."

"Uh-huh. You disobeyed orders. Scorpion and Juggler bought the farm anyway. There was nothing you could do about that. But as a direct result of your *judgment,* that Blackjack had time to launch its antiship missiles. Because of your judgment, the *Esek Hopkins* is burning right now, as we speak. We may lose her. No word yet on casualties, but the butcher's bill is going to be a big one. Because of your *judgment*—"

"Sir!" Coyote interrupted. "That's not fair! You can't blame me for the strike against the *Hopkins*!"

Tombstone spread his hands above the desk top. "It could damned easily have been the *Jefferson* in flames. The way I heard it, Don Strachan deliberately seduced those missiles onto himself. Very likely he saved this carrier."

"But those were goddamned AS-15s! That Blackjack could have launched at any time. They could have waited until I got close enough to worry them and then launched no matter what I did!"

"Maybe." Tombstone had already considered the possibility. Coyote was right. The range of the surface-launched version of the AS-15 was suspected to be in the neighborhood of eighteen hundred miles. If true, the Soviets could have launched them at the *Jefferson* from bases in the Kola Peninsula—hell, they could have popped those things from Moscow or the northern coast of the Caspian Sea—and dispensed with the bomber entirely.

"Maybe," Tombstone said again. "And I can't even say I wouldn't have done the same thing in your shoes. But you disobeyed my orders and men died because of that. You got your Tomcat so badly chewed up you almost didn't make it back. Lieutenant Nichols *didn't* make it. Your RIO's down in the sick-bay morgue right this minute."

"That wasn't my fault either!"

"Mmm." Tombstone crossed his arms. "If you'd engaged the Blackjack at long range, maybe those Fulcrums wouldn't have jumped you."

"Maybe, maybe! Damn it, Stoney, I'm not a wizard. I can't see the future. What . . . you're yanking me from flight status?"

"I've been considering it."

But Tombstone had already made up his mind on that point. Coyote was skipper of VF-95, the same command that Tombstone himself had once held. He knew that the individual members of the squadron, from aviators and RIOs to the enlisted plane crews, tended to close ranks against outside authority, whether that authority was CAG, the Captain, or the admiral in command of the battle group. There was nothing mutinous or seditious about this resentment; it was simply a reflection of human psychology, and of the realities of men working closely together in situations that daily risked life and limb.

If Tombstone grounded Coyote or relieved him as skipper of VF-95, the wing's morale would suffer. In other circumstances, in peacetime, Tombstone might have done it anyway, but *Jefferson* was locked now in a war in all but name. The men had been driving hard for over a week, morale was already shaky, and what they certainly did not need right now was the sense that Big Brother was looking over their shoulders, second-guessing their officers, looking for reasons to find fault. The United States Navy worked as well as it did because, at every rank from seaman recruit to admiral, personal initiative was stressed rather than blind adherence to orders.

Tombstone was well aware that breaking Coyote for anything less than outright mutiny would be the worst thing he could possibly do.

"No," he said at last. "No, I'm not grounding you."

Coyote looked almost disappointed. Some of the fire in his eyes died. "Then why the critique? If you don't like the way I did things, just—"

"Damn it, Coyote, it's not *you* I'm criticizing. It's your performance. You made a bad call up there this afternoon. Okay, it happens to all of us. I'm telling you not to let it happen again. The middle of a war is no place for hotdogging or personal heroics."

"Hotdogging! God damn it, Stoney, I—"

"Hotdogging! Shut up and listen, Grant! You assume that CIC knows what it's doing and you do what you're told, especially when the safety of this air wing and this ship are what're at risk." Tombstone stopped, scowling. "What the hell were you doing on BARCAP this afternoon anyway?"

Coyote seemed surprised by the sudden change in subject. "Uh . . . I needed the hours. Lansky had the duty but he got sick. I filled in."

"Damn it, Coyote! You're the skipper, the CO of the goddamned squadron. You don't 'fill in'! You delegate!" Tombstone tapped a sheaf of papers on his desk. "I've got down gripes on four birds in your squadron. You should've been aboard making sure those aircraft were fit to fly, not out flying BARCAP . . . and sure as hot damn not getting your own aircraft shot out from under you!''

Coyote looked stunned. ''I . . . I did what I thought was best—''

''Next point. First thing you do when you climb into a bird is arm the ejection seats. You remember the procedure? You pull a little arming pin to enable the trigger mechanism, and replace it after you're down. Your plane chief reported that the arming pins were still in place, which was why your ejection seat didn't fire. Was that deliberate? Or another fuckup?''

''I guess we forgot. Sir.''

''Forgot. Coyote, how long since you've had a decent night's sleep?''

Some of the fire returned. ''We've been at Combat Readiness Condition II for three days now and you ask a damned-fool question like that?''

''You're tired, Coyote. Tired men make mistakes. Mistakes get men killed.''

''Sir! Permission to ask a question, sir!''

''Aw, cut the *ka*-det shit, Coyote! What is it?''

''Sir, if you are not satisfied with my performance, *sir,* then I request that you take me off flight duty and assign me to other duties, *sir*! Or consider my request for transfer, *sir*!''

''Denied.''

''May I ask why, sir?''

''Damn it, Coyote, what the hell's the matter with you? You're a good officer, a damned good aviator. You're acting like a spoiled kid caught with his hand in the cookie jar! I'm not grounding you and I'm not transferring you. I need you here, bossing the Vipers. Leading the Vipers. Not being one of the guys, not filling in for your buddies, not screwing up like some damned snot-nosed ensign, but *leading* them! You hear me?''

''Yes, sir.''

"First thing I want out of you is for you to have dinner, if you haven't eaten already, then go sack out, six hours minimum. Next, tomorrow, I want a report on those downed birds. Talk to maintenance. Find out what they need to get them up again. Third, you will continue on flight duty and you will continue participating in CAPs, but you will not fill in for your people. You will delegate. Got me?"

Coyote looked away, anger clouding his gaze. "Sir, I respectfully ask that you reconsider my request for transfer to other duties. It is my privilege to voluntarily step down from flight status if . . . if I . . ."

Tombstone's eyes narrowed. "You want to turn in your wings? Why?"

The aviator seemed to shrink a little as the stiffness went out of his spine. "I just don't think I was cut out for this, sir."

"Because you screwed up? Or because Nichols is dead?"

"I'm . . . not sure. Maybe a little of both."

"Then the answer isn't turning in your wings. If things are getting tough and the bad guys are closing in from every side, sometimes the only thing you can do is wade back in with both fists swinging. Like they say in the Marines: attack, attack, *attack*!"

"It's not that easy."

"It never is. And it's not easy to jump back in when you're been knocked on your ass."

"Damn it, CAG, you're right! Okay? I fucked up! I could've killed every man on the *Hopkins*. Or the *Jefferson*—"

"And you don't want the responsibility. I'll tell you something, old buddy. Responsibility is one thing in this man's Navy you can't duck." Tombstone gestured at his desk and the stack of paperwork on it. "Ask me how I know."

"I screwed the pooch this afternoon, Stoney! I *lost* it! I'm afraid . . . *scared!*"

There, he'd said it, the one thing that no aviator ever

dared admit to another. At least Coyote had called him Stoney, an appeal to the camaraderie they'd once shared.

Tombstone closed his eyes, then took a deep breath. "If I told you that I'm afraid every time I go up, Coyote, you'd think I was patronizing you. But it's true. Every man in the wing is scared every time he climbs into the cockpit. You know it, and I know it. They wouldn't be human if they weren't."

"Bullshit, Stoney. I—"

Tombstone stood suddenly behind the desk, the palm of his hand coming down on the desk. "I need you, damn it. Your people need you! You're not going to let them down! You're not going to let me down! You hear me?"

"Yes, sir!" Coyote's face pinched, and there was a paleness beneath his tan. "Will that be all, CAG?"

"Get the fuck out of here."

Coyote turned on his heel and left, banging the door behind him. Tombstone sat down again behind his desk. He remained there for a long time after that, watching the coffee in his half-full mug shift with the gentle roll of the boat.

CHAPTER 7
Wednesday, 18 June

2000 hours Zulu (1600 hours EDT)
Press briefing room
The Pentagon, Washington, D.C.

Admiral Thomas Magruder glanced a final time over his
notes, then brushed past the curtains and onto the stage,
walking with measured pace to the podium. The press room
was crowded, filled with reporters and, vaguely seen behind
the glare of lights, the cameramen and technicians who
would be recording his every word and gesture. It was an
uncomfortable feeling, one he'd never yet adjusted to as
long as he'd been the Joint Staff's Director of Operations.

He paused a moment at the podium, blinking into the
lights. Microphones were arrayed before him like reptilian
heads rising from a den of snakes, and the steady *pop-pop-
pop* of strobes was accompanied by the clicks and purring
whirrs of cameras. Beyond the sea of faces in front of him,
he saw the unblinking gaze of a dozen tiny red lights, the red
eyes of TV cameras and camcorders; he was on the air.

"Ladies and gentlemen," he said. "I've been directed to
brief you this morning on the crisis which has arisen over
the past few days in the Norwegian Sea." He waited as the
buzz of conversation faded. The tension in the room was
almost palpable.

For forty-eight hours, there'd been a virtual news blackout from the Norwegian Sea. There'd been plenty of

77

speculation—and rumors—about fighting between U.S. and Soviet forces north of Great Britain, but no hard news, and no official announcement.

It was Admiral Magruder's job to break the news to the American public.

"Two weeks ago, on June fifth, the Soviet Union invaded the countries of Norway and Finland. You've been briefed on the events since . . . on the Russian claim that their forces had been invited into Norway to restore order after the assassination of the Soviet president, on the condemnation of Soviet aggression by both the UN and the President of the United States, and on the subsequent creation by the Soviets of a military exclusion zone encompassing all of the Norwegian Sea, an area bounded, roughly, by Iceland, Scotland, and Norway itself. The Soviet Union, in a communiqué issued through their embassy in Washington, warned the President that any military violation of this zone would be regarded as, and I quote, 'a most serious trespass into internal affairs relating to the security of the Union of Soviet Sovereign Republics constituting severe and destabilizing provocation.' "

Flashbulbs continued to pop and snap; the cameras continued their soft, mechanical clatter. Magruder gripped the sides of the podium and stared back at the expectant faces.

"At that time, the United States categorically rejected all Soviet claims that their invasion of Norway and Finland was anything other than raw, naked aggression. Within a short time, the President had dispatched an aircraft carrier battle group to the Norwegian Sea. Their orders were to test the Soviet exclusion zone and to demonstrate our solidarity with our old friends and allies, the free people of Norway."

And what a battle it had been convincing the President that such orders were necessary, Magruder thought, as he continued to summarize the rapid-paced events of the past two weeks. The apparent dissolution of the Russian empire and the death of Soviet Communism had seemed to herald a new age in foreign relations . . . and an end to the old world of military alliances and defense treaties. For three years, both the President and Congress had favored a staunchly isolationist policy; since the breakup of NATO and the loss of U.S. bases in Great Britain, there'd been an almost pre–World War II eagerness to concentrate on the social and economic problems facing Americans at home and let an ungrateful Europe find its own solutions.

Worse, the loss of European bases meant that Norway teetered at the end of a long and fragile logistics bridge. With Britain refusing to help—a situation undreamed of in the energetic years of the NATO alliance—almost any useful American intervention in Norway seemed doomed to failure.

But Norway was still a loyal friend. There were plenty of men and women in the military—and among the President's own advisors—who could not sit by and silently watch the rape of one of the most actively pro-American countries in Europe. The deployment of a carrier battle group would be a way to demonstrate support, to send a warning to Moscow that the marshals had overstepped themselves . . . and maybe, just maybe, *Jefferson*'s presence in the area might serve to deter further aggression.

"Until June 12, Soviet activities were confined exclusively to Scandinavia," Magruder continued. "At that time an incident over the Norwegian Sea near Iceland escalated into a major air battle. Long-range Russian bombers launched cruise missiles which damaged U.S. facilities at Keflavík, and several of our aircraft were shot down.

"The next day, the President moved the defense readiness posture of our military to DEFCON 2 and authorized our carrier group, led by the U.S.S. *Thomas Jefferson,* to proceed east and actively aid our Norwegian allies in the defense of their country.

"We now come to the events of two days ago. We made no immediate public announcement because we feared that a premature release of information to the press could be of some use to the enemy, who, as you all know, watches

CNN, ACN, and the other American networks as avidly as we do here in the Pentagon.''

There was a gentle ripple of laughter at that, and Magruder smiled. The Pentagon was always sensitive to charges of deliberate censorship. Admiral Brandon Scott, the current chairman of the Joint Chiefs, had been most explicit about the problem when he'd briefed Magruder that morning. "Whatever you do, Tom, don't let them smell a cover-up. If they think we were maintaining a press blackout to hide the fact that we lost a battle, they'll be at our throats!''

So far, it seemed, the men and women in the room were with him. There were a few disbelieving looks, a few raised eyebrows, but most were simply listening as they took notes, snapped photos, or held the microphones of portable tape recorders aloft in eager hands.

But the fact of the matter was that, so far, the crisis off the Norwegian coast *was* a defeat.

"I can now tell you that, two days ago on Monday, June 16, elements of Carrier Air Wing 20, operating off the deck of the *Thomas Jefferson,* attacked a large Soviet amphibious group moving down the Norwegian Coast. Our intelligence believes that this flotilla was deploying to land Soviet naval infantry forces here, near Bergen. Such an operation would have served to isolate remaining Norwegian forces, cut them off from supply by sea, and quite possibly force their surrender.

"Our combat operations were executed skillfully and to good effect. Our aircraft caught the Soviet amphibious forces about one hundred fifty miles north of Bergen, near the island of Bremanger. In the battle, a number of Russian navel vessels were sunk, heavily damaged, or run aground and captured by Norwegian forces.

"At the same time a Soviet aircraft carrier providing air cover to the amphibious operation, the *Soyuz,* was struck by Harpoon missiles launched by our A-6 Intruders, and damaged. At last report, *Soyuz* was out of the fight and limping toward the north. This operation was, by any definition you would care to use, a major victory for our forces, and for the military forces of free Norway.''

A victory. Well . . .

The Battle of Cape Bremanger, as it was already coming to be called, would go down in the history books as a splendid victory of American arms, but in political terms, that battle had been as bleak a defeat as Pearl Harbor. Obviously, the Soviets had counted on American isolationism to give them a free hand; the *Jefferson* had been deployed to make them think twice about their plans for Norway.

At least, it *should* have worked that way. There should never have been a battle in the first place. Somehow, someone in the game of bluff and counter-bluff had miscalculated, and now the Soviet Union and the United States were engaged in what every strategist in both countries had dreaded and anticipated ever since the end of World War II—all-out conventional war between the world's two greatest superpowers.

It was ironic. Most scenarios for such a conflict had envisioned the Russians pouring through the Fulda Gap and onto the plains of West Germany, the nightmare of the Cold War, when Eastern Europe had still been in the Kremlin's iron grasp. Others had imagined a Soviet thrust into the Mideast.

No one had expected Armageddon to begin in Scandinavia.

Admiral Thomas Magruder felt a sour stab of pain at that thought. His nephew Matt was aboard the *Jefferson,* had been since Iceland. The Pentagon still hoped that CBG-14's presence could force the Soviets to back down. But if things turned hot . . .

The war was only thirteen days old. It could still easily spread . . . to Europe, the North Atlantic, the Mideast. Washington was determined that that would not happen.

''Since the Battle of Cape Bremanger,'' Magruder continued, ''Russian and American forces have been keeping a watchful eye on one another but have remained out of contact. At approximately 1230 this afternoon our time, however, the situation changed as the crisis in Norway entered a new and possibly very dangerous phase.

"At that time, two of our F-14 Tomcats, on routine patrol off the aircraft carrier *Thomas Jefferson,* were attacked by Soviet aircraft over Norway. One of our aircraft was shot down. An unconfirmed number of Soviet aircraft were downed in the same engagement.

"At the same time, other Russian aircraft launched several antiship missiles at our naval forces off the Norwegian coast. One of our vessels, the guided-missile frigate *Esek Hopkins,* was hit. We are still assessing the damage reports, but we can assure you that damage is relatively light and will in no way impair the effectiveness of our battle group."

A small lie, that, but one necessary to avoid alarm . . . or unwanted questions.

Like what good can a lone carrier do against the massed force of the Soviet fleet?

Magruder looked up, squinting into the batteries of lights. "That concludes my official statement at this time. I'm afraid I can't take questions now, but I can tell you that there'll be a special press briefing at 0900 tomorrow, and we will be able to take your questions then. Thank you."

He turned away from the podium abruptly as a storm of protest erupted from the floor. "Admiral!" a dozen voices called, clamoring as reporters tried to crowd closer to the stage. "Admiral Magruder!" "Does this mean a declaration of war between the U.S. and the USSR?" "How badly was the *Hopkins* hurt?" "What's our next move in the Norwegian Sea, Admiral?"

Ignoring the shouts and questions, Magruder walked backstage, handed his notes to an aide, and was preparing to leave the wings when a woman, a civilian, approached him from the side.

"I'm sorry," he said, turning. "You'll have to— Pamela!"

"Hello, Admiral. Sorry to barge in on you, but you're a hard man to run down."

The sight of her, tall and blond and sharply dressed, had caught him completely off guard. He'd first met Pamela Drake in Southeast Asia when he'd been commander of CBG-14. Afterward, he'd come to the Pentagon and she'd returned to her news desk in Washington; he'd seen her several times over the past few years and each encounter had been uncomfortable for him. He knew that Pamela and his nephew had broken off their engagement, and he thought he knew why.

Magruder wondered if she knew that Matt was aboard the *Jefferson*. He sighed. "Really, Ms. Drake, you must know better than to—"

"I'm not trying to wangle an exclusive, Admiral. I just wanted to say good-bye."

"Good-bye?"

She smiled. "I'm on my way to Norway. I thought you'd like to know."

"Good God! Norway! Why?"

"Really, Admiral!" The smile broadened. "This time it's you who should know better. Norway is where the news is. I assume you've heard about the Soviet invasion? I'm going to join the pool in Bergen. Anyway, I was hoping, well, could you tell Matt for me? I haven't been able to find him."

"Tell Matt?" His brow wrinkled. "Damn, you don't know."

Her eyes widened. "Know what?"

"That Matt's already there. He transferred to the *Jefferson* two weeks ago."

"Oh, God." Her shoulders sagged a little, but she tried to retrieve the smile. "I guess I can tell him myself then, huh?"

"Well, maybe. I doubt that they'll be giving out press passes for the *Jeff* while she's in a combat zone. But you should be able to get a message to him."

She reached up, brushing an errant wisp of blond hair

from her face. "Maybe. I'm not so sure I should. That SOB went off to a damned war and didn't even tell me!" She turned and stalked away, obviously distressed.

Magruder watched her go with misgivings of his own. He had a feeling that he'd just opened an old and bitter wound in that young lady, and wondered if there was anything he could say or do to fix it.

No, better to stay out of it. All the same, he wished that Pamela was not going to Norway. If Matt still had any feelings for her, if he found out about her assignment . . .

Magruder stifled the cold thought and continued on his way toward his office.

2135 hours Zulu (2035 hours Zone)
Soviet Aircraft Carrier *Soyuz*
The Norwegian Sea

White smoke continued to boil from beneath the overhang of the wounded carrier's flight deck, falling across the sea astern like a thick blanket of fog. At last report, the damage-control parties had the fires under control and the ship was out of danger, but hard-working crews were still moving about the deck, cleaning up the debris left in the aftermath of the attack.

Admiral Vasili Ivanovich Khenkin leaned against the port-side railing of his bridge promenade and studied the purposeful, orderly movements of the men below the carrier's island. They were tired; that was obvious from their sluggishness, and by the way the petty officers had to bully and prod their men along.

Small wonder, Khenkin thought. The officers and crew of the Soviet aircraft carrier *Soyuz* had been working without pause for two days. Khenkin himself felt exhaustion dragging at his legs and back and eyes like lead weights.

Below the admiral's perch, a deck party was gathered around the burned-out carcass of a MiG-29. The fighter had been caught in the blast when the last American Harpoon missile had slammed into the carrier's island, scattering flaming debris and chunks of metal across the flight deck. Khenkin watched sadly as the sailors strained against the fire-blackened wreckage, timing their effort to the gentle roll of the ship. The shattered MiG edged forward, slowly at first, then with a rush plunged nose-first off the flight deck. It struck the sea close by the *Soyuz*'s starboard side in an explosion of white foam that was quickly swallowed by the carrier's wake.

Khenkin heard footsteps on the walkway behind him and a familiar clearing of the throat. "Admiral Khenkin?"

"Yes, Dmitri Yakovlevich." He kept his eyes still fixed on the spot, now falling astern of the Soviet carrier, where the MiG had fallen into the sea. "What is it?"

"A priority message, Admiral. Just arrived."

Khenkin turned then, his wintery eyes taking in the tall, almost gaunt form of *Kapitan Pervovo Ranga* Bodansky, his Chief of Staff. "You look tired, my friend."

Bodansky swallowed. "There has been little time for sleep these past few days, Admiral." There were circles under his eyes, and his blue, braid-heavy uniform jacket, normally meticulously clean and sharply pressed, looked as though he'd been sleeping in it.

Khenkin extended his hand. "Let us see what the *zampolits* have to tell us, eh?"

"*Da*, Admiral." Bodansky handed Khenkin the page. "I must also inform you that Flight Operations now reports twenty-one aircraft destroyed or damaged beyond our ability to repair them at sea. That is, of course, in addition to the aircraft we lost in the battle."

Khenkin nodded slowly as he took the paper. A serious blow. *Soyuz* had lost nearly half his complement of naval-ized MiG-29s and Sukhoi-27s. Worse, though, was what the columns of figures in his hands could not list—the blow to morale felt by every officer and crewman in the Red Banner Fleet, the sluggishness of exhaustion, the critical dulling of the carrier group's fighting edge.

Those factors would be far more serious than the loss of

a hundred fighters. Planes could always be replaced. But the men, the *men* . . .

Khenkin gazed for a moment at the eastern horizon, lost now in the deepening twilight haze of late evening. Here, this close to the Arctic Circle and at this time of year, it never grew truly dark, though at least the sun did dip below the horizon for a few hours each night. Five hundred kilometers to the east, unseen beyond haze and horizon, lay the rugged cliffs, islets, and fjords of Norway. There, the future of the *Rodina*, the blessed Russian Motherland, still hung in the balance. The Soviet invasion of Finland and Norway, the subjugation of all of Scandinavia and the reemergence of Russia as the strongest nation in the world, all now depended on how well he handled the ships and men of the Red Banner Fleet.

But damn it all! Why had no one in Moscow foreseen the possibility of American intervention . . . or made room in their calculations for the possibility, the *certainty* that in combat, plans always go wrong?

Khenkin began reading the decoded document.

To: Commander Red Banner Fleet
Congratulations on your victory over American carrier forces in the Norwegian Sea operational area.
You are hereby directed to make necessary repairs with all possible speed in preparation for immediate renewed offensive in coordination with planned deployment of Lenin Fleet, code-named ANVIL.
Red Banner Fleet now designated HAMMER. Joint operation against American forces in region now code-named VULCAN will be under overall command Admiral Ivanov. Ivanov's flag transferred to *Kreml,* effective this date.
The eyes of the Motherland are upon you. Your part in the glorious victory over imperialist forces will not be forgotten.
Vorobyev

Khenkin's lips curled in a grim half-smile. Hammer and Anvil, working together in the forge of Vulcan, blacksmith of the old Western gods. The symbols appealed to Khenkin, who had the Russian's abiding love of mystic symbolism, with its promises of future success, of destiny. They would need those promises in the coming days. Vorobyev and the Soviet high command might be calling the recent battle a victory, but every officer in the fleet knew better.

The giant LSD *Vitaly Oganov* and dozens of smaller vessels destroyed, the Bergen landings called off, *Soyuz* struck and damaged by American Harpoons . . .

And this, Khenkin thought wryly, was what Vorobyev and his cronies called a glorious victory?

Obviously, they were seeking to maintain morale in the fleet, but Khenkin could easily read between the lines of the terse orders. *The eyes of the Motherland are upon you.* That in itself was as much threat as praise. If Vulcan proved successful he would be a hero. If not . . . well, Moscow would know where to lay the blame. The fact that they'd put Ivanov, three months Khenkin's junior in the date of his commission, in overall charge of Operation Vulcan was a stinging, if unstated, rebuke.

An order barked from the deck loudspeaker, capturing his attention. The damage parties scuttled off the flight deck, clearing the way for an incoming aircraft. Looking aft, past the arrestor wires stretched across the aft end of *Soyuz*'s flight deck, he could make out two tiny specks hung in the sky to the south, slowly growing larger.

Reinforcements—the first of the MiGs and Sukhois shuttled from the Black Sea to Murmansk to the *Soyuz* to replace the aircraft lost two days before. He'd heard that a massive air force operation had been put in place to divert American attention from these aircraft as they made the final hop from bases in the Kola Peninsula to rendezvous with the *Soyuz.*

It had been Khenkin's decision to bring them aboard immediately, even though there was still considerable danger from bolts and other thumbnail-sized debris still lying on the flight deck after the explosions that had nearly crippled the Russian carrier. Such fragments could easily be sucked up by the fighters' intakes, destroying fan blades and ruining engines, but it was imperative that the air group be brought to full strength as quickly as possible.

Khenkin was surprised that the Americans had not launched further attacks against the Red Banner Fleet, but he doubted that they would hesitate much longer. Moscow might still be convinced that the Americans remained divided and isolationist . . . but Admiral Khenkin had only respect for American technology, and for the will and the skill of their fighting men. Against such an enemy, he needed every combat-ready aircraft he could muster.

As well as every scrap of his own experience, skill, and training.

So it was to be Ivanov in command of the operation against the Americans? So be it. Khenkin had little confidence in Ivanov's grasp of tactics, but until the Lenin Fleet could force its way past the narrow bottleneck of the Baltic, Khenkin remained here in the north, a continuing threat to the American carrier group. And when Ivanov did arrive, he would be coming from the south, up the Norwegian coast, with the *Jefferson* caught squarely between the two Soviet fleets.

Hammer and Anvil indeed.

With the grace of a falcon stooping on its prey, the first aircraft dropped gently toward the *Soyuz*'s stern. Sleek, deadly, and superbly maneuverable, a Sukhoi-27 lightly touched the carrier's deck, its tailhook snagging the arrestor cable and dragging it to a halt. Khenkin released his pent-up breath. The twin Tumanski engines continued to howl; there was no sharp report of metal striking metal as fan blades shattered. Khenkin felt the knot in his stomach relax like an unclenching fist.

His gamble was paying off. If they could bring fresh planes and pilots aboard without more losses, they had a good chance to crush the American carrier battle group.

After what the enemy had done to *Soyuz* and to his men, Khenkin found that he wanted to destroy the *Jefferson*, wanted to see her burning and sinking in the cold waters of the Norwegian Sea.

His fist closed on his orders, crumpling them.

And he smiled.

CHAPTER 8
Thursday, 19 June

0330 hours Zulu (0430 hours Zone)
U.S.S. *Thomas Jefferson*
Viking Station, the Norwegian Sea

It was four-thirty in the morning—"zero-dark-thirty" as Navy hands liked to say—but it was already fully light; at sixty degrees north June nights were never really dark. There was a heavy mist lying across the surface of the sea, though high above the deck a crisp breeze snapped the flags on the yards and made the air feel more like March than June. Tombstone had returned to his solitary lookout on Vulture's Row.

From here, he could watch the activity from one end of the flight deck to the other. Forward, *Jefferson*'s catapult crew went through their ongoing ballet, readying a pair of VFA-161's F/A-18 Hornets for launch. The jet-blast deflectors rose from the deck like steel walls behind each aircraft as first one, then the other began trembling with the raw power of howling turbofans. Near Cat One, the yellow-jerseyed launch officer snapped a salute to the aviator, made a final check left and right, then dropped to one knee, thumb to the deck. Howl cascaded into thunder, and the Hornet rolled down the catapult track, trailing a boiling cloud of steam as it accelerated from zero to 270 miles per hour in two seconds flat. A heartbeat later, the second Hornet shrieked after it, and the two rose gracefully, wing-and-wing, skimming the swirling sea mist.

They were still climbing as the JBDs folded themselves
flat to the deck and two more aircraft taxied up to take their
place at Catapults One and Two. One was a KA-6D, an
Intruder modified with extra tanks to serve as a tanker for
in-flight refueling. The other was an EA-6B Prowler, one of
VAQ-143's five electronic-warfare aircraft, on its way aloft
to help screen the carrier battle group from the prying radar
eyes of the Soviets.

Aft, a similar dance of precise timing and thundering
machine was unfolding, as aircraft recovery was carried out
at the same time that others were being launched. An S-3A
Viking of VS-42, the Kingfishers, dropped toward *Jefferson*'s roundoff. Tombstone had a special love for the
stubborn, superbly maneuverable sub-hunters. He'd spent a
good many hours aboard them as Deputy CAG. It was
Vikings armed with Harpoons that had turned the tide
against the Russian amphibious forces.

At first, the Viking scarcely appeared to be moving at all.
Then the perspective changed and it swelled larger, looming
over the carrier's stern with alarming speed. Its wings
wobbled slightly as its pilot adjusted the throttles on the
gaping engines mounted under each wing in response to
directions from the LSO on the deck. The tailhook dangling
beneath the huge tail swept just above the number-one wire,
scraped the deck, and engaged the two wire with a jolt that
brought the Viking's nose sharply down. Engines howled
briefly, then spooled down with a dwindling whine as the
pilot cut back the power. The aircraft backed slightly,
spitting out the wire, then taxied slowly after an arm-waving
deck director, its wings already folding across its back.

Tombstone took a moment to study the men moving
about on the deck below. All wore jackets, headsets, and
other protective gear that reduced them to anonymity,
whether they wore the red jerseys of ordies, the white of
safety officers or corpsmen, the purple of fuel handlers, or
any of the other colors used to differentiate their tasks. To
a man they looked tired, though their movements were as
precise, as carefully choreographed, as ever. Life aboard a

Navy carrier tended to be a never-ending routine of work with all too little sleep between each stretch of duty. In an emergency, in combat, work continued around the clock. There were men aboard, Tombstone knew, who had had no sleep at all in forty-eight hours.

How much longer could they continue without letup? In modern warfare, Man was the weak cog in the machinery, the piece that would fail first. The flight deck of a carrier was the most dangerous workplace in the world. The traps were numerous and wicked: the invisibly whirling blades of propellers and rotors; the invisible, blasting exhausts of F-14s; the gaping maws of S-3A jet intakes; the sudden-death deadliness of snapped arrestor cables or aircraft brake failure on a pitching deck, or a simple misstep backward over the side. The exhaustion of men driven too hard and too long would sooner or later cross with the hazards of the environment and people were going to die. He remembered the screwup with Coyote's ejection-seat arming pins. Nothing had happened that time. But the next . . .

Tombstone wondered about the men on the Russian carrier, somewhere to the north. The Soviets were new to carrier aviation. They could draw on none of the tradition or experience that had been part of the U.S. Navy's foundations since the U.S.S. *Langley* began air operations in 1922.

Jefferson and her battle group were at a sharp disadvantage here, fighting superior numbers at the end of an Atlantic-wide logistics pipeline. Somehow, though, Tombstone thought that those disadvantages were going to be outweighed by the qualities of training and experiences.

If the men could pull it together. He was still worried about Coyote.

"Hey, CAG."

He turned at the familiar voice behind him. "Hello, Batman," he said. "You're up early. What brings you to Vulture's Row?"

"Just getting a last look at the light of day before vanishing into the depths of the Magic Kingdom," Batman replied. He was wearing his aviator's jacket against the cool, early-morning breeze. "You know how they like to keep us in the dark."

Tombstone grinned. The carrier's intelligence department was identified by the letters OZ, and from this had come joking references to the Magic Kingdom and the Yellow Brick Road. And intelligence—specifically *military* intelligence—was always fair game for bantering servicemen. A briefing for all department heads, squadron skippers, and their execs had been scheduled for that morning at 0500.

It was just possible, Tombstone thought, that there might at last be some news about the lost Soviet carrier . . . and what *Jefferson* was supposed to do about her. Since the battle off Bremanger three days earlier, no one in the battle group seemed to know where *Jefferson* was going, or what her mission in these waters was supposed to be.

"Well, they'll tell us if they know anything," Tombstone replied. He leaned back against the railing. The surge and roll of the carrier seemed magnified this far above the water. The air tasted of salt and jet fuel. "Have you seen Coyote lately?"

Batman's eyes narrowed. "Not since last night. Why?"

"Nothing. I was just wondering."

"Yeah." Batman joined him at the rail. He looked like he wanted to say something but didn't quite know how. "Y'know, CAG. Maybe you should lighten up on the Coyote. I think he's up against the wall, and it's makin' the rest of us nervous."

Tombstone raised an eyebrow. "He tell you that?"

"Shit, of course not. But it's pretty damned obvious."

Tombstone frowned. Blast the mystical, macho aura of pride, silence, and invulnerability that every fighter pilot wrapped about himself like a cloak. Of course Coyote wouldn't talk to the other men in his squadron about whatever was bothering him. That sort of thing wasn't *done*.

"I'll take it under advisement," Tombstone said coldly. "But if he's got a problem, maybe he should come see me."

"Maybe you're his problem."

"What do you mean?"

"Ah, I don't know. But something's got him uptight. We all figured you must have given him a royal ass-chewing after that CAP incident yesterday." Batman shrugged. "Or maybe he's just taken the *Hopkins* real hard. I guess what happened to that frigate could've happened to us."

Tombstone's eyes involuntarily strayed to the southeastern horizon, where a tiny black smudge marked the still-burning frigate. At last report, *Kearny* and *Decatur* were taking off the wounded, while damage-control parties continued to fight the blaze. The Hornets launched moments before were part of an ongoing Combat Air Patrol deployed to protect the *Hopkins* from further attack.

"If I didn't think Coyote could do his job," Tombstone said carefully, "I'd have pulled his wings and right now you'd be the Vipers' skipper. You can pass that around to your people, Batman. Straight gouge."

Batman's mouth quirked in a half smile. "We all know what a sweetheart you are, CAG. How about it? You coming down to CVIC?"

"Wouldn't miss it." Tombstone glanced at his watch. "Time to go. After you?"

In Navy parlance, the word *carrier* is abbreviated CV, so CVIC stood for Carrier Intelligence Center, pronounced "civic." It was a suite of compartments run by *Jefferson's* OZ department. The Intelligence Officer, Lieutenant Commander Paul Aiken, was giving the early-morning briefing in the large auditorium—also called CVIC—which served as conference room, planning center, and even as television studio.

Tombstone followed Batman in, taking a seat next to the Tomcat pilot on one of the folding metal chairs in the second row from the front. Other officers were filtering in, most with the obligatory mug of Navy coffee in hand.

Coyote walked in the door at the back of the room and paused, looking around. His eyes met Tombstone's, but coldly, without recognition, before he made his way to a seat on the far side of the compartment. Black circles under his eyes showed that Coyote hadn't been getting much sleep either.

What's going on in his head? Tombstone wondered. Once he'd been able to read his friend with ease, but no more. There was more going on than pique at being chewed out for a bad call. As a friend he wanted to help. As CAG he felt he had to know, because one man's personal problems could spill over and affect every man in his squadron . . . or come to a head at a bad time and get someone killed. That, he knew, was what was worrying Batman.

"Attention on deck!" someone called from the back of the room, and every officer stood with a clatter of folding chairs.

"As you were," Captain Brandt said as he closely followed Admiral Tarrant in. Accompanied by several aides, they made their way down the center aisle to the front row. Tombstone and the others sat down again as the senior officers took their seats.

"Thank you, Admiral, Captain," Commander Aiken said, standing at the front of the room. A slide-projection screen had been set up against the bulkhead behind him. "Welcome, gentlemen. Admiral Tarrant ordered this briefing for all department heads and senior assistants. We thought you'd like a close look at the opposition. Lights, please? First slide." CVIC's overhead lights died, and a black and white image came up on the projection screen, an overhead shot of an aircraft carrier.

Tombstone had seen those lines before, two years before when *Jefferson* had deployed briefly with the Soviet carrier *Kreml* in the Indian Ocean. Obviously smaller than the *Jefferson,* she did not have the characteristic angled flight deck of American carriers. Like British and Indian carriers, her bow was raised in the "sky jump" configuration, a design that helped boost planes into the air without a catapult.

It was also clear that the ship in the photo was damaged. Though details were fuzzy, dense smoke seemed to be hanging astern of the carrier as she plowed through the sea. There was a scar on the flight deck, off the aft port corner of the island, that looked like it might have been caused by a fire.

"This was taken late yesterday evening by one of our spy satellites," Aiken said. "We have positively identified her as the Soviet aircraft carrier *Soyuz*. As you can see here, she did take some damage during our attack two days ago, but our best guess is that flight operations were not seriously impaired. For the past seven hours we have been tracking aircraft shuttling in from the Kola Peninsula, probably navalized MiG-29s and Su-27s, to replace the losses they suffered in the battle. Note, please, the significance of her name: *Soyuz*, Union. She's definitely the showpiece of the new breed of Soviet militarists, big, mean, and powerful. We estimate sixty thousand tons or more, and a complement of at least sixty-five aircraft. Her sister ship is the *Kreml*, currently at the Leningrad naval yards in the Baltic. Next, please."

The *Soyuz* vanished from the screen, to be replaced by another shot. This one was on a smaller scale, showing five broad wakes curving across dark water.

"With *Soyuz* are four large surface vessels. We believe that these include the *Kirov* and three guided-missile cruisers of either the Kresta I or Kresta II class. Next."

The next slide showed an oblique view of an enormous warship, broad, with huge decks and a complex superstructure rising like a pyramid amidships. Tombstone heard several low whistles, and a low buzz of conversation from around the room.

"I think I should say right from the start that *Kirov* is a monster. She's designated as a battle cruiser, but she's the largest non-carrier warship built in the world since World War II; nuclear-powered, seven hundred fifty-four feet long, displacing twenty-four thousand tons, and carrying a crew of over eight hundred. There are only three others of her class: *Frunze,* in the Pacific, and *Kalinin* and *Irkutsk,* both in the Baltic.

"The Krestas are smaller, seventy-six or seventy-seven hundred tons each, but all three ships are designed for one thing—to engage and destroy enemy surface vessels. And that, gentlemen, means the ships of this battle group. Next."

The next shot was a map of the Norway coast, and the waters north of Great Britain. Aiken pulled a pointer pen from his shirt pocket, unfolded it, and used it to touch the center of a large circle in the open sea, on the upper half of the screen.

"*Soyuz* and her escorts were last tagged here, just below the Arctic Circle and moving slowly east. Unfortunately, in the eight hours since those sat photos were taken, we've lost them. They could be anywhere in this four-hundred-mile circle. We've had numerous radar contacts, but fleeting . . . and Soviet ECM is going full blast, as you can imagine. Neither our Hawkeyes nor our radar satellites have been able to get a very clear picture, and just to thoroughly screw us up, this whole region is now under a thick cloud cover. Met says we can rule out satellite reconnaissance until a low east of Iceland moves out and takes this dirty weather with it."

The pointer touched several spots on the map, south of the circle and along the Norwegian coast. "We have had several contacts here . . . here . . . over here. Some solid, some partial. We think these are snorters, and we can assume that plenty of their nuke-powered comrades are in the area as well. So far, our SOSUS net hasn't picked up much in the way of Soviet subs making for the Atlantic. That could mean they're restricting their ops to the Norwegian Sea, or it could mean they've found a way to evade SOSUS surveillance. But it is definite that a lot of subs are staying in Norwegian waters. In the last forty-eight hours, this battle group has scored four definite sub kills, plus seven probables. North of this battle group we're beginning to encounter something of a target-rich environment."

Target-rich indeed. Snorters were conventional submarines—Kilos, Tangos, and Foxtrots—using their snorkles to recharge their batteries while staying underwater. Tomb-

stone looked at the target locations and shook his head
slowly. *Jefferson*'s S-3A Vikings were already flying
around the clock, using their seven-hour-plus loiter times to
extend the range of their ASW patrols to the limit. The six
SH-3H Sea King helicopters of HS-19 were patrolling
constantly as well, using dipping sonar to test every square
mile of ocean along the battle group's course, searching for
enemy subs.

The problem lay in the enemy's numbers. Despite the
kills already made by the battle group's ASW forces, sooner
or later the Russians would get lucky . . . and the *Jefferson* would be in their sights.

The pointer skipped up the Norwegian coast, tapping
several isolated surface contact symbols. "All of these are
elements of the Soviet Red Banner Fleet. After the battle
three days ago, which, incidentally, we are now calling
the battle of Cape Bremanger, they scattered over this entire
quarter of the Norwegian Sea. Some managed to hide under
the clouds, like *Soyuz*. Others took shelter among the fjords.
All together, we've counted nineteen definite surface contacts, ranging from the *Soyuz* and the *Kirov* to small stuff,
survivors from the enemy amphib operation, even coastal
patrol boats.

"The main body of the Soviet Red Banner Fleet almost
certainly remains to the far north, probably behind North
Cape. Our adversaries seem to be playing a fairly cautious
game, possibly because they're still working out the, ah,
political ramifications of open conventional war with the
United States. It is Washington's assessment that they're
still working out a political strategy that will force us to
abandon Norway. Certainly that would be consistent with
Moscow's primary goal, which is to gain control of all of
Scandinavia with minimum foreign intervention."

The pointer slid down the coast to the south. "Down
here, we have several hundred scattered contacts. Most of
these are civilian shipping, Norwegian fishing boats and the
like. Some are what's left of the Norwegian navy. We'll be
able to call on them for support, but the largest combat

vessels the Norwegians have are fourteen-hundred-ton guided-missile frigates—smaller than our Perrys. Lights, please.''

The lights came on, and Aiken snapped his pointer shut. ''Our biggest problem working with the Norwegians remains that of codes, recognition signals, IFF, and the like. We are now almost certain that the Tomcat downed over the mountains yesterday was shot down by a Norwegian SAM battery, not by the Soviets. We're going to have to work out an exchange of battle codes with their people before we begin coordinating operations with them. That concludes my part of the briefing. Admiral?''

Admiral Tarrant stood and walked to the front of the room. ''Thank you, Paul.'' He paused a moment, looking over the faces of the men seated in the room. ''Well, first a bit of good news. I have word from Washington that as of twenty-four hours ago, there was a vote of no confidence in the British Parliament. The Labor government in Great Britain has fallen, and new elections are due to be held soon. It seems quite likely that the outcome of these special elections will be a return of the Tories to power, and the entry of Great Britain into the war. On our side, of course.''

There were subdued chuckles from the audience, and several officers applauded. Great Britain's defection from NATO had paved the way for the Soviet invasion of Scandinavia in the first place. CBG-14 was terribly isolated here in the Norwegian Sea, and the arrival of the Royal Navy would go a long way toward evening out the odds.

''Now, the bad news,'' Tarrant continued. ''We can't expect help from the Brits for some time. The socialist Labor Party all but dismantled the Royal Navy while they were in power. A lot of their fleet is laid up, or in mothballs at Scapa Flow. And I'm afraid we can't look for American reinforcements to back us either, at least not soon.'' He held up his hand as the murmured conversation renewed, louder this time. ''I know, I know. We've all heard the same scuttlebutt, that Washington was sending the *Ike* or the

Kennedy to back us up. But I've been in touch with the Pentagon on and off all night, and this is the situation.

"The *Eisenhower* is the closest other carrier to our position. Right now she's in the North Atlantic, south of Greenland. The next nearest battle groups would be either *Nimitz* or *Kennedy*. They're both in the eastern Med right now. *Kennedy* was scheduled to rotate home, but when Scandinavia went hot, she was ordered to sit tight. The Russians have a new supercarrier on trials in the Black Sea. If that monster should sortie, well, this private little war of ours could get real public, real fast.

"Therefore, both the *Nimitz* and the *JFK* battle groups have been ordered to remain on station in the Med, while the *Ike* stays in the Atlantic. Washington is worried that Russian submarines may run our SOSUS line into the Atlantic and attempt to interrupt our shipping line, even raid the U.S. coast.

"We do have some help on the way. The Second Marine Expeditionary Force, that's II MEF, left Norfolk two days ago and is now en route. They are scheduled to join us within four days for operations along the Norwegian coast. Until then we are to do our best to gain air superiority over this area, and that means, first and foremost, running down that Russian carrier and putting her out of the fight, once and for all.

"Accordingly, I have written up new orders for CBG-14. Effective immediately, the *Lawrence Kearny* will be detached from the battle group in order to escort the *Hopkins* to Scapa Flow. The remainder of the battle group will head north. I want each squadron CO to begin working on strike plans and options. CAG, you coordinate them. Have the preliminaries on my desk by 1300 hours."

"Yes, sir," Tombstone replied. A stir ran throughout CVIC, and Tombstone heard worry in the murmurs. CBG-14 consisted of seven ships: the *Jefferson*; the Ticonderoga-class Aegis cruiser *Shiloh*; two destroyers, *Kearny* and *Winslow*; two frigates, the crippled *Hopkins* and the *Decatur*; and the nuclear attack submarine *Galveston*.

Hopkins was out of the fight now, and Tarrant was detaching one of the DDGs to accompany her to port. That left five ships, a pathetically understrength battle group.

Tarrant held up a hand, quieting the rumble of conversation. "I know what you're thinking. Five ships against the Red Banner Fleet is pretty lean. But we have the advantage, gentlemen. We have the better crews, the better morale."

"Christ," Batman whispered at Tombstone's side, his hand covering his mouth. "He's going to win this thing by throwing morale at the bastards?"

"Shh."

"We have the better aircraft," Tarrant continued, "the better weapons, the better strategy. We will *win*." Someone in the back had his hand up, and Tarrant pointed his finger. "What is it, son?"

Commander Max Harrison, skipper of VS-42, stood. "Excuse me, Admiral, but what strategy? OZ there just finished telling us we're up against a Russkie carrier, the *Kirov,* and seventeen more ships."

"A good question, Commander. And I'll tell you. In four more days the Marines will arrive, and we'll be able to augment our force, especially our ASW assets, with the Marines' escort.

"Until then, gentlemen, we're going to hide. And here's how we're going to do it."

The silence in the compartment was absolute as Admiral Tarrant explained how they were going to hide an eighty-thousand-ton aircraft carrier from the Russians, and carry the fight to them as well.

And at the end, every man in the room was on his feet, applauding and cheering. Perhaps, Tombstone thought, standing and clapping with the others, strategy and morale could turn the tide after all.

Especially morale.

CHAPTER 9
Friday, 20 June

0530 hours Zulu (0630 hours Zone)
U.S.S. *Thomas Jefferson*
Romsdalfjorden

Mountains rose on every side of the *Jefferson* like the walls of a box, the lower ones blanketed in mist and green, the taller ones crisp and sheer in the early morning light, ice-covered even on this last day of spring. Fog hugged the water's surface and swirled past the carrier's bridge windows, transforming the massive shapes of the *Decatur,* to port, and the Norwegian frigate *Stavanger,* ahead, into lean, gray ghosts.

Romsdalfjord was one of Norway's great fjords, a twisting, water-filled canyon winding inland from the sea, 150 miles north of Bergen. Thirty miles astern of the *Jefferson,* the large island of Otrøy guarded the fjord's entrance like a sentinel. Ahead, to the east, the early, near-Arctic sun glistened from snowcapped peaks. At its widest, Romsdalfjord was six miles wide. Here, far inland, a narrowing passage and a large island midstream had reduced that width to a bit over a mile, some five times *Jefferson*'s length.

The water, when it could be glimpsed through the mist, looked cold and dark.

Tombstone watched *Jefferson*'s passage up the fjord from the bridge. Captain Brandt was perched in his high-backed seat on the port side of the bridge, as officers and ratings stood at their posts, calling off their reports in calm, professional voices.

"Depth," Brandt snapped.

"Depth, one-five-one-five," a seaman replied.

"Still way too deep to anchor," Brandt said, turning to Tombstone. "We'll have to go farther in. What's the matter, CAG? Not used to tight quarters?"

"I wouldn't have thought these fjords were this deep," Tombstone said.

"Carved by glaciers," Brandt said. Wonder touched his voice. "It's relatively shallow out by the mouth . . . maybe five hundred feet. In here it's more like eighteen hundred and some feet deep. At least we don't have to worry about grounding."

Tombstone tried to imagine a third of a mile of water beneath his feet and failed. "Those mountains still look damned close," he said.

"Like threading a Cadillac into a Volkswagen's parking place," Brandt agreed. He reached inside his uniform jacket and produced a pipe, which he began filling from a small pouch. "So, CAG, how about it? Can we continue air ops from inside this bottle?"

Tombstone glanced at the cliffs looming above the fog to port and starboard. "Should be no problem, Captain. I'd hate to try it in rough weather or at night."

"Night could be a problem," Brandt agreed. "Fortunately, this far north, at this time of year, it's light until after 2200. And zero-dark-thirty ain't dark."

Tombstone smiled politely. That particular joke had been making the rounds of the wardroom and flight officers' quarters lately. "We'll be able to keep night ops going too, Captain, as long as you can keep the *Jeff* lined up with the fjord instead of against it. We can take off and land up and down the valley."

"Wind going to be an issue? I won't be able to maneuver much in here."

"Seems pretty quiet down here inside these walls. A

storm might make us suspend operations, but I can't imagine anything less causing a problem."

"Good."

The plan was sheer audacity. Thinking about the operation—of actually hiding the carrier inside a fjord—made Tombstone shake his head in wry admiration.

Actually, the idea of hiding American aircraft carriers in Norwegian fjords was not new. During the height of the Cold War various strategies had been proposed to counter what was viewed as an inevitable Soviet invasion of Norway in conjunction with the expected thrust across Central Europe.

Always, throughout its history, the Soviet Union had faced one single, overwhelming disadvantage in its military naval planning: All of its ports were located behind bottle-necks of land—those on the Black Sea by the Dardanelles; Vladivostok and the other Siberian ports by the island chain of Japan and the Kuriles; Leningrad and the other Baltic ports by the narrows between Denmark and Sweden. Only their far-north ports—Murmansk, Polyarny, Severomorsk, and others on the Kola Peninsula, and Arkangelsk on the White Sea—were not landlocked by potentially hostile territory, and even ships from these ports had to run the gauntlet between northern Norway and the Arctic ice in any attempt to break out into the Atlantic. During World War II, the mere *threat* of German air and naval forces hidden among the fjords of northern Norway had scattered Murmansk-bound convoys and tied down escort warships.

Control of Norway was vital to any Soviet war in Europe, and NATO had planned accordingly. Forward defense was the name of the concept, which was first tested in NATO exercises during the mid-eighties. Normally, an aircraft carrier's single greatest advantage was its maneuverability, its ability to change its position by as much as seven hundred miles in a single day. Forward defense, however, called for the carrier to trade maneuverability for conceal-ment. Locating something as large as an aircraft carrier would be extremely difficult among the cliffs, crags, and

islets of a fjord, even in this age of spy satellites, and the
mountains provided protection, natural castle walls, against
air-to-surface missiles.

The concept had first been tested during the Falklands
campaign in 1982, when British amphibious ships slipped
into the mountain-ringed shelter of San Carlos Water
proved far less vulnerable to air attack than had been
expected. Subsequent exercises carried out jointly by the
United States, Great Britain, Norway, and Denmark had
further tested and vindicated so-called "fjord thinking."

Still, Admiral Tarrant was testing the very limits of the
theory. The idea had always been that several American
battle groups would be inserted into the fjords in times of
crises, where they could operate together with Norwegian
and other NATO forces to deny seas and skies to the Soviets
once the shooting began. Worse, most military experts were
already questioning the forward defense policy in the early
nineties, when the navies of all of America's European
allies were being sharply reduced. Once Britain had dropped
out of NATO, the idea had been all but forgotten.

It was risky, then, pushing a single, weakened battle
group up against the Norwegian coast when much of the
country had already been overrun.

But to remain at sea posed dangers of its own. The
Blackjack attack was being viewed both in Washington and
aboard the *Jefferson* as a warning from Moscow: pull out of
our exclusion zone or you run the risk of widening the war.
Blackjacks firing antiship AS-15s could as easily strike at
the *Eisenhower*'s battle group, now well outside the Soviet-
claimed Norwegian Sea, as they could at *Jefferson.*

Cruise missiles remained the deadliest threat to American
surface vessels in the combat area. They were fast enough
and deadly enough that a carrier's ability to move three
hundred miles in a single night would not be of much help.
Sooner or later, Soviet spy satellites or reconnaissance
aircraft would peg *Jefferson*'s location long enough to
launch a massed strike, and then the cruise missiles would
begin arriving in such huge numbers that no antimissile

defense could possibly hope to cope with them all. American strategy in such a situation was to degrade the incoming missile waves in a series of successive steps, using Tomcat-launched Phoenixes in an outer defensive ring, ship-launched Standard missiles in the middle, and finally Phalanx CIWS for last-ditch, close-in defense. Soviet strategy would be to overwhelm this layered defense with so many missiles that there simply weren't enough Phoenixes, Standards, and CIWS units to get them all.

With CBG-14 down to five ships, it was easy to guess which strategy would be more effective in the long run. The Soviets could launch a *lot* of cruise missiles.

The second greatest danger facing the Americans in the area was that of submarines. The Russians had the largest attack submarine fleet in the world, and the majority of them were based from ice-free Kola ports like Polyarny. Half of these were diesel subs, noisy, easy to track, and relatively vulnerable to American ASW sweeps. The rest, however, were nuclear-powered and silent. Some were fitted with SS-N-21s, the torpedo tube-launched version of the AS-15, which gave them an antiship capability across a range of sixteen hundred miles.

Long before *Jefferson* approached Romsdalfjord, the deep, dark expanse of water had been thoroughly probed for lurking subs, first by SH-60 helos off the *Jefferson* using dipping sonar, then by the frigates *Decatur* and *Stavanger* working together. Finally, the U.S.S. *Galveston* had penetrated the cold waters of the fjord, bringing her high-tech array of sub-hunting sonar to the task of searching the bottom for hidden Soviet subs, while the frigates mounted guard at the fjord's mouth.

By moving into the fjord, *Jefferson* vastly simplified the task of defending herself against enemy subs. The mountains screened her from sub-launched cruise missiles as effectively as they did from air attack, and torpedo-armed subs had only a single approach they could use—past the line of frigates and ASW helicopters mounting guard outside the fjord in the waters around Otrøy.

Tombstone knew all of these arguments, and he accepted them. Still, the cliffs closing in on either side of the carrier as she slowly made her way deeper into the fjord were claustrophobic. An aircraft carrier was a creature of the open ocean; moving her inland felt like a violation of the fundamental laws of nature.

His feelings must have shown on his face. Brandt laughed as he held a lighter to the bowl of his pipe. "What's the matter, CAG? Feeling penned in?"

Tombstone grinned. "Hard to get used to the lack of sea room, Captain." He glanced up involuntarily at the overhead. "And I can't help wondering how easily a Russian spy satellite might see us."

Brandt nodded, pulling at the pipe. Blue smoke wafted toward the open window by his left elbow. "They've been busy with their satellites, that's for damned sure. Washington says they started repositioning their spy sats three weeks ago so they could keep a constant watch on everything from the Barents Sea to Scotland. The thing you have to remember, CAG, is that even the best satellite imagery has to be gone over meticulously, square centimeter by square centimeter. The more enlarged the image is, the more of it there is to look at."

Tombstone nodded. "With all these islands, twists and turns, I can see how they'd have trouble picking us out."

"There's a fair-sized shipyard at Romsdal," Brandt said. "Manufactures oil rigs, ore barges, stuff like that. We'll be staying clear of the ports, of course, but there's always a hell of a lot of big, metal structures cluttering up the waterways here."

"So it'll be like finding one tree in a forest."

"Right," Brandt agreed. "More than that, though, we're gambling on the way the Russians think. You see, we figure they'll think moving an aircraft carrier inland is a *crazy* idea, so crazy they'll spend more time hunting for us out at sea."

"Makes sense."

"Admiral Tarrant's also counting on the well-known

Russian paranoia. They're probably terrified that we're going to sidestep the *Soyuz* and her consorts and run for North Cape, maybe launch an air strike at Murmansk or their boomer bastions in the Barents Sea. No, they'll be looking at a *lot* of other places real, real carefully before they look for us here. As long as they didn't see us coming in here in the first place."

Which explained why *Jefferson* had spent the entire previous day racing north, then doubled back in the dark, taking advantage of intermittent cloud cover, and finally slipping into the fjord at dawn under a heavy blanket of fog.

"You know," Tombstone said. "They're right."

"Who's right?"

"The Soviets. This *is* crazy. I wonder if it's crazy enough to work."

"Well, it damn well better work, CAG," Brandt replied. He was leaning close to his port-side window, peering up at the northern wall of cliffs and mountains gliding past in the mist. "Getting out of this slot under fire is going to be a royal bitch."

"Bottom coming up," a seaman reported. "Depth one-two-zero-zero."

"Bridge, Comm," a voice called over the 1-MC speaker mounted on a bulkhead. "Message from *Stavanger*. 'Approaching anchorage.' "

"Acknowledge," Brandt replied. "And tell them thanks for the help."

Jefferson had been in touch with Norwegian military authorities ashore for several days. Arrangements had already been made for Tombstone, in his official capacity as CAG, to fly to Bergen to meet with the Norwegian military commander in order to work out an exchange of codes, radio frequencies, and the like—necessary if the tragedy of Scorpion and Juggler was not to be repeated.

Yesterday, a rendezvous had been arranged by radio with the *Stavanger*, one of Norway's few remaining Oslo-class frigates. Though not as large or as well-equipped as the American Perry-class FFGs like the *Decatur, Stavanger* was a very welcome addition to the battle group indeed. She carried Penguin antiship missiles—Mach .7 infrared homers with a range of twelve miles—Sea Sparrow for antiair point defense, and ASW torpedo tubes. While only marginally useful in a general surface engagement, she would be a big help if the Soviets were able to locate the battle group and attack it with cruise missiles.

"Bridge, Comm. Reply from *Stavanger*. They say, '*God hell.*' That's 'good luck,' Captain."

"Right. Acknowledge, please."

As they watched, the slim, sharp-angled frigate ahead began to slowly come about, presenting her side to the carrier as she carefully reversed course within the narrow, rock-walled channel. She would return to the mouth of the fjord, where she would take up her station with the rest of the American battle group, defending the entrance against Soviet subs and aircraft.

"Depth now eight-five-zero. Shoaling fast."

"Okay, people. Let's get this bird farm parked," Brandt said to the bridge at large.

Slowly, majestically, the *Thomas Jefferson* entered her haven.

0900 hours Zulu (1000 hours Zone)
Soviet Aircraft Carrier *Soyuz*
The Norwegian Sea

Admiral Vasili Ivanovich Khenkin leaned back in his thickly padded chair, sipping tea from a glass and contemplating the obligatory portrait of Lenin in its gilt frame on the bulkhead of his office. The reasoning of the men who had ordered portraits of Lenin, Marx, and the other gods of the Communist pantheon placed in prominent places aboard every ship remained murky. Surely, the new military leaders in the Kremlin were aware that such icons held almost no power at all over most Russians today. The wild, anti-Communist pogroms, the chaos that had swept the nation from Riga to Vladivostok in 1991, surely had convinced even the most obdurate of Communist hard-liners that Communism was, in fact, dead.

Apparently not. Claiming the need to restore order, preserve the state, and prevent general civil war, the marshals had seized power from the faltering and disintegrating Soviet republics at gunpoint, proclaiming a new era of Communist glory, of efficiency, of productivity, of glory.

Well, if that was to be the rallying call for the revitalized Union, so be it. Chances were, Khenkin thought, no one else—not even Vorobyev or his marshals—believed much in Communism themselves, but they needed a symbol to bind the Union together, at least until a final victory over the West made such symbols obsolete.

If they lost, Communism would be dead forever.

Khenkin had been thinking a great deal about defeat for the past several days. The Soviet campaign in Norway was stalled, stalled . . . and two things were responsible. On land it was the terrain—a rugged, mountain-spined country with easily cut roads and a fanatically stubborn populace that came and went in the night like ghosts.

And at sea it was the continuing presence of a single American aircraft carrier.

Where was the damned *Thomas Jefferson*? His superiors in Leningrad and Moscow bombarded him hourly with that single question.

Khenkin scowled at the portrait, which seemed, in the saturnine lines of eyebrow, beard, and mustache, to scowl back. According to the planners of this operation, the United States never should have involved herself in the Scandinavian campaign in the first place.

Soviet strategy had been built on the expectation that the United States, isolated from the European community and lacking air and naval bases in Great Britain, would accept the loss of Scandinavia with her usual rhetoric and bluster, but without risking an embarrassing and costly military defeat in the field. Naturally—because the unexpected is always part and parcel of warfare—contingency plans had been formed against the possibility that the Americans would come into the conflict anyway. The *Soyuz* battle group had been assembled specifically to deal with the American supercarrier threat.

But first, they had to find that carrier, and that was far easier said than done.

Jefferson had last been sighted by a Russian satellite twenty hours earlier, one hundred fifty miles east of the *Soyuz*'s position, and rapidly heading north. By the time *Soyuz* had received the information, however, the data was already hours old. *Jefferson* and her escorts had vanished.

Khenkin could feel an uneasy, crawling sensation pricking at the nape of his neck, the fear that the Americans had dashed past him in the night and were already approaching North Cape. It would be just like the damned Americans to pull that kind of maneuver, a . . . what was that analogy from one of their sports? An end run, that was it. An air strike against Russian bases near Murmansk or the White Sea could disrupt all of Moscow's plans, might even force a cease-fire before all of Norway was comfortably digested. That must not happen. The *Jefferson* had to be found.

There was a knock on the door.

"Da. Voydeet'yeh!"

The door opened and a tall, young officer strode into the room and snapped a crisp, manual-perfect salute. Captain Second Rank Sergei Sergeivich Terekhov was blond and pale-eyed, with the automatic and unthinking arrogance that seemed to accompany every talented pilot.

"Reporting as ordered, Comrade Admiral," Terekhov said.

"At ease, Sergei Sergeivich. Thank you for coming." Khenkin set his tea aside and leaned forward bracing his elbows on his desk top. "As you are aware, Comrade Glushko has been declared officially dead. His body has still not been found, but several eyewitnesses saw him in the passageway leading to the flight deck a few moments before the last American missile struck."

It was too bad about Glushko . . . but Khenkin couldn't

help smiling as he thought it. Captain First Rank Fyodor
Arturovich Glushko had been the carrier's air commander—
the equivalent of the American CAG—but he'd also been an
incompetent fool who'd owed his rank to powerful relatives
in the Navy's high command. Khenkin had never liked the
man, who had apparently had the extreme bad luck to open
a hatch and step onto the carrier's flight deck at the exact
instant that an American Harpoon missile came in the other
way.

Glushko's death had left a rather sudden vacancy in the
air commander's slot, one which Khenkin had immediately
filled by promoting Terekhov to the post.

"I heard the report, Comrade Admiral."

"I want you to take his place. Your promotion to captain
first rank is effective immediately, and should be confirmed
by Moscow within a day or two."

Terekhov's cold eyes lit up. "Thank you, Comrade
Admiral! This is . . . this is most unexpected!"

Like hell it is, Khenkin thought. He could see the wheels
turning behind Terekhov's eyes. Yes, he'd been expecting
the promotion, and the power it brought.

But he approved of the young pilot. The man had
distinguished himself in the battle with the Americans four
days earlier. Though the enemy had destroyed or scattered
the Soviet amphibious group close to shore, the young
MiG-29 pilot was being credited with saving the *Soyuz* from
a desperate American air attack. He seemed to possess the
one quality that Khenkin admired above all others—*luck.*

Luck, certainly, was one quality the unfortunate Glushko
had not possessed.

"I expect a full report on the combat readiness of the
wing as soon as possible," Khenkin said.

"Yes, sir."

"You will also submit to me a plan for locating the
American aircraft carrier. Finding and destroying the
Jefferson is to be our absolute top priority. Special consideration is to be given to the possibility that the Americans
have already moved past our position and are attempting to

round North Cape.'' Khenkin saw a shadow in the man's eyes. ''You disagree?''

"Disagree, no. However, there is another possibility.''

"And that is?''

"I have spent much of these past weeks flying over the Norwegian coast, Comrade Admiral. It occurs to me that many of the fjords would be an excellent hiding place. Perhaps the Americans only want you to think they have moved farther north.''

Khenkin considered the possibility. He knew about the NATO exercises in these waters, about the concept of forward defense. ''Our rear areas and lines of communication must be protected,'' he said. ''But you could be right. We must not fall into the trap of underestimating our opponents. I will have our intelligence people give special consideration to the idea. If you think reconnaissance flights would help . . .''

"I will incorporate the plan in my report,'' Terekhov said. ''Will there be anything else?''

"No, Sergei Sergeivich. You are dismissed.''

Khenkin continued to stare at the door for long minutes after the young pilot had gone. From the bulkhead, Lenin continued to scowl.

CHAPTER 10
Friday, 20 June

Tombstone sat on one of the hard, fold-down seats mounted against a bulkhead in the back of the Sea King helicopter. The thunder of the rotors was so loud he and the crew chief with him wore helmets with built-in radios.

"Almost there," the crewman called. He pointed out the helo's open door for emphasis. "Skipper says we'll be landing in five minutes."

Tombstone nodded. The landscape visible through the Sea King's cargo door was of silver-blue ocean shadowed by lowering thunderheads in the distance, of green hills and rocky points of land and forest-covered slopes in the near ground. The outlying suburbs of Bergen, neat, almost medieval-looking hamlets rising from the lower slopes of the hills encircling the city, were already in view.

Bergen was the second largest city in Norway, and the country's largest port and shipbuilding center. As the helicopter flew low across the waterfront, Tombstone could see dozens of merchantmen lying at anchor in the waters beyond the city and within the inlet called the Vågen that pierced the heart of Bergen like a dagger.

Several of those ships were low in the water or heavily listing. Smoke still clung like a greasy cloud to the superstructure of one small tanker that lay offshore with its foredeck almost completely submerged. Even at this distance, Tombstone could see numerous tugs, barges, and small craft milling about the wrecks like beetles on the water, as men worked to salvage cargos or effect repairs.

Bergen had been raided a dozen times in the past two weeks. According to OZ Department, there'd been strikes by Soviet cruise missiles every day. He could see the scars, buildings with windows gone, gaps in neatly ordered rows of houses where whole buildings had been reduced to charred rubble, where the spire of the Johanesskirken had toppled into the parklike grounds of Bergen's University.

But, like London during the German Blitz, life continued in the beleagured town. Half the buildings in the city, it seemed, had the Norwegian flag, a St. George's Cross on blue, fluttering defiantly from roof or flagstaff or balcony.

The helicopter circled an open field on a hillside south of the city, then settled toward a circle marked on the ground with white paint. A number of men in military fatigues waited there. No sooner had the UH-60's wheels touched down than a tall, blond man in military fatigues was leaning in the helo's open cargo door, extending a hand to Tombstone as he unbuckled his safety harness and retrieved his briefcase.

"Welcome to Bergen!" the Norwegian officer shouted to be heard above the whine of the helicopter's rotors. "It's very good to see you!"

Tombstone had memorized a table of Norwegian military rank insignia before leaving the *Jefferson*. Three stars on white-bordered shoulder slides made the man a colonel, equivalent to a U.S. Navy captain. "Commander Magruder, sir!" he shouted back, saluting. "It's good to be here!"

"Forget the formalities, my friend. This way, please!" Bending low beneath the slowing rotors, they trotted across the field to the waiting soldiers who were standing next to several jeeps and an M-113 personnel carrier parked by a road. Tombstone clambered into the back of one of the jeeps, and in moments the entire convoy was heading east, racing up a six-lane toll road into the hills above the city. The road was almost deserted save for military traffic, and the tollbooths stood empty and ignored.

It was surprisingly warm and humid, with the mugginess that hangs heavy in the air before a thunderstorm. Bergen, Tombstone reminded himself, lay farther north than the southern tip of Greenland, but it possessed a remarkably mild climate. The hill-blanketing forests were lush and green. "I'm Colonel Bondevik," his host said once they were under way. His English was perfect, carrying only a trace of the musical lilt of the Scandinavian tongues. "I'm sorry we couldn't let you fly directly to our headquarters, but we were concerned that enemy infiltrators might observe the helicopter and locate our position."

"Infiltrators?"

"The Spetsnaz." Bondevik spat the word. "And traitors as well. I fear the spirit of Vidkun Quisling is not entirely dead in our country."

The journey into the hills was interrupted only once, ten minutes after they left Bergen. Receiving a code phrase by radio, the lead jeep in the convoy pulled off the road and into the shelter of the hardwood forest that lined that part of the highway. The others followed suit, and waited in the shadows silently, unmoving, for several moments more.

Then the silence gave way to a growing thunder in the distance. Seconds later, four jet aircraft boomed out of the east, skimming the hilltops in a tight-knit diamond formation, so low that Tombstone could see the red stars painted on wings and tails, and the sun-glint from their canopies.

Sukhoi-27s, Tombstone thought, "Flankers" in the NATO lexicon. Twin-tailed and arrowhead-flat, they looked like enlarged copies of the American F/A-18 Hornet, and like the Hornet they were designed as multirole aircraft, as handy at ground attack as they were in a dogfight. The formation vanished to the west. Several minutes later, the distant boom and thud of explosions echoed among the trees, and the Norwegian soldiers with him grew grimly silent. Bombs were falling in the city they'd just left.

"Have the air attacks been bad?" he asked Bondevik as the convoy began moving up the highway once again.

"Bad enough," the Norwegian replied. "Nothing on the scale that you Americans demonstrated in Iraq a few years ago, but bad enough. We think they are not so interested in pounding us into rubble as they are in keeping us off balance. So far the bombing has done nothing but strengthen us."

Tombstone wasn't certain he'd understood. "Strengthen?"

"You would be amazed, my friend, how a man can be strengthened by hatred. Our men fight the bastards with the ferocity of *berserks*."

It was raining by the time they reached their destination, a steady, melancholy drizzle. The headquarters of the Norwegian defense was located in the woods outside a village called Arna. There was little to see—tents scattered in small groups beneath the dripping canopy of the forest. Vehicles were carefully draped with branch-festooned camouflage netting, and the machine shops, motor pools, and warehouses were hidden in tunnels cut into the faces of rocky bluffs. Tombstone saw no cook fires, and care was taken not to run the motors of jeeps or personnel carriers more than was absolutely necessary. He was surprised to learn that thousands of men and women were living and working in this forest base, coordinating the activities of all of Norway's defense forces.

General Nils Lindstrom was blond and blue-eyed, three inches taller than Tombstone's six-foot-plus height, with the rawboned power in his hands of a farmer rather than a general. The only rank he wore was the three white stars of a full general on his collar. "*Velkommen,* Commander," he said as he stepped out of his tent, smiling broadly. "Welcome to Norway. The weather you bring is good, *yar*? It hampers our enemy more than ourselves."

His accent was thicker than Bondevik's, but easily understandable. Tombstone hoped that his hastily memorized Norwegian was half as good. "*Goo darg, Generaal,*" he said, saluting. "*Day gayderr may aw trehffer dehm.*"

"*Nay*, Commander," Lindstrom said grinning. "It is we who glad to meet you are. And I suggest, to protect your throat, that English we speak, *yar*?"

"With pleasure, General." Tombstone hefted the briefcase he was carrying in his left hand. "I have here the codes and frequencies we'll need to coordinate our operations. Would you care to discuss them now?"

The general consulted his watch. "Have you supper yet, Commander?"

"No, sir."

"Then come, dine with me, please. And with another new-come guest." Turning, he pulled back the flap to his tent. "Your countryman has come, my dear."

Tombstone's jaw dropped. The pounding in his chest was surely loud enough for Lindstrom to hear. Pamela Drake stood in the entrance to the tent, wearing muddy army fatigues and a Finnmark cap with the earflaps snapped up. A stray wisp of blond hair danced beside a smudge on her cheek, and she impatiently shoved it aside. "Hello, Commander," she said, extending a slim hand. She seemed amused by his surprise. "First Thai, now Norwegian. I'm impressed."

She was referring to when they'd first met two years before, during *Jefferson*'s deployment to Thailand. They'd toured the floating *khlong* markets of Thonburi where he'd made a local girl laugh with his clumsy attempt to speak her language.

"Don't be," Tombstone said, shaking her hand. He could barely find his voice. "I doubt that the general understood a word I was saying. But what the h—" He stopped himself with a sideways glance at Lindstrom. "I mean, what are you doing here?"

"My job." One eyebrow arched slightly. "I *am* a news reporter, remember?"

"Miss Drake has come to tell our story to your people," Lindstrom said gravely. "Glad we were that your aircraft carrier is come. But much more help is needed."

"These people have been holding off the Soviet juggernaut by themselves for three weeks now, Matt,'' Pamela said. ''Their story needs to be told.''

''Miss Drake tells me you know one another.'' Lindstrom's eyes twinkled.

''You could say that, sir.'' Tombstone didn't know how to react to Pamela's presence. It had been months since he'd last seen her in Washington. He'd not even bothered to look her up and tell her about his reassignment to sea duty, so sure had he been that their affair was over. Looking at her now, her face dirty, her figure hidden by the bulky ODs, he wondered why he'd been fool enough to let her get away.

''We were engaged, General,'' Pamela put in. ''But it turned out that the commander was already married. To his career.''

Lindstrom's face clouded, as though he was uncertain how to reply. ''These are difficult times,'' he said. ''But friends make them less so. Please, come inside, before we all are soaking.''

They ate at a folding table set up inside the general's tent as the stiffening rain drummed against the canvas overhead, the surroundings surprisingly elegant despite the camping-out atmosphere. When Tombstone commented on the strange combination of silver tableware and canvas floor, Lindstrom laughed and pointed out that theirs was, after all, a defense of civilization. ''You must forgive me if I put on the show for my American guests,'' he said. ''Normally, I eat with men. In any case, nothing is hot. Cooking fires are too easily seen by the enemy's infrared devices.''

That, Tombstone decided, didn't matter in the least. In the rush of working up recommendations for strike operations for the entire wing earlier that day, he'd had only coffee and a donut for breakfast and had skipped lunch entirely. Only now did he realize how hungry he was. Dinner was *okserull,* a kind of beef roll stuffed and served cold; and *sildesalat,* a salad of cucumber and vegetables, onions, salted herring, and mayonnaise. Afterwards, they talked about the war over glasses of *linjeakevitt,* a drink served in Tombstone's honor according to Lindstrom. *Akevitt* was a flavored alcoholic beverage distilled from potatoes. *Linjeakevitt,* the general explained, was stored in oaken casks aboard ship, where the rolling motion was said to give it a unique flavor. Tombstone did not drink as a rule, but the liquor's smoky taste was not unpleasant.

Lindstrom had a large map of Scandinavia mounted on an easel in the tent. As stewards cleared away dinner, Tombstone and Pamela sat in folding canvas chairs while the Norwegian general explained the death grip that was strangling his nation.

"Until two days ago," he explained, using a red marker to sketch arrows on the map, "we had Soviet forces moving down the coast from the north, so . . . and in the area around Oslo, so. At Oslo, we contained them. A few of them only arrived by ship and commercial airliner. Two days ago we learn of new movement, here . . . here . . ."

With bold slashes, he drew red arrows on the map, bridging the Gulf of Bothnia from Finland and the Baltic from the Red Army–occupied ports of Riga and Tallinn, crossing to the eastern shore of Sweden at Sundsvall, Gavle, and Stockholm.

"Our Swedish cousins have fought valiantly," he continued. "Their army, once mobilized, is larger far than Norway's. Still, Stockholm was taken in a few hours, and breakthroughs were made here . . . on the highway through Jamtland toward Trondheim. We fight them in the mountains here, at the border, but our lines behind Trondheimfjorden are flanked. Already I have given orders for retreat."

Norway's strategic position looked hopeless. The Bergen Pocket, as Lindstrom called the perimeter that encompassed all of the country south of Trondheim save for the region around Oslo, was being pressed from north, south, and east out of Sweden. Hard as the Norwegian Home Defense might fight, that perimeter could only dwindle as the Soviets closed in, throwing more and more forces against their defenses. Air strikes had increased as well, now that the Soviets were overflying Swedish airspace at will.

"But why are they doing it?" Pamela wanted to know. "That's what I can't understand. Everything was falling to pieces inside the Soviet Union. I thought the last thing they wanted was a war!"

"Actually, that's exactly what they wanted," Tombstone said. The subject had been a frequent topic for discussion in *Jefferson*'s wardroom. "A war gets the people's minds off how bad things are. Look, France was falling apart in the 1790s, but they went to war with the rest of Europe and ended up with an empire. Or take Hitler. He tried to pull Germany out of a depression and started World War II." He frowned and shook his head. The *linjeakevitt* had thickened his tongue. "The fall of Communism didn't make the world safer. When the marshals couldn't put the Soviet economy in order after the '91 coup, the only way they could stay on top was to invade Europe."

"Wars are expensive," Pamela said. The liquor, Tombstone noticed, was getting to her as well. She seemed to be having trouble focusing. "The people still need food."

"Sure. But with a war on people accept the rationing and the shortages."

"You think the attack on us, then, is aimed at all of Europe?" Lindstrom asked.

"Certainly." Tombstone gestured at the map. "Look, with Scandinavia in the Soviet orbit, all the lost countries of Eastern Europe are going to go scampering back to Mother Russia. Western Europe too. They're outflanked, with their whole northern coast exposed to Russian air and amphibious attack. Better yet, the Russians'll have proved that the United States can't be depended on to come to Europe's rescue." He shrugged. "My guess is that Germany and France will surrender without a fight. Maybe Britain too, though the memory of World War II might keep them going for a while."

"The Soviet empire," Lindstrom said softly. "Reborn."

"Maybe not." Tombstone told them what he'd heard that morning, that Britain's socialist Labor government had fallen.

"This I have heard," Lindstrom said, nodding. "With Britain in the war, we will see the old NATO alliance alive once more."

"It'll take time for Britain to get her act together, though," Pamela pointed out. "What do we do in the meantime?"

"We hang on," Tombstone said. "We hang on and do everything we can to keep the Russians from shutting down Norway. Because if they do, it's going to be damned hard to pry it out of their grip again."

"They will have problems closing their hand on us," Lindstrom said, his eyes ice. "I promise this!"

"There could be a problem with the United States too," Pamela said. Her eyes locked with Tombstone's. "The people are convinced that Europe never did take its share of its own defense. There could be a push for a political settlement."

Tombstone dropped his eyes to the half-full glass in his hand. "That's more your department than it is mine, Pamela. Public opinion, and all that. But I know every man in my air wing is after Russian blood right now. We've lost too many good men to those bastards and their damned power games for us to pull out and leave the field to them!"

"Perhaps, Commander," Lindstrom said, "it would be well if we finished our business, you and I. You think as do we. You understand the danger. Working together, your people and mine, these *Russik avfaller* have no chance."

2245 hours Zulu (2345 hours Zone)
Norge Hotel
Bergen, Norway

It was almost dark—well past nine-thirty—when Lindstrom ordered a convoy to return Pamela and Tombstone to Bergen. The rain had stopped, but it was still overcast. With further meetings between Tombstone in his capacity as CAG and the senior staff of the Norwegian defense forces scheduled for the next morning, the general had arranged for him to be put up for the night at the Norge, an impressively grand hotel on the Ole Bulls Plass in the heart of the city.

Pamela and her ACN crew were registered at the Royal Hotel, but, as she'd somehow known would happen, she ended up spending the night with Tombstone.

She was confused about her own feelings. She'd been finished with him, finished with the Navy, unwilling to allow the military to take her husband as, fourteen years earlier, it had taken her brother. But seeing Tombstone again had brought back all of the memories, of long walks and lovemaking and being together, of understanding, humor, and tenderness.

God, she thought, snuggling her head against his chest as they lay together in bed. *God help me, I still love him. . . .*

"Remember the first time we spent the night in a hotel together?" she asked. That had been in Bangkok, where she and Tombstone had become pawns in a Communist-inspired coup against the government.

"Mmm. We were interrupted by rude people with guns."

"I hope you locked the door this time."

"I locked the door then," he murmured sleepily. "Didn't help." He moved his arm, drawing her closer, caressing the base of her spine with his hand.

"Matt?"

"Mmm."

"Can *Jefferson* make a difference? I mean, just one ship . . ."

"Not one ship. It's *Jefferson* and her battle group. If the Russians don't run us down and sink us, yeah. She can make a hell of a difference. Why?"

Run us down and sink us. Not her, the ship, but *us.* The way he identified himself with the battle group bothered her.

"Oh, Matt. What does Washington expect you to do here anyway? What can one carrier do against the whole damned Russian navy?"

"Quite a bit, actually. Just being here could make a

difference. The Russians don't want a general war any more than we do.''

"But you told General Lindstrom—''

"They need a *small* war to unite them. A big war could destroy them.''

"Don't you ever question why you were sent out here?''

"What is this, an interview for your news program? I'm an aviator, Pam, not a politician. Not my place to question.''

"Come off it, Matt!'' She pulled back from him, raising up on one elbow and brushing the hair back from her face. "That's a cop-out and you know it.''

"It's true. Sure I question, but I have a job to do, and I do it.'' His fingertips slid lightly over her hip, sending delightful shivers up her back. "I do believe in what I'm doing, though, or I wouldn't be here.''

She sighed, her head dropping back to the pillow. "Like Bobby.''

"Your brother.''

Robert Drake had believed in what he was doing too. But he and 240 other Marines had been killed fourteen years ago by a suicide bomber in Beirut, sacrifices to a muddled foreign policy composed by politicians who thought in terms of *long-term strategy* and *stability* and a *strong U.S. presence* rather than in terms of lives . . . or cost.

"Hold me, Matt . . .''

A long time later, their embrace was shattered by the eerie wail of a siren. At the first note, Tombstone leaped naked from the bed, scooping clothing from the floor and tossing it at her. A pulse of light throbbed from the hotel room's windows, like the strobing of a camera flash.

"What . . . ''

"Air raid!'' he snapped. "Get dressed.''

Seconds after the flash, the windows rattled with the thud of a far-off concussion. Blearily, Pamela remembered being told at the front desk that the hotel basement had been designated as a bomb shelter. Movement half-glimpsed through the window caught her eye as she pulled on her panties. Caught in the glow of a searchlight, something like a pencil with stubby wings streaked low over the city, vanishing in the direction of the harbor. Another thud, much closer this time, set the chandelier in the room swaying as plaster dusted from the ceiling.

OD trousers, T-shirt . . . and Tombstone made her put on shoes in case there was broken glass. Then he was leading her through hallways dimly lit by emergency lights, down an echoing, concrete block-walled stairway, and into the basement.

The thud and rumble continued intermittently throughout the rest of the night as they waited it out with a hundred other people, hotel guests and employees and people off the streets. Few spoke English, so they passed the hours on the cement floor in a corner, talking quietly.

Pamela was surprised at how good it was to get to know him again.

CHAPTER 11
Saturday, 21 June

1025 hours Zulu (1125 hours Zone)
Flag Plot, U.S.S. *Thomas Jefferson*
Romsdalfjord

Tombstone returned to the *Jefferson* late the next morning, stepping from the Sea King and onto the flight deck as a light rain misted from slate-gray skies. The weather was ideal, providing cover from both satellites and high-flying recon aircraft.

What, he wondered, had been his chances of running into Pamela at Lindstrom's HQ? Perhaps it was not that big a coincidence. Bergen was the heart of Norway's resistance, the logical place for a reporter to look for news. Still, the unexpected reunion had caught him flat-footed. He'd thought he was over missing her. *Loving* her.

"Welcome back, CAG," a lieutenant in charge of the deck detail securing the helicopter said, saluting. "They said to tell you you're expected up in Flag Plot soon as you touch down."

Tombstone groaned inwardly. He'd never gotten back to bed after he and Pamela had been unceremoniously rousted in the middle of the night, and most of that morning he'd been locked in further meetings with Lindstrom's air defense people, working out the protocols that would allow *Jefferson*'s aircraft to overfly Norwegian positions without getting shot down. He was definitely running way minus on sleep.

But he returned the salute. "Thanks, Lieutenant. On my way."

During his absence, Brandt had worked *Jefferson* around so that she was now facing the outlet to the fjord, anchored in the relative shallows where retreating glaciers had deposited a reef of sand and gravel. The only other vessels with her were a trio of Norwegian Hauk-class guided-missile patrol boats, tiny craft laying to in the shadow of their huge consort. Their Penguin missiles and Bofors 40-mm cannon would augment *Jefferson*'s antiair defenses. With one exception, the rest of the American battle group had taken station at the mouth of the fjord to maintain the ASW watch. The exception—the attack submarine *Galveston*—was patrolling farther north, searching for the acoustic trail of *Soyuz* and her escorts.

Tombstone's eyes felt gritty and he needed a shave. He'd packed an electric razor in his toiletry kit, but the power had gone off in the hotel sometime during the wee hours and had not been restored by the time of his appointment with Lindstrom's people. When he walked into *Jefferson*'s Flag Plot, however, he was somewhat relieved to see that, except for the ever immaculate Admiral Tarrant, the dozen or so officers already gathered there looked as rumpled as he felt.

"Welcome back, CAG," Tarrant said, looking up from a large, photomosaic spread out on the plot table. "You're just in time for the party."

"Thank you, Admiral. What's going down?" Tombstone had felt the tension in the room the moment he'd walked in. He dropped his hat and flight jacket on a chair, gratefully accepted a cup of coffee from an enlisted aide, and walked over to the table.

A mosaic of dozens of smaller, high-resolution photographs, the map showed most of the Norway coast, from North Cape to just south of Bergen. The crispness, the clarity of detail were astonishing. Looking closely, Tombstone could see the shadowed moiré of wave patterns on the sea, the precisely ordered patchwork of fields and forests, the layered strangeness of glaciers in mountain valleys.

Obviously taken from space by an American satellite, the photographs showed no trace of clouds or of darkness. Numbers printed on one corner of the map indicated that the sweep had been made only hours ago.

"High-resolution radar imagery," Tarrant explained. "From a new spy sat. They flashed the pieces through from NSA early this morning, and OZ put it together."

The NSA—the National Security Agency—was responsible for much of the United States' electronic intelligence, especially that gained through satellite reconnaissance. Spy satellites, carrying radars more sensitive than the equipment that had mapped the surface of Venus from the Magellan spacecraft, could create photomosaics of incredible detail, with a theoretical resolution of detail of a few feet.

This map was not that fine—it would have had to have been larger than *Jefferson*'s flight deck to record individual buildings and vehicles—but it did strip the clouds from the Norwegian Sea, robbing the *Soyuz* of any place to hide. His eyes went at once to a clump of symbols marked with grease pencil onto the mosaic three hundred miles west of the sheltering island chain of the Vestfjord. The symbols were adapted from NATO computer display symbols, each symbol indicating different targets—surface vessels, aircraft, or submarines. One symbol stood out from the others, a red, cross-hatched diamond.

The CDS for a Soviet aircraft carrier. Close by were other diamonds, each with a central dot. Those would be the escorts, two Krivaks, one Kirov battle cruiser, and a protecting ring of frigates and destroyers for ASW and antiair defense. An arrow and cryptic figures indicating bearing and speed showed that the group was heading east, roughly in the direction of the Vestfjord.

"You found them" was all Tombstone could say. He felt the thrill of excitement, like that of a hunter who'd glimpsed his quarry. In modern combat, whether at sea or in the air, the advantage always went to the side that spotted the other side first.

"Damn right." Commander James K. Brody, *Jefferson*'s

Operations Officer, rubbed his mustache thoughtfully. "Now we gotta figure how to nail 'em down."

"Ideas, CAG?" Captain Brandt asked.

Tombstone glanced at the mosaic's scale and estimated the range to the Soviet carrier battle group at something like four hundred miles. A-6 Intruders had a combat range with full warload of over a thousand miles; their Tomcat escorts had an operational radius of over seven hundred miles, and both aircraft could extend their ranges with in-flight refueling. "No problem hitting them," he said. "Surprise would be the real problem. It could get pretty bloody."

"That's what we were just discussing when you came in," the admiral said. "We can expect a lot of triple-A from those escorts, not to mention their CAP."

The *Kirov* alone possessed formidable SAM defenses— SA-N-6 Grumbles and SA-N-4 Geckos, plus Gatling guns similar to the American Phalanx CIWS. Any Intruder attack would suffer savage losses.

"Not much we can do about the escorts," Tombstone said slowly. "But we could whittle down their air a bit."

"Draw them away?" Paul Aiken asked. "With what, a diversion?"

"Several diversions, actually." Tombstone gestured at the ragged coast of Norway. "If we launch, oh, maybe three alpha strikes at their land bases, one after another, they might feel compelled to beef up their air assets ashore with carrier air. We could catch them scattered halfway across the Norwegian Sea."

Tarrant nodded, staring at the map. "I like it. Cape Bremanger in reverse. Gentlemen, I move we plan things in that direction. But we're going to have to develop this thing fast, before they realize we have the *Soyuz* spotted."

"And," Brandt added darkly, "before they spot us the same way."

A week earlier, Tombstone had deployed a carrier-air attack—an alpha strike in Navy parlance—against the Soviet amphibious ships and their escorts making their way south along the Norwegian coast off Cape Bremanger. In order to help clear the way for *Jefferson*'s aircraft, he'd ordered a diversionary strike against the Soviet battle group, a feint designed to draw the Russian carrier air back to the defense of the *Soyuz*. Against impossible odds, the diversion had actually scored at least two Harpoon hits against the Russian carrier.

Now, Tombstone was suggesting a reversal of that strategy. The Soviets had captured dozens of Norwegian military air bases from North Cape to the front lines north of Trondheim. Most of those bases were occupied now by Soviet Frontal Aviation units shuttled in from the Kola Peninsula, units engaged in close-support and air-superiority missions against the Norwegians . . . or in the search for the American battle group. If *Jefferson* launched a crippling attack against the most important of those bases, *Soyuz* would almost certainly deploy its MiGs and Sukhois to help protect the captured airfields and to track down the source of the strike.

And while part of the *Soyuz*'s air arm was defending the Norwegian airfields, *Jefferson* would attack the carrier.

"Okay," Tarrant said, after they had worked out the broad sweep of the plan. "My staff and I will transfer to *Shiloh* this afternoon."

"Sir?" Tombstone looked up, surprised. He'd expected Tarrant to run the battle from *Jefferson*'s CIC.

"I'll be able to follow things overall better from *Shiloh*'s CDC," Tarrant said. "And if a general surface action develops, I'll want to have some sea room for maneuver. But I want you to manage the air battle from here."

Tombstone felt cold. "Yes, sir."

Tarrant seemed to sense his surprise . . . and his worry. "I've got every confidence in you, Commander. In your ability. And in your judgment." His eyes flicked across to Brody. "How about it, Jim? You don't mind some help down here from CAG, do you?"

"Nope." The Operations Officer was studying the mosaic. "Frankly, Admiral, I'll be glad to have Stoney take it. This is a pretty far-flung op."

Meaning you don't know whether or not it's going to work, Tombstone thought. *The hell of it is, neither do I.*

It was a long-odds gamble that risked everything. If CVW-20's losses were too high, if *Jefferson*'s hiding spot in Romsdalfjord was discovered . . .

Soyuz had to be sunk or disabled first, or the American intervention in Norway would be over before it had properly begun.

1050 hours Zulu (1150 hours Zone)
Norwegian Theater of Operations (NTO)
Central Norway

The EA-6B Prowlers went in first. Designed as electronic-warfare aircraft, their primary mission was to jam enemy radar, but this time they were also going in armed. Based on the Navy's venerable and highly successful A-6 Intruder, Prowlers were equipped to carry only one offensive weapon, the HARM AGM-88A.

High-speed Anti-Radiation Missiles homed on radar emissions. Each was over thirteen feet long, weighed eight hundred pounds, and had a cross section so narrow it was almost invisible to enemy radar. With a range of eighty nautical miles, the HARM missiles came skimming over the mountains of central Norway before the Soviet radar operators knew they were under attack.

All of the captured airfields across north-central Norway were located north of the Arctic Circle where, on this midsummer's night, the sun never set but dipped sullenly beneath the leaden overcast and drifted from west to east along the northern horizon, not quite setting even at midnight. It was daylight, then, but still the middle of the night at Bodø, Narvik, Andselv, and Tromso, when radar dishes and operation vans suddenly shattered under the detonation of 145 pounds of high explosive. Backup radars and SAM systems switched on and, minutes later, vanished in the fireballs of a second wave of incoming HARM warheads.

Two hundred miles out at sea, the attack sub U.S.S. *Galveston* added her volley to the barrage. The Los Angeles–class submarine had been stalking the newly pinpointed *Soyuz*, but she paused now to loose a salvo of deadly Tomahawk Land-Attack Missiles.

TLAM was launched underwater from a 21-inch torpedo tube, blasted into the sky by a solid-fuel booster, and sent cruising toward its target by an air-breathing turbofan that gave it a range of up to 450 nautical miles. TLAM/C cruise missiles carried conventional warheads—either one thousand pounds of high explosive or sub-munitions dispensers with combined-effects bomblets. Eighteen feet long, with a diameter of less than twenty-one inches, Tomahawks were very hard to spot—especially when Soviet radars across northern Norway were either being jammed or coming under HARM attack. They'd been used for the first time in combat during the Gulf War of 1991, when cruise missiles from two American attack subs and the decks of several surface ships had joined in with the aerial pounding of Baghdad.

What happened at Bodø, a commercial seaport on the Saltfjord just north of the Arctic Circle, was typical. There, two squadrons of a Soviet Frontal Aviation unit had recently deployed to the former NATO air base outside of town. Most of the aircraft were sheltered in hardened revetments, but two Su-25 close-support aircraft were already on the runway readying for takeoff, while four more waited their turn on the taxiway below the tower. Su-25s, designated "Frogfoot" by NATO, were similar in mission to the American A-10 "Warthog," ugly, straight-winged aircraft with twin engines tucked in close alongside a chunky fuselage. Each carried over four tons of air-to-ground rockets, GP and cluster munitions, and laser-guided bombs.

The alert sounded seconds after the radar dish spinning above a trailer parked beyond the hangars exploded in a fiery detonation that sent chunks of metal pattering across the runway. At a signal from the tower, the first Frogfoot began accelerating down the runway, building to takeoff speed.

At Mach .7, the first TLAM hurtled in from the sea, traversing the runway from southwest to northeast. Panels in the side of the cruise missile blew out, scattering bomblets across the tarmac in a rain of death. Shrapnel scythed through walls, glass, and the thin metal fuselages of aircraft caught in the open.

The first Frogfoot had just lifted clear of the tarmac when the firestorm began, a savage whirlwind of firecracker blasts that snapped hydraulic lines and ruptured fuel tanks. The pilot battled the controls for a fraction of a second as death descended around his hurtling aircraft, and then the fuel ignited and the Su-25 exploded into a disintegrating cross of fire and wreckage cartwheeling down the runway. In the tower, Soviet controllers and the base commanding officer died as glass shattered and nail-sized bits of metal shredded flesh and bone. The second Frogfoot, just moving to the end of the runway, crumpled as bomblets exploded around it, then erupted into flame. The blasts stalked across the tarmac like some striding, death-dealing god of war.

Secondary explosions rent the air long seconds after the last bomblets fell, sending black smoke boiling above the fueled and armed aircraft parked by the tower, from a storage hangar, and from a large fuel tank nearby. Munitions slung beneath the wings of burning aircraft detonated, adding to the destruction. The Bodø tower was rocked by multiple blasts. Rockets ignited within the destruction of a burning Frogfoot and hissed across the pocked and cratered tarmac. Nearby, a truck containing half a ton of belted 30-mm rounds for Soviet Gatling cannons vanished in a fireball that continued to hiss and pop like fireworks at a Chinese parade.

From first blast to last, scant seconds had passed. The destruction was not absolute; within minutes, Soviet ground crew and troops were at work, clearing wreckage and bits of metal from the tarmac, extinguishing fires, patching craters in the runway with sheets of wire mesh, and readying another pair of Su-25s for a mission against the Norwegian perimeter. At most, Bodø's airfield had been put out of commission for two hours.

Still, for two hours Bodø *was* out of action, and during that time, the first wave of Hornets from the *Jefferson* struck.

Four F/A-18 Hornets of VFA-161, "the Javelins," approached Bodø from the southwest, skimming low over the waters of the Saltfjorden. Their primary mission was SAM suppression, and they carried HARM missiles that homed on the frequencies used by Soviet SAM batteries and rode the beams in from twelve miles out at sea.

Minutes behind the Hornets came four Intruders of VF-84, the "Blue Rangers," wave-hopping up the fjord at an altitude of barely fifty feet. They split into two groups of two for a two-pronged approach timed to sweep over Bodø from different directions, spaced three minutes apart. One Intruder in each pair carried four GBU-10E Mark 84 Paveway II laser-guided bombs.

As Hornets from Javelin Squadron circling over the fjord directed invisible beams of laser light against the revetments and shielded bunkers housing Soviet aircraft, the Paveway IIs, each weighing two thousand pounds, glided unerringly toward the electronically painted bull's-eyes and exploded with shattering, devastating effect. Even a partial penetration of armored doors or sandbagged hangar walls filled the hangar enclosures with hurtling bits of metal. Secondary explosions brought down walls as stored munitions detonated.

The remaining Intruders each carried thirty Mark 83 bombs in fore-and-aft-paired multiple ejector racks. As vast, black pillars of smoke from burning revetments blotted out the midnight sun, they made their pass, taking out fuel storage tanks, barracks, and hangars, and putting several five-yard-wide craters squarely in the middle of the Bodø runway.

Four more Blue Rangers threaded their way through the

mountains on the Swedish side of the border, emerging over Narvik, 160 miles further to the northeast, nearly thirty minutes after the strike at Bodø. The scenario there was much the same, save that one A-6 was lightly damaged by shrapnel from a hastily launched SAM. At Bodø, all four Intruders escaped unscratched.

From across occupied Norway and Sweden, swarms of Soviet fighters rose to exact revenge for the sneak raids. Circling Tomcats from both the Vipers of VF-95 and the War Eagles of VF-97 watched the enemy fighters assemble, as recorded by the prying, long-range eyes of two orbiting Navy Hawkeyes. One by one, as radar contacts were fed by Hawkeye operators to the RIOs of each Tomcat, lock-ons were achieved and massive, AIM-54 Phoenix missiles streaked northeast on roaring pillars of flame, striking MiG after MiG from as much as 112 miles away. Twenty-four kills were recorded, confirmed by the watching Hawkeyes, and the Soviet counterattack was broken before it had a chance to properly form.

Returning from their strikes, the Intruders and the Hornets rendezvoused far at sea, then wave-hopped back to Romsdalfjord to avoid being tracked by enemy radar. One after another, their weapons racks empty, they trapped aboard the *Jefferson* as the carrier's crew went wild, swarming around each aircraft as it taxied to a halt, all but dragging the pilot from the cockpit, and carrying him in triumph across the flight deck to the island.

Meanwhile, the second strike was assembled as quickly as the attack aircraft could be refueled and rearmed. Tombstone worried as the second wave began shrieking off the *Jefferson*'s bow on clouds of billowing steam. The first strike had been an unqualified success, but there'd been no response at all from the *Soyuz*.

As the long, nightless twilight dragged on, *Jefferson*'s attacks continued.

CHAPTER 12
Sunday, 22 June

0745 hours Zulu (0845 hours Zone)
Tomcat 200
Over Trondheim, Norway

Wider than the Romsdalfjord one hundred miles to the southwest, Trondheimfjord was a slash of silver-blue water between rocky cliffs, half-glimpsed through intermittent clouds. Trondheim, third largest of Norway's cities, was a picturesque mingling of buildings old and new, divided by a twist of the Nidelva River and squeezed between hills to the south and the fjord waters to the north.

Coyote flew four miles above the city. With Tomcat 201 so badly smashed it had been shoved over the side, he was flying "Deuce double-nuts," the CAG bird usually reserved for the air wing commander. It didn't seem likely that Tombstone was going to be doing much flying. The poor guy had been buried in *Jefferson's* Air Ops ever since his return from Bergen the day before and showed no signs of coming up for air.

Flexing his gloved hand on the Tomcat's stick, Coyote savored the feel of raw power throbbing through the aircraft's seat, the feel of the harness pressing against his torso and shoulders, the weight of mask and helmet on his head. Those sensations stirred him, reminders that he was alive. *Alive* . . .

He was afraid. There was no denying now that simple

fact. He'd felt the fear early that morning during the mission briefing in the Viper Squadron ready room, felt it even more keenly as he'd walked out to the line and clambered into the F-14's cockpit. He knew the symptoms. He'd seen them often enough in other aviators, men who'd lost the edge, who'd faced Death . . . and flinched.

When he'd gone in to see Tombstone, that afternoon after the dogfight with the MiGs, he'd been ready then to turn in his wings. He'd come so damned *close* . . . first when a Fulcrum had sent cannon shells sleeting through his Tomcat, then when he'd lost control of the faltering aircraft and sent it slamming into *Jefferson*'s deck.

He should have died. John-Boy Nichols *had* died, and there seemed to be no good reason why the RIO was dead and Coyote was not.

Coyote knew he was operating now on borrowed time. He'd been shot down once in enemy action, captured, and wounded during an escape, not the sort of experience a man could shrug off. He'd come even closer the other day in the dogfight, and in the near-disaster of his landing. Each time he launched from the *Jefferson*'s deck he was tossing the dice with his life as the wager. Sooner or later his luck was going to desert him.

Julie . . .

Get hold of yourself, Grant, he told himself savagely. *That brush with combat statistics a few days ago has you royally screwed up in the head.*

But he couldn't get Julie out of his mind. He wanted to see her again, to be with her. And Julie Marie. A kid needed her father, not a name on a wall somewhere, or a picture in a scrapbook.

Trying to break the morbid train of thought, he looked out first one side of the cockpit, then the other. His wingman hung in position off his right wing, Tomcat 209 piloted by Lieutenant Randy "Trapper" Martin. Below, vapor trails scratched white lines across the dark waters of the fjord, a flight of Norwegian F-16s out of Trondheim.

The front lines were close here. There were Russians at

Namsos, a few miles beyond the northern end of Trondheimfjord, and the battlelines might be closer still. Soviet forces
crossing from Sweden were at Kopperå, forty-five miles to
the east. The situation was fluid, the latest news of enemy
positions usually out of date by the time *Jefferson*'s people
heard it, but a fight was shaping up at Trondheim, as the
enemy pressed in from two directions. Those F-16s might
well be deploying for an attack on the Russian lines. The
remnants of the Norwegian air force had been hurling
themselves at the enemy for the past several days in an
almost suicidal frenzy, blasting narrow mountain roadways,
bombing enemy columns, and challenging the Soviets'
mastery of the skies. *Jefferson*'s air wing would have long
since been overwhelmed by the Russian superiority of
numbers had it not been for them.

Unfortunately, the Norwegians were outnumbered at
least ten to one. The aircraft aboard Jefferson—two squadrons of Tomcats, two of Hornets, two of A-6 Intruders, and
the rest—would not be enough to turn the tide.

Something else, something *more* was needed.

"Cowboy One-one, this is Delta Tango One," a voice
crackled over his headset. Delta Tango One was the current
call sign for one of the two E-2C Hawkeyes coordinating
alpha strike operations. "Do you copy, over?"

"Delta Tango, Cowboy One-one," Coyote replied.
"Copy."

"Large contact bearing from your position, three-four-
one, range eight-five."

"Got 'em," Coyote's RIO called from the backseat.
Lieutenant Terrance C. James, call sign "Teejay," was a
young, self-assured black kid who'd started off running the
electronics suites aboard E-2C Hawkeyes but managed to
wangle a reassignment to RIO school and Tomcats because
he loved fighters. "Four bogies. Looks like they're wave-
hopping, comin' in hard and fast."

"Delta Tango One, Cowboy One-one," Coyote said.
"We have your contact, four bogies, at three-four-one."

"Oh-oh," Teejay added. "Looks like it's jammin' time. I'm losing 'em."

"Cowboy One-one. One-two, come to three-four-one and close with contact. Dragon's Lair requests hard ID, over."

"Cowboy One-one copies." Dragon's Lair was *Jefferson*'s CIC. Coyote brought the stick over, felt the Tomcat's left wing drop. "Coming left to three-four-one."

"One-two copies," Trapper's voice added. "Hey, Coyote! You think this is it?"

Coyote glanced at the other F-14, still holding position on his wing as he leveled off from the turn. "Could be, Trapper. They're coming from the right direction."

As they streaked northwest toward the sea, they were rapidly closing the range between themselves and the snow-blurred contact. Closer to the target than the E-2C, they were trying to get close enough to burn through the jamming.

"Delta Tango One, Delta Tango One," Teejay called. "This is One-one. Contact is definitely multiple targets. Ah, bogies appear to be deployed from Citadel. Can you confirm, over?"

"Roger, One-one," the Hawkeye controller replied. "Citadel is confirmed."

Citadel, code name for the Russian carrier. If *Soyuz* was sending aircraft toward Norway, it could be that the strategy worked out in *Jefferson*'s CIC was working. The alpha strikes had succeeded in drawing the Russian carrier's planes into the fight.

Sheer cliffs and a rugged headland flashed away beneath the two F-14s. Coyote glimpsed white surf, the crystal blue of the sea. "Cowboy One-one, feet wet," he called.

"Contact now resolving as two groups of six targets each," Teejay reported. His voice was cool, hard-edged and professional, not at all like the surging emotions Coyote was feeling at the moment. "That's twelve, repeat, twelve targets in two groups. Designate targets, Red One through Six, Blue One through Six. Range five-eight miles."

Coyote licked lips gone dry beneath his face mask. He

felt the fear, a snake uncoiling in his belly, the familiar inner tightness aviators joked about as their puker factor, but worse, much worse than he'd ever known it before. It was a replay of the encounter of the Jostedalsbre, two Tomcats on a collision course with a number of enemy aircraft, with fuzz cluttering the radar and the knowledge that a wrong choice now meant death. His next order should have sent Trapper high and right, increasing the separation between the F-14s to get a clearer radar picture of what was ahead.

But he couldn't do it, couldn't give the order. That was what had happened last time, with Scorpion and Juggler over the mountains.

"Hey, Coyote," Trapper called. "What say I break right for a look-see?"

"Negative, One-two." He snapped the reply. "Hold position."

"Cowboy, this is Delta Tango. Be advised that contact is on converging course with Linebacker. Dragon's Lair requests that you assume contacts are hostile, repeat, hostile, and execute TACCAP."

TACCAP—TACtical Combat Air Patrol. Linebacker was a flight of Blue Ranger Intruders now making its way down Norway's mountain spine, returning to Romsdalfjord after its second alpha strike against Bodø. Eight A-6 Intruders, unarmed and low on fuel, would make splendid targets for interceptors launched from the Soviet carrier. *Jefferson*'s CIC was asking Coyote and Trapper to place themselves between the Intruders and the oncoming Russian fighters, to protect the attack aircraft until they could get under the cover of the carrier battle group's protective antiair screen.

Coyote swallowed. Two Tomcats on twelve MiGs—odds of six to one. "What do you say, Teejay?" he asked. "Can you get Phoenix lock through the clutter?"

"Working on it, Coyote," his RIO replied. "Wait one . . . got it! We have AWG-9 lock on target Red One. Missile armed, ready to fire."

"Delta Tango One, this is Cowboy One-one. We have Phoenix lock on contact."

"Ay-firmative, Cowboy. You are cleared to fire."

"Copy." Coyote took a deep breath. "Okay, Teejay. Punch it!"

"Fox three!" his RIO called, and the Tomcat lurched as the heavy missile dropped away, then arrowed toward the northeast on a rippling plume of white.

"Tango Delta, this is Cowboy. We are engaging."

The battle was joined.

0751 hours Zulu (0851 hours Zone)
MiG 501
Over the Norwegian Sea

Captain First Rank Sergei Terekhov heard the warning tone in his headset and knew that American aircraft had locked onto his flight. Tomcats—only the American F-14 carried the long-range Phoenix missile and the characteristic fingerprint of the AWG-9 radar—and that meant that the American carrier was somewhere close, *close.*

He could almost smell it, eighty thousand tons of fighting steel, hidden somewhere among these damned fjords. He knew he was right about the American carrier hiding in the fjords, *knew* it, and Tomcats over the Norwegian coast proved it.

Terekhov had an intense admiration for American technology born of extensive travels in the West during the brief period of relaxed tensions between East and West a few years before. He knew what the F-14 was capable of . . . just as he knew to the finest degree the advantages possessed by his MiG-29.

The American Tomcat was a superb fighting machine, a legend among the flyers of nations around the world, but it had weaknesses. The F-14 was huge for a fighter, almost two full meters longer than the MiG-29, and more than twice as heavy. The MiG's twin Tumanski 33D engines gave it a higher thrust-to-weight ratio and better handling. The Tomcat was slightly faster at high altitudes, but the

MiG-29 could outclimb the F-14 and, vital in a dogfight, it could outturn it.

Where the Americans excelled was in the quality of their pilots. Their Fighter Weapons School—Top Gun—where their Navy aviators honed their aerial combat skills by pitting themselves man-to-man against experienced adversaries, was legendary. Similar programs had been tried in the Soviet Union, at Frunze, at Leningrad, and at the Black Sea training center for Soviet carrier aviation, but so far, at least, the Americans' success with such training programs had not been matched.

The individual superiority of American naval aviators would not count for much in the coming engagement, however. Radar jamming made the picture ahead fuzzy, but so far only one Phoenix had been launched, and Terekhov doubted that there were more than two Tomcats on patrol—four at the most—and he was thundering toward the Norwegian coast at the head of a squadron of twelve MiG-29s.

And the enemy's vaunted Phoenix missiles would not be a deciding factor either. Soviet jamming and their wave-hopping approach had brought them to within sixty miles of the enemy before they'd been spotted. The four AA-10 missiles under his wings, dubbed "Alamo" by the West, had a range of better than sixty miles, and the two massive AA-11s slung inboard were Russian copies of the Phoenix. The Soviet MiGs had long-range talons as swift and as deadly as the Americans.

"Cossack, Cossack," Terekhov called, using *Soyuz*'s code name for this operation. "This is Harvest Reaper. Enemy targets acquired. Engaging."

Centering the targeting pipper on his tactical screen over one of the blips marking an enemy aircraft, he acquired a lock. *Fire!* The missile ignited, streaking toward the enemy. The exultation of man-to-man combat sang in Terekhov's blood as a second MiG launched, then a third. *Victory!*

"I have bandit launch, repeat, bandit launch," Teejay reported from the backseat, still the cold professional. "Now multiple launches. They're gone active and have acquired locks. Looks like AA-11s. One-point-four minutes to intercept."

"Okay." Coyote took a deep breath, forcing nerves and hands steady, forcing the image of Julie from his mind. "Okay, Cowboy One-two. You with me?"

"We're tracking the launch, Coyote. Three missiles inbound so far."

"Let's take 'em down on the deck. Hold course and speed until my mark. Then break right while I go left. Steady . . ."

Mentally, he counted down the seconds. The two F-14s were cruising directly toward the oncoming missiles at a hair under Mach 1.

"Those missiles are gettin' damned close, Coyote," Trapper said.

"I see 'em." Blips on his radar display, closing . . . closing . . . He could see them now, three white contrails scrawled across the sky ahead. "Okay, on my mark, three . . . two . . . one . . . break!"

He pulled the Tomcat nose-high, then brought his right wing over, falling into an inverted plunge toward the sea. Coyote couldn't see the Russian missiles now, but he knew their radars would have registered the maneuver, that the missiles would be angling down now, plunging after the diving F-14s.

"Hit the chaff, Teejay!" he called. Packets of aluminized mylar fibers, cut to the length of the AA-11s' radar waves, wafted into the Tomcat's slipstream and exploded, scattering false targets across the sky. Coyote kept his eye on the altimeter indicator, like the steps of a ladder flicking up the right hand side of his HUD. Eight thousand . . . six . . . four . . .

"Hang on, Teejay! Here's where it gets rough!"

0752 hours Zulu (0852 hours Zone)
MiG 501
Over the Norwegian Sea

"Evasive!" Terekhov snapped the order as he brought his MiG sharply left. He pressed the countermeasures button hard several times, firing chaff to decoy the oncoming American Phoenix.

For a moment, the aircraft of Harvest Reaper scattered and milled. The Phoenix plunged through them, then detonated with a dazzling flash. Terekhov winced as MiG 599 exploded, sending Lieutenant Vadim Filatov's plane plunging toward the sea.

"Harvest Reaper," he called. "Form up! Maintain formation, damn you!"

It is like a cavalry charge, he thought. Or no, he corrected himself, it is like mounted Don Cossacks surging across the steppes wielding steel that flashed and glinted in the morning light.

The range closed.

0752 hours Zulu (0852 hours Zone)
Tomcat 200
Over the Norwegian Sea

Coyote brought the F-14's nose up again, pulling out of the dive as the weight of eight men pressed down on top of him, mashing him into his ejector seat. He'd angled the aircraft in such a way that he was pulling up into the oncoming missiles once more, presenting the smallest possible radar cross section to their rather small brains, as chaff packets continued to blossom behind.

"Hit!" Teejay called, the word grunted to force it out against the crushing G-force of the pullout. "We . . . got . . . the . . . bastard! . . ."

Coyote had seen it repeated on his own display, the merging of the tiny spark of the AIM-54C with the larger blip of a Russian fighter, the slight fuzzing, the sparkle of tiny fragments, the flicker as the distant aircraft changed aspect . . . and fell.

This, he thought, was the ultimate test of Man and Machine, the one-on-one joust between skilled men in high-tech armor. G-forces built relentlessly as he pulled out, aware now that one of the Russian missiles, still dropping toward the sea in response to Coyote's wild dive, was starting to curve around and up, arcing toward impact with the fleeing American fighter . . .

. . . but not fast enough. Its downward momentum was too great, its course correction too late. The missile hit the water and detonated with a shivering crash.

Coyote saw the plume of white water a hundred yards to starboard. One down . . .

And two! The second explosion was closer, but farther astern. Teejay reported the detonation with a jubilant yell and Coyote sagged against his safety harness, relief coursing through his body.

Alive . . .

"Where's Trapper?" Coyote called. "Where's Trapper?"

"Don't see him!" Teejay replied. "No, there! At zero-nine-five with one on his tail!"

"Trapper, this is Coyote! Watch your twelve!" Trapper's Tomcat was hurtling at wave-top height toward a large island, one of dozens dotting the Norwegian Sea a few miles off the coast. Coyote wondered if Trapper, his attention focused on the Russian missile swooping toward his tail, had missed the island cliffs looming dead ahead.

"Roger that, Coyote," Trapper called. "I'm giving the sumabitch the brush-off!"

Coyote saw the silver glint of sun on aircraft wings as the F-14 skimmed the cliff tops of an island a mile to the north. The sky above the island suddenly swirled with movement—seabirds startled from their nests by the shriek of afterburners. A thread of white on blue, the AA-11 followed, its tracking radar momentarily confused by the blurred images of target aircraft and rock. There was a flash as the warhead slammed into a cliff.

"Nice move, Trapper!" Surprisingly, Coyote's fear was gone now. In its place was relief after this first, wild encounter . . . and adrenaline shouting in his veins.

"Come and get it, you bastards!" he called. "Target lock! Fire Phoenix!"

"Fox three!"

Relentless, the Russians continued their approach.

CHAPTER 13
Sunday, 22 June

"We have what appears to be two large groups of Russian aircraft, on a direct heading for Trondheim, Admiral," Tombstone said, speaking into the telephone handset. "Cowboy is attacking with Phoenix. They've just splashed their first bandit."

"We've got it all on the screens over here," the voice of Admiral Tarrant replied. "How do you plan to proceed?"

"We're still going according to plan, Admiral. I've issued orders to the rest of Cowboy, told them to rally on Cowboy One."

"Okay. Just remember, son. No plan survives contact with the enemy."

"Yes, sir."

Tombstone hung up the handset, annoyed. The old aphorism was true, there was no denying that. But Tarrant's warning was disturbing, like a bad omen.

He turned in the high, leather-backed chair from which he could survey the domain of the CIC's Air Ops suite. Commander Brody was standing with a burly Navy chief, Earl Matchett. A heavyset man with a down-home Kentucky drawl, Matchett was in charge of coordinating communications between the disparate parts of *Jefferson*'s combat operation.

"How's our surprise shaping up, Chief?"

"Uh . . . *Hvit Lyn*," Chief Matchett said, stumbling over the strange Norwegian syllables and butchering the pronunciation. "They say they're hot and ready, CAG."

"That's *'veet lewn,'* Chief," Tombstone said, smiling. "White Lightning."

"My granddaddy used to make white lightning," the chief said with a wry grin. "I wonder if these fellers'll have the same kick to 'em that his product did."

"We're about to find out." Tombstone watched the air display as the sixteen blips representing the Norwegian Falcons began moving toward the northwest, each blip accompanied by an identifying tag of data. Sheltered by the walls of Trondheimfjord, the Falcons would have been invisible to the approaching MiGs until they literally popped onto their screens out of nowhere.

"I'll bet the Russkies are getting a hell of a shock about now," Brody said, echoing Tombstone's thoughts.

"Are we ready to go with Summer Thunder?"

"All planes armed, up, and ready," the Operations Officer confirmed.

"Notify Pri-Fly. I want the whole strike airborne, ASAP. I want our people ready to go when we're sure the Russians have committed."

"Right, CAG."

Tombstone continued watching the air radar screens. The 1-MC brayed warning. "Now hear this, now hear this. Commence flight deck operations."

Moments later, he heard the rattle of steel on steel, felt a faint shudder through the deck. On the PLAT monitor hanging from overhead in one corner of the compartment, first one, then a second A-6 Intruder rushed forward down the steaming slot of the number-one catapult and vaulted into the skies off *Jefferson's* bow.

Operation Summer Thunder had begun in earnest. For the next hour, sweating deck crews would work flat out at all four catapults, putting Intruders, Prowlers, Hornets, and Tomcats into the air. *Soyuz* would be attacked by successive waves of aircraft, the timing and direction of each strike carefully choreographed by CIC to confuse the Russian combat centers and distract the enemy's antiair defenses.

Tombstone glanced at another monitor, this one showing the location of surface elements in the operation, and the ragged coast of Norway outlined in white light. The three parts of the equation were spaced apart at the corners of a huge triangle. Northeast was Trondheimfjord, where Cowboy and White Lightning blocked the Russian attack on the Intruders returning from Bodø. One hundred miles southwest lay Romsdalfjord and *Jefferson,* where the aircraft of Summer Thunder were gathering for their strike, and where the other surface elements of CBG-14 deployed beyond the fjord's mouth.

And at the northwestern corner of the triangle, two hundred miles from both *Jefferson*'s location and Trondheim, lay the *Soyuz* battle group, four capital ships behind a screen of frigates and destroyers. Beyond them, a hundred miles more to the west, a pinpoint marking *Galveston*'s last-recorded position followed in the Russian carrier's wake, seeking an opportunity for Harpoon launch or torpedo strike. Tombstone was not counting on that possibility, though. So far, the Russian's ASW work was damned good, and the attack sub might never get a clear shot.

Their best hope lay in the strike force of Intruders, Hornets, and HARM-loaded Prowlers now launching from *Jefferson*'s flight deck.

A seaman interrupted his thoughts. "Commander Magruder? Excuse me, sir. They said you were waiting for this."

Tombstone accepted the manila envelope from the messenger and looked at the typewritten report inside. It was a listing of *Jefferson*'s aviations stores, including her supplies of Harpoons, AIM-54Cs, and other combat expendables.

The picture painted by the report was not good. Two weeks of war, including three major combat operations, had seriously depleted *Jefferson*'s military stores. They would need to rendezvous for UNREP damned soon after Summer Thunder, or CVW-20 was going to be fangless.

UNREP—UNderway REPlenishment—referred to resupply from oilers or cargo ships while at sea. Two UNREP vessels, the fast combat support ship *Provender* and the replenishment oiler *Kalamazoo,* had accompanied the Marine forces from Norfolk. Tombstone made a mental note to discuss the details of the rendezvous with Tarrant as soon as the present crisis was past. They would have to make arrangements to take on ammo and missiles from *Provender* by tomorrow at the latest, or risk facing a Soviet counterattack with neither Phoenix missiles or Harpoons in *Jefferson*'s inventory.

Replacing the report in the envelope, Tombstone turned his attention back to the Air Ops display. Two groups of aircraft, Russians on one side, Americans and Norwegians on the other, were merging now over the waters off Trondheimfjord. On the PLAT monitor, Intruders and Hornets continued to vault off *Jefferson*'s bow two-by-two.

It was a curious feeling for Tombstone. He was supposed to be managing this battle, but now that he'd set things in motion, there was little for him to do.

Except wait . . . and worry.

0759 hours Zulu (0859 hours Zone)
Tomcat 200
Over the Norwegian Sea

"This is our last shot, Teejay," Coyote called. "Make it count!"

"Lock on," his RIO replied. "Fox three!"

The last of their six Phoenix missiles sped from the Tomcat's body, leaving the F-14 weaponless now, save for the 675 rounds in the magazine drum of the six-barreled Gatling cannon tucked into the aircraft's nose on the port side.

Coyote flicked the weapons-selector switch to guns. How

many kills had they scored so far? He was amazed to discover that he'd lost track. The skies above the azure waters of the Frohavel were scratched and scored now by the vapor trails of tangling aircraft. The screen of his AXX-1 was tracking an enemy MiG, still beyond eyeball range but crisp and clear on the TCS display.

"Delta Tango, Delta Tango," he called. "This is Cowboy One-one. We're clean now. Where's the cavalry? Over."

"One-one and One-two, cavalry on the way. You are clear to break off and RTB."

"Roger that," Coyote replied. "One-one, RTB."

"Amen," Trapper replied. "We're dry too. One-two, RTB."

RTB—Return to base. They'd survived another dogfight, though this one had been a remote, long-distance affair. Coyote brought the Tomcat into a hard turn to port.

"Hey, Coyote!" Teejay called on the ICS. "We got company, man!"

"What, more bandits?"

"Negative. Looks like the cavalry, just like the man said!"

"Cowboy One, Cowboy One," a strange voice called over Coyote's headset. It was heavily accented, almost unintelligible, and distinctively Scandinavian in its musical lilt. "Dis ist Flight *Hvit Lyn,* coming to your rear."

Coyote glanced at his VDI and saw the V-shaped formation several miles astern of the two Tomcats, coming up fast. They were squawking IFF codes that identified them as friendly, Norwegian F-16s.

White Lightning. He'd been briefed on the Norwegian operation that morning, but he'd not realized that their allies could assemble so many interceptors so quickly.

"We see you, White Lightning," he replied. "The Russians are all yours. We're going back to rearm."

"Affirmative, Cowboy. *God hell.*"

"He sounds pissed, man," Teejay observed.

"Negative, Teejay. He just wished us good luck."

Coyote keyed the tactical frequency again. "*Takk,* White
Lightning," he said. "*God hell!* We'll be back!"

The new aircraft must have been hiding, sheltered by the
mountains around Trondheimfjord. Terekhov could see
them now, black specks spreading across the sky directly
ahead. Selecting one, he locked on, then triggered the
launch.

Its contrail curling left as the missile tracked its prey, the
Alamo missile streaked into the distance. Moments later,
Terekhov was rewarded by the sight of a far-off flash and a
puff of smoke. *Udar!* A hit!

Then the line of Russian MiGs penetrated the enemy
force. One of the specks grew rapidly almost directly ahead
through the MiG's windscreen, swelling from speck to
fighter in seconds. It passed Terekhov to the left, his
adrenaline-fired senses translating the blur of metallic
motion into myriad details.

It was an F-16, the American aircraft known as a
"Fighting Falcon." Norway had had four squadrons of the
vicious, highly maneuverable aircraft, he knew, a Mach-2
killer in both the air-to-air and ground-attack roles. He
glimpsed the red, white, and blue roundels of the Royal
Norwegian Air Force painted on tail and wings, and the
clear, bubble canopy—designed to give the pilot an almost
unrestricted view in every direction—perched far out on the
flattened fuselage.

Then the Falcon was gone, flashing astern as quickly as
it had appeared. If the Norwegian pilots were any good at
all, this was going to be a tough fight.

"Harvest Reaper, Harvest Reaper," he called as he stood
his MiG on its tail, swinging up and over in a sharp course

reversal designed to put him on the Falcon's tail. ''All aircraft, engage independently! Execute!''

The Soviet line parted, the separate MiGs scattering across the sky as they strained to come to grips with the Norwegian dogfighters.

0803 hours Zulu (0903 hours Zone)
Intruder 502
Over the Norwegian Sea

Lieutenant Commander Barney J. Dodd held the A-6E Intruder steady only a few feet off the deck. The sea was a blue-gray blur beneath the aircraft, which was hurtling north at its top speed of Mach .85. Spray splashed at the windscreen like heavy rain.

Dodd's call sign was ''Sluf,'' a nickname that reached back ten years to the first attack aircraft he'd driven for the Navy, the Vought A-7 Corsair II. The Corsair, gape-mawed, squat, and deadly, had been known throughout the Navy as the Sluf, the Short Little Ugly Fucker—or ''Fella'' when discussed in polite company. Dodd had started flying Slufs with VA-97 off the *Carl Vinson* in 1987; he'd taken the nickname with him when he switched to Intruders five years later.

The name fit. At five-six, Dodd was short for an aviator, wiry, and horse-faced ugly. Now he belonged to VA-89, the Death Dealers, and his A-6 sported that squadron's insignia in low-contrast grays on its tail—a grinning Grim Reaper holding five aces of spades. The Intruder was even uglier than the Corsair, in Sluf's opinion, but it was a rugged flying machine, capable of delivering eighteen thousand pounds of ordnance with pinpoint accuracy across over a thousand miles in any weather. Sluf's favorite example of the march of technology was the fact that the mighty B-17 Flying Fortress of World War II had normally carried bomb loads of four thousand pounds . . . though it could manage seventeen thousand pounds for special, short-range missions. The B-17 had had three times the Intruder's range on internal fuel, true, but then, a Flying Fortress couldn't refuel in flight, had twice the wingspan, and outweighed the A-6 by three tons.

"Target acquisition, Sluf," his B/N, for Bombardier/ Navigator, said at his elbow. Lieutenant "Spoiler" Fracasetti lifted his helmet from the round black-rubber hood that enclosed his radar screen, shielding it from outside light. "Range six-one miles."

Unlike the Tomcat, which positioned the pilot's seat directly in front of the RIO, the Intruder placed aviator and B/N almost side by side, with the pilot slightly above and ahead of the weapons system operator.

"Roger that," Sluf said. "What we got?"

"Can't sort it all out yet. At least three strong contacts, but I can't see shit through the clutter and the jamming. You wanna pop up for a look-see?"

"Hell, no!" Sluf shook his head for emphasis. "I like it down here, playing submarine. Safer."

"Affirmative." The B/N lowered his face to the radar hood again. "Looks like the fighter jocks are on the ball. I got one air contact at three-five-oh. Looks like a helo . . . probably ASW. No fighter cover at all."

"Well, they're gonna see us soon enough, and then it gets fun. How're the babies?"

"Gyros engaged. Target-acquisition mode, set. All four hot, primed, and ready."

Behind his mask, Sluf smiled. Today, his Intruder was carrying roughly the same weight of ordnance as those old B-17s: four AGM-84A Harpoon long-range antiship missiles, slung two beneath each wing, each weighing 522 kilos—about 1,150 pounds. They made his Intruder the high-tech nemesis of any vessel afloat. His last naval target, a week before, had been barges and amphib ships off Cape Bremanger.

This time he was getting a shot at the *Soyuz* herself.

If they could manage to sort the Russian carrier from the

clutter on the screen. Enemy jamming was heavy, and distinguishing targets was difficult.

"Sliding into our approach vector now, Sluf. Come left two degrees . . . hold it . . ."

Sluf kept his eyes glued to the VDI monitor on his console. Unlike other aircraft, the Intruder was flown with a Heads Down Display, the scene ahead painted on the screen in lines of light, as the aircraft's computer fed data lines—weapons cues and flight information—across the display. Sluf could fly the aircraft, from launch to trap, without even looking up through the windscreen. The A-6's electronic imaging was what made the Intruder such a versatile attack aircraft, able to make low-level penetrations in pitch darkness, rain, snow, thick fog . . . or, as now, sleeting sea spray.

Keeping the steering bug lined up with the nav pipper on the screen, Sluf brought the A-6 precisely into line with the still-unseen target. Voices crackled intermittently over his headset. With the radio set to the Death Dealers' attack frequency, he could monitor the calls of the other A-6 pilots as they made their runs.

So far, two other Death Dealers had already gone in: Collins and Jakowicz in 505, and Bernedewski and Keogh in 516. No casualties yet, but the enemy sure as hell knew they were on the way. Things were liable to start getting interesting any time now.

"Four-eight miles, Sluf," the B/N announced. "We're in range now." Harpoon had a range of about fifty nautical miles.

"Let's ride 'em in a ways," Sluf replied.

"You're the boss."

Eight miles of water whipped past with each passing minute. The Intruder thumped heavily. The air at wave-hopping levels was rough, and Sluf had to fight to keep the Intruder steady. The smallest mistake and the A-6 could slam its belly into the waves; the slightest loss of control and Sluf could drag a wingtip in the sea.

But this close to the water there was a measure of safety,

at least for a time, from the prying radars of enemy fire-control systems.

"Looking good," Spoiler said, his face still buried. "Range three-three."

A light winked on the console, accompanied by the electronic warble of a threat signal. "Shit," Sluf said. "Someone's tracking."

"I-band. Sounds like Top Dome."

Top Dome was the NATO designation for the missile-guidance radar associated with Soviet SA-N-6 surface-to-air missiles. It was installed in some of their largest surface ships, including the Slava and the Kirov classes.

"They may not be getting us through the clutter. What's air activity look like?"

"Got some bogies, far-off stuff. Tangling with our Tomcats."

"They don't see us. Hot damn! I think we're gonna pull this off!"

"Range two-seven. C'mon, Sluf! Let's do it!"

"Roger that." Sluf brought the Intruder's stick back and pushed the throttles forward. The sea dropped away as the A-6 clawed for enough altitude to release its warload without dropping the Harpoons into the water. "You acquired?"

"Tracking. Safeties off. Your pickle is hot. Range two-five. Shit, Sluf! I've got missile launch! They're shooting at us!"

"Thar she blows." Sluf's thumb mashed the pickle trigger on his stick. The Intruder lurched skyward as half a ton of airframe, solid-fuel propellant, and high explosive dropped clear of the Intruder's wing. "Harpoon one away."

"Reset. Go!"

"Firing two! And three . . . and four!"

One after another, the Harpoon missiles fell free and ignited, following one another on arrowing plumes of smoke toward the north. Sluf rolled the A-6 to starboard and cut in the afterburners. With a shuddering roar, the Intruder swung toward the south. The SA-N-6 had a range of about thirty miles. In one minute, the Intruder could cover eight miles, the Russian antiair missile thirty. It was a race between a slow plane with a big head start, and a fast missile with limited fuel.

The Intruder won the race, breaking the enemy's radar contact at about the same time that the SA-N-6 fell into the sea some hundreds of yards astern.

And by that time, the Soviets who'd fired that missile had other things to worry about.

0808 hours Zulu (0908 hours Zone)
USSR Battle Cruiser *Kirov*
The Norwegian Sea

The attack was the third in as many minutes, and Captain First Rank Yevgenni Vashirin had ordered the *Kirov* to move ahead of the *Soyuz* to better shield the carrier.

The Americans were firing cruise missiles—Harpoons—launching them from extreme range in groups of four, some bearing on the cruiser, others locking onto the *Soyuz. Kirov* had enjoyed good success so far. The SA-N-6 could be used with fair effect against cruise missiles. Three Harpoons had already been knocked out of the sky.

In the next few minutes, eleven more were destroyed at close range, close enough that Vashirin and the other officers on the bridge could see the flashes and hear the thumping detonations as the incoming Harpoons were engaged with point-defense SA-N-9 missiles and Gatling guns. *Kirov* mounted eight AK-630s, six-barreled cannons similar to the Americans' CIWS, the turrets squat and ribbed instead of tall and smoothly rounded. As the missiles came into range, the barrels spun with shrill whines, each gun spewing radar-corrected rounds toward the tiny, fast-moving targets fifty a second. One Harpoon after another hit that wall of hurtling metal and exploded.

But there were too many targets, too little time. The attacking Intruders had hoped to lock onto the *Soyuz,* but the

Kirov had been closer, a readier target for his AN/APQ-158 tracking radar through the heavy jamming. The first missile was damaged by a near miss by an SA-N-9 and fell into the sea. The second approached to within two hundred meters before an AK-630 whipped around and put a burst through warhead and engine, detonating it in a fiery splash. The third and fourth Harpoons closed the gap toward the *Kirov*, weaving low across the surface of the water until the last possible moment, when their on-board computers sent them popping high into the air to give them a better angle of attack on their target. Then, as the AK-630s slewed wildly, trying to reacquire targets suddenly lost, the Harpoons began their final dive.

The cruise missile first plunged into *Kirov*'s towering, pyramidal superstructure, striking just below and behind the bridge. Tearing through bulkheads, the warhead plunged deep into the ship before detonating in the officers' wardroom, a savage blast that nearly tore the bridge away and knocked out its primary fire control.

The second, by luck alone, arced into the forward deck, smashing through the neatly spaced array of twenty hatches set just forward of the bridge.

Those tubes were the vertical launchers for SS-N-19 missiles, huge antiship missiles, each with a range of three hundred miles, that were the *Kirov*'s principal standoff armament. The Harpoon explosion triggered a second, far larger blast as the high-explosive warhead on an SS-N-19 detonated. That explosion, in turn, triggered another . . . and another. Blast after blast sent shudders through the stricken cruiser's hull, as smoke boiled into the sky above the blazing wreckage.

Ten miles astern, Admiral Khenkin aboard the *Soyuz* saw the flame-shot pillar of cloud rising from the southern horizon and, moments later, felt the massive, successive thuds of the explosions transmitted through the air like thunder.

He knew then that *Kirov* was doomed.

CHAPTER 14
Sunday, 22 June

0856 hours Zulu (0956 hours Zone)
Tomcat 200
Marshall Stack, off Romsdalfjord

"Cowboy One-one, charlie now."

"Roger," Coyote replied. "Cowboy One-one, coming in."

The horizon canted sharply as Coyote dropped into a starboard turn. Normally, the Marshall Stack was located within twenty miles of the carrier. This time, however, it was located well away from the *Jefferson,* over forty miles to the east. Airspace inside the fjord was limited, and the battle group's commanders did not want the high level of air activity to give away the carrier's precise location.

Välderöy airport, located on a small island north of the port city of Alesund, provided a measure of cover. All airfields in the region had been taken over by the military, and any unusual air traffic in the area noticed by the Russians might be attributed to Norwegian F-16s or F-105s. The Norwegian interceptors that were turning the tide of the air battle over Trondheim had come principally from Välderöy.

He leveled out heading east, a course that took him across a scattering of islands near the port city of Alesund, and just south of the airport. Two aircraft crossed the Tomcat's path a thousand feet below—F-105 Freedom Fighters by the sharp-nosed, angular look of them. Descending slowly, he

161

went feet dry over the small port of Søvik, crossed a rolling patchwork of farms and forests, then emerged over the Romsdalfjord. The island of Otrøy lay to the north. Coyote could see the lean, gray shapes of the *Shiloh* and the *Winslow* in the lee of the headland. Ahead, where the fjord's waters narrowed between steeply rising banks, *Jefferson* lay at anchor, bow-on.

Passing the carrier two miles off her port side, he could see the toy shape of the Angel One helo hovering between him and the carrier. An A-6 was just crossing *Jefferson*'s roundoff, descending toward its controlled crash on the number-three wire. It had to be one of the Intruders from the raid on the Russian carrier group up north.

Coyote wondered if they'd managed to hit anything.

"Goin' to goose mode," Teejay said from the backseat. The Tomcat's computer was extending the aircraft's wings as airspeed dropped below 280 knots.

Coyote let it ride. The narrow confines of the fjord left no room for error, and there were unpredictable crosswinds and downdrafts off those crags and rocky cliffs.

Navigating the final turn less than a mile off *Jefferson*'s stern, Coyote reached out with his mind, sensing the aircraft—flaps and rubber and ailerons. He slapped a switch and felt the thump of the gear locking, felt the sudden extra drag. Wheels down.

"Cowboy One-one, call the ball."

"Tomcat Two-zero-zero, three-point-eight, ball."

"Roger ball. Deck steady. Bring her on in, Coyote."

The last time he'd tried this . . .

No, it wouldn't do to think about the last time. There was only now, and that, Coyote realized, was what had been getting him into trouble before. He realized that, at some undefined point during the past hours, he'd arrived at a decision. He was going to leave the Navy, and soon. As soon as he could arrange it, in fact, once this current crisis was past. He'd danced with Death too often in the past.

Coyote felt a tremendous peace in his decision. When he'd considered leaving the Navy before, that evening when he'd gone up to the CAG office to see Tombstone, he'd been driven there, chased by fear and his own guilt at being afraid. All of that was gone now.

He was still afraid. Hell, who wouldn't be? Crash-landing Tomcats on postage-stamp-sized aircraft carriers in the middle of a war was *dangerous*; the chances that he would be killed were very, very good. But now the pressure was off. He'd keep on doing what he was doing because he did it very well and because his shipmates were counting on him, just as he counted on them. And if he survived, he would go home to Julie and Julie Marie and pick up—well, it wouldn't be the life he'd had with her before, because he'd been an aviator longer than he'd been married. No, they would all start over.

Meanwhile he would do what he had to do, free of the fear that had threatened to paralyze him the last time he'd guided twenty tons of aircraft onto a steel deck.

Jefferson's roundoff grew rapidly. There were no corrections from the LSO, just the impression of a last-second rush of speed as the lines painted onto the flight deck rose to meet the F-14, the squeal of wheels as he opened the throttles, followed by the solid snap-*unh!* as the tailhook snagged the three wire and dragged the Tomcat to a halt.

Coyote felt a surging, adrenaline-charged buoyancy.

He felt *free*.

0935 hours Zulu (1035 hours Zone)
Near Molde, overlooking the U.S.S. *Thomas Jefferson*
Romsdalfjord

There were four of them, tall, athletic men with wind-tanned features, wearing the high, zip-necked shirts of the Norwegian army under olive-drab jackets. One wore the double green rank stripes, one thick, one thin, of a sergeant. The others were privates. The bulky tube of an 84-mm Carl Gustav antitank gun was slung over the shoulders of one. The others had NATO-issue G3 rifles.

The sergeant lay on his belly in a clump of spring flowers on a bluff high above the fjord and peered down through 7 × 50 field glasses. From this vantage point on the north side of the fjord, he was staring down onto the *Jefferson* from her starboard side. From less than a mile away he could clearly see an F-14 floating toward the deck, wings spread wide, nose high . . . then jerk to a halt as it snagged the arrestor cable.

"I would say that we've found what we are looking for, comrades," the sergeant said, speaking Norwegian. His real name was Ivan Finenko, and he was a lieutenant, not a sergeant. All four men were Spetsnaz, one of hundreds of teams throughout Norway. Their mission was to investigate fjords between Trondheim and Nordfjord, searching for a hidden American aircraft carrier. Finenko was not sure why such tactics were necessary in this day of spy satellites, but he was not the sort of man who questioned orders. They'd begun with Trondheimfjord and worked their way slowly south, examining each inlet large enough to conceal an American carrier.

They had found it. Perhaps now their superiors would let them get on with their primary mission, which was to infiltrate the headquarters of the Norwegian resistance near Bergen. A hundred other teams must be trying the same thing, and this detour to examine the fjords had put them behind the rest. Finenko checked his watch, a Casio digital. There was plenty of time to pass the word back to head-quarters on the regular broadcast at 1200 hours. The roar of an engine made him look up.

The tracked vehicle thundered and roared over the wooded ridge line one hundred meters behind them, belch-ing black diesel fumes. It was a Norwegian army M109, a SAM carrier mounting Roland 2 antiair missiles. *Skynd Dem!* was painted on the side of the turret. A young lieutenant was shouting at him from the vehicle's turret, but Finenko could not understand a word above the deep-throated clatter of the engine and the squeal of metal tracks.

Standing, he held one hand to his ear and shook his head in a clear "I don't know" gesture.

The Norwegian lieutenant vanished into the turret for a moment, and the M109 slewed to a stop, its engine idling. The officer reappeared, scrambling out of the turret hatch, then dropping to the ground beside the massive treads. "Steady, Aleksandrov," Finenko murmured to the man with the Carl Gustav. "Be ready if I give the word."

"Da, tovarisch leytenant," the man growled, so excited that he'd forgotten both his Norwegian and Finenko's role of sergeant. He was on his stomach at Finenko's feet, the Carl Gustav across his shoulder, squinting against the sight.

The Norwegian lieutenant was coming down the ridge toward the Spetsnaz team. He obviously believed the four of them were Norwegian soldiers; he either thought they were stragglers and intended to round them up for some mission of his own, or he was lost and wanted to ask directions.

Finenko fingered the greasy slick receiver of his G3. They could play along and pretend to be Norwegians separated from their unit, but so much could go wrong with that approach. None of the Spetsnaz commandos had heard much in the way of recent military news, and even playing dumb they could easily make a mistake or fail to "remember" a battle their supposed unit had recently fought.

And headquarters *had* to learn about the American carrier in the fjord here. If they were pressed into service by some over-diligent prick of a Norwegian junior officer, they wouldn't be able to reach their radio, and the carrier might get away.

He weighed the dangers. Destroying the M109 would be simple enough, but would a fire attract the attention of the enemy carrier? Finenko doubted it. The battle lines were some distance away, and there were other reasons for fire than enemy action. Only that morning, the team had encountered some farmers burning trash in a field.

He took several steps toward the Norwegian, one hand casually on the grip of his G3, the other raised in greeting. His enemy was armed with a typical Norwegian tank commander's weapon, a Maskin M40—a copy of the MP40 made famous by the Germans in World War II as the so-called "Schmeisser." Finenko knew he would have to take the man down quickly and efficiently to avoid a devastating spray of return fire. Casually, his left hand dropped to the barrel of his weapon.

"*Tyepyehr!*" he shouted, his own Norwegian forgotten. "*Strelyat!*"

His finger closed on the G3's trigger as he dragged the muzzle around, aiming from the hip at the young Norwegian as the assault rifle stuttered and cracked, shattering the stillness of the ridge-top woods. The enemy's mouth gaped open as his jacket exploded in bloody spurts with each bullet impact.

In the same instant, the Carl Gustav whooshed, and a brightly burning point of light streaked across the forest clearing, slamming into the M109 between turret and tracks. There was a flash and a hollow-sounding bang. There was no flame and little smoke. That was good; there would be nothing to alert the Americans now.

The Norwegian lieutenant was flat on his back, arms spread, eyes wide open.

"Up!" Finenko snapped to the others. "Quickly! We must leave the area at once."

Like ghosts, the four infiltrators slipped away through the trees, leaving the wreckage of the SAM vehicle beside a tree-shaded lane on a Norwegian hilltop.

0941 hours Zulu (1041 hours Zone)
Viper Squadron ready room, U.S.S. *Thomas Jefferson*
Romsdalfjord

Coyote walked into the ready room, Teejay close behind him. Both men still wore their flight suits, though helmets, life vests, and survival gear had been parked in lockers outside. Quite a few of the other VF-95 aviators and RIOs were already gathered in the compartment, along with crew chiefs and squadron deck personnel.

"Coyote!" Batman cried, reaching through the crowd to clap him on the shoulder. "Teejay! Welcome back, guys! Have some caffeine."

He handed Coyote a mug filled with steaming coffee, and Coyote took it gratefully. "What's the occasion?"

"Waiting to hear from the powers on high," Ken Blake, "Malibu," said. Batman's RIO grinned and jerked a thumb toward the 1-MC on the bulkhead. "Things've been damned quiet since we hit their airfields. Word is there's another briefing coming up soon. God knows what it'll be this time."

"Coyote! I watched you come in on the PLAT," Batman said, a mischievous grin on his face. "Your landing was *much* better this time. I really think you're improving!"

Coyote surprised himself by laughing. "Practice makes perfect."

"Hey," Teejay said. "If I'd've known you were still *practicin'*, man—"

"Make a hole!" someone yelled, and the crowd parted from in front of the ready room door. Tombstone stepped through. His khakis were rumpled, and Coyote thought again that he'd never seen him looking so worn.

"As you were, everybody," Tombstone said. He waved the clipboard he was carrying in one hand. "Thought you gentlemen would like to see the latest posting for the Viper tally board."

He began reading off the names of pilot-RIO teams in the squadron. Eight of them had been in combat earlier that morning, flying TACCAP for the A-6 strikes against the Russian air bases. Most of the rest had been on BARCAP over Romsdalfjord and had not taken part in the battle. Loon and Saint, in Tomcat 205, had scored two kills, confirmed by the circling Hawkeye coordinating the battle. Batman and Malibu had chalked up three, while Big D Sheridan and Fast Eddie Glazowski in 212 had gotten one.

Tombstone looked up at Coyote and grinned. "And you,

hotshot, have just gone ballistic. Coyote and Teejay, we pegged you guys this morning with five kills.''

The room exploded with cheering and applause. Someone pounded Coyote on the back, making him slosh some of his coffee onto the deck.

"Of course," Batman said, kidding, "the Coyote still has to learn that *real* Navy flyers don't go in for this candy-ass, long-range, Phoenix stuff!''

"Right on!" Lieutenant James Dubois, "Mad Dog," exclaimed. "I ask you! Would John Wayne blast the bad guy out of the saddle from a hundred miles away?''

"If John Wayne had a Phoenix?" Teejay asked. "Damned straight he would!''

"You know," Lieutenant "Loon" Baird said, "the *real* heroes are those Norwegian Falcon drivers. They were mixing it up with those MiGs like pros.''

"Amen," Trapper Martin said. He raised his cup in salute. "To White Lightning!''

The feeling of belonging in that crowded room, of *strength,* was overpowering. Coyote set his mug on a table. His decision to leave the Navy was unchanged, but he felt closer to these men than he had for some time. A *part* of them and what they stood for.

"Congratulations, Coyote." Tombstone stood in front of him, hand extended.

"Thanks, CAG." Coyote took the hand and shook it. "Ah, listen . . ." He hesitated, uncertain how to proceed. "Stoney, I've been way out of line these last few days. I want to apologize . . . and thank you for keeping me on the flight line.''

"Nothing to apologize for, hotdog," Tombstone replied. "Anyway, I *needed* you. We all do.''

"I'm beginning to understand that, CAG.''

"Good. Because we still need you, more than ever.''

"Why?" There was something about Tombstone's tone. "What's up?''

"There'll be a full wing briefing later, but I can tell you guys the details now. VA-89 nailed the *Kirov.*" He was interrupted by a cheer. "All right, all right. Settle down. *Kirov* is out of the fight, adrift and burning. The guess is the Russians'll have to scuttle her. The bad news is that we didn't get close enough to tag the *Soyuz*."

"See?" Mad Dog said. "John Wayne would've gotten them up close and personal."

Tombstone grinned. "We're readying another mission and targeting the *Soyuz*. This time we'll take the missiles in so close we'll be able to shove the Harpoons down their throats. Or into any other suitable bodily orifice." The men laughed at that.

"When, CAG?" Batman asked. "When are we gonna go? This afternoon?"

"Negative," Tombstone replied. He shook his head. "Stores and military expendables are way down, especially after that last A-6 strike. We're due to rendezvous with the stores ships tomorrow, early. We'll take on more missiles and then hit 'em."

"By tomorrow morning, that Russkie carrier could have scampered clear back to North Cape," Malibu said. "Bad scene, man. We'll have to catch 'em all over again."

"Don't count on it. OZ says that our strikes on Bodø and the other air bases have hurt them, bad. They're going to want their naval air to help cover the airfields. That means *Soyuz* is going to stay where she is, at least until they figure out where we are."

Trapper laughed. "Which they won't do because they're *stupid*!"

"Not stupid," Tombstone cautioned. "But definitely confused." He grinned at the men ringing him in. "If I was up against this bunch of maniacs, I'd be confused too!"

That elicited more laughter. Someone extended Tombstone a coffee mug. "Have some java, CAG."

"Thanks, guys. I'd like to but I can't. Planning session in Ops. You men stand down and hang easy until we pass the word for launch tomorrow, hear? VA-97 has the duty today on BARCAP."

Which meant the closest thing to liberty the Vipers could

enjoy while they were at war. They cheered as Tombstone
ducked out of the compartment, and the congratulations for
Coyote's kills continued.

Five kills . . . five dead men.

But Coyote could feel only the promise of being alive.

1500 hours Zulu (1600 hours Zone)
The Øresund
Between Sweden and Denmark

Stretching between the Swedish cities of Helsingborg and
Malmö to the east and the northeastern tip of the Danish
island of Sjæland to the west, the Øresund, a strip of water
two miles wide, divides the southern tip of Sweden from
Denmark. This narrow sound is the deepest of several that
connect the Baltic Sea with the Kattegat and the approaches
to the North Sea.

It is also one of the rock-bound bottlenecks that have
hampered Russia since that country became a seafaring
empire. As with Japan in the far East, or the Bosporus and
the Dardanelles connecting the Black Sea to the Aegean, the
fact that the straits are controlled by neutral or hostile
foreign powers has long hampered the projection of Russian
sea power to those regions where it is most effective—the
open ocean.

When General Vladimir Vorobyev and the marshals
behind the resurgent Soviet empire first began planning
Operation Kutuzov, it was assumed that Norway would fall
within a week to ten days of the invasion and that, at that
time, Sweden and Denmark could be bullied into surrender
without having to deploy a single soldier against them.

Two weeks after the first Soviet forces poured across the
frontiers in Finnmark, it was clear that neither Sweden nor
Denmark was going to surrender without a fight. The war
was spreading, whatever the Moscow planners did to stop it,
and unless something was done to break the deadlock, the
Soviets would soon find themselves fighting a defensive

war. Within the Motherland, the situation was not good; food was scarce and strictly rationed, gasoline impossible to get. The people would put up with great privations if the news from Scandinavia continued to be good, but once it was clear that the Soviets were on the defensive, that the war might drag on indefinitely, the public mood could quickly change.

So the decision was made to expand the war. Sweden was invaded by amphibious army units operating across the Gulf of Bothnia on the night of June 18.

Four days later, early on the twenty-second, and with final preparations in place, elements of the *Morskaya Pekhota,* the Soviet Naval Infantry, landed on beaches at Køge and Karlslunderstrand, a few miles south of Copenhagen. Soviet *desantniki,* airborne forces redeployed to the Baltic after their operations in Finland and Norway, descended silently out of overcast skies in the fields outside Malmö and Helsingborg, on the Swedish side of the straits.

The Swedes were already fighting for their lives, heavily outnumbered and stretched to their very limits in southern Sweden, and the new assaults left them reeling. The Danes, while not unprepared—their military had been mobilized and on the alert since the events leading up to the invasion of Norway and Finland two weeks earlier—were still caught off guard by the sheer, ruthless viciousness of the attack. The seaborne landings were backed by parachute landings throughout Sjælland, by naval infantry unloading from Russian cargo ships in Copenhagen's waterfront, and by the appearance of thousands of Spetsnaz commandos in civilian clothes. The Spetsnaz forces, especially, effectively paralyzed Danish resistance as they took over central telephone offices, radio and TV stations, military headquarters, and even the Christiansborg Palace, where the Danish parliament was in emergency session.

After twelve hours, fighting was still savage across the entire length and breadth of Sjælland and the issue in the Danish capital of Copenhagen was still in doubt. All major military installations overlooking the Øresund, however,

were in Soviet hands, and by late afternoon the first
elements of the Soviet Baltic Fleet were entering Danish
waters. Russian naval infantry captured the strategic island
of Bornholm almost as an afterthought, while more troops
debarked from the packed cargo holds of Soviet merchantmen directly onto the docks at Trelleborg and Malmö. Strike
aircraft—Su-24 Fencers, Su-27 Flankers, and MiG-27s—
circled endlessly, delivering bomb loads, strafing ground
targets, and providing close air support for both Soviet
troops on the ground and the swarms of Hind gunships
stooping from the leaden skies over Sweden. A desperate
sortie by a squadron of sleek, canard-winged Swedish Saab
Viggens was stopped cold high above the cold waters of the
Baltic by a wave of MiG-27 Fulcrums.

Despite the fighting, the Øresund was secure by mid-
afternoon, the Danish and Swedish coastal defenses neutral-
ized. By 1500 hours, the first minesweepers and ASW
frigates were passing the island of Saltholm, in mid-channel
between Malmö and Copenhagen, where the old red flag of
Communism fluttered above a bomb-shattered coast guard
station.

At 1800 hours, lead elements of the main Soviet Baltic
Fleet, including the Kirov-class battle cruisers *Irkutsk* and
Tallinn, and the aircraft carrier *Kreml,* were proceeding
north through the sound, threading their way between cities
from which the crack and chatter of gunfire continued to
echo.

Throughout the West the alert spread, first from watching
satellites, then through the network of military attachés and
observers throughout northern Europe.

The Baltic Fleet was out.

CHAPTER 15
Monday, 23 June

Admiral Magruder had been in the White House Situation Room before. It never seemed to change much from Administration to Administration, this carpeted, wood-paneled bunker with its hidden television screens; its massive, central conference table; its flanked U.S. and Presidential flags; its small army of Marine guards and Secret Service personnel protecting its miles of passage-ways and work spaces hidden beneath the streets and buildings of Washington, D.C. The passes and authorization sent to him earlier that afternoon by Admiral Scott had gotten him this far past the maze of security. Now he showed the ID card pinned to the lapel of his dress blue uniform jacket a final time and entered, crossing the deep gold carpet and finding his place at the table.

The war in Norway had everyone in the city jumpy. Was Scandinavia the precursor of all-out war in Europe, or of a nuclear strike against the United States? No one knew, but security was tighter than he'd ever remembered it. The tension in the room was a cloying, almost choking presence, unseen but very real.

Most of the others scheduled to attend the discussion were already present and seated. Vincent Duvall, the CIA

173

Director, nodded at him as he walked in. Admiral Brandon
Scott, big, bluff, and white-haired, and the current Chairman
of the Joint Chiefs, was engaged in a whispered conversation with his immediate boss, Secretary of Defense George
Vane. Secretary of State Robert Heideman was reading a
report, a worried frown creasing his face behind the thick
lenses of his glasses. After years in the Pentagon, it was still
hard for Magruder to think of these names and faces as
people rather than as personalities glimpsed on television
news interviews or shows like *Face the Nation.*

As Magruder took his chair next to Admiral Scott, the
National Security Advisor, Herbert T. Waring, entered the
room, followed closely by White House Chief of Staff
Gordon West.

"Hello, Tom," Scott said to him, his voice low. "Welcome to the funny farm."

"I got your message, Admiral. Why'd you drag me down
here?"

"Because a few years back you ran the battle group
we've got off Norway right now. I thought your insights
might be valuable."

Magruder sighed. He'd been in similar situations before
but never liked them. The decision-makers and policy-
setters of Washington frequently needed the point of view
of a man who had been there, where their policies met the
real world . . . but it invariably left him trying to read the
minds of other men, men whose lives depended on his
guesses and assumptions. He thought of his nephew, now
Acting CAG aboard the *Jefferson.* Matt Magruder had never
had much patience with the Beltway desk jockeys micro-
managing military forces half a world away.

For that matter, neither had Admiral Thomas Magruder.

He shook his head. "There's not a hell of a lot I can say
about it, sir. Admiral Tarrant's a capable man, I've heard,
but I don't know him personally."

"It's the capabilities of the battle group I'm interested in,
Tom. We've got one carrier facing two now, with this new
Russian deployment out of the Baltic. We're outnumbered

fifteen to one in surface combatants. What you have to say could—''

''Gentlemen!'' Herbert Waring rapped the tabletop with his knuckles. ''If you please, gentlemen, let's get this show on the road. We're on a tight deadline. You've all seen the briefings and read Mr. Duvall's report. We've got one hell of a situation here, with the Russian Baltic Fleet coming out into the North Sea. The President needs our advice on how best to handle this new . . . development.'' He looked at the Secretary of State. ''Bob? Let's start with you. What about our European allies?''

Robert Heideman held a pen between his hands before him on the table. He still looked worried and seemed unable to meet the eyes of the others in the room. ''There still is no word from Germany,'' he said. ''There have been numerous, um, rumors of Soviet invasions along their Baltic coast but nothing substantive. So far at least, the Russians seem to be restricting their activities to the Scandinavian land mass and to the Danish islands of Bornholm and, of course, Sjæland. Our best guess is that Germany and France intend to pursue a wait-and-see policy, that they do not perceive an immediate threat from the Russians at this time.''

''Damn it, Mr. Secretary,'' Admiral Scott growled. ''The Russians have just invaded Denmark, marched in and grabbed Copenhagen, for God's sake, and the Germans don't feel threatened?''

''It's a matter of perspective, Admiral,'' Heideman replied. He pursed his lips. ''Both Germany and France feel somewhat, um, isolated by the Soviet moves in Scandinavia. Berlin and Paris have been in almost constant consultation since the beginning of the crisis. Even united, however, they cannot hope to stop the Russians by themselves. And I imagine they are uncertain about our intentions in the region. One carrier group is not enough to stop the Russian tide.''

''Are you suggesting we go in with more? As I recall, Bob, you've taken the position all along that we shouldn't be in Norway at all.''

"I still don't think an active military presence in Scandinavia is going to help, no. As a message to the Russians that we intended to support our Scandinavian friends, yes, sending the carrier battle group in was a valid strategy. Now, though . . ." He spread his hands helplessly. "Now we're trapped, engaged in direct military confrontation with the Soviets. If we back down, we show our weakness. If we push on, send reinforcements in to back up our assets in the battle zone, we risk losing . . . *everything*."

"What about Great Britain?" Waring slouched in his chair with one arm draped over the back. "Any guesses on what are the Brits going to do?"

Heideman shrugged. "They'll come out solidly against the Russians, that's certain. With the Socialists out, Lloyd Whitmore has been asked to form a new government. He's Tory, solidly conservative and anti-socialist. He'll choose a cabinet that will push for England to stand up against the Russians. But it will take time, too much time. The current polls show most Britains favor standing up to the Russians, but the socialists are still pretty active. There could be another few weeks of debate."

"We don't have a few more weeks," Gordon West said, his long face showing his pessimism. "If we could revive NATO, we might have a chance. But this thing has happened too fast. I mean, damn it! Nobody thought the Communists could stage this kind of comeback!"

Waring leaned forward, elbows on the table and his fingers steepled in front of him. "Gentlemen, in two hours Gordon and I have to go upstairs to see the Man. He's going to ask us for a consensus . . . a solid direction to go in. Now what are we supposed to tell him? Wait and see what the British do? Wait on the French and Germans and let them take the lead? Maybe we should wait until the damned Russians invade New Jersey, and *then* decide!"

Admiral Scott cleared his throat, and Waring turned his gaze on him. "Admiral? You have something to say?"

"Only that we should give some thought to our carrier group in Norway," he said. "This new Soviet push out of the Baltic puts them squarely between two superior naval forces. Basically, they can stay and fight only if we give them some kind of support.''

''That MEF is still on the way, isn't it?''

''Yes, sir. II MEF is passing between Scotland and the Faeroes now, still out of range of Soviet naval air. But they won't be for much longer with this new Russian force coming out of the Baltic. We have to make a decision, and it's got to be now. Either we keep *Jefferson* where she is, send in the Marines, and back them up with at least one more carrier group. I'd suggest the *Eisenhower*. She could be in the area in another couple of days. Or we say the hell with it and pull out. But damn it, we've got to do it *now*. If we don't, we're going to lose the *Jefferson*, her escorts, and ten or twelve thousand of our boys. They won't last long against the combined weight of two Russian fleets!''

Vane ran his hand through thinning hair. ''As I understand it, CBG-14 is already badly weakened. The loss of the *Hopkins* . . . and the destroyer they dispatched to escort her to Scotland.''

''The *Kearny*,'' Scott said.

''Yes. That leaves only, what? The carrier and three surface vessels, plus an attack sub. And they've been hiding in some damned fjord for the past four days. The situation is clearly impossible.''

''If we pull out,'' Duvall said thoughtfully, ''what kind of message does that send to the Germans? Or the British?''

''That they're alone,'' Vane pointed out.

''Yes,'' Heideman added. ''But you know, it's really too late for heroics over there. Maybe the best we can hope for is a cease-fire, one that leaves the Russians in control of Scandinavia but preserves our forces intact. I think we should pull the *Jefferson* out.''

''How about it, Admiral?'' Waring said. ''Create a mobile, defensive force, *Ike* and *Jeff* and the Marines. Let the bastards have Norway, but draw the line at Scotland and the Faeroes. Could they do it?''

''Yes.'' Scott exchanged glances with Magruder.

"Though the Marines won't do much good aboard ship, except maybe as a threat that they're going to land somewhere. My suggestion would be to stand where we are and fight."

They continued to argue the problem back and forth, and Magruder despaired. Most of the men in the room seemed to favor withdrawing from Norway, possibly setting up some kind of barrier along the GIUK gap, from Greenland to Iceland to the United Kingdom. Just as the Soviets had tried to establish an exclusion zone within the Norwegian Sea, perhaps they could be kept from passing through into the Atlantic.

The Marines of II MEF were a sticky problem. Secretary of Defense Vane suggested landing the Marines of II MEF in the Faeroes, which were owned by Denmark, both as a warning to the Soviets and to prevent them from doing it first. Heideman seemed to favor keeping the Marines at sea until Britain could be persuaded to take them in with an eye to keeping the Soviets nervous and bottled up, while West suggested returning them to the United States as a conciliatory gesture to Moscow.

Only Admiral Scott and Vincent Duvall seemed to favor standing and fighting it out in the Norwegian Sea, and even they conceded that it would take massive reinforcements for the lone *Jefferson* battle group to have even a ghost of a chance.

The conversation in the soundproofed room was becoming steadily louder, steadily more chaotic. One of Scott's aides was shouting at one of Heideman's aides, while George Vane looked as though he was about to throw a punch at Gordon West. Tempers were flaring, the shouting so loud that it was impossible to follow any one conversation in the room.

"Gentlemen, *please*!" Waring shouted from the head of the table, trying to restore order once again. "One at a time!"

Magruder was forcibly reminded of a scene in the old black-and-white Kubrick movie *Dr. Strangelove.* *"You can't fight in here, gentlemen!"* one of the characters had shouted. *"This is the war room!"*

"Mr. Waring," Admiral Scott said in the abrupt silence that followed. "May I say something?"

"Please do," Waring said, resuming his seat. "But *quietly . . .*"

"Gentlemen," Scott said, "we can argue this thing until the cows come home. But I want to make one point. In any crisis, the aircraft carriers, the ships, the men, all are tools . . . *weapons* in our hands. In the President's hands. But by God, we'd better know how to use those weapons effectively, or we might as well face the enemy unarmed.

"Now, I've invited Admiral Thomas Magruder, the Joint Staff's Director of Operations, to join us this evening. He once commanded the *Jefferson* battle group. Perhaps he can tell us something about this weapon of ours, how we can use it to best advantage. Admiral? Do you have anything to add to the discussion?"

Magruder stared across the table into the hostile silence. "If you want my opinion in this . . . debate, I'd have to say that I don't think retreat is an option—"

He was cut off by the rising babble of angry voices. He held up his hand and waited as Waring pounded on the table again.

"I don't believe retreat is an option," he repeated. "Maybe if you'd backed down before the first shots were fired last week, you could have allowed yourself a more flexible response. But not now."

"The loss of an aircraft carrier is hardly an acceptable alternative," Heideman pointed out. "How much does one of those things cost . . . five billion? Ten?"

"I'm not worried about the cost in dollars, Mr. Secretary. The human cost is far more important."

"Tell that to the taxpayers. Besides, if our foreign policy is discredited by a major defeat at sea—"

"With all due respect, sir, our foreign policy is already discredited. But I'm not as interested in foreign policy as I am in what you expect the *Jefferson* to do."

"That's what we're asking you, Admiral," West said. "What can we tell them to do, and have some assurance that they'll be able to carry out those orders?"

"Well, if you don't give CBG-14 some support, and damned fast, all they'll be able to do for you is die."

"Then they should be withdrawn. Is that what you're saying?"

"No. What I'm saying is that you can't give them orders without giving them what they need to carry them out. That aircraft carrier has been on the battle line for over a week now. That's an eternity in modern warfare. They've lost men. Whether they stay or retreat, they will lose more men before this thing is done. *Don't let what they've gone through already be in vain!*"

"The question, Admiral, is whether to keep them where they are or pull them out," Vane pointed out. "I can understand your feeling that they need help if they are to stay put. But that is not a viable option."

"You could send in the *Eisenhower,*" Magruder said. "And you could detach *Kennedy* from the Sixth Fleet. She could be on station in five days. You could—"

"As I said, that is not a viable option." Vane looked around the conference table. "I think I would have to strongly recommend that they pull back."

"You will lose the battle group if you do that. The Soviet Baltic Fleet will intercept them before they're halfway to Scotland."

"In other words," Duvall said, "we'll still have our defeat, and we'll have sent the wrong message to Europe and to the Soviets. Christ!"

"Then they should stay put," West said.

"You can't just abandon them—"

"Really, Admiral. No one has said anything about simply abandoning them. But there are political realities here that—"

"I'm not talking about politics, Mr. West," Magruder said sharply. "Damn it, I'm talking about men who have put their lives on the line to carry out policies you people have set. That *we* have set. Fine. Now give them what they need to carry out those policies, and let them do their job.''

"What *is* their job, Admiral?" Waring said. "That, I think, is the point."

"To carry out the government's policy. It's not up to me to tell you what that policy should be. But by God, don't abandon our people . . . and don't micromanage them to death. Decide whether you want to stand by Norway and Sweden and the rest, or give them up, but don't squander the lives of our boys on the front lines!''

"Touchingly put, Admiral," Waring said. "And I take your point. However, as Gordon here tried to point out, there are political realities which must be addressed. Realities which shape our policy and give it substance." He hesitated, placing the tips of his fingers together delicately before him. "Perhaps Admiral Magruder has hit upon something, though. We should not, ah, micromanage the situation. Perhaps the thing to do would be to allow the commanding officer of CBG-14 the fullest possible freedom in carrying out his orders."

"Which are?" Vane asked.

"Why, to support the Norwegians. To avoid excessive losses to his own command. To maintain CBG-14 as a viable fighting force and a credible deterrent to the Soviets. And to maintain for us as wide a selection of options in the region as possible. I think that about covers it, yes?"

Inwardly, Magruder groaned. They were abandoning the *Jefferson*. There'd be no help for her. He could read between the lines of the discussion and see that the bureaucrats and politicians were arranging for *Jefferson*'s martyrdom.

He felt sick to the core of his soul. *God, Matt,* he thought. *I'm sorry . . .*

CHAPTER 16
Monday, 23 June

0330 hours Zulu (0430 hours Zone)
CVIC, U.S.S. *Thomas Jefferson*
Romsdalfjord

The atmosphere in CVIC was charged with an invisible but almost palpable electricity as Tombstone and his senior CAG staff gathered with Tarrant and Captain Brandt, the admiral's senior staff, and the senior Ops staff to sort out the new and unsettling news flashed simultaneously from Bergen and from Washington. Tarrant and his flag officers had flown in by helicopter from *Shiloh* less than an hour earlier. They'd brought with them new orders from Washington.

The room was darkened, and a large-scale map of Denmark and the southern portions of Norway and Sweden was up on the projection screen. Broad, sweeping strokes in red outlined the latest concentrations of Soviet naval infantry and the new fronts, now engulfing all of Sjæland and most of the southern tip of Sweden, from Halmstad to Kristianstad. Arrows and cryptic notations—numbers, ship names, and times—showed the movements of Soviet ships north through the Denmark-Sweden strait, with lead elements already positioned off Lindesnes, the southernmost tip of Norway, and well into the North Sea proper.

"The main body came through the Øresund nine hours ago," Paul Aiken said. The shadow of his pointer traced movements across the map. "The aircraft carrier *Kreml* was positively identified by Swedish observers ashore, in close company with two Kirov-class cruisers—*Tallinn* and *Irkutsk*.

"Apparently, Swedish Viggens attempted to organize an attack on Soviet ships here in the Baltic, but the attack was broken up before it could be properly organized. A second strike was made late yesterday evening. AJ37 Viggens outfitted for antishipping operations attacked Soviet warships off Göteborg. An Udaloy-class destroyer, the *Marshal Shaposhnikov,* was struck by Swedish Rb04E antiship missiles and sunk. A Kresta II–class guided-missile cruiser, we think she is the *Admiral Isachenkov,* was heavily damaged and appears to be making for port. We also have reports of several smaller Soviet vessels—corvettes and patrol craft—sunk or damaged by Swedish torpedo boats or air, but we don't have any solid data on that as yet."

Aiken closed his pointer as he turned to face the officers gathered in the room. "Best information, based on Swedish reports and satellite data, suggests that the Baltic Fleet deployment includes at least thirty-five ships of all classes, exclusive of patrol small stuff. As you can see, their losses so far barely scratch the surface. Lights."

CVIC's lights came up, and Aiken looked toward Tarrant. "This concludes my briefing. Admiral?"

"Thank you, Paul." Tarrant stood and took Aiken's place at the front of the room. He braced one elbow on the podium and paused, seeming to consider carefully what he had to say. "Well, gentlemen, you see what we're up against. This battle group is now facing two major threats. I won't underplay the seriousness of our position. CBG-14 is now effectively pinned between two superior Soviet forces, the *Soyuz* and supporting elements of the Red Banner Northern Fleet to our north, and the *Kreml* and the bulk of the Red Banner Baltic Fleet to the south. If *Jefferson* is caught between them—or if they manage to join forces, well, I think all of you can draw your own conclusions." He gestured toward one of the Flag Staff officers in the front row, Lieutenant Commander Emerson, and cracked a grin.

"Joe here put it best when the word came through just after midnight. Something about a snowball's chances in hell, was it?"

Several in the room chuckled, and Emerson folded his arms and shook his head with a wry smile.

"Defeatist talk, right? But I'm afraid this time I have to agree. The men of this battle group have conducted themselves superbly; they've given everything they've got and acquitted themselves valiantly. But the odds now are simply too great. Sooner or later, our opponents are going to find us. It'll only be a matter of time before they run us down and overwhelm us by sheer weight of numbers.

"I have been in consultation with the President and the Joint Chiefs." He extracted a printout from his shirt, unfolded it carefully, and began reading. "'Flash secret. One . . . satellite reconnaissance and intelligence assets confirm presence of second Soviet carrier task force in CAMELOT operational area. Evidence suggests major sortie by RED BANNER/BALTIC naval units possibly directed at CAMELOT, as well as Free Norwegian Forces Ashore (FNFA). This sortie is recognized as a threat to U.S. Navy operations in the area.'" He looked up. "Well, I'd say they got that right."

There was scattered laughter in the room. Tarrant pressed ahead. "'Two . . . COCBG will use discretion in preserving full operational integrity CBG-14 while fulfilling basic mission directives and supporting FNFA. If possible, Soviet naval operations are to be hindered but without risking major loss to CBG surface assets.' I'm interpreting that paragraph to mean they'd rather I not lose *Jefferson* or the *Shiloh*.

"'Three . . . COCBG is advised that II-MEF has been deployed to Norwegian combat zone in order to conduct amphibious operations in support of FNFA. CBG-14 will maintain independent operational command but is directed to coordinate activities with II MEF through COMLANT.

"'Four . . .'" He looked up. "Well, there's more, but that covers the major points. It's signed Admiral Lawrence

R. Harriman Jr., USLANTCOM, Norfolk, but the directives are straight from the President and the Joint Chiefs.

"Our orders are . . . ah . . . comfortably vague. The bottom line seems to be that they're leaving the final decision to us. We're directed to continue harassing Soviet naval forces in the forward battle area, but to preserve the fighting capabilities of this carrier group." He nodded toward Tombstone, who was sitting in a second-row seat. "CAG tells me that our store of antiship missiles and other expendables is almost exhausted. Given that, and the numbers we face, it seems to me the prudent thing to do is to retire. The lead elements of II MEF are five hundred miles away and already in range of air sorties off the *Soyuz*. I can't emphasize this enough. It is imperative that we shield the MEF from attack by Soviet air and naval forces. Uh, lights, please? Let me have that map up here again." CVIC's overhead lights dimmed, and the map reappeared. "Can I have a view of the whole North Sea, please?" Tarrant asked the projectionist.

A moment later, a new map appeared, this one showing all of Scandinavia and the North Sea, as well as part of the Norwegian Sea as far west as Britain. "As of 2400 hours," Tarrant continued, "II MEF was here, one hundred miles north of Scotland.

"Now, the word is that mobilization is under way at home, but it's going to be a while before the Army is going to be in a position to do anything. By the time the Army gets it together, all of Scandinavia will be under the Soviets' thumbs. That Marine Expeditionary Force is the only shoreside card we have to play against the Russians right now. If they're knocked out of the game early, well, we might as well all go home, because there won't be a free Norway to defend.

"Accordingly, it is my intention to withdraw from Romsdalfjord and run southwest. We will rendezvous with II MEF somewhere about here . . . in the vicinity of the Shetlands. From there, we can carry out a purely defensive operation. We'll have the *Eisenhower*'s battle group as

backup to prevent a general Soviet breakout into the
Atlantic. Lights.''

As the lights came up, Tarrant faced his audience. He
looked, Tombstone thought, like a beaten man.

And the tactics he'd just outlined reflected that defeat.
Every man in the compartment could see the risks in what
Tarrant was proposing—breaking from cover and fleeing
southwest across three hundred miles of open sea. The
Soviet Baltic fleet was already in a position to interdict that
line from Romsdalfjord to Scotland; it would mean a
running fight across the North Sea, one that they would not
be able to avoid, one certain to end in the loss of more
American ships.

As he stared at the map, however, Tombstone could see
an alternative. There was tremendous risk involved, but it
offered them a chance to keep the enemy on the defensive,
instead of merely reacting to his moves and thrusts.

His scowl must have revealed his thoughts. When he
glanced up, he found himself staring into Tarrant's eyes.
''CAG? You don't look happy. It was my intention to open
this session to debate and comments, and it seems to me
you've got some comments to make. Spill 'em.''

Tombstone was remembering the confrontation with
Coyote in his office a few days before. *Sometimes the only
thing you can do is wade back in with both fists swinging.
Like they say in the Marines: attack, attack, attack!*

It's not that easy.

No, it never was. Especially when the lives of thousands
of men were riding on it.

What else had he said to Coyote that evening? *There's no
way to duck responsibility in this man's Navy.*

Yeah, right. He took a deep breath. ''Sir, I would like to
suggest another possibility. I think we should attack, hit the
Soyuz again before they get organized, and before *Kreml*
gets close enough to hit us. Then we head, not southwest,
but north.''

''North!'' Emerson said, shocked. ''Damn it, CAG, that's
suicide.''

Tombstone shrugged. "It's unexpected."

"You got that right," Parker, *Jefferson*'s Exec, muttered. But he was grinning.

"It's also the move the Russians are dreading most," Tombstone continued. "They still seem to be holding the bulk of their Red Banner Northern Fleet in reserve, up in the Barents Sea someplace, waiting for us to try a swing that way to get at their Kola Peninsula bases. If we make that move, they're going to bunch up, go on the defensive. And if they do that, we've got them!"

"Well, I can't think of a better way to get the Baltic Fleet to follow us," Tarrant said slowly. He was studying the map. "They'd follow us instead of heading for the Atlantic, or trying to ambush II MEF. But as you pointed out, we'd still have the rest of the Red Banner Northern Fleet in front of us. And the *Kreml* and her consorts behind. That's assuming that we manage to sink the *Soyuz* in the first place."

"The key, Admiral, is to stop playing catch-up with the bastards and put them on the defensive."

As he spoke, Tombstone could not help thinking about Pamela. He felt a soul-wrenching longing for her. He had to assume that she was either still in Bergen or with Lindstrom's people in the hills. What would happen to her if the Russians crushed the last of the Norwegian resistance?

Well, what would happen to all of them if they abandoned Scandinavia? The problem was far larger than the threat to any single individual. It would be a long time before U.S. forces would be able to organize for a return, and the captive nations would suffer in the meantime. With the Soviets' past record, there could be no doubt of that.

Tombstone knew that he should not, *could* not let his worry for Pamela lead his thinking about battle group strategy. But, he reasoned, if it did not *lead* his thinking, at least it could help clarify it. Was it Samuel Johnson who'd once said that if a man knows he is to be hanged in a fortnight, it concentrates his mind wonderfully?

It was much the same for him now. Tombstone was

convinced that he was right, that *Jefferson*'s best hope lay in staying close to the Norwegian coast and striking hard at the *Soyuz* once again, before the two Russian forces could unite. Stonewall Jackson had used much the same strategy in the Valley Campaign of the American Civil War, hitting first one Union army and then another . . . and in the end defeating them all.

"If we run," he pointed out, "we've got two Russian forces on our heels. In fact, we'll have to cut right past the Baltic Fleet's bows. They're bound to spot us once we're clear of the coast, and they'll be launching alpha strikes of their own. Any ships in this battle group that are damaged will be snapped up in pretty short order.

"But if we head north, we can deal with one force at a time. Hit the *Soyuz*, sink her, sink or scatter her escorts. We'll draw *Kreml* after us and give II MEF a chance to get through to the coast. Maybe we can find a new hideout in a different fjord and coordinate with the Marines as they approach the beach."

"What about expendables?" Emerson said. "The admiral just pointed out we're almost out of Harpoons."

"Almost. We have enough for one more alpha strike, though. Maybe two. If we get in really close this time, I'm convinced we can break through their air defenses and do some real damage. But we're going to have to move damned fast."

"Another twelve hours," Brandt said from his seat in the front row of chairs, "and *Kreml* will be in range to launch an alpha strike of her own. God help us then."

"Stores is a big problem," Tarrant pointed out. "We're going to have to rendezvous with the UNREP ships sooner or later."

"Yes, sir." Tombstone pulled a notebook from his khaki shirt pocket and thumbed it open. He'd been making some notes already, toying with the resupply problem. "The UNREP ships carry CH-46 Sea Knights for vertical replenishment, and there are Sea Knights with the Marine amphib ships. Their cargo capacity would let them carry two

Harpoons each internally . . . or eight slung externally
from a cargo net. Even ASW Sea Kings could manage one
Harpoon apiece if they skimp a bit on fuel for the trip. We
could press them into service off the Marine amphibs, or
from our frigates.''

"That takes care of Harpoons," Brandt said. "What
about jet fuel? We must be running close to critical. Helos
can't bring in enough fuel for the whole air wing.''

"Yeah, fuel's a problem," Tombstone conceded. *Jefferson* was nuclear-powered and needed no fuel, but her
aircraft burned tens of thousands of gallons of JP-5 each
day. *Shiloh* and the other ships in the battle group—all save
Galveston—were not nuclear powered either. They needed
fuel, a lot of it, to keep going. "But we should be able to
proceed with air ops at this level for two more days before
that becomes critical. We could also stretch things a bit by
tapping helo fuel from *Shiloh* or the escorts.''

"Negative," Tarrant said sharply. "I will not reduce our
ASW capability. Not with the threat from Russian subs as
great as it is in these waters.''

"Okay," Tombstone said. "We still have enough JP-5
aboard for one more alpha strike, especially if it's a short
one. In two days we can rendezvous with the UNREP ships
and resupply. But north somewhere, near the coast. Maybe
in the Vestfjord.''

One of Tarrant's staff officers shook his head as he turned
in his seat to look at Tombstone. "Nice idea, Commander,
but I still don't see why the *Kreml* battle group doesn't just
chase us all the way up the coast. If they could catch us
while we're running southwest, they could do the same with
us going north.''

"They might. But they're going to be cautious if we
manage to deep-six the *Soyuz*. And, if we time things right,
if they do follow, it will be them getting trapped between
CBG-14 and the Marine carriers." He grinned. "The
Russians are not dumb. Sink the *Soyuz,* and I don't think
they'll be in a mood to follow us too closely.''

"Well, that's the problem, isn't it?" Tarrant said. "Sinking the Russkie carrier. We've tried twice now and missed both times."

"With respect, sir, we haven't tried hard enough. Their ECM has been pretty good throughout the battle so far. I think we're going to have to get in a hell of a lot closer to make sure our Harpoons hit the right target. And I have an idea on that too—"

A telephone buzzed on one of the CVIC bulkheads, and an aide picked it up. "Captain Brandt?" he said after a moment. "CIC. Urgent."

Jefferson's Captain went to the phone, spoke in low tones, then listened. "What?" His shout startled the officers gathered in CVIC. "Okay. Sound GQ."

He handed the receiver back to the aide and turned to address the listening officers. The clangor of general quarters began sounding from the 1-MC, and Tombstone could hear the metallic pounding of running feet in the corridors outside.

"Admiral, you and your staff had better hustle back to *Shiloh*. Our Hawkeye has picked up a large target, many contacts, approaching from the north. They appear to be vectoring on Romsdalfjord."

The admiral went pale. "God, no . . ."

"Looks like the question of heading north is academic, CAG," Brandt said. "They've found us and they're launching an alpha strike. We're going to be damned lucky if we survive."

The officers began filing out of CVIC, heading for their combat stations.

And Tombstone realized with a sinking feeling that they might well have just lost their one chance to save the battle group, to save Norway . . .

. . . to save Pamela. He followed the others into the passageway outside and headed for his duty station in CIC.

CHAPTER 17
Monday, 23 June

0351 hours Zulu (0451 hours Zone)
Officers' Quarters, U.S.S. *Thomas Jefferson*
Romsdalfjord

The rasp of the klaxon brought Coyote wide awake out of the hardest, deepest sleep he'd enjoyed in a long time.

"Now hear this, now hear this!" sounded over the 1-MC as his bare feet hit the deck. "General Quarters, General Quarters! All hands man your battle stations. Set condition Red Two throughout the ship. This is no drill!"

He reached the door leading to the passageway, which was filled now with running men. Standing there, wearing nothing but his shorts, he realized that Tombstone's orders to get a full night's sleep could not possibly apply to this. "All hands," the announcement had said . . . and it could only mean an attack on the *Jefferson* was imminent.

Coyote saw a familiar face. Batman was trotting down the passageway, still pulling on his shirt. "Batman! What is it?"

"Hey, Skipper! Put your pants on. We've got a Russkie air wing coming at us."

He didn't question how Batman had gotten the information. News traveled faster than light aboard a Navy warship, purely by word of mouth. Coyote ducked back inside his cabin and snatched a shirt and trousers from his closet.

There was no time even to think about being afraid.

Tombstone clutched a mug of hot coffee someone had
handed him and leaned over a map on the plot table in CIC.
He was bone-tired, but adrenaline, rather than caffeine, was
keeping him going now. The Soviets were making their
move, striking at *Jefferson* and striking hard.

The life of the ship throbbed and pounded around him. He
could feel the gentle throb of engines through the deck as
Jefferson got under way. It would take some time to
maneuver the great carrier down the fjord and into the open
sea, but at least they were now presenting the Russians with
a moving target, however slow.

His initial fear that the Soviet attack might have ended
their chances of saving Norway was ebbing as he studied
the cryptic markings penciled onto the map. The nearest
Russian planes were eighty miles out—less than ten minutes
away at their present speed. *Jefferson*'s CAP was deploying
to meet them now at the fifty-mile point, and more Tomcats
and Hornets would be airborne in minutes to back them up.
There was also a flight of Norwegian F-16s, designated
White King, launching from Välderöy, but it was clear
already that the battle was going to reach all the way to
Jefferson's position in the fjord. He'd already heard the
word passed to set the carrier's CIWS on manual, and to
ready her missiles for launch. It was going to be one hell of
a fight.

Still, Tombstone thought he saw a window of opportunity
here, a chance to carry out the plan he'd been presenting up
in CVIC. He would have to approve the thing with Tarrant,
of course, but in the meantime he wanted to make certain
that the window stayed open.

Damn, though, it meant they were going to lose some

aircraft, and some good men. The thought brought a bitter scowl to his face. *Who are we going to lose this time?*

"CAG? They said you wanted to see us."

He turned and looked down into the hard, brown eyes of Sluf Dodd, the A-6 pilot who'd been credited with taking out the mighty Russian battle cruiser *Kirov*. Behind him, towering over Sluf's squat frame, was Commander Max "Hunter" Harrison, CO of the VS-42 King Fishers.

"Hello, Sluf," he said, setting the coffee aside. "Hunter. Thanks for coming. Got a question for you."

"Sure thing, CAG," Hunter said. "Shoot."

"I want you men to tell me if you think something is possible . . ."

0412 hours Zulu (0512 hours Zone)
Tomcat 200, U.S.S. *Thomas Jefferson*
Romsdalfjord

Tomcat 200 trembled with the thunder as another aircraft, a Hornet, roared off the catapult just ahead and into the pearly light of the early morning sky. Coyote finished going down the preflight checklist, reminding Teejay to check the electrical fuses in the receptacle in the seatback behind the RIO's head. He double-checked that the safety was pulled on his ejection seat, then confirmed that Teejay's was pulled as well.

The sky overhead through the F-14's cockpit was dazzlingly beautiful, partly cloudy, the patches of blue an intense, vibrant azure, the clouds limned with pearly light. The deep U-shaped gulf of the fjord was still entirely in shadow, the water misted over by patches of fog, the details of rock and tree and cliff almost lost in the depths of shadow made darker by the brilliant light from the sky.

"We've got clearance to roll," his RIO said.

The jet-blast deflector that had protected the Tomcat from the exhaust of the F/A-18 ahead of them in line was coming down. Gently, Coyote guided the aircraft forward, position-

ing it over the slot in the deck where green-shirted hookup
men were guiding the catapult shuttle into place. A green-
shirt held up a chalkboard where Coyote could read it:
66,000. He nodded to the man, indicating verification of the
Tomcat's total weight, aircraft, fuel, and weapons load. The
same information was being relayed to the catapult officer,
who would adjust the pressure in Cat One to the proper
setting to get Tomcat 200 airborne.

A red-shirted ordie held high a bundle of wires, each with
a red tag. These were the safing wires from their ordnance
load, four AIM-7M Sparrows and four AIM-9M Sidewinders, and they let Coyote verify that all eight AAMs were
now armed and ready. They were carrying no Phoenixes on
this mission. The long-range AIM-54Cs were in short
supply after Summer Thunder, and the few remaining were
being hoarded. Coyote hoped the admiral would see fit to
rendezvous with the resupply ships damned soon. Rumor
had it that the battle group was low on everything, especially Harpoons.

That, however, was not his immediate concern. The fight
this morning would be close up, at knife-fighting range, as
Navy aviators liked to say, and the combination of Sparrows
and Sidewinders would give him optimum flexibility.

With a clatter of chains, the hookup men secured the
launching bar on the Tomcat's nose wheel to the catapult
shuttle. The launch officer made a circling motion with his
hand, signaling Coyote to bring his throttles up to military
power.

The F-14 was trembling again, this time with a barely
suppressed ongoing shudder of raw power. Coyote checked
his control stick in the old litany of Navy aviators:
forward—*Father,* back—*Son,* left and right—*Holy Ghost,*
rudder pedals left and right—*Amen.*

All correct. A red light still shone from the carrier's
island, beside Pri-Fly.

"Tomcat Two-zero-zero" sounded in his headset. "This
is God."

God—also known in his mortal guise as Commander

Jack Monroe, *Jefferson*'s Air Boss. "Two-zero-zero copies."

"Two-zero-zero, be advised of hostile aircraft in the immediate area. We are expecting overflight momentarily."

"Roger, God. It'll save time tracking them down."

Coyote glanced left and right, his eyes searching the skies above the cliff tops on either side of the carrier. Contrails marred the random beauty of the cloud deck overhead, arrowing southwest to northeast. Norwegians, he thought, out of Välderöy. "Whatcha got on radar, Teejay?" They should have been getting a feed from one of the Hawkeyes controlling the battle.

"Nada, Commander. Junk City. I don't know if—"

A pillar of water erupted into the sky one hundred fifty yards from *Jefferson*'s starboard side. Coyote felt the shock through the water, and half a second later he heard the thunder of the explosion.

"Christ!" Teejay shouted over the ICS. "What the hell was that?"

"Incoming!" Coyote yelled back. There was an ear-tearing sound from the starboard side forward of the island, and a blur of motion. Coyote turned his head in time to see the white contrail of a Standard missile streaking off toward the north. There were more contrails in the sky now, some of them twisting about, others skimming low across the northern line of cliff-top ridges. *Jefferson* was under direct attack.

The red light by Pri-Fly switched to green.

"There's our go. Hang onto your breakfast, guy. We're getting off this damned fat target!" The yellow-jerseyed launch officer on the deck saluted and Coyote returned it smartly, signaling that they were ready for launch. The launch officer took a last look around, dropped to one knee with arm and leg extended as gracefully as a gymnast, and touched the deck with his fingertips. There was a pause . . . then the Tomcat hurtled down the catapult track, blasted from zero to 170 miles per hour in two heart-pounding seconds.

0414 hours Zulu (0514 hours Zone)
MiG 501
Over the Norwegian Sea

Captain First Rank Sergei Sergeivich Terekhov checked his
heading once again—one-seven-five—straight for the island of Otrøy at the mouth of the Romsdalfjord. Black rocks
stabbed from white foam a hundred feet beneath his MiG's
belly. His eyes flicked to the weapons indicators. All
correct.

His MiG-29 carried a warload of six AA-10 air-to-air
missiles. The scramble to launch on board the *Soyuz* had
been urgent once word had come through that the American
carrier had been found, and there'd been no time to reload
with antiship missiles. Terekhov regretted that. It would
have been good to have a chance to hit the *Jefferson*.

As it was, though, there would be plenty of opportunities
to kill Americans. The first wave of Soviets had brushed
past the screen of F-14s and Norwegian F-16s with almost
ridiculous ease, but his radar display was showing an
increasing concentration of enemy aircraft over the target.
He would be very busy indeed for the next few moments,
clearing a path for the wave of attack aircraft that was
following close behind his flight of MiG-29 interceptors.
The first antiship missiles had already been loosed—AS-10s
and AS-14s launched from a distance. The chances that they
would lock onto a target after being fired blind into the fjord
were small, but they would interrupt the Americans' coordination, and who knew? They might get lucky.

Terekhov was sure, though, that they would have to take
the air battle into the fjord, sweep the American Tomcats
and Hornets out of the way, and attack the *Jefferson*
directly. The Americans had been clever, hiding their carrier
inside a fjord with the surrounding mountains as cover. It
was what Terekhov himself would have done, had the
situation been reversed.

The island of Gossen separated itself from the mountainous coastline ahead, then from the larger island of Otrøy beyond. His threat board was showing lock-ons by several radars, and as he approached Otrøy he could see several lean, gray shapes in the island's shadow.

It made sense that the Americans would post their escorting vessels there, at the mouth to the fjord. Time enough to deal with them later, after they'd taken out the heart, soul, and strength of the battle group—the carrier itself. Bringing the stick to the left, Terekhov banked sharply toward the east, swinging onto a new heading that would take him well north of Otrøy and across the cliffs and hillsides that formed the northern side of the Romsdalfjord canyon.

The warbling screech of a missile radar lock-on sounded in his ears. Glancing around sharply, he saw the threat, the thread-thin contrail of a surface-to-air missile lancing into the sky from one of the ships off Otrøy. "Hunter Leader to all Hunters!" he called. "Independent action!"

Like wasps stirred by a stick, the MiG-29s in his flight scattered. Soviet tactical doctrine generally called for a tighter, more controlled deployment of forces. But the airspace in the fjord was going to be limited, too limited to allow maneuvers by large groups of aircraft. Better, he thought, to catch the Americans by surprise and overwhelm their defenses, with aircraft coming at them from every point on the compass.

Angling slightly toward the north, he waited . . . waited . . . an eye on the missile, but his attention centered on his instruments and on the rippling flow of land and water, of rocks, hills, and cliffsides flashing past only centimeters, it seemed, beneath his wings. The missile was definitely locked onto his aircraft now. Wait . . . wait . . .

Now!

He cut sharply to the left, sweeping low across the cliff top. A village exploded into view. He was so low that for one frozen instant, he could see steeply pitched tile roofs, the squat thrust of a Lutheran church steeple, the crisscross complexity of narrow streets and winding, hilltop roads, automobiles, people, bicycles. . . .

Terekhov punched the countermeasures button, releasing clouds of chaff. A cliff loomed in front of him and he cleared it, with ten meters to spare.

He heard the roar seconds later, a far-off thud as the American missile slammed into the cliffside. The hills that protected the American carrier could be used to advantage by the hunter as well. With victory surging in his veins, Terekhov whipped the MiG-29 back toward the fjord. Trees blurred beneath his aircraft, interspersed with scattered houses, a road, the burned-out shell of a Norwegian SAM carrier. . . .

There!

The MiG shrieked into clear sky above the vast, four-mile-wide gulf of the Romsdalfjord, and ahead, almost directly below, was the American carrier . . . a gray monster over three hundred meters long, her deck crowded with aircraft. He could see some of them now, like toys hanging in the sky between his eagle's vantage point and the water. The carrier was under way, its V-wake ruffling the calm of the dark waters as it cruised slowly west toward the open ocean some twenty miles distant. A column of water erupted in the distance, a wide miss by a blindly launched air-to-surface missile.

"Victory!" He shoved the control stick forward and watched the U.S.S. *Thomas Jefferson* swell in his forward windscreen.

0416 hours Zulu (0516 hours Zone)
Tomcat 200
Over Romsdalfjord

Coyote saw the Russian MiG almost as soon as he cleared *Jefferson*'s bow and started grabbing altitude. The enemy aircraft flashed into view above the wooded ridge top north of the carrier like some huge, silver-bodied bird of prey.

"Viper Two-zero-zero!" he called. Without a specific call sign for his flight, he would use the squadron name for VF-95. "Tallyho at zero-zero-five! Engaging!"

"Copy, Viper Two-zero-zero. Go get him."

Coyote was on top of the target almost before he had a chance to react. Modern air battles tend to be sprawling things that crisscrossed hundreds of cubic miles of sky. This battle was something beyond Coyote's experience, an all-out, toe-to-toe slugging match confined to the narrow strip of sky above the Romsdalfjord, walled in by cliffs and filled with hurtling, high-performance jet aircraft.

There was no time to think, no time to react as he almost closed with the MiG from the other plane's starboard bow. The range was too close for missiles, and Coyote instinctively snapped the weapons-selector switch on the stick. "Going to guns!" he called. The circular target ring of his Lead Computing Optical Sight, or LCOS, floated in the center of his HUD, accompanied by the data line that told him he had 675 rounds available. He had only an instant to aim, more by instinct than by skill, and squeeze the trigger.

The GE M61A1 Vulcan cannon recessed into the port side of his Tomcat's fuselage screamed . . . and then Coyote was past the MiG, climbing hard. He didn't know if his brief burst had hurt the target or not. Probably not, he decided. The shot had been rushed, but it might have taken the guy's mind off the carrier for a moment.

"You missed him, man!" Teejay yelled. "You missed— *oof!*"

The hard grunt was blasted from Teejay as Coyote snap-rolled the F-14 in a savage 9-G turn. He hoped to drop onto the MiG's tail, but by the time he'd swung around 180 degrees, the Russian was gone . . . gone! "Where's the bastard, Teejay?" he called. Sunlight exploded into the cockpit as they climbed above the mountains. "Where'd he go?"

"Eleven o'clock, and high!"

Coyote snapped his head back. There he was, twisting into the morning light in a perfect Immelmann, sun-glint flashing from cockpit and wings. Coyote was about to follow when Teejay interrupted. "Watch it, Coyote! We got two more comin' in hard, seven o'clock, angels two!"

"I see 'em!" Two MiG-29s seemed to be sliding off the cliff tops and out over the open waters of the fjord. From half a mile away, Coyote could see the stubby, finned deadliness slung beneath their wings; ship-killer missiles, though he didn't recognize what they were.

His Tomcat was still sluggish, low on energy after the extremely tight turn, and the wings had slid to their full open position. Coyote slapped the override, sliding the wings back. The loss of extra lift sent the slow-moving Tomcat dropping, plunging like a spear point into the shadow-darkened valley. Snapping the weapons-selector switch to engage with his Sidewinders, he watched the targeting diamond appear on his HUD, drifting across the nearer of the two MiGs. He let the Tomcat's plunge carry the pipper across the Fulcrum, heard the Sidewinder's growl as its heat-seeker eye found the target. Lock!

"Target lock!" he called. "Fox two!"

The Sidewinder *shooshed* from the launch rail and sprinted across the dwindling gap between the two planes. The MiGs must have become aware of Coyote's approach at the last second, for they suddenly rolled right, showing their light gray bellies and the neatly grouped, pencil-slender missiles slung from pylons. The Sidewinder's contrail followed the maneuver with electronic deadliness, closing . . . closing . . .

Slamming into the MiG's tail, the missile detonated with a flash that engulfed the aircraft. The Fulcrum emerged from the fireball an instant later, its twin stabilizers gone, fire streaming from one engine. The cockpit flew away, and with a tiny puff of smoke the pilot rocketed into the air, his chute deploying a moment later. "That's a hit, that's a hit!" Teejay was calling. "Two-double nuts, splash one MiG!"

"Pilot ejected," Coyote added. "Good chute. I'm on number two."

But when he found the second Fulcrum he saw that it was already being closely pursued by another interceptor, one of the tiny, almost toy-like Falcons, with Norwegian roundels on wings and tail. The nimble little interceptor seemed too close for a missile launch, but Coyote saw a flash and a streak of white, and then the second MiG was swallowed by a fireball that spewed, an instant later, a blazing pinwheel of wreckage that tumbled wildly into shadow, impacting in the fjord with a violent splash and a scattering of smoking debris.

"We've got new players in the game," Coyote called. "Norwegian Falcon just splashed one."

"Roger," an air controller called back. Was he someone aboard *Jefferson,* or in a circling Hawkeye? "Be advised we have twelve F-16s in the air, designated White King. Watch who you're shooting, people . . ."

The battle was rapidly becoming a confused melee in the skies above the fjord, a furball of tightly woven contrails as the aircraft of three nations tangled, closed, and evaded. Coyote saw a Falcon fall to pieces as a MiG pounced on it from above and behind, its 30-mm Gatling cannon savaging the lightweight aircraft in less than a second. At almost the same moment, Coyote locked and fired, sending a second Sidewinder streaking into the Soviet plane and blasting it apart in a fiery burst of flaming debris and whirling fragments.

"Javelin Three-oh-eight!" he heard over his headset. "I've got one on my tail! Got one on my tail! I need help!"

"There he is!" Teejay warned. "Two o'clock, one mile!"

Javelin referred to aircraft of VFA-161, one of *Jefferson*'s Hornet squadrons. Coyote could see the Hornet in a tight turn, a MiG close behind.

The range was great enough that Coyote decided to use a Sparrow. "Hang on, Javelin Three-zero-eight," he called. "When I give you the word, break left."

"Hurry up! Hurry up! This guy's all over me!"

"Three . . . two . . . one . . . break!"

Twisting hard to the left, the Hornet dropped clear of Coyote's cone of fire, clearing the way for a solid radar lock on the MiG. Coyote triggered the lock, then sent the AIM-7 shrieking through the sky as Teejay continued to illuminate the MiG with the AWG-9 radar. "Fox one!" he called, and held the Tomcat steady for a desperate several seconds as the semiactive homer closed on the target . . . merged with it . . . then detonated in a searing flash.

"Yah!" Teejay screamed. "That's splash three! Splash three!"

A threat warning warbled in Coyote's headset.

"Someone's locked on," Coyote called. "God damn it, Teejay! Where is he?"

"I don't know, man, I don't know. Christ, it's gettin' too crowded up here!"

The entire sky was now a confused tangle of contrails, of aircraft jinking and weaving, of the crisscrossing trails of antiship missiles, of plunging streamers of smoke—funeral pyres of aircraft and men. It was impossible to single out any one missile trail . . .

"He's on our six, Coyote! Comin' shit-hot fast!"

Twisting in his seat, Coyote saw the MiG. God . . . was it the same one he'd nearly caught earlier? He couldn't tell, but this one was crowding in close, lashing him with fire-control radar, lining up a perfect shot, one that couldn't miss.

"Hang on, Teejay!" Coyote rammed the throttle to Zone Five afterburner and hauled back on the stick.

The Tomcat clawed for the sky.

CHAPTER 18
Monday, 23 June

Coyote held the Tomcat in a sharp, full-powered climb until Teejay shouted that the Russian pilot was committed, goosing his Fulcrum in hot pursuit of the F-14. Then he pulled the throttles back hard, cutting power to seventy percent, and brought the nose up higher, until they were hurtling straight toward the zenith. A thin layer of clouds exploded past them. Cold sunlight bathed the aircraft in a dazzling radiance.

Bleeding off air speed, Coyote held the Tomcat in its climb, drifting toward ten thousand feet, hanging the aircraft at the ragged edge of a stall. Then he kicked the rudder over, letting the F-14 fall to port in a low-speed vertical turn. Sky, clouds, blue mountains, and water wheeled around the Tomcat's canopy. In the space of three seconds, Coyote had reversed course and was now hurtling straight down toward the Romsdalfjord, which filled his forward windscreen like a huge and colorful map. Punching through the broken clouds once more, he saw *Jefferson* below and to the west, a tiny, gray rectangle walled in by black cliffs.

He saw the pursuing MiG, a thousand feet below and still climbing toward him. With their combined velocities, the gap between them narrowed in a flash. There was no time to take aim and fire, no time to do anything but nudge stick and rudder in an instinctive maneuver to avoid collision.

They passed, starboard to starboard. In that instant, freeze-framed by the adrenaline pounding through his system, Coyote glimpsed every detail of the MiG: the high, angular tail fins; the flat body; the helmeted pilot staring back at him through his canopy; the number 501 picked out in red and white against the gray painted nose.

As soon as the MiG was past, Coyote brought the stick up, feeling the massive, crushing weight of G-forces piling up on head and chest. Breathing became difficult. He bore down with the muscles of neck and diaphragm, grunting hard to deliberately force blood from heart to head as his peripheral vision started closing down. It was as though he were peering through a black, fuzzy tunnel. A reading on his HUD showed 9 Gs as he opened the throttles and added thrust to the torture of the high-G pullout.

Where was the MiG? "Tee . . . jay!" he grunted against the intolerable pressure. "Do you . . . see . . . him?"

There was no answer and he assumed he'd put his RIO to sleep. The G-force eased as the Tomcat bottomed out in its dive and began climbing again. Coyote twisted his head back and forth, scanning for the other aircraft. Where was the guy?

Tracers streamed past his cockpit, glowing gold and looking as large as grapefruit only feet away from Coyote's head. He felt a jarring crash transmitted through the Tomcat's frame, just as he whipped the stick over, twisting away from that deadly cascade of shells.

The MiG-29's laser aiming gave the Russian pilot an undeniable advantage in close-up dogfighting, the chance of getting a hit with every burst. The only way Coyote could counter was to stay on the move and stay alert, never giving the other pilot a chance to close and lock on.

But damn, this guy was *good*, a shit-hot pilot with an airplane to match.

"Teejay! Are you with me?"

"Uh . . . yeah, man. Rough ride . . ."

"We've got a real top gunsikov here. Help me watch him!"

"I see him, Coyote. Comin' up on our right!"

The MiG flashed past the Tomcat, eighty yards to starboard. Coyote yanked the stick back to the right, swinging the F-14 into a turn across the other plane's tail. He flicked the weapons selector to guns, watched the LCOS predict the target's forward movement, and squeezed the trigger. It was a difficult shot, designed to slash across the target's expected path with a stream of Vulcan shells sprayed like the sweep of water from a hose.

Magically, the Russian anticipated his move, rolling on his back and going nose-down just as Coyote fired.

"Shit! I overshot!"

"Clean miss, Coyote. Keep it chill, guy . . ."

Since the days of the Red Baron, the essence of ACM—Air Combat Maneuvers, the classic dogfight—had been to put yourself in the head of the opponent, to anticipate his next move and use the laws of physics—energy and gravity, drag and thrust—to place yourself in a position where you could take advantage of your foreknowledge of his actions. What made the exercise a challenge was the knowledge that he was doing precisely the same. Guess wrong and you might end up in his sights; guess right and you might survive.

The Russian's roll evolved into a break to the left. Coyote knew that if he'd been in the same position he'd have tried to pull that break into a wide turn, one that would bring him around onto his opponent's tail. That position, on the other guy's six, was the ultimate goal of every dogfighter, the point in space where the enemy could be shot at, without having him shoot back.

Coyote was in a gentle turn to the right, with plenty of airspeed . . . translating into plenty of energy for any maneuver he cared to make.

There was a trick Coyote remembered, something he'd learned about in ACM classes and exercises. Tombstone had talked about pulling it once, during a dogfight with

North Korean MiGs several years ago. Almost by reflex, he sharpened his turn and slapped the override that governed the position of his wings.

The Tomcat's variable-geometry wings slid forward to their extended position but at a higher speed than that for which they were designed. The aircraft shuddered with the unaccustomed stress.

"Hey, man!" Teejay called. "What the hell are you doing?"

The position of a Tomcat's wings was controlled by an on-board computer, which adjusted them in or out depending on the aircraft's speed and need for additional lift. At low speeds the wings extended almost straight out; at high speed they were swept back, transforming the F-14 into a sleek, hurtling arrowhead. The design allowed the pilot to increase his wing area and lift, though normally the Tomcat handled this function automatically. Though it increased the plane's maneuverability, one tactical problem with the design was the fact that an opponent could take one look at an F-14 in a turn and, if he was good, take a guess at the energy the Tomcat driver still had simply by noting the position of his wings.

Coyote held the turn, wings spread wide, ignoring the vibration, while a mile away the MiG completed its own turn and began lining up for another pass.

He knew what the Russian pilot was seeing—the ungainly, cruciform shape of a wings-forward Tomcat in a low-energy turn, passing left to right across his HUD targeting indicators, a tempting, *slow* target. Rather than trying to drop onto the F-14's tail, he would take the easy shot, locking on with missiles or guns, knowing that the Tomcat simply did not have the airspeed for an evasive maneuver.

As he watched the MiG swelling nose-on, seeming to plunge straight toward his canopy, Coyote knew he'd guessed right.

He slapped the control that restored wing control to the computer and felt the vibrations ease off as the wings slid back once more along the Tomcat's flanks. Opening the throttles and tightening his turn still more, he watched as the MiG swung across his canopy and squarely into the center of his HUD, dead ahead.

Nose-to-nose now, Tomcat and MiG thundered toward one across a space of half a mile. This time, Coyote was ready for the pass, his targeting reticle already circling the edge-on shape of the MiG, his LCOS showing what he already knew, that there was no need for pulling lead on the target. He clamped down convulsively on the trigger, and the M61 Gatling shrieked.

The other plane was firing too. Coyote glimpsed the wink of its cannon flickering at the root of its left wing, but he'd caught the Russian by surprise, before he'd had a chance to lock his targeting laser on the Tomcat. Coyote held the trigger down in a continuous volley that spewed a hundred rounds each second, hurtling toward the Fulcrum behind that stream of lead, then passing the other plane so closely that he felt the buffet of its jet wash. He released the trigger. In a second and a half he'd hosed over 150 20-mm shells at the target and he'd been dead-on. He *must* have hit . . .

Yes! In the last instant before he passed the MiG, he saw bits flaking away, debris torn from one wing. As the MiG roared past, Coyote twisted in his ejection seat, staring after it. A thin, hard stream of vapor trailed from one wing, fuel spilling from a ruptured wing tank.

"You got him!" Teejay called. "He's hit . . . but he ain't going down!"

"I'm on him." He pulled into a hard turn. The MiG was swinging north, trailing smoke. He was hurting, Coyote decided, hurting but still alive. "I think he's getting out of Dodge," he said. "We're on his six now. Almost got him . . ."

"New target!" Teejay shouted. "Coming fast at three-five-three and on the deck!"

Coyote's eyes flicked between his VDI and through the canopy in the indicated direction. During the wild maneuvers of the past few minutes, they'd fallen far through clear,

cold air. They were less than a mile now above the dark
waters of the fjord. He saw the target, a ramrod-straight
scratch of a contrail drawing itself across the landscape
three thousand feet below.

He recognized it immediately—the contrail of an antiship
cruise missile skimming the mountains, by chance or design
aligned perfectly with *Jefferson,* which was still moving
sluggishly down the fjord to the sea.

"Lock it!" he snapped.

"Tracking! We have a lock!"

He snicked the selector switch. The F-14's AWG-9
computer-controlled pulse-doppler radar could look down
on targets at lower altitudes, sorting them from the clutter of
the ground below. This look-down/shoot-down capability
gave the Tomcat the capability of shooting down cruise
missiles in flight.

If they could catch them in time. "Fox one!" An AIM-7
Sparrow streaked from the beneath the F-14's wing, trailing
smoke as it lanced down through the sky. Coyote held the
F-14 steady, letting it slide into a gradual, descending turn
to keep the incoming cruise missile within the cone of radar
energy emitted from the aircraft's nose. Teejay kept the
radar locked onto the target, tracking it all the way to its
collision with the diving Sparrow.

The explosion erupted above the cliffs, less than two
miles from *Jefferson*'s side. The puffball explosion cast a
long, rippling shadow across the treetops below.

As Coyote pushed the throttles forward, he realized that
the damaged MiG had gotten away, slipping away from the
fjord and off toward the northeast, skimming the mountains
so low that Teejay could no longer track him on radar.

For the first time in long moments, Coyote became aware
of the air battle as a whole, so tightly had he been
concentrating first on that one MiG and its pilot, then on the
incoming ship-killer missile.

The battle in the skies above the fjord was fast, furious,
and far too complex for any merely human mind to follow.
Turning his head from one side of the canopy to the other,

Coyote saw at least twenty different aircraft scattered across the sky: a Falcon trailing flame and smoke as it fell toward the forests north of Romsdalfjord; a pair of Sea Sparrow point-defense missiles rocketing skyward from *Jefferson*'s port-side aft launcher like twin shooting stars; an F/A-18 Hornet in hot pursuit of a Sukhoi Su-21 Flagon; a missile track and a hurtling MiG colliding with a flash and a cottony puff of smoke that sent the MiG spinning, one wing torn away, in a dizzying corkscrew into the side of the fjord cliffs; a Tomcat with the stooping eagle insignia of VF-97 dropping from the sky, its canopy smashed open and empty, like a blind, staring eye . . .

And those were only the closest targets. His radar screen showed an indecipherable tangle of contacts, concentrated in the air above the fjord, but extending in all directions for fifty miles. Aircraft turned, maneuvered, and closed with one another, as missiles took high-speed ballistic paths through the melee or twisted after wildly jinking victims like dogs on the heels of a fleeing deer.

Just above the waters of the fjord, Soviet MiGs and Sukhois were trying wave-top runs against the carrier but did not have enough maneuvering room for a proper deployment. MiGs caught in the leaden torrent hosed from *Jefferson*'s CIWS mounts simply disintegrated.

Only gradually did the pattern of the battle become clear. The Russians had approached the fjord from several directions, evidently hoping to overwhelm *Jefferson*'s defenses. But the mountains had prevented them from firing their antiship missiles until they were close—at ranges of less than a few miles—and the air defense around the carrier was far tougher than they'd been expecting. The Norwegian Falcons too were stiffening the American resistance, though their casualties were fierce, at least two or three Norwegian planes falling from the sky for every U.S. plane destroyed.

But the Russian losses were higher still. Whether it was superior American tactics, poor Soviet training or coordination, or the nature of their target, the Russians were losing, *losing* as MiG after MiG, Sukhoi after Sukhoi exploded in flames or limped from the battlefield, trailing smoke.

Voices buzzed and crackled over Coyote's headset. *"Viper Two-one-one! I'm on him! I'm on him!"*

"Coming around, Trapper! Steady . . ."

"When I give the word, break left. Three . . . two . . . one . . . break! Fox two!"

"I'm hit! I'm hit!"

"Eagle Three-zero-two, get this guy off me!"

"On him, Mustang! No sweat! Rock and roll!"

"Watch it, Javelin Three-one-five! Break high and right. Go!"

"Incoming at three-five-five, angels base minus three. Viper Two-oh-five coming right to two-seven-three . . ."

Coyote found another target and pulled back into the fight.

But he could sense the victory building, sense that the Russians were close to breaking. "Viper Two-double-oh!" he called over the tactical net. "Tallyho at *Jefferson*'s three-one-zero!"

The dogfight continued.

0430 hours Zulu (0530 hours Zone)
U.S.S. *Thomas Jefferson*
Romsdalfjord

For over half an hour, the air-sea battle of Romsdalfjord had raged above the deep, still waters of the fjord in a wild melee more appropriate to World War II than to the annals of modern war.

Modern naval warfare was a cold-blooded exercise of tactics and logic, a cerebral interplay of computer projections and computer-guided weapons, of tense men stage-lit by the eerie glow of radar displays and CRT monitors, of high-technology weapons that made SF spectacles like *Star Wars* seem somehow quaint and old-fashioned.

That interplay of men and machines was precisely the

atmosphere in *Jefferson*'s CIC, where combat directors relayed orders and received reports, where radar data from far-seeing Hawkeyes was received and distilled into glowing flickers on computer screens and remote displays. It set the one, the backdrop for the battle, tense, but somehow remote and detached, not at all as if the lives of thousands of men depended on the decisions and orders made in that high-tech cavern of subdued lighting and glowing monitors.

But on *Jefferson*'s deck, the battle was immediate and very real. Sweating, cursing, weary men yelled to make themselves heard above the cacophony of gunfire and jet thunder, of roaring catapults and the raucous clatter of steel on steel. Most orders were passed through the Mickey Mouse helmets they wore, devices that filtered out the raw noise to protect the wearers' ears, leaving only the weirdly distorted gabble of men yelling against an electronic silence.

The sky was filled with aircraft, a scene that would have been familiar to veterans of Midway or Leyte Gulf save that these machines were larger, faster, and far louder than anything in the air during the Second World War. A Norwegian F-105, its left wing blasted away by a Soviet AA-10, tumbled wildly across the sky and slammed into the rock cliffs to the north in a brilliant orange fireball. Contrails wove and squirmed overhead, like skywriting gone amuck, punctuated by the soft, harmless-looking puffs of white marking plane-killing missile detonations. With a shriek, another Sea Sparrow left the Mark 29 launcher on the carrier's port-side aft sponson, stabbing into the sky atop a writhing string of white smoke. An AS-7 Kerry air-to-surface missile homed on the *Jefferson* from ahead, was decoyed by blossoming clouds of chaff fired from steadily thumping RBOC launchers, and struck the water fifty yards off the port bow with a roar. A white column of water geysered into the air; the spray fell like a torrent, drenching men in the catwalk above the starboard-bow sponson and on the flight deck near Cats One and Two.

To the south, a MiG-27 Flogger-D, duck-nosed, swing-winged, and deadly, shouted thunder above the tiny village of Vikebukt, skimming rooftops and church steeples in a silver blur before emerging over the Romsdalfjord, hurtling toward the *Jefferson* scant meters above the water. The Flogger was not a naval aircraft, but one of a flight of Soviet Frontal Aviation attack planes out of Bodø ordered to join the *Soyuz* strike against the American carrier. Slung from pylons beneath its wing roots was a warload of ten OFAB-0250 quarter-ton fragmentation bombs, weapons better suited for an attack against soft ground targets, but capable of doing terrible damage to the relatively thin skin of a carrier, especially when that carrier was literally a floating bomb crammed with jet fuel and high-explosive ordnance.

Aboard *Jefferson,* the CIWS mounted port side forward slewed to the left, its radar tracking the incoming target, processing data far faster than would have been possible for any human combatant, verifying what it had already deduced from the absence of an IFF code, that the target was hostile. With a shriek like a diamond drill bit biting steel, the Phalanx fired; the head-on shot required no second burst for correction, but sent depleted uranium slugs slicing through a MiG-27's airframe like buckshot fired through tissue paper.

The effect was spectacular, a pyrotechnic nightmare of flame and disintegrating wreckage that came hurtling low across *Jefferson*'s flight deck aft of the island. It missed deck and island superstructure and tight-packed aircraft all by a hair. Fragments snapped a cable on the towering neck of the carrier's Tilly crane, punched holes in the SPS-49 radar dish atop the superstructure, crumpled an SH-3 helicopter and the F/A-18 Hornet parked next to it, and sent deck crewmen scattering for cover as, for half a second, the sky exploded. The wreckage sprayed into the water one hundred yards off *Jefferson*'s starboard side, the detonation of 250-kilo bombs sending a gout of spray skyward higher than the radar mast atop *Jefferson*'s superstructure.

Shaken crewmen rose from the deck and went on with their work. The helicopter was burning, and men wheeled one of the yellow fire trucks called an Oshkosh into position to hose the flames down, as men and mules heaved and strained at the wreckage, levering it over the side and into the fjord with a heavy splash.

A stray shell from an aircraft cannon or a piece of shrapnel—it was never learned which—struck the flight deck amidships with a shrill whine, ricocheting into the back of a seaman running toward the island. For a few moments, his screams echoed above even the roar of battle, at least in the vicinity of the island, until a hospital corpsman could jab a needle into his arm and inject him with morphine. Most of his intestines were strewn in a slippery smear across the deck, unfortunately, and he did not live long enough to reach sick bay.

Seconds later, an AS-7 Kerry antiship missile slipped past *Jefferson*'s hard-pressed defenses, skimming out of the north just above the water, ignoring RBOC blooms as it locked onto *Jefferson*'s radar image, traveling so fast that three separate CIWS bursts served only to lash the water beneath and to either side of the hurtling fish shape into white frenzy.

At Mach 1, its one-hundred-kilogram warhead slammed into *Jefferson*'s side, beneath the overhang of the flight deck just aft of the port-side forward elevator.

Every man on board knew that *Jefferson* had been hit.

CHAPTER 19
Monday, 23 June

0435 hours Zulu (0535 hours Zone)
CIC, U.S.S. *Thomas Jefferson*
Romsdalfjord

He felt the shudder transmitted through the deck in CIC, a far-off thump that echoed for several seconds through the steel caverns of the warship. Tombstone looked up from the display monitor he'd been studying, frowned at the overhead for a moment, then turned his attention back to the displays. If the carrier had been seriously damaged, he would know it in a moment. There was nothing else he could do, save stay where he was and watch the battle as it unfolded around the *Jefferson*.

How long could it continue? He slouched forward in the raised, leather-backed chair, following the crawling blips on the main display, blips representing air targets tangling above the carrier. Over the 1-MC, a voice announced a fire on the hangar deck and ordered damage-control parties and shoring parties to report to a particular frame, but it was easy to ignore the urgent call, concentrating instead on the crackle and buzz of voices calling to one another over the tactical communication net. With the electronic sounds, the flicker and drift of featureless points of light across glowing monitors, it was more like some bizarre video game than a battle.

The engagement had long since passed beyond Tombstone's control. He continued to issue orders that were passed on to the warring aviators somewhere in the unseen skies beyond the CIC's overhead, the "roof" as they called the flight deck. As new threats materialized, he deployed aircraft by twos or fours, forming reserves, spending those reserves as each Soviet thrust appeared among the shifting hordes of blips.

But the real battle had taken on a life of its own. *Jefferson* would live or die now according to which side had the better aviators, the better machines, the greater will. *Jefferson*'s computers could report, but not manage, the struggle. It was now up to Coyote and Teejay and the others, not to Tombstone.

"Admiral on the deck," a voice called, but no one in the dimly lit expanse of the CIC Air Module moved from the phosphorescent glows of their radar screens. Tombstone swiveled in his chair and saw Admiral Tarrant standing behind him.

"Hello, CAG. I got the word you wanted to talk to me."

"Yes, sir," Tombstone said, sliding from the chair. He'd left a message with one of the admiral's aides shortly after GQ had sounded. "I didn't intend to drag you from the battle, though."

"It's out of my hands now," he said with a grim smile. "And yours too, I expect." He nodded toward the rows of consoles, the silent, bowed heads of the electronics technicians and radarmen manning the CIC suite. "Actually, since they jumped us before I could get back to the *Shiloh*, I figured I could get a pretty good look right here."

"Well, glad to have you, sir."

"What did you have to tell me?"

"An idea, Admiral. A way we might be able to turn this fight to our advantage."

"I'm interested," Tarrant said bluntly. "Spill it."

"I've already started setting things up, but I'll need your approval." In swift, concise statements, Tombstone began presenting the idea that had been nagging at him since the interrupted CVIC conference that morning. When he'd finished laying it out, at least in broad strokes, Tarrant pulled at his chin with a deeply tanned hand. "This is a reversal of what you pulled at Cape Bremanger, isn't it?"

"I suppose you could say that, Admiral. I don't think they'll be expecting it."

"And the Intruders are ready to go?"

"We have ten Harpoons left in inventory. I've ordered five Intruders readied, two Harpoons to a customer."

"That'll do it for us, then, as far as air-launched antiship missiles go."

"We could rig some Mark 46s for surface attack," Tombstone said, referring to ASW torpedoes launched from helicopters or S-3 Vikings. "But yes, sir. When the Harpoons are gone, all we'll have are the Sea Sparrows. And the Standards of our escorts." Sea Sparrows could be used against air or surface targets, but they only had a ten-mile range. The longer-ranged Standard missiles fired by *Shiloh* and the others could also be used against ships, but the antiship weapon of choice was the Harpoon.

"Kind of like putting all the eggs in one basket, isn't it, CAG?"

"Sure is, Admiral. But if we don't use 'em, they go rotten. To tell you the truth, sir, I don't think we're going to have a better chance than this."

Tarrant considered it for a moment. "I agree," he said at last. "We've got one possible problem. I suppose the Intruders were being armed down on the hangar deck?"

"Yes, sir." The flight deck, exposed to hurtling bits of metal, was not the place to load munitions in the heat of a battle.

"Well, that thump you felt a few moments ago was a Russkie missile coming into the hangar deck. I don't know how bad it is. Captain's looking into it now."

Tombstone tried to visualize the scene on the hangar deck, the cavernous space that occupied fully a quarter of *Jefferson*'s interior, a steel-walled chamber packed with men, aircraft, machinery, and inflammables. An explosion

down there could destroy a dozen aircraft and spray scores
more with bits of metal flying like machine-gun bullets.

"Then the whole idea must be bust anyway," he said.
"We can't pull it off without the Intruders or the Harpoons."

"We'll see when we get the damage reports." Tarrant
reached out and laid one hand on Tombstone's shoulder, a
strangely human gesture from a man Tombstone had come
to think of during the past weeks as some kind of hard-
driving machine. "Commander, I've acquired a high regard
for your tactical intuitions over these past few weeks. You
may just be the greatest naval strategist since John Paul
Jones. But even he made mistakes. If you're wrong this
time, God help you. God help all of us."

"God help us if I'm *right,* Admiral. We're going to need
His backing on this, no matter which way it goes."

"I'm going back up to the flag bridge," he said. "If we
have the planes and the ordnance, I'll approve your plan."

"Thank you, Admiral."

"I'll let you know when we hear about the Intruders.
Carry on."

"Aye, aye, sir." Tombstone returned to his seat and
continued to watch the battle.

0440 hours Zulu (0540 hours Zone)
MiG 501
Off the Norwegian coast

Sergei Terekhov looked at the water below with sharp
distaste, but there was no escaping the facts. He'd had to
coax and prod the stricken MiG-29 to get this far, and the
damaged aircraft was simply not going to take him much
farther. That head-on pass with the Tomcat had sent a
torrent of lead through his left wing and fuselage, shredding
the port wing tank, damaging his left stabilizer, knocking
out radar, radio, and all weapons systems, and playing hell
with his hydraulic system. He doubted that he was going to

be able to get his left wheel down; even if he'd been able to limp back to the *Soyuz,* it was clear that his only recourse would be to eject, letting the MiG ditch at sea.

If that was his only alternative, he might as well do it sooner than later, while he still had marginal control and the aircraft was still more or less in one tattered but functional piece. Briefly, he'd considered trying to reach the Russian lines north of Trondheim, maybe setting down at a captured NATO air base, but he'd discarded the idea almost at once. *Soyuz* was closer, and a gear-up landing in the battered MiG was no more appealing on a concrete runway than it was on the pitching deck of a carrier.

There was another possibility.

Limping through the sky just off the Norwegian coast, he spotted what he was looking for nearly one hundred kilometers north of the fjord, just beyond the large Norwegian island of Smøla, just over halfway back to the *Soyuz.*

Smøla, well south of Trondheimfjord, was still in Norwegian hands, but he could see a shark-lean shape ahead, a Soviet Krivak-I frigate, its silhouette unmistakable with the blocky, four-tube SS-N-14 launcher on the forward deck.

The *Doblestnyy,* a name translating as *Powerful* in English. Terekhov had noted the vessel earlier, during the southbound leg of this mission.

Now *Doblestnyy,* part of *Soyuz*'s ASW screen, might well be his salvation. Throttling back until he was barely keeping the MiG in the air, he passed the frigate close by his starboard side. Contacting the ship was out of the question with the radio gone. All he could do was position himself close to the vessel and fire the ejection seat.

With a silent and very un-Communistlike prayer, Terekhov grabbed the ejection handle and pulled.

As the canopy blasted away, as the powerful rocket engine smashed at the base of his spine and hurled skyward, he hoped someone on the ship's deck was watching.

0445 hours Zulu (0545 hours Zone)
U.S.S. *Thomas Jefferson*
Romsdalfjord

The cruise missile had struck on the port-side aft of the
elevator support frame, shearing struts, buckling hull plates,
and blasting an external fueling platform into the sea. The
explosion tore a yard-wide hole through the hull, spalling
fragments of hot metal across the hangar deck. Fuel gushing
from ruptured pipes ignited, sending jets of flame up the
slope of the flight deck overhang, and exploding into the
hangar spaces.

Damage, fortunately, was minimal. Automatic cutoffs
sealed the ruptured fuel lines, and the fire was quickly
extinguished by the hangar bay sprinkler system and by
furiously working damage-control parties armed with foam
and CO_2. Two men were killed, five wounded by shrapnel
or blast. The port-side elevator was jammed in the up
position and the massive, steel-armor doors over the huge,
oval-shaped hangar deck elevator access were locked shut.
In all, six aircraft were damaged, including a Prowler and a
KA-6D tanker, but a preliminary check suggested that all
could be repaired at sea, given a few days without the
urgency of battle stations.

The most serious problem once the fire was out was the
crippled forward elevator. Only one of the five Intruders
being armed with Harpoon missiles on the hangar deck was
damaged, but tow paths had already been cleared for these
aircraft to the now-unusable port-side elevator. The Deck
Handler, in Flight Deck Control on the O-4 level, turned to
the large plan view of *Jefferson*'s hangar deck and began
sliding the scale cutouts of A-6s, Tomcats, and other aircraft
across the model, like an interior decorator arranging the
furniture in an especially cramped house. Also known as the
Mangler, the Deck Handler was charged with choreograph-
ing the dance of men and machines that maneuvered the

readied aircraft to a working elevator and up onto the flight deck.

By the time *Jefferson* had reached Otrøy Island, the first A-6 Intruders, each with a pair of Harpoon missiles slung from its wings, was riding the starboard-side forward elevator into sunlight, as a small army of sailors commenced a walkdown along the flight deck, retrieving thumbnail-sized bits of shrapnel and metal that might damage turbine blades in flight deck operations. Overhead, the only aircraft in sight were friendly, Norwegian Falcons and American Hornets and Tomcats providing continuing protection for the slow-moving ship. The first phase of the Battle of Romsdalfjord was over.

The second phase was just about to begin.

0450 hours Zulu (0550 hours Zone)
H.M.S. *Ark Royal*
Scapa Flow

Four hundred miles southwest of Romsdalfjord, in the huge natural anchorage within the Orkney Islands called Scapa Flow, another battle had just ended, and ended victoriously. The sun was well up, casting a golden radiance across the scattering of barren-looking hills and small villages that surrounded the anchorage. Lieutenant Commander DuPont stood on a concrete pier, staring up at the moored vessel that, for the past five days, had been his first command.

Esek Hopkins was a wreck, her bridge shredded as though by a giant's hand, windows blindly gaping, her mast with the broad SPS-49 radar dish smashed and twisted, her hangar aft sheared away and her gray hull streaked and blackened by fire. Her pumps were still running. He could hear their familiar, steady chugging muffled by *Hopkins*'s hull, and steady streams of water continued to pour from her scuppers and outlets. Even now, moored to the pier, she maintained the fifteen-degree list that she'd carried all the way across the North Sea. She seemed to be straining against the lines that tied her to the land.

To *life,* as though she wanted to give in at last to the sea.

For four days after the attack off Norway, the battle to save the combat-savaged Perry-class frigate had seesawed between desperation and utter disaster. More than once, DuPont had been certain that *Hopkins,* steadily taking on water, was going to turn turtle and sink, especially on the second day when the wind had picked up and a squall line had struck. It had been an epic voyage, one of heroism and of survival. And of will.

Somehow, *somehow* they'd made it, with men manning the hand pumps by turns when the automatics simply could not keep up with the flooding. They'd made it under their own power too, though the turbines had threatened moment by moment to quit. Progress had been painfully slow through heavy seas. He'd had a choice between putting in at Bergen and heading across the North Sea to Scapa Flow. Hearing reports of almost constant air attacks on Bergen, DuPont had chosen the Orkneys. The crippled *Hopkins* would have made an ideal target to Soviet attack planes and to the submarines known to be lurking off the coast. If he'd known their speed was going to be as slow as it had been, he would have opted for Norway and to hell with the Russian blockade.

But they'd come through. *Kearny* had stuck with them until the end, ready to take off the skeleton crew of volunteers that had remained aboard if the decision was made to abandon. Late the previous evening, the *Hope-kins,* as her weary crew had renamed her, had limped into Scapa Flow. She'd been met in the approaches by an escort of Royal Navy destroyers, *Cardiff* and *Exeter,* and the tug *Gwendoline.* After rendering honors, *Kearny* had come about and returned at once to the open sea. Commander Tennyson, her captain, had been eager to return to the *Jefferson* battle group as quickly as possible.

And DuPont wished that he could go too.

Now, with the *Hopkins* secured, her wounded "in hospital'' as their British hosts had put it, and her crew in a naval barracks ashore, she seemed like a ghost, empty . . . and dead. He'd promised to save her and he had, but she would never go to sea again, of that DuPont was sure. He was seaman enough to know that nothing short of a complete rebuild would make her seaworthy again. He was going to miss her.

He also felt lost. The first of what would probably be countless full reports on the battle and the damage to the ship had already been cabled to Washington, but so far, neither he nor his crew had received new orders. It was unlikely that they would, either, at least for several days. The Navy Department was preoccupied now with the battle off Norway. Washington had not yet made up its collective mind about which way to jump—with full-fledged support of Norway, or with all-out retreat from the Norwegian Sea.

Time would tell. In the meantime, DuPont and his men were at loose ends.

Leaving the ship was hard, like abandoning a member of the family. He'd seen the butcher's bill that morning: thirty-seven dead out of a crew of 220. He suppressed a shudder. He'd also seen Captain Strachan's body when they pulled it out of what was left of the bridge. Strachan had been a friend as well as a commanding officer, and a man DuPont respected.

Looking beyond the cloven, fire-seared superstructure of the *Hopkins,* DuPont studied the lines of other ships gathered in the Orkneys, ships with proud names, and proud histories. *Ark Royal,* one of Britain's three remaining aircraft carriers, rose like a steel cliff at a pier beyond the American frigate.

Scapa Flow, an important base for Britain's fleet in World War II, had become a major anchorage again, this time for ships of the Royal Navy that a peace-minded British government was retiring. Dozens of ships were here, in mothballs or in the process of being decommissioned. Great Britain's once-mighty Royal Navy had come down in the world since the days of the Falkland Islands war. The

far-left socialist government that had come to power a few
years before had gutted the fleet, sending many of its ships
here. From what DuPont had been able to gather, a new
government had been elected, but decisions to reactivate the
Royal Navy were going to be some time in coming. A
nation's foreign policy could not be reversed overnight.

"Might you be Commander DuPont?"

He turned. The speaker was white-haired and ramrod
straight, a tall, imposing man in dress blues. The bands and
loops on his sleeve, the heavy gold on cap and shoulder-
boards, proclaimed him to be an admiral of the Royal Navy.

DuPont snapped to attention and saluted. "Excuse me,
Admiral. I didn't hear you. I'm DuPont, yes, sir."

"Admiral Montgomery Parker. They told me I might find
you here. Sorry if I startled you."

"Not at all, sir." DuPont was curious. Where was the
usual retinue of aides and junior officers? Parker was alone.
A limousine with blue flags on the front fenders was parked
by the accessway to the jetty, a hundred yards away.

"Hm. Saying good-bye to her?"

"I suppose I am, sir. It . . . seems a shame."

"Know what you mean. When you've lost friends,
shipmates . . . you can't just walk away."

"Yes, sir." Was Parker reading his mind?

"And I expect you're thinking about the lads in the battle
group off Norway."

"Yes, sir."

"I've heard all about your action. And what you must
have gone through to get your ship and your men safely to
port. An excellent job, Commander. Very well done."

"Thank you, Admiral. Uh, may I ask, sir, what is this all
about?"

Parker gestured past the *Hopkins,* toward the massive
silhouette of the *Ark Royal.* "That one's mine, you know.
Her and her chicks. *Ark Royal* battle group. Until NATO
went down the tubes, the best damned ASW team in the
alliance. Still would be the best . . . but we're a little
short-handed just now." He was smiling.

"I'm not sure I know what you mean, sir."

"The crew's aboard. Most of them. But her captain's short-handed. Especially in some of the ET specialities. Radar, sonar, commo. And we need some liaison officers to talk with the American battle group in the area. Help if we could follow what they were bloody talking about, eh?"

DuPont still didn't follow the man. "Yes, sir?"

"I have in mind putting my battle group to sea, young man. The sooner the better. Unfortunately, we don't have our full complement here. Scapa Flow's not a regular anchorage, you know. Just occasionally, for mothball fleets, the odd war, and the like. A lot of our specialists were distributed through the fleet." The line of his mouth hardened. "They were going to mothball the *Ark,* more fools they."

DuPont was becoming uncomfortable. Admiral the man might be, but he was making little sense.

"You know, you people in the colonies got a bit testy a few years back," the admiral continued. "Eighteen twelve, and all that. Remember?"

"I, ah, wasn't around at the time, sir."

"Impressment, man, impressment! You Yanks didn't care for it much when the Royal Navy'd heave to alongside one of your ships, come aboard, and carry off a boatload of seamen to serve His Majesty. But, well, it seems to me that a bit of impressment might be just the thing here, to solve my problem, and yours."

Understanding dawned with the force of an exploding bomb. "You want us, *Hopkins*'s crew, to come aboard the *Ark Royal*?"

A distant thunder grew, swelling in volume. DuPont glanced up, saw the down-angled wings of a British Sea Harrier making an approach toward the carrier. Killing its forward velocity, the ungainly aircraft hovered for a moment, an impossible sight, then began descending toward the *Ark Royal*'s deck, drifting down like a helicopter.

Parker grinned, and raised his voice against the noise. "Those who want to. Volunteers only. And it won't be soft,

I promise you that. You chaps'll have to learn the ropes on a new ship, as they say, while we go on exercise.''

"Exercise?"

"Well, we're not at war, you know. Not officially, at any rate. But I believe I have sufficient leverage with Whitehall to swing a small readiness exercise. Just to check out the systems and the men's training, and all that. And of course . . ." He stopped, shrugged. "Of course if we come under attack while we're in international waters, we have every right to defend ourselves. Wouldn't you say?''

"Damned straight, sir!"

"Ah, good. Well, then, unless you Yanks see fit to start another bloody war over our impressing your seamen, I take it then that we have a deal?''

"I'll speak to my men immediately, sir. Uh . . . you might have to swing some of that leverage you mentioned toward Washington.''

"The wheels are already turning, Commander. Talked to your Joint Staff's Director of Operations this morning. You'll get your TAD orders while we're at sea.''

DuPont felt a surge of fierce exultation. All those lives lost . . . but they would not be lost in vain. *Hopkins*'s crew was going back! He saluted. "I consider it a privilege to be impressed by you, Admiral!''

"Excellent!" Parker returned the salute, and then he extended his hand. His ice-blue eyes glittered with humor. "Welcome aboard!"

CHAPTER 20
Monday, 23 June

0609 hours Zulu (0709 hours Zone)
Viking 700
Over the Norwegian Sea

Commander Max Harrison, call sign Hunter, glanced to port, catching the movement of his S-3 Viking's shadow as it rippled across the surface of the sea, less than one hundred feet below. At their cruising speed of 350 knots, the four Vikings, holding a tight, diamond formation, roared north toward their target.

CAG had outdone himself, Hunter decided. His strategy was simple, based on the expectation that the Russians would see what they'd seen on their radar screens the day before and assume that yesterday's attack pattern on *Soyuz* was being repeated.

In fact, the Vikings were decoys, their crews volunteers. In the Battle of Cape Bremanger their unexpected assault against the Soviet amphibious squadron with Harpoons had meant victory. This time, when they got close enough for the Russian radars to pick them out of the surface clutter, the Soviets might assume that they were Intruders loaded with bombs or antiship missiles. Russian CAP aircraft that spotted them would recognize them as Vikings—there was no mistaking their high-tailed, fat-canopied profile—but might assume they were repeating their Cape Bremanger role, pulling off a low-level attack with Harpoons.

If so, the joke would be on them. The S-3s were flying empty, no missiles, no torpedoes or sonobuoys, with only a pilot and copilot in the cockpit instead of the usual four man sub-hunting crew.

Everyone was being very careful not to talk about the operation as a suicide mission, but Hunter was under no illusions about their chances. To make it look realistic—hell, to get in close enough that Soviet radar would pick them up at all through the jamming—meant that they would have to ride all the way in to the *Soyuz,* straight into the crossfire of point-defense AK-630s, surface-to-air missiles, and MiGs. Four aircraft, however fast or maneuverable, would not survive that inferno for long.

As Hunter kept telling himself, it was not whether or not they survived that counted, but whether they could survive long enough.

"Hunter One-one, this is Bifrost, do you copy? Over."

"Bifrost, Hunter One-one," he replied, his voice calm. *Bifrost,* the rainbow bridge that connected earth and heaven in Norse mythology, was the call sign for the Hawkeyes controlling the mission. Things were being kept simple, with a minimum of radio jamming at this point, just in case the Soviets were listening in. "We read you."

"Hunter, you are go for attack run. Target bearing your position zero-zero-five, range eight-one."

"Roger, Bifrost. Commencing attack run now." Reaching out with a gloved hand, he eased the throttles forward, and the two big GE TF34 engines slung beneath his wings increased their keening thunder. In seconds, the Viking had accelerated to 450 knots, the other three sub-hunters increasing thrust to maintain the pace.

Blue water blurred beneath the Viking's wings as the miles ticked away.

0610 hours Zulu (0710 hours Zone)
Intruder 502
Over the Norwegian Sea

Six miles above the Vikings and several miles to the southwest, Lieutenant Commander Barney J. Dodd felt particularly vulnerable at the moment. Looking from side to side in his Intruder's cockpit, he could see other American aircraft scattered across the sky, A-6Es from his own Death Dealers squadron mingled with F-14D Tomcats of the VF-95 Vipers. The sea was an achingly lovely expanse of azure beneath intermittent scatterings of puffy white clouds.

What made Sluf uneasy was the alpha strike's attack profile. The Death Dealers were flying north, on a direct heading toward the heart of the Soviet battle group, and they were going in at an altitude of 35,000 feet.

Intruders were frequently called upon to make high-level attacks, usually with precision, standoff weapons like the Mark 84 Paveway laser-guided bombs that had been so effective in the Gulf War of '91. When the enemy knew you were coming, though, a more usual strategy was to get down on the deck, flying so low that enemy radar could not separate you from the ground clutter. Going in at angels thirty was a sure way to invite attack.

Sluf looked out the starboard side of his canopy, peering down through streaming clouds, searching for a quartet of tiny shapes far below. He couldn't see them. From his vantage point almost six miles above them, they would be all but invisible. But somewhere down there, four S-3 Vikings from the King Fishers were mimicking the moves of an A-6 squadron deploying for an attack run one hundred feet off the deck.

Decoys, Sluf thought. Dead meat. But damned important dead meat since their weaponless run against the Russian battle group would give the Intruders their chance to get in close to the target.

The Intruders had been deployed with the F-14 TAC-CAP, hurtling north as part of the interceptor formation. He could hear the radio chatter between Bifrost and Hunter, but the Intruders' orders were to maintain radio silence until they deployed for their attack. Unarmed save for their Harpoons, unable to engage in a dogfight even to defend themselves, they would be indistinguishable from the Tomcats by Russian radar. With luck, the Soviets might ignore the fighters altogether, concentrating their battle-dwindled assets instead against the Vikings.

At least that was the idea according to CAG, who earlier that morning had compared the strategy to a plot device in a story by Edgar Allan Poe. Sluf had never read *The Purloined Letter,* but the theory seemed plausible enough. For the Intruders to get close enough to lock onto the right target, they would have to be hidden in plain view.

He glanced around again. Plain view, right. Despite heavy jamming by both sides, they must be in plain view of every radar from Bergen to North Cape.

If it came to a dogfight, the Tomcats would protect the Intruders. An Intruder half-glimpsed in the heat of air-to-air combat would almost certainly be mistaken for its close cousin, the EA-6B Prowler. Two Prowlers were flying with the Tomcat formation, providing ECM cover for the whole group. It wouldn't save the Intruders from enemy missiles in a dogfight, but the family resemblance of Intruders and Prowlers might keep the bad guys confused for the critical few minutes they needed.

He glanced at Lieutenant Fracasetti in the B/N's seat beside him. "So what do you think, Spoiler? Of CAG's hot-shot idea."

"I think it's kind of hard on the King Fishers." He kept his head forward, his face pressed against the radar scope.

"Roger that. That Magruder's ice, man. Like a glacier."

"I'm just glad I don't have to give that kind of order, Sluf. Wouldn't be able to sleep nights. Okay, here we go. I've got three solid targets burning right through the hash, bearing zero-zero-eight, range eight-five. Start setting up the approach.''

Sluf spared another glance for the nearest pair of Tomcats—Coyote Grant's 200 bird and his wingman, Trapper Martin in 209. At the moment, Sluf felt tired enough that he thought he'd be able to sleep for a week, no matter what the provocation. But he knew what Spoiler meant.

Sometimes command carried with it a damned heavy price tag.

0611 hours Zulu (0711 hours Zone)
CIC, U.S.S. *Thomas Jefferson*
The Norwegian Sea

Jefferson had burst from the confines of Romsdalfjord less than thirty minutes earlier and was making her way due north now at thirty-three knots. Coming out of the northeast, the wind had picked up a bit. The carrier was pitching in roughening seas, spray bursting past the bow each time the carrier plunged into another wave.

The motion was noticeable in CIC but easy to ignore. A stiff head wind might slow the alpha strike, delaying them by a few minutes, but it would not become a danger unless it became much worse. It actually aided the aircraft still launching from the pitching deck, translating as a few extra miles of airspeed as the catapults slammed them headlong into the wind on streamers of steam.

Tombstone pulled a handkerchief from his pocket and mopped his forehead. Despite CIC's air-conditioned chill, he was sweating enough to soak the back of his khaki shirt. Sitting there in his chair, he could sense his own stink, mingled exhaustion and fear. Replacing the handkerchief, he returned his gaze to the large tactical display, a screen that repeated data transmitted both from Bifrost and from the U.S.S. *Shiloh,* now cruising parallel to *Jefferson*'s track, five miles to the west. It showed the many pieces of the alpha strike, code-named Asgard, the home of the gods in Norse myth.

The individual pieces of Operation Asgard had been given less classical code names. The Intruders were called Dealer, tucked in with Viper and doing their best to look like Tomcats. Down on the desk was Fisher, closing now with the targets at attack speed. Nearby was another four-plane group, EA-6B Prowlers of VAQ-143, call sign Smokescreen. Forming up over *Jefferson* were Eagle and Javelin, the F-14s of VF-97 and the Hornets of VFA-161. They composed the second wave, a chance to strike *Soyuz* again if Dealer only damaged the prey.

The Hornets were armed with Paveway laser-guided bombs, but the real money was on the Intruders and their Harpoons. If the A-6s couldn't get through, the Hornets' smart bombs could seriously damage the *Soyuz* but were not as likely to get a kill.

Everything depended on the Intruders, and on the deception Tombstone had worked out to get them close to their target. The plan had been hastily conceived, hastily assembled. Tombstone wondered if it could possibly work as he'd planned it.

Fisher was creeping ahead of the cluster of contacts marking Viper and Dealer. ''Damn it,'' he said, shifting forward in his chair. ''Fisher's racing ahead of the pack. Get them back in line.''

''Fisher, Fisher, this is Camelot,'' a first class air controlman sitting at the console in front of Tombstone said, speaking into a microphone. ''Come in, Fisher.''

''Camelot, this is Fisher One-one.'' Tombstone recognized Harrison's voice, relayed through Bifrost. ''We are commencing our attack run.''

Damn, he was playing to a Russian audience, and he was making the attack look good. But it was also exposing him to quick annihilation.

''Fisher, you are out of position. Please maintain original course and speed.''

"Camelot, we are commencing attack run." The Vikings were now well ahead of the others.

"Okay," Tombstone said. "Have the attack group match 'em." The Intruders could hit 590 knots plus . . . and the Tomcats were having to loiter to stay with them. But Harrison's enthusiasm for his risky mission disturbed Tombstone.

Not for the first time, he wished he could be in the cockpit of one of those aircraft, piloting a Viking . . . or better yet, one of his beloved Tomcats. Coyote was piloting the CAG bird right now. Damn it, he wanted to join them. . . .

But modern combat was a team effort, with thousands of men pulling together to get the fighters armed and airborne, tracking them, seeing the mission through to its close. CAG had no special prerogatives. His place was here, making the decisions that would result in the brightest and the finest going in against impossible odds.

He already knew, with an acid gnawing in his stomach, that a lot of those boys weren't coming back. He'd set the plan in motion. Now it was up to them to carry it out.

On the screen, Dealer and Viper were again closing the gap with Fisher. A cluster of blips, three distinct contacts, marked their destination, now seventy miles ahead.

Soyuz would be in sight of the Vikings in minutes. Tombstone ignored the burning in his stomach and watched the dance on the electronic display continue.

0610 hours Zulu (0710 hours Zone)
Flag bridge, U.S.S.R. Aircraft Carrier *Soyuz*
The Norwegian Sea

Admiral Khenkin stood at the huge, outward-slanting windows of his flag bridge, staring at the dazzling interplay of light, clouds, and water to the south. When they came, they would be coming from *that* direction. . . .

Soyuz was plowing northward against a stiff and unseasonably chilly breeze. East, off the carrier's port beam,

Marshal Timoshenko, one of two escorting Kresta-II cruisers, took spray over his bow as he plunged along on a
parallel course.

Other men were on the bridge, staff and aides, but there
was no sound save the hushed roar of the wind outside the
bridge, and the sounds reaching them from the flight deck.
Soyuz was preparing to launch interceptors, assembling a
force to probe the literal cloud of ECM noise that seemed to
be spreading across the southern horizon. Other aircraft
were in the process of recovery aboard the carrier. As he
watched, a MiG-29 floated toward the Russian carrier's
stern, nose-high, tailhook dangling. For a breath-holding
moment it seemed to hang there in the sky . . . and then
with a rush it slammed into *Soyuz's* aft flight deck, engines
shrieking, wheels screaming against steel. Dragged to a halt
by the arrestor gear, the MiG paused to spit out the cable,
then began following a deck director toward a free space to
starboard. Khenkin's eyes narrowed as he noted gouges in
the thin, flexible metal of the MiG's right wing.

That plane had been in a fight. He sighed. They should
have had the *Jefferson* cold. That they did not said less
about the quality of the men he'd sent against the Americans
than it did about the sophistication of the American defenses.

He heard his chief of staff come up behind him. "Enemy
aircraft are attacking from the south, Comrade Admiral.
Range now one hundred ten kilometers." Bodansky seemed
agitated, almost afraid. That would never do.

"Easy, Dmitri Yakovlevich, my friend," Admiral Khenkin said in a voice so low that only the two of them could
hear. "The men must see you calm. If they smell your fear,
they become afraid themselves."

"D-da, tovarisch Admiral." He drew himself up, glanced
around the bridge, and licked white lips. "But perhaps it
would be best if you came down to CIC, Admiral, where
you can better direct the battle."

"The men know their jobs, Dmitri." He patted the
binoculars hanging around his neck. "They do not need

their admiral leaning over their shoulders, managing every decision. I shall remain here."

Indeed, Khenkin had long believed that the most serious weakness of the Soviet military system was the inefficiency of the rigid hierarchy that had subordinates relaying requests for direction up the chain of command at every turn. He had drilled his officers hard during the past month, however, creating in them a willingness to make decisions, to take initiative, wherever possible.

Besides, he wanted to watch the unfolding battle from here, where he could see it, *feel* it with his own senses, instead of as some kind of fantastic light display on a computer screen.

"There . . . could be some danger, Admiral."

"This is war, Dmitri. There is always danger." Something occurred to him, a sudden thought. "How are you settling in as air wing commander?"

"Well enough, sir. I wish Captain Terekhov were still here."

"He will be. His signal this morning stated that he ejected safely and had been recovered by one of our frigates. But you believe you can handle his duties in CIC?"

Again, the man's tongue flicked across his lips. "Yes, Admiral."

"Good." Khenkin turned, staring toward the south once again. "Very good. Captain Lazerov is an excellent Combat Direction Officer. Listen to him. You will do well."

Khenkin felt strangely at peace. He'd not expected that, not at all, for he could feel the weight of Russia's imperial destiny, riding above his small task force like the ponderous mass of thunderheads above the steppes just before a sudden storm. But the knowledge that the Americans were now at last rushing headlong toward a final confrontation with the Red Banner Northern Fleet was almost reassuring.

All his life, Khenkin had been a Communist. During the coup of 1991, when the dedicated Communist cadre of the KGB and Politburo had briefly—and ineptly—seized power in Moscow, he, along with most of the other military

officers of his generation, had watched from the sidelines.
The coup plotters had meant well, but their timing, their
poor planning, had betrayed both their haste and lack of
understanding of the forces that were shaping the Soviet
Union at the time. Instead he, and many others, had waited,
knowing that the restructured, so-called democratic government would do nothing to put bread in people's bellies, or
provide work, or stabilize spiraling prices. The ordinary
workers of Russia and the other republics couldn't care less
who their rulers were. All they wanted was stability . . .
and food on the grocery shelves.

And that, of course, had been why the marshals and
generals had so easily taken power in the months and years
that followed, how the Communists once again found
themselves leading the greatest power on Earth.

But it had occurred to Khenkin that he was about to be a
very small part of a kind of scientific demonstration. If, as
the Marxists claimed, Communism evolved naturally from
capitalism, it was because there was a kind of law of
survival of the fittest that governed the way nations and
governments changed, adapted, and grew. Many of his
countrymen felt still that Communism had been exposed as
a bankrupt philosophy by the events of 1991, that the return
of the generals to power was a kind of death rattle, a spasm
soon extinguished.

Which was right? Khenkin himself did not know. The
devotion he'd once felt for the Communist Party had been
tarnished by the aftermath of the Coup of '91; by now it had
very nearly rusted away, corroded by the continuing lies and
hypocrisy that were a part of day-to-day life in the Soviet
Union under the CPSU.

Soyuz. Union. Was it the wave of the future or a dying
cult? If the Americans and their *Jefferson* triumphed this
day, there would be no resurgence of the old Soviet Union.
If *Soyuz* won, there would be nothing to stop the complete
subjugation of Scandinavia and, very soon after that, of all
of Europe. The technology, the food, the industries engulfed
by the victorious Soviet armies would fuel a renaissance of the

Soviet economy and make the *Rodina* truly mistress . . . no, *Mother* of the world.

It was like a return to older, crueler days, to the ordeal of trial by combat. Two ships, their escorts, their men, their machines, pitted against each other in a battle to decide the fate of Europe and the world for the next one thousand years. The thought was at once thrilling and terrifying.

For Khenkin, the best thing, the *only* thing to do was to leave the battle where it belonged, in the hands and minds of the people who would fight it. He would be superfluous in CIC. Let Bodansky perch in the semidarkness of CIC, giving his orders, making his decisions. He was not as cold and calculating as Terekhov, was not the fawning, cowardly idiot that Glushko had been. It wouldn't matter either way. Nothing that any one commander could do or say would count for much this day.

The matter would be settled at a higher level, almost at a spiritual plane, by the warriors who were now squaring off, man to man.

"Admiral Khenkin," a voice said over a loudspeaker. "This is Lazerov in Combat. We are tracking at least twelve targets approaching from the south. Four are at extremely low altitude. Analysis suggests that they are either A-6 Intruders or S-3 Vikings commencing an attack run. Both *Admiral Yumashev* and *Marshal Timoshenko* have acquired the targets and have positive tracks. Range now fifty-five kilometers. We may open fire at any time."

Khenkin glanced at Bodansky, who was still standing on the flag bridge. "I think you'd better get down there, Dmitri. I will come if I am needed."

"Yes, Admiral." He saluted and left.

Khenkin picked up a telephone handset. "Lazerov. This is Admiral Khenkin. You have my permission to commence fire."

He turned as he replaced the handset, looking again out the bridge windows at the *Marshal Timoshenko,* three miles off. Raising his binoculars to his face, he could make out the twin arms of the cruiser's surface-to-air missile launcher tilt and swing on its forward deck. There was a flash, and the first missile arrowed into the sky, twisting sharply in midair toward the south. Seconds later, a second missile pursued the first toward its unseen target somewhere beyond the southern horizon.

"Quartermaster," he snapped.

"Yes, Admiral!"

"Note the time in the log," he said into the hush on the bridge. "*Marshal Timoshenko* commenced fire on hostile aircraft approaching this task force."

Joy sang through his veins. *And now,* Khenkin thought, *now it begins.*

CHAPTER 21
Monday, 23 June

Hunter gripped the S-3A's stick as the aircraft shuddered through a patch of rough air. A threat indicator winked on, accompanied by a warbling tone in his headset.

"Shit, Spock," he told the man next to him. He'd been hoping to make it another ten or twenty miles before being picked up by enemy radar. "They nailed us already."

"That is affirmative," TACCO Lieutenant Commander Ralph Meade said, as cold and as expressionless as ever. "Frequency-hopping, monopolar, which is how they're scanning us through the jamming. Sounds like Head Lights. SA-N-3." He studied his radar screen for a moment, then added, "SAM, SAM. I have a positive track, two missiles incoming, SARH-active, range two-nine miles."

Hunter glanced at his tactical officer. The man's professional reserve, the emotionlessness that had given him his call sign of Spock, never failed to amaze him. Here they were, deploying on a suicide missile with a pair of SAMs on the way, and the guy was rolling off the targeting data as though he were sitting in a simulator back in Norfolk. He found that Spock's relaxed manner had a calming effect on him as well. But his heart was still pounding beneath his seat harness.

241

"Well," Hunter said evenly, "they were going to pick us up sooner or later." The SA-N-3, called Goblet by NATO, was a semiactive radar-homing missile big enough and fast enough to be used against air or surface targets. Head Lights was the code name for the fire-control radar that guided the missile to its target.

He keyed the Vikings' tactical frequency. "Fisher One-one to all Fishers. Here's where things get exciting. On my command, execute Dispersal Pattern Alpha. On three . . . two . . . one . . . execute."

At his own order he brought the Viking's stick slightly to the left, as each of the four S-3s swung onto a different, new heading. To Soviet radar, it would look like they were deploying for a Harpoon launch. It would also separate them as targets and make it clear which of the four had been targeted by the SARH missiles.

"Smokescreen, Smokescreen, this is Fisher One-one," Spock called over a different frequency. "We are on their screens and have detected SAM launch. Do you read Head Lights activation, over?"

"Fisher One-one, Smokescreen, that is affirmative," a voice replied in their headsets. "Special delivery is on the way."

"Shut down or die, assholes," Hunter growled. With Smokescreen on the job, they had a good chance of coming out of this alive.

He still didn't want to think of this as a suicide mission.

0611 hours Zulu (0711 hours Zone)
Smokescreen 1/1
Over the Norwegian Sea

They were known as wild weasels, a term derived from the Vietnam era that applied to aircraft designed to identify, locate, and suppress enemy air-defense systems by locking onto their guidance radar. In the U.S. Air Force, the venerable F-4E and G Phantoms often filled this role, but in modern carrier air operations it was the EA-6B Prowler that sought out enemy radar emissions with their sophisticated electronics suites and homed on them with the powerful HARM antiradiation missiles.

The AGM-88As weighed almost eight hundred pounds apiece and traveled at better than Mach 2. The first HARM dropped away from the belly of the lead Prowler, homing on the Soviet Head Lights radar thirty miles ahead. It was a difficult target, for Head Lights rapidly shifted between a number of random frequencies, partly to burn through enemy interference, partly as a countermeasure to antiradar missiles.

For several seconds, it was a vicious "war of the beams," as the men of VAQ-143 called it, electronics matching electronics at speeds that defied human comprehension. The Soviet radar shifted frequencies, the AGM-88 hunted, matched, and locked, the cycle repeating again and again, all in a space of microseconds as the HARM shrieked north at better than Mach 2. Soviet operators aboard *Soyuz* and *Marshal Timoshenko* detected the missile launch and were faced with a choice—continue to illuminate the target for the SAMs already on the way, or shut down to save their radars.

The decision was easy. Radar systems were far more expensive—and less easily replaceable—than surface-to-air missiles. For a time, control of the missiles shifted back and forth between *Soyuz* and the *Timoshenko,* with first one ship illuminating the approaching target, and then the other. In minutes, though, the incoming HARM was close enough that both ships had to shut down their emissions. Their Head Lights winked off and the two Goblet SSMs went ballistic.

Hunter glimpsed it seconds before it hit. Twenty feet long
and only about a foot thick, the SAM looked like a flying
telephone pole trailing white smoke. It struck the sea two
hundred yards ahead and to starboard, sending up a massive
explosion of white spray and buffeting the air around the
thundering Viking.

"Missile down!" he called. "Clean miss!" He never did
see what happened to the second missile.

Milky contrails streaming from tails and wingtips in the
wet air just above the sea, the Vikings pressed on with their
mock attack.

Soyuz and *Marshal Timoshenko* continued on course. The
Admiral Yumashev, far enough north of the carrier that it
had been unable to participate in the opening high-tech
round of the battle, came about and began retracing its
course, maneuvering to a better position from which it could
help defend the *Soyuz.*

The Soviet carrier, meanwhile, was launching aircraft to
reinforce the CAP it already had aloft, a dozen MiG and
Sukhoi interceptors deploying toward the south.

It was also recovering aircraft, a delicate and dangerous
operation in the urgency of the attack. MiGs and Sukhois
were still returning from the raid against the American
carrier in Romsdalfjord, and other aircraft were parked on
the deck as ordnance technicians rearmed them and tanks
were filled with jet fuel. The Americans were attacking at

precisely the worst possible time, for *Soyuz* was a floating bomb, with ammunition stacked on her decks and explosive fumes gathering in her hangar spaces.

But *Marshal Timoshenko* was an able shield, fast, well-armed, literally bristling with surface-to-air missiles of several types. The big, Kresta-II cruiser continued to spar with the American ECM aircraft, switching on her fire-control radars and launching Goblet missiles when possible, then shutting down as Prowler-launched antiradar missiles came streaking in.

And *Soyuz* continued to hurl aircraft into the sky. Much depended on the fighter battle, as the Soviet interceptors attacked the American fighter cover. With their F-14s out of the way, the defenseless U.S. attack planes could be easily swept from the sky.

0616 hours Zulu (0716 hours Zone)
Tomcat 200, "Viper"
Over the Norwegian Sea

Coyote split his attention between the data on his HUD and the screen displaying the telescopic television image from the Tomcat's AXX-1, which was automatically tracking the cluster of pinpoints that seemed to be spreading out through the sky just above the northern horizon. The enemy aircraft were too distant for him to identify yet, but he knew what they would be: Soviet navalized MiG-29s and Su-27s.

"Bifrost, Bifrost, this is Viper One-one," Coyote called. "Tallyho. We have visual contact, bearing three-five-eight to zero-zero-five, range eight miles at angels twenty."

"Roger, Viper One-one. We are tracking bandits. We make it . . . twelve targets, repeat, twelve targets. Estimate Mach one-point-seven. You are clear to engage."

"Roger, Bifrost. Engaging." He switched frequencies. "Viper One-one, Viper Two-one. Where are you, Batman?"

"On your six, Coyote, half mile back and a mile high."

"Right. It's show time. Get on in there and show us how it's done."

"Roger that. Watch and learn while we wax their tails. Two-one to Viper Two. We're outta here."

As one, in perfect unison, the four Tomcats that comprised "Viper Two" executed left wing-overs and broke away from the main group, leaving the four F-14s of Viper One still closely grouped with the four Intruders of Dealer Flight.

Coyote looked right. His wingman, Trapper Martin in Tomcat 209, was hanging off his starboard wing. Beyond him were the Intruders in their close-spaced diamond formation, and beyond that were the remaining two Tomcats of his flight, Baird and Whitman in 205, Sheridan and Glazowski in 212.

"Viper One, Viper Leader," he called. "Hang tight, boys, and look casual. Two's blocking for us while we go for the quarterback."

"Viper Leader, Dealer Leader," another voice said. "We've got the target. Preparing for target run."

Coyote felt his stomach muscles tightening. Batman was wheeling off to take the approaching Russian fighters on at one-to-three odds, but in some ways he and the other three F-14s of Viper One had the tougher job: riding all the way in to the Soviet carrier, escorting the Intruders long enough for them to discharge their deadly packages. As soon as the Soviets realized that Fisher was a decoy, all hell, as the saying went, would be out for noon.

He was tense, wound so tight that every detail of cockpit, sea, and sky seemed to stand out in his vision with a stark, crystal clarity. But fear stayed in the background, an undercurrent that focused mind and will but otherwise could not touch him.

"Copy, Dealer. You tell us when and we'll follow you in."

Ahead and below, the contrails of Viper Two merged with the more numerous traces of the Russian planes. *Go get 'em, Batman,* he was chanting silently, willing the Soviet planes to fall from the sky. *Get them!*

0616 hours Zulu (0716 hours Zone)
Tomcat 204, "Viper Two"
Over the Norwegian Sea

Batman deployed his flight in two elements of two F-14s each: him and Mustang Davis in 210, Beaver Camerotti and Mad Dog Dubois in 233 and 236.

"Two-two, this is Two-one," he called. "Malibu here has a SARH target. Would you care to do the honors?"

"Roger that, Batman," Mustang replied. "The Walkman's got it."

Lieutenant Bruce R. Davis was a newbie, on his first carrier deployment at sea. The kid had picked a hell of a time to get himself assigned to a carrier, Batman decided, but he'd handled himself well so far; at Cape Bremanger, in the action over Trondheim, and finally that morning at Romsdalfjord. He still hadn't gotten a kill, however—probably more because of bad luck than lack of skill—and Batman was setting him up for an easy one. In the back seat, Malibu was painting one of the MiGs so that Mustang and his RIO, Terry "Walkman" Walker, could lock one of their Sparrows onto the reflected radar energy.

"Looks like a good shot," Mustang called. "Fox one!"

The AIM-7 Sparrow shooshed away from Tomcat 210. Batman kept his F-14 aimed at the target, visible on his telephoto display as an Su-27. On Batman's HUD, it was still a computer symbol, invisible to the naked eye at a range of almost eight miles. The enemy aircraft were swinging left and right now, scattering across the sky as they broke into their combat approach. Batman stayed with the Sukhoi until he saw the Sparrow ride the beam squarely into the target. The flash lit up the AXX-1 display.

"That's one!" Malibu called over the tactical net. "Splash one for Mustang and Walkman!" Seconds later, a

MiG's wing exploded as a Sparrow launched by Mad Dog sliced into it and ignited the fuel. In an instant, the Fulcrum was spinning wildly toward the sea, trailing flame and a comet's tail of smoke. Russian missiles were in the air now, AA-10s and AA-11s. The two groups of aircraft approached one another with a combined velocity of well over Mach 3.

"Missile at eleven o'clock!" a voice yelled in Batman's headset. Was that Beaver? *"Break, Mad Dog! Break!"* Other voices mingled, confusing, urgent, giving the spinning dance of sea and sky outside the canopy a surreal air, at once dangerous and remote.

"Hit the chaff! Hit the chaff!"

"Christ, that one almost got us!"

"Watch yourself. Two o'clock low. I've got two Fulcrums coming up fast."

"Break left, Beave! Break left!"

"I see him, Mad Dog. Cover my six! I'm on him!"

Aircraft twisted and turned, trying to claw one another from the sky. A MiG flashed along Batman's port side, so close he saw the sun flash from the pilot's visor. His threat warning chirped and he twisted left into a dive, dropping five thousand feet before pulling out, as Malibu dumped chaff all the way. The missile shot past Batman's canopy, close enough to touch. Its proximity fuse set it off with a bang that rocked the Tomcat, but—miraculously—no lights winked from Batman's trouble board.

Climbing again, Batman spotted a Fulcrum, a mile ahead and climbing sharply. A glance showed Batman that the bandit was tracking Tomcat 233.

Like Mustang, Lieutenant Paul Francis Camerotti, called "the Beaver" because of a legendary incident with a captain's daughter while he was in flight training at Pensacola, was new to the squadron. His RIO, Lieutenant Commander Vince "Hard Ball" Bollinger was an old hand, though he'd been with CVW-20 for less than a year. Batman had never cared much for the Beaver, who liked to brag and sometimes let the Navy aviator's inborn arrogance carry him a bit too far in casual conversations over a drink or in the ready room.

There was no thought for that now at all. "Beaver!" Batman called. "You've got one comin' up on your six, way low. Come right and I'll pick him off!"

"Thanks!" Beaver sounded tight, a bit shaken. The battle had lasted less than a minute, but the strain was already telling. "Coming left . . ."

"Target lock!" Batman yelled. "Good lock! Fox two!" A Sidewinder slid off the Tomcat's rails, streaking toward the MiG just as the Russian fired. An AA-8 Aphid rocketed toward Tomcat 233, drawing a delicate white line in the sky.

Seconds later, Beaver cut in his afterburners, his tailpipes lighting up suddenly like a pair of angry orange eyes.

"Negative on the burners!" Malibu called. "It's a heat-seeker!"

Beaver was already dropping flares, a string of burning white pinpoints of light, but the missile was ignoring them as it streaked toward the F-14's exhaust.

"Beaver!" Batman called. "Cut your burners, man! You've got a heat-seeker coming up your ass!" The Tomcat's afterburners were far hotter than the engine at lower throttle settings, a beacon no IR homer could miss.

Too late. The missile, an AA-8 Aphid, slashed into the tail of Tomcat 233 and exploded. Batman saw the aircraft shudder, then belch smoke as the left stabilizer tore free. For a long second, Beaver struggled to bring his aircraft under control, but the fight was clearly hopeless.

"Beaver!" Batman called out. He scarcely noticed as his own heat-seeker struck the MiG just as it began to break clean from its pursuit of the stricken F-14. An orange fireball engulfed the rear third of the Fulcrum. Pieces, many burning, showered from the cloud and began arcing toward the sea. "Punch out, man! Punch out!"

Beaver's and Hard Ball's Tomcat continued to fall, twisting in midair until it was upside down, pancaking toward the sea seventeen thousand feet below. An engine fire or a broken fuel line flared suddenly. Fuel ignited, and flame erupted like a bomb blast from the port engine.

"Beaver! Hard Ball! Eject! Eject!"

"Watch it, man!" Malibu called from the backseat. "We've got two comin' hard on our six! Watch it! Watch it!"

"Shit!" Batman twisted the F-14 hard right, then cut in his own afterburners, reaching for blue sky. He lost sight of Beaver's stricken aircraft as he went ballistic, boosting hard, hot, and vertical.

"Beaver and Hard Ball are hit," Malibu called, as clouds rotated around the canopy of the climbing F-14. "Beaver and Hard Ball are hit and going down. Negative chutes."

Three Russians down, and one American. And the odds were still three to one. Relentlessly, grimly, Batman began jinking his Tomcat every way he knew. He had to even the odds, or some of these Russians were going to leak through and hit Viper One.

But even as he maneuvered, he saw six of the bandits breaking off from the dogfight with the Viper One F-14s.

The thin American line had been overwhelmed. The enemy was breaking through.

0618 hours Zulu (0718 hours Zone)
Viking 700
Over the Norwegian Sea

Hunter checked his VDI. Twelve more miles to target . . . but that meant they were in range or nearly so of the Russian point defenses, the short-ranged missiles like the Gecko and SA-N-9. The air was going to be thick with deadly flying objects any time now. His grip tightened on the Viking's stick.

"Fisher One, this is Bifrost. Fisher, Bifrost. You are clear to break off and RTB."

Hunter frowned. The Intruders would not be at the target yet. He needed to give them more time. "Ah, copy,

Bifrost.'' He switched frequencies. ''Fisher, this is Fisher Leader. The word is break off and RTB.'' He continued to maintain Viking 700's flat, straight course toward the north.

''What's the matter?'' Spock asked, as cool as ever.

''Oh, I don't know. I just figure the Intruders haven't gotten close enough yet. What say we extend the envelope a little, huh?''

White contrails laced the sky ahead, rising from the horizon like the weave of some fantastic, animated spider's web.

But the TACCO only nodded. ''We'll keep them guessing if three of our aircraft break off but this one does not. It's worth a try, anyway.'' Several miles to the east, a silent flash lit up sea and sky for an instant. Spock peered at the radar display. ''I believe they just took out Lieutenant Commander Burroughs.''

''Damn.'' Hunter's jaw clenched, and he riveted his eyes on the northern horizon. Rabbit Burroughs had been a friend of Hunter's, the irony of their running names a squadron joke. He'd been piloting Viking 704. ''*Damn*. Okay. Let's just see how hard we can push it.''

He kept the Viking on a heading toward the north.

CHAPTER 22
Monday, 23 June

As the attacking aircraft drew closer, the Russian ships had to switch on their radars, American HARM missiles or not. First the Head Lights systems that directed the Goblet antiair missiles. Then Head Net C and Top Sail, both Soviet air-search radars on the Kresta-IIs, and Bass Tilt, which handled fire control. Each radar had its own characteristic electromagnetic signature, and each was registered by the EA-6B Prowlers that were still bearing down on the heart of the Soviet task force.

A second AGM-88 HARM rocketed away from a Prowler's belly, boosted for two minutes, then descended.

On a Kresta-class cruiser, the Top Sail radar is the largest antenna array, an enormous, diamond-shaped curve of wire mesh mounted at the highest point on the ship's superstructure.

Marshal Timoshenko was halfway into a turn to port when the HARM plunged from the clouds, cleaving through the air with a whistling shriek, and exploded inside the antenna's focus. The main radar dish was completely destroyed. Fragments sprayed across the deck, killing or wounding several crewmen, and showered into the water on either side of the cruiser. Shrapnel ripped like a shotgun

blast through the Head Lights array mounted atop the bridge
forward of the Top Sail, temporarily, at least, putting it out
of action. With both air-search and missile-fire control
down, the *Timoshenko* was blind. It had other radars still
active, but specialized for navigation or as fire control for
57-mm guns.

Captain First Rank Petr Shelepin immediately ordered the
Timoshenko to come right, to the northwest. For a critical
few minutes, until the *Yumashev* could get into position, the
Soyuz was naked to the American attack.

0620 hours Zulu (0720 hours Zone)
Viking 700
Over the Norwegian Sea

Hunter could see the carrier now, a gray cliff looming above
the horizon, it seemed, a mountain of metal now less than
ten miles distant.

"Say, Hunter . . ." his B/N said.

"I think you're right, Spock," he said, his voice touched
with awe. How had they gotten so close? "Time to
boogie—"

"Threat warning."

"Fire chaff! We're out of here!" He brought the stick
over, turning sharply. He saw the carrier slide to starboard.
Beyond, he could see the towering pyramid of a capital
ship's superstructure.

The missile slammed into the Viking's right wing.
Plexiglass shattered and a shrieking wind filled the cockpit.
He felt his control going, but they were low, low. . . .

"Eject! Eject!" he yelled. Spock sat beside him, head
down. Was he—

He yanked the ejection handle and the canopy dissolved
in smoke and flame. It seemed to take forever for the rockets
beneath his seat to fire. When they did, it was with a savage
jolt. Then he was weightless, falling through absolute
silence.

His chute deployed with a savage yank to his harness. Spock! Where was Spock? He looked around, twisting beneath the parachute shrouds, but he could not see his B/N. He saw the tail of the S-3, though, several hundred yards away, already sticking straight up out of the water and going down.

Hunter did not have time to watch. His boots hit the water with another jarring shock. Training took over, survival school and countless hours spent in classrooms and in swimming pools, learning how to land in water and get free of the parachute before it dragged you under. He grasped the beaded loops at the waist of his life jacket, yanking them out and down. With a hiss, the jacket inflated, the stiff collar chaffing at his neck. Clumsily, he fumbled under water for the Koch fittings that secured the parachute shrouds to his harness. His mask filled with water and he pulled it free, gulping down great gasps of clean, cold air.

He was numb with shock. It took him several more moments to realize what had happened. He'd been shot down . . . he'd ejected . . . he was alive.

Alive and adrift in the middle of the Soviet task force.

At least no one was shooting at him now. His life raft, attached to his ejection seat when he'd punched out, had inflated automatically and was drifting nearby, moored to him by a line. Grimly, hand over hand, he began to pull himself toward it.

0619 hours Zulu (0719 hours Zone)
Tomcat 200, "Viper"
Over the Norwegian Sea

Coyote had stuck with the Intruders most of the way to the target. As the range dropped to twelve miles, the four Intruders of Dealer Flight had split up, taking widely spaced attack positions to further confuse the already hard-pressed Soviet air-search and fire-control radar networks.

Now, he and Trapper had taken position wing-and-wing

behind Dealer Leader, Intruder 502, behind and above the Intruder as it began its attack run.

"Uh-oh," Teejay called over the ICS. "Bad news, Boss. We've got some mean-lookin' dudes coming in on our five, and they look pissed!"

Damn. The Soviet MiGs and Sukhois must have broken past Batman's TACCAP defense. "Okay. Whatcha got?"

"I make it two bogies at two-zero-five, coming in at Mach one-point-five. Range eight miles and closing fast."

"Trapper," Coyote called. "You got that?"

"Affirmative, Coyote. I think they mistrust our intentions."

"Damn straight they do. Let's see what the gentlemen want. Breaking left." He pulled the F-14 into a hard, wings-back turn.

"I'm with you. Breaking left."

Computer-generated symbols drifted across Coyote's HUD. Switching his AXX-1 to telescopic, he could pick out the targets visibly. The bogies were close together, apparently heading straight toward him.

He dragged the targeting pipper across one of the targets on his HUD. "Going for a radar lock, Teejay." Contact! A tone sounded in his ear and the targeting pipper flashed from its diamond shape to a circle. "I've got tone. Sparrow lock." His finger closed on the trigger. "Fox one!"

A threat warning chirped. The Tomcat was being painted by an enemy missile's guidance radar. "Trouble, Boss!" Teejay warned. "Launch! Launch! I've got enemy missiles, two . . . no, three missiles in the air. SARH-active. They're targeting us."

"Damn it, Teejay, we're stuck on the straight and narrow here." As long as they were painting the enemy aircraft for their own AIM-7, evasive maneuvers were impossible.

"Understood, buddy. I'm tracking the incoming missiles at six miles . . . five-point-five . . . five miles . . ."

Coyote felt the skin of his face growing slick beneath the padding of helmet and mask. He was locked in a game of high-tech chicken, his Sparrow hurtling toward the enemy at Mach 2, as three enemy missiles approached him at the same speed. To break away was to lose the target, with no certainty that he'd be able to dodge three Soviet missiles.

He held the Tomcat on a steady course, still aiming at the pair of Soviet fighters.

"I've got Sidewinder lock," Trapper called. "Fox two! Fox two!"

"Incoming missiles now at two miles," Teejay called. Coyote thought he heard the slightest crack in his RIO's voice. "One-five. One mile . . ."

There was a distant flash against the sky, and Coyote hauled the Tomcat into a gut-wrenching left turn. Sea and sky swung past the canopy, a dizzying blur of blue and white as acceleration crushed him down into his ejection seat. They were falling now. The ladder up the side of his HUD that showed altitude was flicking past too fast to read. "Chaff!" he yelled as he fought to control the Tomcat, both hands on the stick, hoping that Teejay could still hear him and handle the countermeasures.

Something flashed past his canopy . . . followed closely by another something, closer, a streak of white. Miss! Coyote exalted, bringing back the stick, bucking the Tomcat out of its two-mile plummet toward the sea. G-forces built, clamping down on his chest and making breathing difficult. The natural high of adrenaline roaring through his system banished fear, banished doubt as he tensed arms and shoulders and neck, forcing blood from where it was pooling in his extremities and back into his brain. Still hauling back on the stick, he started to bring the Tomcat out of its dive. . . .

The shock kicked Coyote in the back so hard that stars flashed and spun in front of his eyes, and the tunnel vision of the high-G pullout closed down completely, plunging him into blackness. The stick flopped loose in his hands, offering no resistance at all, as sea and sky were whirling past his windscreen so quickly now that he could not separate one from the other. Something was terribly wrong. He was no longer being crushed down in his seat, but pressed hard to the right side of the cockpit. Dimly, he realized that the Tomcat was spinning, that centrifugal force had slammed him against the side of the cockpit, that only his harness kept him from being plastered against the canopy, as helpless as a bug pinned to the bottom of a cigar box.

His hands fumbled for the yellow-and-black-striped ejection handle. Where was it? He couldn't reach it . . . couldn't reach . . . there!

He yanked, and his universe exploded in a coruscating blaze of fireworks, of blackness shot through with lightning and a red haze of pain. The canopy was gone and the wind was raging at his helmet and mask and body like an angry demon, a raging beast trying to tear him into pieces. Teejay . . . where was Teejay? . . .

Coyote's last thought was of Julie as he plunged through blackness and flame. . . .

0621 hours Zulu (0721 hours Zone)
CIC, U.S.S. *Thomas Jefferson*
The Norwegian Sea

"Tomcat Two-double-oh is hit! They're hit!"

Tombstone's fists clenched, the nails biting into the palms of his hands as he listened to Trapper's urgent call.

"Splash one MiG." That sounded like L-D, Trapper's RIO. *"Splash two, that's splash two MiGs."*

"Oh, God, Coyote and Teejay are down, coordinates x-ray one-five-niner, Yankee three-one-one. I don't see any chutes. . . ."

Not Coyote! Damn, damn, *damn!*

"Camelot," another voice was calling. *"Camelot, this is Bifrost. Fisher One-one has gone off our scope. We've also lost Fisher One-two and Viper Two-four."*

Tombstone's fist came down on the arm of his chair. Aviators, *his* aviators, were falling from the sky faster than he could conjure up their faces and names.

But there was no time to mourn, no time even to think. Dealer was almost at the target, and Coyote and Hunter and all the rest had bought them the time they'd needed to close. It was time for the payback on their sacrifice.

0621 hours Zulu (0721 hours Zone)
Intruder 502
Over the Norwegian Sea

Sluf had heard the call that one of the Tomcats was down, but his attention was fully focused now on his Heads Down Display. The Kaiser AVA-1 Visual Display Indicator revealed a glowing, electronic picture of the target, tiny against a tilted horizon, painted by the Intruder's computer. He kept the steering pipper on the target, which his electronics had pegged as the source of several different radar emissions.

"That's a contact," Spoiler said, his face buried in his radar hood. "Solid lock . . . shit. Lot of fuzz. Switching to FLIR. Yup. Looks like our carrier, all right." The B/N had already set his ordnance panel to release the pair of Harpoon AGMs slung beneath the Intruder's wings. Sluf could almost imagine feeling them down there, ticking and purring as the Intruder's computer fed them data on course, speed, and target.

"I think they're finally waking up down there," Sluf said. More missiles were arching up from the sea ahead. Threat warnings chirped and flashed on his console. "They're figuring out that we might not be Tomcats or Prowlers after all."

"Yeah, and the fighter jocks kept their air-to-air boys off our tail," Spoiler said. "We've got the bastards. Weapons armed. Safe off. Pickle's hot."

"Range ten miles. Hang on!" He keyed the tactical frequency. "This is Dealer Leader, going in hot."

"Roger," a voice replied over his headset. "Dealer Two, going in hot."

"Dealer Three. We're in. Save a piece for us."

"Dealer Four. In and hot."

Good. All four Intruders had made it this far, though at least one of the F-14s had been taken out. He pushed the stick over, picking up speed as the Intruder's nose dropped below the horizon line. The old days of Navy dive bombers were long gone, Sluf thought, but this pounding excitement, this rush of blood in ears and chest must have been what SBD dauntless pilots felt as they lined up their lumbering aircraft and primitive sights on the Japanese carriers at Midway.

"Picking up some heavy SAM fire here." That was Scooter Van Buren's voice, in Dealer Three. "Shit! I got one on me!"

"Break it off, Scoot," another voice called.

"Negative. Popping chaff. I—"

The sudden cutoff of the transmission was chilling in its abruptness. Sluf wanted to look around to see if he could see Dealer Three—Scooter and Rider ought to be off to the east somewhere—but he couldn't shift his attention from the VDI.

When he glanced up through the Intruder's HUD, though, he could see the Soviet carrier with his own eyes, looming on the horizon. The missiles were much closer now, crawling across the sky with deceptive slowness. Puffs of smoke, deceptively small, almost friendly-looking, were beginning to appear above the horizon to the north. There was enough triple-A rising above the Soviet ships to defend a small city.

"Hold it steady," Spoiler warned as the Intruder bumped slightly in some rough air. "Steady . . . Harpoon one away!" The Intruder thumped heavily as the missile dropped clear and ignited. His view of the Russian carrier was momentarily obscured by the boiling white haze of the missile's exhaust.

"Pickle hot on number two," Spoiler said. "Firing two!"

The A-6 lurched again. As soon as the missile was clear,

Sluf put the stick over, breaking into a hard right turn that would take them clear of the battle zone. The threat warning continued to chirp from the console.

"We got a couple SAMs coming in fast, Sluf."

"I see 'em. Chaff."

"Rog."

They'd done all they could against the Soviet aircraft carrier. Now it would be a fight for survival in the smoke-laced skies over the Norwegian Sea.

0623 hours Zulu (0723 hours Zone)
Soviet Task Group Soyuz
The Norwegian Sea

Deprived of air cover from its consorts, *Soyuz* did its best to defend itself. The Soviet carrier mounted CIWS-type weapons, as well as launchers for both SA-N-3s and SA-N-4s. Her 3-D air-defense radars, switched on moments before when the carrier's CIC lost the feed from the damaged *Marshal Timoshenko*, painted six Harpoon missiles incoming from three different bearings.

Had the *Kirov* still had been part of the carrier task force, perhaps the outcome would have been different. Kirov-class cruisers could lob volleys of SA-N-6s at cruise-missile-sized targets over fifty kilometers away.

But *Kirov* was forty kilometers astern now, a helplessly drifting, fire-blackened wreck, and *Soyuz* simply did not have enough antiair assets to deal with all of the incoming targets herself.

Her Gatling cannons shrieked, spraying 30-mm shells across the sky. Larger, slower antiaircraft guns joined in, hurling round after round into the sky, which was coming alive with the puffs of antiaircraft fire, tiny white clouds against the blue.

One Harpoon went down eight kilometers from the ship, sliced in two by a buzzsawing stream of lead from *Soyuz*'s stern. A second Harpoon exploded an instant later, scattering shrapnel across a carrier-sized patch of frothing white sea. A third was hit, exploding in flame, CIWS cannons adjusted, tracked, slewed to new targets . . .

Running the gauntlet of fire, a Harpoon struck the carrier's stern, slamming into the open gallery just below the flight deck that housed one of the Soviet carrier's CIWS AK-630s. The explosion plucked the Gatling turret up by its roots and hurled it into the sea. The roundoff curled up, knocking men to their knees with the concussion.

The next Harpoon struck three seconds later, striking *Soyuz*'s island aft and on the starboard side. The warhead plunged through two bulkheads before exploding in *Soyuz*'s air department intelligence center. Twenty men were incinerated outright as the blast knocked out decks and overheads and smashed computers and severed electronics links. Two hundred men more died as the explosion shattered an entire level and destroyed the carrier's primary flight control center.

The killing blow was delivered by a third Harpoon, whipping in five seconds after the first and on a slightly higher trajectory. It passed over *Soyuz*'s stern and through the expanding cloud of smoke and debris, plunging to self-destruction among the ranks of MiGs and Sukhois parked aft of the bridge. Bombs and missiles slung from wings, fuel tanks already topped off with JP-5, fuel hoses coiled across the deck like strands of spaghetti, cannon rounds tight-packed in magazines, all erupted in a savage detonation that overwhelmed the initial flash and boom of the exploding Harpoon.

On *Soyuz*'s flag bridge, Admiral Khenkin dragged himself erect from a deck covered with shards of broken glass. Men littered the deck, dead and dying, stunned and wounded. Someone shrieked agony in the smoke-choked darkness. Khenkin's arm was broken, and his face was slick with blood, but he scarcely noticed. What he did notice was a distinct cant to the deck. *Soyuz* was listing to port, and settling by the stern as well.

The damage was almost certainly fatal.

Glass crunched under his shoes. Every window on the bridge had been blown out by the concussion, and the pall of smoke was so thick that daylight had been blotted out. From one gaping window, he peered down into an inferno, where the flight deck had been laid open as though by a titanic, white-hot knife and filled with raw flame.

The great social experiment was over. *Soyuz* was doomed. The Russian mystic in Khenkin had already accepted the trial-by-combat judgment of Fate.

At the same time, he knew that his death would mean nothing to Vorobyev or the other militarists, or to Admiral Ivanov steaming north aboard the *Kreml* at this moment. The struggle would go on, with thousands more dying to confirm what he already knew: The Americans fought like demons, their technology was superior . . . and the twin battles this day, at Romsdalfjord and here, had proven that they had a will to fight for what they believed at least equal to that of the Soviets.

The struggle and the dying would go on. The realization filled him with sadness.

Beneath the inferno, gasoline and JP-5 spewed from ruptured fuel lines, turning hangar spaces into vast reservoirs of fuel-air explosives. Flames raging through the paint locker spaces at the carrier's stern ignited the mixture. As Khenkin reached for a telephone on the flag bridge, the Soviet aircraft carrier died around him.

With a crack like the thunder of Judgment Day, flame-licked smoke mushroomed five hundred meters into the sky. Airplanes and pieces of airplanes and house-sized pieces of the island and flight deck were whirled end over end over end high above the stricken carrier, as explosion followed explosion in a deep-throated barrage of savage detonations, each building one upon another, a waterfall, a booming, rumbling tidal wave of raw and furious sound.

In the sea a mile away, Hunter Harrison clung to his inflatable life raft, his face gone slack with awe as he watched the rending of the skies, felt the heat wash across his exposed face and hands, felt the terrible power of that multiple, ongoing thunderclap.

And aboard Intruder 502, Sluf Dodd felt the shudder that reached out and took the fleeing A-6 like a dog worrying a bone. He gritted his teeth and held the aircraft on course, as flame lit up the inside of the cockpit like a newly risen sun.

Twisting in his seat, he glimpsed the pillar of smoke rising from the sea, like the volcanic destruction of some exploding island. Opening the tactical frequency, Sluf repeated a phrase that had already gone down in Navy history, one first spoken some fifty-five years before after the sinking of the Japanese carrier *Shoho* at the Battle of the Coral Sea.

"Camelot, Dealer One," he called. "Scratch one flat-top."

Behind him, flames scoured the sky.

CHAPTER 23
Monday, 23 June

0900 hours Zulu (1000 hours Zone)
CBG-14
The Norwegian Sea

The last blow struck by the American forces in what was to be known as the Battle of the Fröya Bank was something of an anticlimax. During the air strike against the Soviet task force, the attack sub *Galveston,* which had been dogging the enemy carrier group for days, at last slipped past a pair of Kashin-class destroyers, located *Soyuz* and her consorts at a range of nearly 120 miles, and loosed her last two sub-launched Harpoons.

Soviet radar operators on the cruisers escorting the *Soyuz,* distracted by the explosion that had demolished the carrier and turned her into a flaming wreck, never saw the cruise missiles skimming the waves from a totally unexpected direction—the northwest. Both Harpoons slammed into the cruiser *Admiral Yumashev,* one in her helicopter deck astern, the other into her hull just below her superstructure.

The detonation of warheads, helicopter fuel, and a magazine locker holding several dozen antisubmarine torpedoes was not nearly as thunderous as the blast that had destroyed *Soyuz,* but the *Yumashev* was a much smaller vessel. Her spine snapped, she broke in two at 0842 hours and went to the bottom, taking 303 of her complement of 380 officers and men with her.

Soyuz, meanwhile, continued to burn.

The first American ship to reach the *Soyuz* was the frigate *Stephen Decatur,* but she could not approach closer than a hundred yards because of the fierce heat from the burning carrier. Explosions aboard had opened *Soyuz* to the sea. Already, the waves broke over her stern quarter, while her island superstructure canted far to starboard.

There was little *Decatur* could do but try to rescue some of the survivors. Thousands of men were in the water, adrift in crowded masses of oil-blackened humanity clutching floating debris, in lifeboats and rafts or swimming alone, men who were no longer enemies, but fellow sailors to be rescued from the relentless sea.

Decatur lowered lifeboats and rafts, then stood by until a small fleet of Norwegian ASW ships, helicopters, and patrol torpedo boats could arrive from Trondheim to take up the rescue effort.

More of *Soyuz*'s crew might have been saved had *Jefferson* and the other members of the battle group been able to join the rescuers, but the necessities of war and cold, common sense dictated against such a gesture. There were Soviet subs in the area. An SH-3 off the *Shiloh* found and sank a Victor III less than thirty miles from the Soyuz at 0935 hours, and *Winslow* scored an unconfirmed kill less than an hour later.

By now, every Soviet sub in the Norwegian Sea would be vectoring toward the Fröya Bank, searching for the *Jefferson* now that she was out from behind the parapets of Romsdalfjord. An aircraft carrier's only defense against those silent, deadly hunters was speed . . . and an encircling net of ASW ships and helos.

For her to linger might mean a few more lives rescued from the *Soyuz* holocaust, but it would mean exposing the six thousand Americans aboard the *Jefferson* to a similar fate. *Jefferson* slowed enough to extend the search for a few hours with SH-3s flown off her deck, but by the middle of the afternoon she passed beyond the range for her rescue helos, which had given up their melancholy quest.

The helos had had mixed success. Twenty oil-soaked Russian sailors were plucked from the water, as were two MiG pilots downed in the dogfight with Viper One. Miraculously, Hunter Harrison was picked up, tired, cold, and barely conscious, still clinging to his aviator's life raft. His TACCO, Ralph Meade, however, was never found.

And Hard Ball, Beaver, Teejay, Coyote, and so many others were gone.

1430 hours Zulu (1530 hours Zone)
U.S.S. *Thomas Jefferson*
The Norwegian Sea

Coyote was gone.

Tombstone still couldn't believe it. He'd lost friends in combat before, but Willis E. Grant—Coyote—had been part of his Navy life almost from the beginning, when they'd been stationed together at the San Diego Naval Air Station . . . and then again after that during their first operational deployment aboard the U.S.S. *Kennedy*. He thought of Julie Wilson Grant, the girl both of them had dated and Coyote had married. He would have to write her.

What was he going to say to her?

That he'd given the orders that put Coyote at the wrong place at the wrong time? That he'd sent the irrepressible Coyote to his death?

It was in a decidedly somber mood, then, that Tombstone threaded his way across *Jefferson*'s hangar deck.

He wore a Mickey Mouse helmet against the noise. The hangar deck was filled with men and machines, with aircraft parked almost wingtip to wingtip, divided only by narrow lanes made hazardous by mules and tow tractors and plane crews scurrying about like ants among the tunnels of their nest. Refueling and rearming operations were being carried out here to keep the deck clear for the vertical replenishment operation, and so that Air Ops could continue to launch and recover aircraft on CAP.

Tombstone had completed checking on reports of minor battle damage to two of the Death Dealer Intruders and he wanted to make certain that the A-6s would not have to be down-griped. CVW-20 had lost so many aircraft already, and even though *Soyuz* had been destroyed, the fight for the control of the Norwegian Sea was not over yet. There was still the Baltic Fleet to deal with, and there was a serious sub threat, with only six S-3 Vikings left of the King Fishers' original complement of ten. He'd completed his check and was heading for the ship's ladder that would take him back up to his office when he spotted a familiar, lanky form crossing toward the port elevator.

"Batman!" he called. "Hey, Batman! Wait up!"

Batman saw Tombstone's wave and waved back. Tombstone caught up with him and they stepped across the pattern of yellow and black warning stripes on the deck that marked the elevator deck's rim. "Hello, CAG," Batman said, shouting above the noise. "What brings you down here?"

"A couple of dinged-up Intruders and not enough Vikings," Tombstone said. They backed out of the way as a tow tractor began maneuvering an S-3 onto the elevator. "Congratulations on your kills this morning," he added. Batman was being credited with bringing down a Sukhoi and a cruise missile over the Romsdalfjord moments after the Russian attack had begun.

"Another day, another Sukhoi," Batman quipped. "Getting routine, you know?"

Tombstone walked to the edge of the elevator deck and looked down. The water, transformed into a frothing white by the passage of the gray steel cliff of *Jefferson*'s hull, roared and hissed a few yards below. Looking up, he could see the damage, crudely patched, where a missile had struck the carrier in the fjord. The elevator had been repaired, however, and seemed to be working well. The carrier's damage-control parties had certainly earned their pay this morning.

Outside, the noise levels were lower. Batman pulled his

ear protectors off so he could hear. Tombstone removed his own helmet. "Too bad about Coyote," he said.

"Yeah." Batman turned his helmet in his hands. "Y'know, Stoney, he could still be alive."

"Maybe. I hope so." Tombstone turned his gaze on the aviator. "But for now, you're CO of the Vipers."

Batman nodded. "I figured." He jerked his head, indicating the oval opening in the ship's side leading into the hangar deck. "I was down here checking on some of the turkeys. Two-oh-three and Two-one-oh both took some damage. Plane crews're checking them out now. They should have them back on the line in another six hours."

"Good."

A warning klaxon sounded, and with a jerk, the elevator deck began moving up, carrying the Viking, the tractor, several crewmen, and the two officers with it.

Tombstone remembered how once before he'd thought Coyote was dead, during the crisis with North Korea a couple of years earlier. Somehow his friend had walked out of that one. Batman was right. Maybe he would do it again.

But he knew better than to think too much along those lines. It was futile and it was distracting at a time when he needed to focus his full attention on his duties as CAG. It was his responsibility to order men into situations they might not survive. It wasn't a pleasant responsibility, but it was part of the package . . . and part of the price paid for that morning's victory.

The air wing had lost thirteen other naval flight officers that morning, good men, all of them, with wives, sweethearts, families, promising futures back in the World, *lives*. . . .

None of them would be coming back.

Batman dropped a hand onto Tombstone's shoulder. "I, ah, just wanted to tell you, Stoney. You're doing a hell of a job as CAG."

"Thanks, Batman." He gave a shallow grin. "I'd rather be driving a Tomcat."

"Yeah. That's where I got you beat, old man. Me, I like life simple. None of these power games for me!"

Maybe, Tombstone thought, *the ultimate test of leadership is being able to send shipmates,* friends, *out to die.*

Batman's acceptance of the situation somehow made it—not better—easier.

A blast of raw noise assaulted their ears, and both men donned their helmets again. The elevator clattered to a stop at the flight deck level, the black and yellow stripes matching with counterparts along the elevator-shaped cutout at the deck's edge.

The roar came from a big, twin-rotored CH-46E Sea Knight, descending from the solid roof of overcast. *Jefferson* was finally within helicopter range of II MEF and her UNREP ships, and vertical replenishment operations had been proceeding since that afternoon. In the distance to the west another Sea Knight, an HH-46 off one of the UNREP vessels, was dwindling toward the pearly glimmer where sea met sky. On the deck, seamen labored and sweated over piles of off-loaded munitions. Pallet after pallet of supplies had already been dropped off. Most numerous were the Harpoons, still in their packing cases, accumulating on the deck faster than men and mules and forklifts could stow them away below. As he and Batman stepped off the elevator, Tombstone couldn't help but wonder what would happen if a Soviet cruiser missile skimmed in just now and touched the whole load off.

Fortunately, *Jefferson* had left the Soviet Baltic Fleet far to the south in her rapid dash toward the Arctic Circle. *Shiloh,* with her far-seeing Spy-1 radar and up-to-the-second access to American reconnaissance satellite data, guaranteed that the enemy could not sneak up on the battle group. The sneak attack at Romsdalfjord had been possible only because *Soyuz* had already been within a hundred twenty miles of *Jefferson*'s position, a ten-minute flight at Mach 1. Now, their nearest aircraft were ashore, at airfields so heavily damaged they would be out of action for days.

Tombstone and Batman waited well clear of the landing

zone until the Sea Knight settled to the deck, and sailors began unloading its cargo. Men in purple jerseys—fuel handlers or "grapes" in *Jefferson*'s color-coded society— dragged hoses across the steel and connected them to receptacles in the helo's fuselage.

"Now hear this, now hear this," the voice of someone up in Pri-Fly boomed across the deck from a 5-MC speaker. "Helo incoming, that is, helo incoming. All personnel stand clear of the designated landing zone."

Looking back toward the west, Tombstone saw the new arrival, an SH-3 drifting down through the gloom of overcast Arctic twilight, its anticollision lights strobing brightly. The wind was stiffening, wet with spray and scattered droplets of rain.

"Now hear this, now hear this," the voice brayed again. "II-MEF, arriving."

The announcement quickened Tombstone's interest. The word was out that a high-level staff meeting would be held aboard *Jefferson* later that evening. "II MEF" could only refer to Major General Chester R. Wagner, commanding officer of the Second Marine Division. His flagship, the LPH *Iwo Jima,* was still three hundred miles to the west, but on a converging course with the *Jefferson* battle group and drawing closer with every hour.

With a roar, the SH-3 Sea King settled to the deck some distance astern of the Sea Knight. As the rotors whined to a halt, a double line of *Jefferson*'s Marines, dazzlingly outfitted in their full dress uniforms, trotted into position and snapped to attention. Captain Brandt and Admiral Tarrant strode up the line and were beside the helo when a side door slid open. A lean, weathered-looking man in khakis dropped to the deck, saluted his greeting party, then walked with them toward the island, closely pursued by staff officers carrying briefcases and urgent expressions.

"A Marine general on board," Batman said. "God, I bet things happen now!"

Two hours later, Tombstone and Batman sat side by side on folding steel chairs in CVIC. General Wagner and

Admiral Tarrant had conferred together, then assembled most of *Jefferson*'s department heads. Rumor and speculation had been running unchecked through the labyrinthine tangle of *Jefferson*'s passageways and compartments all day, and it looked as though this conference would answer the questions that seemed to be on the mind of every officer and man in the task force. Was *Jefferson* pulling out? Were they pressing the attack, pressing the advantage they'd won by destroying *Soyuz*?

What in *hell* was going on outside the tight, enclosed little worlds of *Jefferson, Shiloh,* and the other ships of CBG-14?

"Gentlemen," Tarrant said, beginning the meeting. "Thank you all for coming. This afternoon, if you don't mind, I'm going to serve as my own briefing officer. Not that I'm putting him out of work, but I wanted the pleasure of this session myself.

"First, I would like to take this opportunity to present Major General Wagner, whom I'm sure most of you know by reputation, if not personally.

"Next, I've been asked by Washington to do something a bit out of the ordinary. This is not ordinary procedure, you understand, but these are not ordinary times." His eyes found Tombstone's. "Commander Matthew Magruder! Front and center!"

Tombstone was caught completely off guard. He rose and made his way to the podium, where Tarrant was fishing a small box from his uniform coat. "Yes, sir."

Tarrant turned and addressed the room. "I'm not very good with speeches," he said, unfolding a computer printout, "so I'll simply give you the straight word. Commander Magruder is being credited with devising the strategy that broke the Soviets' naval defense of Norway and led to the disabling of the *Soyuz*. The commendation reads, in part . . . 'Commander Magruder's brilliance in implementing the tactical doctrine of carrier forces operating from advance positions in the Norwegian fjords has played an important role in delaying the Soviet timetable in the area, and in winning for United States forces the time necessary to organize an effective counterattack.' ''

Folding the paper carefully, he turned again to face Tombstone. ''Commander Magruder, as Commanding Officer of Carrier Battle Group Fourteen, and by the direction of the Commander in Chief, Atlantic, it is my great privilege and personal pleasure to present you with . . . these.'' He extended the open box. Inside were a pair of small silver eagles. ''Congratulations, *Captain* Magruder.''

Tombstone accepted the devices, stunned. ''I, uh . . .'' He stopped, embarrassed. ''I don't quite have the time in grade, Admiral.''

''Waived. By special directive from the Navy Department. You've been handling your duties as Acting CAG so well, it looks like they've gone and made you captain so you could be CAG in fact. Can't have a commander filling a captain's billet, after all.''

''I don't know what to say.''

''Then say nothing. You've got the damned job, whether you want it or not!''

CVIC exploded in laughter and scattered applause. Tombstone smiled and accepted the admiral's handshake. He returned to his seat as the applause continued, his eagles clutched in an unsteady grip.

''Heeeey, Cap'n Stoney!'' Batman said as he sat down once more. He tossed Tombstone a salute, strictly nonregulation since he was uncovered. ''Way to go, Stoney!''

''Thanks, Batman.'' Several other nearby officers, grinning broadly, clapped him on the back. ''Thanks, guys. Damned if I'll ever understand the military mind!''

Promotion to captain. It marked an important turning point in his career . . . *the* turning point. Only a small percentage of all naval officers stuck it out long enough to make captain, and as often as not, their rise to that rank was as much due to politics as it was to skill. For most of his career, Tombstone had wondered if his rapid rise through the ranks had been due to the influence of his uncle,

Admiral Thomas Magruder. Talk about being junior for a command—he'd been made skipper of VF-95 when he'd still been wearing two and a half stripes, a necessity when there'd been a shortage of qualified full commanders aboard. Two weeks earlier, he'd become Acting CAG, filling a captain's slot while still a commander. Now he was a captain years before he should have even been able to dream about getting on the promotions list.

It didn't hurt to be well connected. He knew that fact, and accepted it. But for perhaps the first time in his naval career, Tombstone knew that he was being rewarded for *his* abilities, and his talent. His uncle would have had nothing to do with these eagles. Even if he had, it didn't matter.

Though saddened by the loss of Coyote and the others, he was proud of what he'd done. He deserved those eagles, not as reward, but because of the job he still had to do.

"Now to the business at hand," Tarrant said. Tombstone looked up, willing an inner trembling to subside. "During the past few hours, we and the Norwegians have been following through on our rather spectacular victory over the *Soyuz* this morning.

"At 1420 hours today, the Norwegian submarine *Ula*, a German Type 210, put three torpedoes into the replenishment oiler *Ivan Bubanov* twenty miles off Stavanger. The *Bubanov*, carrying something like thirteen thousand tons of fuel and fresh water, plus hundreds of tons of munitions, sank in about twenty minutes. An hour later, a Russian submarine support ship was damaged by a torpedo from a Type 207 Norwegian sub, the *Skolpen*. In an action off Stavanger late this afternoon, a Kashin-class destroyer was hit by two Penguin Mark II SSMs from a Norwegian missile boat and sunk. Another Russian ship, the corvette *Odesskey Komsomolets*, was damaged by Norwegian F-16s loaded with five-hundred-pound Snakeye retarded bombs. She ran aground off Kristiansund and her crew surrendered to Home Defense forces.

"In the past five hours, ASW helos and Vikings of CBG-14 have racked up four confirmed sub kills, and two more probables. The cruiser *Yumashev* was sunk this morning by Harpoons from the *Galveston*. Her sister ship, *Marshal Timoshenko,* was last reported heading northeast at thirty-four knots, along with several smaller vessels. The *Soyuz* battle group appears to have been completely scattered.

"Two late notes. First, satellite reconnaissance indicates that the *Kirov* is under way again. She appears to be limping north, either to rejoin elements of the Red Banner Northern Fleet beyond North Cape or to return to Murmansk. We cannot be sure how badly *Kirov* is hurt, but the damage appears to be extensive and serious.

"Second, according to our spy satellites, at 1627 hours this afternoon, just over an hour ago, the aircraft carrier *Soyuz* rolled over and sank. Norwegian . . .'' Tarrant had to stop for a moment as the room erupted in cheers and renewed applause. As the noise subsided, he went on. "Norwegian forces are still in the area picking up the survivors.

"I think it's clear that we have the bastards on the run. We intend to use the momentum we've gained so far to keep them on the run, to keep hitting them so hard they can't hit back.

"Ah . . . you might also be happy to hear that *Kearny* rejoined the battle group this afternoon and has taken up ASW patrol to the south. The *Esek Hopkins* is now safe at Scapa Flow." There was more applause. This, Tombstone reflected, was turning into more of a cheerleading session than an operational planning meeting.

It didn't matter. These men deserved a few cheers.

"As for the disposition of the remaining Soviet naval forces," Tarrant continued, "we are still tracking two main groups. One is a large, mixed task force built around the light aircraft carrier *Kiev* and the helicopter carrier *Moskva* in the Barents Sea beyond North Cape, six hundred miles northeast. The other, of course, is our friends from the Baltic. For the past twelve hours, they appear to have been holding position off Bergen, four hundred miles southwest of our current position. At this point we're not sure what their intentions are. It's possible, now that *Soyuz* has been sunk, that they don't know what their intentions are either." Laughter rippled through the compartment.

"Thanks, at least in part to Captain Magruder there, and thanks also to the efforts of every man in this battle group, we can make some solid plans of our own. And Major General Wagner here is going to fill us in."

General Wagner took Tarrant's place beside the podium. "Thank you, Admiral. Well, it's not every day that the Marines have a good word for the Navy, but today is certainly one of them. I tell you all now, from the bottom of my heart, 'Well done!'

"It is my pleasure to inform you that at 1200 hours today, local time, new orders were transmitted to II MEF. Those orders are signed by the President of the United States. By those orders, the Second Marine Division has been directed to proceed to the coast of Norway and effect an amphibious landing in the area of the city of Narvik. We are to break enemy resistance in the area, seize key airfields, and isolate Soviet forces in central Norway from reinforcements and resupply by land and sea.

"Gentlemen, the United States is going back into Norway. We are going in after the Russians, we are going in hard, and we are going in to win."

Wagner then proceeded to present the plan for Operation Thor.

1830 hours Zulu (1930 hours Zone), 25 June
2 MARDIV Landings
Vagsfjorden, Norway

Norway is a tiny nation and, from a military point of view, a difficult one, either to invade or defend. Though the northern reaches are cold, wet, and dreary in the popular mind, summer temperatures can reach 30°C in daylight that lasts twenty-four hours, and changes in the weather can be rapid and completely unpredictable.

With a coast heavily indented by the fjords, the land broken by steep mountains and rugged terrain, with no railroads at all north of Bodø and only a single primary road system, the E-6, which is unable to accommodate heavy military traffic, transportation links between the north and south of the country are limited.

The Soviet forces that had occupied northern Norway, then, were relatively isolated, totally dependent on resupply by air or by sea. With the defeat of the *Soyuz* battle group, most of the Norwegian coast was opened to interdiction by American air strikes, and resupply by sea became increasingly difficult. Air drops continued to be made by cargo planes—big Ilyushin 18Ds and Antonov Cubs—flying in over the occupied portions of Sweden, but fewer and fewer of these were making it through the waves of Swedish Viggen interceptors, or past the long-range lightning of U.S.

Phoenix missiles, launched by Tomcats over the coast 120 miles away.

Key to any military strategy in the region is Norway's shape. Kirkines, in the far north, is over seventeen hundred miles from the Baltic, and yet at Narvik, at the head of the huge, inland slash of the Vestfjorden, the country is only four miles wide.

Narvik. The port had known the thunder of battle before. In 1940, a British fleet headed by the battleship *Warspite* had sailed up the fjord and engaged German ships in the harbor, sinking nine destroyers. Fifty-seven years later, Narvik occupied a strategic chokepoint that could block Soviet military traffic. A single road runs east into Sweden, but through a vast and desolate area not yet under the control of Soviet forces. Capture Narvik, then, and southern Norway could easily be isolated from the north.

From Narvik, a finger of close-set islands, the Lofotens, extends southwest like the jagged, armored tail of a dragon. The gulf between the Lofotens and the mainland is the Vestfjord, sixty miles wide at its mouth. At its head, it narrows sharply, forming the Ofotfjord, the sea approach to Narvik.

The dragon's head juts northeast, a clutter of islands called the Vesterålen. Between these Western Islands and the scattering of islands close to the mainland is another gulf, the Andfjord. Vagsfjord branches south from this sheltered backwater, between the islands of Grytøya and Rolla. Among these sheltered coves and hill-backed fjords the II MEF operations team had placed the landing beaches, at the point where the dragon's feet met the jagged coastline of Norway: Green Beach, south of Harstad; and Red and Blue Beaches, at the head of the Vagsfjord near the town of Tennevik.

The invasion began at 0630 hours on the twenty-fifth, with preassault landings on Rolla and Grytøya, and on the Vesterålen island of Andøya. These landings, some by combat swimmers, others by helocasting or parachute insertion, were carried out by Marine Recon forces and by

detachments of U.S. Navy SEALs. Their objectives in-
cluded clearing the sea approaches to the invasion beaches,
carrying out hydrographic reconnaissance, silencing SAM
sites and radars, and, in particular, capturing the small
airfield on Andøya, which now was home to a squadron of
Soviet MiG-29s.

The fighting at Andøya was still going on when the Norwegian Mine Countermeasures Squadron entered the Vagsfjord at just past 0930 hours and began sweeping the beach
approaches. The squadron, including three minesweepers, two
minelayers, and a dozen smaller craft, was accompanied by
two Perry-class frigates and led by a flight of massive
MH-53E Sea Dragon helicopters towing Mark 105 mine-
clearing sleds. The steep hills surrounding the fjords rang
and echoed to the ongoing bombardment by Marine and
Naval air units. Marine Harrier II jump jets and Huey Cobra
gunships stooped, hovered, and struck, blasting enemy
installations and command centers, vehicles on the road,
and concentrations of troops.

Behind the mine sweepers and air strikes came the
amphibious assault ships *Saipan* and *Nassau* and the LPDs
Austin and *Trenton*. The assault helicopter carriers *Iwo Jima*
and *Inchon* remained offshore, dispatching regimental landing teams by CH-46s and CH-53s. The helos clattered
inland, escorted by more Huey Cobras.

The first U.S. Marines hit the beaches near Tennevik at
1630 hours on June twenty-fifth. They were members of the
1/25th Regimental Landing Team, and they swam ashore in
twelve LVTP-7 amphibious armored personnel carriers
released by the LHA-4 *Nassau*. Streams of LCUs came
ashore moments later, disgorging more troops and Marine
LAVs—Light Armored Vehicles—and HMMWVs.

Initial fighting was surprisingly light and scattered.
Rather than spreading themselves throughout the country
and defending every village, hill, and potential beach
landing site, the Soviets instead appeared to be maintaining
a conservative defense of centralized strongpoints, around
Narvik and the airfields at Evanskjaer, Andselv, and on the

island of Andøya. The Marines encountered little resistance at first, though light artillery and mortar fire from Tennevik caused some casualties before being silenced by helicopter gunships and it was evening before Andøya was reported secure. The heaviest losses were suffered when rising winds and sea swells swamped two LVTP-7s, and there was a sharp fight in the Vagsfjord port of Harstad before Huey Cobras moved against the defenses with rocket and machine gun fire.

Harstad was in American hands by 1800 hours. RLTs ferried inland by helicopter secured key sections of the E-6 road net north of Narvik, at Bjerkvik and Fossbakken, and by early evening, most of the peninsula jutting west from the mainland was in American hands. Marine units were positioned within sight of Narvik itself, in the hills south of Bogen on the north edge of the Ofotfjord. The first serious fighting of the day occurred at 1830 hours, when 2nd LAV Battalion antitank vehicles tangled with a platoon of Soviet T-72s just outside of Narvik. Four of the thin-skinned LAVs were knocked out, exchanged for two T-72s, but the follow-up air strike by Huey Cobras firing TOW missiles killed six more Russian tanks before they could retire.

Meanwhile, the Marines—a full division of them, some seventeen thousand strong—kept coming ashore.

The Soviets could no longer challenge the Navy or the Marines for control of the skies. Air strikes by A-6 Intruders and both Marine and Navy Hornets knocked Soviet tanks off the roads as fast as Marine spotters could call in their positions, and the black pall of smoke rising from an enemy fuel depot outside Narvik suggested that they would soon be in deep trouble if they did not get help from somewhere.

There were one obvious source for that help . . . and a single remaining opportunity for the Soviet militarists. The Baltic Fleet remained off Bergen, perfectly positioned for a strike at the Marine landing forces four hundred miles to the north.

In Moscow, Vorobyev and the marshals agreed that the risk was worth taking. Even yet, success against the

Americans could deliver all of Scandinavia into Soviet hands. All it would take was speed, decision, and a little daring.

Late on the twenty-fifth, at Vorobyev's command, the machinery was set in motion.

2030 hours Zulu (2130 hours Zone), 25 June
Soviet Aircraft Carrier *Kreml*, Baltic Red Banner Fleet
The Norwegian Sea

Outside the portholes of Admiral Yuri Vasilievich Ivanov's office aboard the *Kreml,* the wind shrieked and howled in the first gusts of a storm sweeping down from the northwest, as raindrops splattered against the glass. On his desk, a large-scale map of the Norway coast had been spread out over the clutter of papers and reports that normally covered it. Neatly penciled notations in Cyrillic characters marked known ship locations and the reported landings near Narvik by thousands of U.S. Marines.

Ivanov stared at the orders in his hand, reading the words again, digesting them. A stronger storm, it seemed, was brewing in Moscow. Vorobyev was angry, and hesitation or vacillation on Ivanov's part would clearly mean the end of his career—one way or the other. The man expects the impossible, Ivanov thought. He waits until *Soyuz* is lost and Khenkin is dead, waits until the American Marines are already ashore, and then he sends . . . this.

Vorobyev's directions were explicit. *Attack American operations in Narvik area in coordination with Red Banner Northern Task Group Kiev. Execute immediate.*

There could be no more delay.

For three days, Ivanov had held back the Red Banner Baltic Fleet on the pretense of blockading the approaches to Stavanger and Bergen—the two largest and most important cities still in free Norwegian hands. It had not been clear, after all, how the enemy's strategy would unfold, and most of Ivanov's staff advisors had felt that the American

Marines were heading for Bergen, where they could go ashore at a friendly port and deploy to help stiffen the Norwegian resistance.

News that the Marines were ashore at Narvik had come as a shock to Ivanov—almost as great a shock as the orders that he attack the American beaches immediately. *Kreml* and *Soyuz* working together would have been more than a match for the *Jefferson,* but Khenkin had thrown away the opportunity by attacking before Ivanov could reach him. Now the American carrier had been joined by at least two Marine LHA assault ships, small carriers each capable of carrying twenty Harrier jump jets. The odds had just shifted dramatically in favor of the Americans.

And worse was on the way. Soviet spy satellite reconnaissance had showed that the main strength of the American fleet had not yet reached the landing areas. The carrier *Eisenhower,* freed at last from her North Atlantic station, was still a thousand kilometers to the west, north of the Faeroes, while the *Kennedy* was still off the east coast of Britain, fourteen hundred kilometers to the south.

There was still one chance, however. Both the *Eisenhower* and *Kennedy* battle groups were coming at flank speed, like the Americans' proverbial cavalry to the rescue, but it would be another twenty-four hours at least before they would be within air strike range, and in that time much could happen. In the early evening of the twenty-fifth, responding to directives from Moscow, the *Kiev* battle group had departed its station in the Barents Sea and rounded North Cape, sortieing toward the Narvik landings. When the American ships escorting the Marine force detected the *Kiev* task force's movement, they would almost certainly respond by moving north.

The Russian fleet admiral listened to the wind and rain blasting against his portholes. *Kreml*'s meteorology department predicted that the storm would last all night, offering excellent cover all the way from Bergen to the Lofoten Islands. By sailing north at full speed, using the storm for cover, Ivanov thought he just might be able to catch the Americans off guard.

With quickening excitement, he studied the map. It might work. It *would* work. The American escorts would be pulled out of position by the *Kiev*'s movements in the north, and the approaches to the Vagsfjord would be clear. He could round the northern tip of Andøya with *Kreml*, the mighty Kirov-class battle cruisers *Tallinn* and *Irkutsk*, and a dozen smaller warships by—he consulted the map, walking up the Norwegian coast and past the Lofoten Islands with a pair of calipers—yes! By noon tomorrow.

The only possible obstacles along the way were a scattering of Norwegian vessels near Trondheim—the storm would take care of them—and the *Jefferson* battle group, last reported at anchor in the Vestfjord.

Ivanov scowled. Always it was the *Jefferson*. Most likely, though, the troublesome enemy carrier would be drawn away to the north. And if not . . .

He smiled. If not, well, *Jefferson*'s air assets must have been sharply reduced in the battle that morning, her pilots, her officers exhausted by a week of hard fighting. Alone, *Jefferson* would be no match for the Soviet Baltic Fleet. And once his ships reached the American anchorage at Vagsfjord, a few hours would suffice to reduce the U.S. invasion force to a scattering of flaming, sinking hulks. The Marines ashore would be trapped, their supplies from the sea cut off. It would be, Ivanov thought smugly, the greatest defeat of American naval forces since Pearl Harbor . . . a defeat that would *end* a war, rather than begin it. With an entire Marine division forced to surrender or be destroyed, the Americans would have no stomach for further fighting. They would withdraw, and Scandinavia would remain the new bastion of Soviet arms, a decisive threat against Europe, a monument to the triumph of the Russian Empire over the West.

Admiral Ivanov reached for the telephone that connected him to *Kreml*'s command center. The orders had to be given immediately.

0530 hours Zulu (0630 hours Zone), 26 June
U.S.S. *Thomas Jefferson*
Vestfjord

Once again, *Jefferson* had taken refuge in a Norwegian
fjord. This time, her shelter was within the Vestfjord, the
broad reach of the waters between the Lofoten Islands and
the mainland, fifty miles north of Bodø.

Fighting ashore continued, though reports, on the whole,
were encouraging. At 0400 that morning, Marines of the
2/8th RLT had fought their way down Riksveg 6, past the
Peace Chapel and into Narvik proper. Marine LAVs had
engaged and destroyed a column of Soviet BMP personnel
carriers, and, after a sharp fight at the city's small airport,
had reported the town of Narvik secured. The picture was
still incomplete, but early reports gave partial credit for the
swift victory to units of Norwegian militia, guerrilla forces
that had descended from the hills of Narvik to attack Soviet
positions as soon as American ships were seen entering the
Vagsfjord.

Tombstone, his new eagles gleaming on the collar of his
khaki shirt, knocked on the door to Admiral Tarrant's
office. He heard a muffled "Enter," and walked in.

Admiral Tarrant was standing with Captain Brandt, bent
over a small worktable smothered in charts.

"Good morning, Admiral. Captain. You sent for me?"

"Hello, Captain," Tarrant said, gesturing. "Get your butt
over here. We've got problems. Have a look at these."

He passed a set of black and white photographs to
Tombstone, who took them and studied them critically.
They showed aerial views of ships at sea, photographed
through broken clouds. Coded information in the corner told
him that these were TENCAP photos, taken within the last
hour.

TENCAP—Tactical Exploitation of National CAP-
abilities—had been a powerful resource for American

military commanders for the past several years. Once, satellite photos had always been routed by the NSA through NPIC, the National Photographic Interpretation Center in Washington, D.C., which distributed them to the President and to senior policymakers. Only slowly, if at all, had they reached the commanders in the field who could use them tactically—and who needed them quickly. TENCAP allowed commanders in the field to request satellite coverage on the spot, and to have the results in their hands within minutes.

"The Baltic Fleet," Tombstone said. He recognized the huge, Soviet carrier in two of the shots. He'd seen the *Kreml* firsthand two years ago off the coast of India. "Where were these taken?"

Brandt's mouth twisted, an unhappy scowl. "Less than one hundred miles from here. It seems our Russian friends managed to steal a march on us. Took advantage of the storm last night to slip up the Norway Coast. Our best guess is they're heading for the landing beaches. They could be there by late this morning."

"The Marine escorts?" II MEF had arrived with about a dozen escorts—several frigates, four guided missile destroyers, and the nuclear-powered cruiser *Virginia*.

"About midnight last night," Tarrant said slowly, "the *Kiev* battle group sortied past North Cape. *Virginia* and most of the other surface combatants deployed north toward Fuglöy Banks to meet them . . . and to avoid being pinned against the coast if they made a stab for the landing beaches."

Tombstone closed his eyes, picturing the tactical situation. "Leyte Gulf," he said.

"That," Tarrant said, "is just about the size of it."

In 1944, during the war in the Pacific, U.S. Marines had gone ashore at Leyte Gulf in the Philippines. The Japanese fleet had deployed in a complex plan to decoy the American carrier and battleship fleets under Admiral Halsey out of position, allowing a column of Japanese battleships and cruisers under Admiral Kurita to strike the undefended beaches at Leyte.

In one of the most heroic and desperate actions of the war, "Taffy 3," a squadron of light escort carriers, destroyers, and destroyer escorts under the command of Rear Admiral Thomas Sprague—all that stood between Kurita and the Marine beaches—had hurled itself against the enemy. In a furious assault by sea and air, they sunk two Japanese cruisers and damaged another, while losing two escort carriers and three destroyers to the heavy pounding by enemy battleships. Then, miraculously, the vastly superior Japanese force had turned and fled. The tenacity of the American defense had convinced Admiral Kurita that he was facing the main body of the American fleet, and he had broken off the attack at the moment of victory.

"There's just one problem with the analogy," Captain Brandt pointed out. "Admiral Kurita didn't know what he was facing, didn't know the true strength of the squadron he was up against. If he'd had spy satellites, Leyte Gulf might've had a different ending."

"That's right," Tarrant said. "The Russians for damn sure know just how strong we are and exactly where we are. I don't think we're going to be able to surprise them."

"Do you think they're heading for the beaches?" Tombstone asked. "Or for us?"

"The beaches," Tarrant said. "Almost certainly. *Virginia*'s hotfooting it back to Vagsfjord at flank, but she won't arrive until sometime this afternoon. *Ike* and *Kennedy* won't be in the area until this evening sometime. The enemy knows that. They'll want to get in their licks against the grunts while they can. Hell, if they can sink the Marine transports, they won't care if they lose their whole fleet. They'll have us by the balls. They can ask for an armistice and we'll have to give it to them. We'll have lost Norway."

"We're betting that the *Kreml* will launch an air strike against us as they pass," Brandt said. "We could expect that, oh, sometime between zero-nine hundred and eleven hundred hours this morning. Their idea will probably be, if they can kill us, fine . . . but don't stop for anything until they reach the beaches."

Tombstone looked down at the top map on the pile covering the table. It showed Vestfjord and the Lofotens, with *Jefferson* in the lee of the islands, her frigates and destroyers spread across the southern reaches of the fjord as an ASW screen.

Outside of a scattering of Norwegian corvettes and frigates, they were all that stood between the Russian Baltic fleet and the Marines.

"So what's the plan?" he asked. He looked up and grinned. "I assume you gentlemen are preparing an attack."

"The best defense . . ." Brandt began, and they laughed.

"I'm ordering the battle group out of the fjord," Tarrant said. His finger traced a route southwest, past Vaerøy Island into the Norwegian Sea. "The Lofotens are pretty rugged. Lots of mountains, and the weather's still pretty dirty. We might be able to hit them with a surface attack before they realize we're not in our anchorage anymore."

"What we need from you, CAG," Brandt said, "is a plan to minimize damage to the *Jefferson* during enemy surface-to-surface and air-to-surface attacks. We plan to keep the *Jeff* well clear of the major fighting, but you can bet that *Kreml*'s air group is going to be all over us. *Jefferson* is going to be vulnerable."

Tombstone thought again of the Harpoons and other munitions he'd seen piled on the carrier's decks the evening before. The next Soviet attack against the carrier would not be hampered by the mountains of a fjord. If *Jefferson*'s decks were cluttered with planes rearming and refueling . . .

An earlier thought returned to Tombstone with redoubled force. *Maybe the ultimate test of leadership is being able to send shipmates, friends, out to die.*

"Actually," he said, "there's something else we could try. It means *Jefferson* might take some damage, but it could give the bad guys some grief."

"Let's hear it," Tarrant said.

Tombstone hesitated. "There's just one thing. I'm going to want to be in on this one myself. In the air."

"Leading the air strike, you mean?" Brandt asked.

"Yes, sir. I figure I've got some flight time coming. With my people."

Tarrant nodded. "I think you've *earned* that right, CAG."

"Thank you, sir." Tombstone began explaining his idea.

CHAPTER 25
Thursday, 26 June

The airstrip was positioned almost at the water's edge, with a view northwest across Ofotfjord toward the rugged hills near Bogen. The overcast was gone, replaced by dazzling sun and temperatures in the eighties. Smoke continued to stain the crystalline sky above Narvik from the burning fuel storage tanks, however. Fortunately, large quantities of fuel remained at the Narvik airfield, and more had been flown in by KA-6D tankers an hour before. A team of Marine aircrewmen surrounded Tombstone's F/A-18 Hornet, topping off the tanks and checking the racks of ordnance slung beneath his wings. One of them held the arming wires aloft, showing Tombstone that his warload of six Sidewinders and two Sparrows were ready for launch.

Tombstone tossed a salute in acknowledgment, then turned his attention back to the controls in front of him, refreshing his memory.

It had been a while since he'd been in the high-tech cockpit of an F/A-18. His personal flying favorite had always been the Tomcat, but as Deputy CAG he'd been expected to be familiar with all of the aircraft under his command. Two weeks ago, he'd largely been flying S-3 Vikings, and before that he'd been getting in plenty of hours with A-6 Intruders, EA-6 Prowlers, and E-2C Hawkeyes.

But he'd flown Hornets before and loved the nimble, high-tech, dual-role aircraft. The "office" was one of the most advanced in the air, featuring HOTAS—Hands-On Throttle And Stick—technology and three multifunctional displays, or MFDs. There were almost no traditional instruments on the console, save for some backups tucked away at the bottom of the panel. Necessary flight data was presented on computer displays. One screen was the Combined Map/Electronic Display, or COMED, which projected radar information and other data against a moving electronic map. All of the displays could be changed at the touch of a menu button. If his memory needed jogging, there was even a built-in vocal warning, a soothing female voice to tell him that he was low on fuel or had neglected to raise his landing gear.

A Hornet-driving friend of Tombstone's had once said that the F/A-18 was so advanced it *almost* made it possible for one man to run the thing; unlike the Tomcat, which had a RIO in the backseat to handle communications, radar, and some of the weapons, the Hornet had only a single occupant. That wasn't so bad in a dogfight, but an air-to-ground attack could get pretty hairy when one man had to fly the aircraft and target and release the warload as well.

But as Tombstone saluted the ground crew and brought the engines to life, he knew that the Hornet represented a truly remarkable symbiosis of Man and Machine. The old fighter pilot's expression "strapping on an airplane" took on new meaning in a Hornet. Tombstone *was* the airplane, its control surfaces and weapons extensions of his brain, no less than his hands and feet.

"Dragon Leader, this is Camelot" sounded in his headset. "Come in, Dragon."

"Dragon copies. Go ahead."

Dragon, the code name for those of the CVW-20 aircraft—almost all of *Jefferson*'s air wing—that were now transferred ashore, scattered among four different air bases. Tombstone had been overseeing the shuttling of those planes from *Jefferson*'s flight deck to Norwegian airfields just recaptured from the Soviets all morning. Glancing through his canopy, he could see other F/A-18s arrayed by the Narvik tower. His own Hornet, the modex number newly repainted to give him a "CAG bird" number of 300, was ready to roll.

"Dragon, we have bandits in the air, bearing three-five-five, our position, range three-zero miles. The party is about to begin."

"Roger that, Camelot. Dragon is on the way." He shifted frequencies. "Dragon, Dragon, this is Dragon Leader. The sword is drawn. Repeat, the sword is drawn." As he spoke, his hand gentled the HOTAS throttle grip under his left hand forward, and the thrust from his twin GE turbofans built to a thundering, shuddering roar.

His command, relayed to every aircraft in the wing either directly or through the E-2C Hawkeyes code-named Bifrost, set forty aircraft moving. Others, the F-14 Tomcats of VF-97, were already in the air, flying CAP above the battle group as it steamed out of the fjord to engage the enemy. At Narvik, Tombstone was leading eight Hornets of VFA-161—the Javelins—plus six surviving Intruders of VA-84—the Blue Rangers—into the air. The remaining squadrons had been posted to the airstrip at Evanskjaer, close to the Marine beaches; to Andøya among the Vester-ålens; and to Bodø, captured only hours ago by a heliborne Marine Regimental Landing Team.

"Tower, this is Dragon Leader," he called. "Request permission to roll."

"Dragon Leader, Narvik Air Control. You are clear for takeoff. Wind one-eight at zero-one-zero. Good luck, Navy."

"Thank you, Marines. Keep the beer cold. This shouldn't take long."

"Roger that, Navy. But if you miss the bastards, you're buying."

His eyes scanned the runway ahead, so strangely different from his usual view, a pitching deck with sea and sky seeming close enough to touch. The Narvik strip was

littered with patches. Marine combat engineers had been
working all morning to repair shell holes and craters in the
tarmac, covering them with swaths of wire mesh and filling
them with asphalt. Ironically, most of those craters had been
made by A-6s during the raids to draw out the *Soyuz*. He
hoped the Marine engineers knew their jobs.

It was strange not having a deck officer, a cat crew, or the
ritual of a catapult launch. He had his clearance; pressing
the throttle forward, he set the Hornet moving, rolling faster
and faster down an uncharacteristically motionless ramp.
His right hand gripped the stick, holding it steady against
the bumps and thumps of the uneven terrain beneath the
fighter's wheels, then easing it back. The Hornet's nose
came up and the roughness vanished. He soared toward
blue sky.

He exulted.

Captain Matthew Magruder, CAG of CVW-20, was
airborne again, unshackled after what seemed like months
of confinement within *Jefferson*'s gray corridors.

The faces of two people hovered at the edge of his mind,
friends, one dead, one living, both a part of him. *For you,
Coyote,* he thought. *And for you, Pamela.*

Tombstone felt complete, victorious, the professional
warrior vaulting skyward to give battle, man-to-man, among
the clouds.

He was where he belonged.

0855 hours Zulu (0955 hours Zone)
MiG 1010
Over the Norwegian Sea

Captain Sergei Sergeivich Terekhov held his MiG-29 on
course, his eyes scanning the horizon ahead. They were
almost there . . . close enough to the American carrier
that he could taste it.

He savored the coming rematch. The humiliation of his
defeat three days earlier burned like a living fire. Pulled

from the sea by the crew of the *Doblestnyy*, who joked about the big fish they'd caught, put ashore two days later at Bodø, where he learned that *Soyuz* had been sunk and the Marines come ashore at Narvik, he'd had to beg for an aircraft from the Soviet base commander there. He'd flown across to the *Kreml* early that morning, learning only after he landed on the carrier that Bodø had been captured by enemy forces shortly after he'd taken off. Later he'd learned that his promotion to captain first rank had not been forwarded to Moscow before *Soyuz* had gone down.

Needless to say, he was no longer air wing commander. *Soyuz*'s air wing had been obliterated with the carrier, save for a few that had been in the air and managed to flee to nearby air bases. Most of those had been captured when the Marines landed.

It was like a personal insult. Twice now he'd narrowly escaped death at the hands of the Americans. Terekhov possessed a rigid and uncompromising pride, a fierce arrogance born of steel and flame that demanded he give back to the Americans what they had given him. His MiG-29 was configured for precision attack, with two AA-8 infrared homing missiles on his outer pylons and two AS-7 tactical air-to-surface missiles slung from mid-wing pylons.

Those AA-7s would bury themselves inside the huge, vulnerable target that was the U.S.S. *Thomas Jefferson*— that Terekhov had promised himself. Admiral Ivanov, strangely, did not seem that interested in *Jefferson*, was content to neutralize the threat the American carrier posed to his rear and pass it by, so intent was he on reaching the Marine landing beaches at Harstad and Tennevik.

Terekhov knew better. Destroy the *Jefferson*, and the heart and soul were gone from the American effort in Norway. The American carrier had been behind every reverse, every delay, every defeat the Soviets had suffered in their invasion of Scandinavia, from the stubborn and irrational resistance by Norwegian freedom fighters and Home Defense forces, to the sinking of the *Soyuz* himself.

He wanted to see the Yankee carrier *burn*.

The wing commander aboard *Kreml* was an idiot, a Party-nurtured *aparatchik* named Chelyag. It had not been difficult for Terekhov to impress Chelyag with his previous experience in combat with the American carrier, and to suggest a course of action. At his urging, Chelyag had agreed to let him try a low-altitude approach with a flight of six MiG-29s. It would, he promised the pudgy-faced wing commander, divide the American defenses, and allow the main force of forty-some MiGs and Sukhois to break through the American air defenses.

In fact, Hangman, as the six MiGs were called, would almost certainly be able to slip close to the American carrier undetected. The enemy would be concentrating on Chelyag's main group, and Terekhov had swung the flight far around the American ships and was approaching them from the south. Only meters above the water, under fierce ECM and jamming, they would be almost impossible to spot.

"Hangman Leader, Fortress," a voice said over his headset. "Range to target forty-six kilometers. Normal air activity with some ECM. You are clear for attack run."

Terekhov acknowledged, then dropped the MiG toward the sea.

0903 hours Zulu (1003 hours Zone)
CBG-14
The Norwegian Sea

The enemy planes stooped like hawks on the American battle group as they slid past Vaerøy on their way to the open sea. *Kearny* was in the lead, the frigate *Stephen Decatur* close astern. South, screening for a submarine threat from that direction, was the destroyer *John A. Winslow*, while *Jefferson* and *Shiloh* brought up the rear.

The first air clash was short, intense, and violent. Phoenix missiles launched at long range by the VF-97 War Eagles' CAP drew first blood, striking MiGs and Sukhois in flaming bursts of smoke and debris, sending wrecked tangles of debris plummeting from the sky at the ends of long, unfurling streamers of white.

There was no room in these narrow seas for multiple layers of defenses or for elaborate maneuver. Despite their losses, the Soviet planes bore in straight from the north as the War Eagles, their AIM-54s expended, vaulted forward to grapple with them plane-to-plane, closing to "knife-fighting range" in seconds. Standard missiles and Sea Sparrows whooshed from the deck launchers of *Kearny* and *Decatur* almost in unison. For perhaps five minutes, a dogfight raged in the clear summer sky, the vapor trails of clashing aircraft interweaving and looping through the sky like a tangle of fishing line, a classic "furball." A MiG disintegrated as a Standard struck it dead center and ignited its fuel tanks in a searing blast; a War Eagle Tomcat pilot called "Fox one" as he loosed a radar-homing Sparrow at his target, guiding the SARH missile across five miles of empty air and squarely into the fuselage of an Su-27; seconds later, the Tomcat's left engine exploded as an AA-8 Aphid curved in on the heat of its exhaust, killing pilot and RIO and sending the F-14 plunging toward the crystalline blue of the sea below.

There had been eight Tomcats in the CAP to begin with. The number was now seven . . . now six as another Soviet missile struck home. There'd been forty Soviet planes in the attack wave to begin with. Fifteen of those fell to Phoenix strikes and surface-to-air missiles from the ships in the opening minutes of the combat, then seven more to Sparrows and Sidewinders as the opponents came to grips.

Aircraft fell from the skies in flames.

0906 hours Zulu (1006 hours Zone)
MiG 1010
Over the Norwegian Sea

Captain Terekhov glanced left and right. The five other MiGs of Hangman Flight held formation, bellies still scant meters above the sea as they flashed south toward the

American carrier, so low that sea spray drenched his canopy as though he were flying headlong through a rainstorm. They were close enough now that their low altitude would soon be no protection to enemy radar.

Yes! The threat-warning light lit up on his console, and he heard the shrill warble of a weapons lock in his headset. But it was too late now, too late to save the *Jefferson.* He could see the American carrier now, a vast, flat-topped gray cutout on the northern horizon, ten miles away. The sky was filled with twisting contrails, and the straighter, faster scratches of deadly missiles. The radar pulses probing his aircraft now were probably from the enemy's Aegis cruiser, which was protecting its larger charge like a dog protecting its master.

Too late! Terekhov gave his console a last check. Weapons armed, gyros running, guidance locked. He brought the MiG up slightly off the deck, giving himself clearance for launch.

Fire!

The AS-7 Kerry ship-killer dropped clear, ignited, and streaked toward the American carrier. The attack plan he'd suggested that morning to *Kreml*'s wing commander had worked perfectly, though not quite as Chelyag had anticipated. Chelyag's planes were falling from the skies like nuts from a shaken tree, while Terekhov's flight had flown all the way around the Americans to come upon them from the south, slipping in under their CAP and radar umbrellas, sneaking in close for the kill. His second AS-7 whooshed clear of the mid-wing pylon. Seconds later, the other MiG-29s of the flight began launching their ship-killers as well.

Ten AS-7 Kerry ship-killers sped north across the water at Mach 1, targeting the *Jefferson.* At Mach 1, they would reach their target in less than one minute.

Flying low, staying in the radar shadow of the rugged, sawtooth mountains of the Lofotens, Tombstone led the formation of Hornets and Intruders west-southwest, following the island chain so closely that it was unlikely Soviet radars would pick them out from the background clutter. They maintained strict radio silence. Other formations, Tombstone knew, were making their way down the Vestfjord, from Evanskjaer and Andøya, and, skimming the wave tops from the southeast, from the newly liberated field at Bodø. So many aircraft, taking off from widely separated airstrips and traveling at different speeds.

Jefferson and her escorts should by now be rounding Vaerøy Island, at the southwestern fringes of the Lofotens. According to the latest update from the E-2Cs, Bifrost One and Bifrost Two, the *Kreml* was now about forty miles north of the *Jefferson* and twenty-five miles west of Moskenesøya Island, moving northeast at thirty knots.

Tombstone checked the COMED display, which showed data both from his Hornet's APG-65 radar and from one of the Hawkeyes, which let him, in effect, see beyond the mountains. There they were, on the nose. The cluster of blips marking *Kreml*, two Kirov cruisers, and an array of smaller vessels was clearly visible. Prompts on his display showed course, speed, and waypoints.

He looked to his right. Off his starboard wingtip, between him and the sheltering, gray-green mass of the Lofotens, was Hornet 301, flown by Commander Jake "Red" Bledsoe, the skipper of the Javelins. Beyond him was Hornet 304, Red's wingman, Lieutenant Commander Norman "Hurricane" Hawker, a fiery young aviator who nevertheless flew with the ice-cold precision of an engineer.

No radio communications yet . . . but he could attract

their attention with a brief waggle of his wings. *Get ready. Almost there* . . .

The other aircraft responded with waggles of their own, and he saw Bledsoe's helmeted figure give him an answering thumbs-up from his cockpit.

Their turning point lay just ahead, a narrow pass, like a saddle, winding between two rugged hills on the island of Moskenesøya. That island was the southernmost of the major Lofotens, a rugged strip of land twenty miles long. Five miles beyond was the tiny islet of Mosken.

The gap between was the fabled Maelstrom. When Tombstone had been a kid, fourteen, maybe fifteen years old, he'd read Verne's *Twenty Thousand Leagues Under the Sea* and wondered if the "Norway Maelstrom" was real.

Apparently it was, though not so wild or deadly as Jules Verne had suggested when he had it swallow Captain Nemo and the fabled *Nautilus*. Tombstone was sorry that he wouldn't get to see it.

He checked his map, comparing the terrain to the land forms drifting past his right wing. There it was, the pass. He cut back on his throttle and descended, sliding in front of and below Red and Hurricane and angling toward the gap. The other Hornets and the six A-6s of the Blue Rangers followed.

Hillsides exploded on either side of the Hornet, gray and green blurs sloping down to meet somewhere a few hundred feet below his aircraft. Houses, a tiny village, checkered farmland flashed by. Ahead, the open sea filled the notch between the mountains with searing blue.

The Soviet fleet was now twenty-five miles away. At 560 knots, the maximum speed of the A-6 Intruders at sea level, they would be there in less than three minutes.

CHAPTER 26
Thursday, 26 June

0908 hours Zulu (1008 hours Zone)
CBG-14
The Norwegian Sea

The U.S.S. *Jefferson*, in company with all of the Nimitz-class supercarriers save the *Carl Vinson*, mounted three CIWS point-defense Gatlings. They'd been named—possibly by a sailor with a love for science fiction—after the three chunky-looking robots of the SF classic *Silent Running*, Huey, Dewey, and Louie, though some aboard maintained that they were white and stubby-looking and therefore named after the nephews of Donald Duck. Louie was mounted on a sponson on the port side forward, just ahead of the main port elevator. Dewey was all the way aft, covering a broad sweep astern and to port. Huey was on the flight deck to starboard, outboard of the island.

The incoming missiles were spotted almost at once, and *Jefferson*'s point-defense systems, set on manual because of the large number of friendly aircraft overhead, were activated. The targets were south of *Jefferson*, which put them on the port side, within Louie's domain. Guided by its powerful radar and tracking computer system, the white-painted silo slewed, the gun elevated, and bursts of depleted uranium slugs shrieked toward the missiles. Radar tracked targets and rounds simultaneously; the computer corrected the aim and triggered another burst. One Kerry flashed into flame, lashing the sea with shrapnel. Another missile exploded . . . and another . . .

Astern of the *Jefferson,* the Aegis cruiser *Shiloh* entered the fight. Standard missiles and one of the two CIWS Gatlings that could bear joined in, killing three more. RBOC guns thumped, spreading blossoms of chaff, but the missiles already had a solid lock on the carrier and could not be so easily distracted.

Unfortunately, Louie's maintenance enclosure was a sponson located only twenty yards forward of the fueling deck that had been hit by a Kerry missile during the fight in Romsdalfjord. Shrapnel had sprayed the CIWS maintenance enclosure. One piece, a chunk of steel no larger than a .45-caliber bullet, had pierced Louie's silo and half-severed a power lead.

Power still flowed to the motors that spun the silo, and earlier diagnostics had checked out okay. But with a war on and men driven to the limits of endurance by lack of sleep and constant work, the puncture had been overlooked.

Now, as the silo slewed left and right, tracking incoming missiles, the motion was enough to part the cable. There was a flash of light, a stink of burning rubber, and the portside CIWS went dead.

Given time, the unit could have been easily repaired. Given time, Captain Brandt could have ordered *Jefferson* to swing north, bringing Dewey to bear, or *Shiloh* could have moved up to help cover the carrier with her point-defense weapons. Given time . . .

But there was no time. At the speed of sound, four Kerry missiles that had survived the gauntlet of their approach howled in, one after the other, and slammed into the *Jefferson* with devastating, steel-rending explosions.

The massive, armored doors sealing the oval opening from the hangar deck to the port-side elevator were smashed, erupting inward in a spray of white-hot, molten steel. Fire erupted as fuel lines cracked and stores ignited. Men fled the wall of flame, their uniforms afire, or dropped to the deck and burned. An A-6 Intruder, parked on the hangar deck while battle damage to its radio was checked, exploded with a detonation like a five-hundred-pound bomb, the concussion contained and absorbed by the massive steel bulkheads of the hangar deck. Another missile hit the flight deck opposite the island, shearing through Catapults Three and Four and sending a shotgun blast of shrapnel cracking into the island. On the bridge, Captain Brandt went to his knees as fragments of glass tore his face and arm, and the helmsman writhed on the deck, shrieking in agony until corpsmen arrived to jab the needle of a morphine syrette into his neck and drag him away.

The third and fourth missiles struck the hull amidships, almost at the waterline, but there the bilges were thick, the hull heavily armored. *Jefferson* shrugged off the blows like a prizefighter in the ring.

But her hangar deck was an inferno, fed by JP-5 pouring from torn fuel lines. A KA-6D, an Intruder equipped for air-to-air refueling, exploded as the flames swept across it, adding to the carnage and destruction in *Jefferson*'s bowels.

A hundred men died in the inferno, as flames roared from the breached elevator doors, as steam boiled from ruptured lines alongside the catapults, as smoke erupted like some monstrous black djinn above the stricken carrier, a nightmare giant pronouncing its verdict of doom.

0910 hours Zulu (1010 hours Zone)
Hornet 300
Over the Norwegian Sea

Miles north of the *Jefferson,* Hornets tangled with MiGs and Sukhois in a sharp, brief encounter.

"*Watch it, Red! Two on your six!*"

"*Comin' around now! Gonna break left!*"

"*Roger that! I'm on 'em, Sidewinder lock! Go! Go!*"

"*I'm out of here!*"

"*Fox two!*"

The Soviet CAP was small and widely scattered. Three Soviet planes were downed before the others fled, and the way was open for the Harpoon-laden Intruders thundering west, still bearing on a trio of gigantic radar targets.

The range closed. Tombstone separated from the other aircraft, gaining altitude to give himself and his radar a clearer view of the entire battle. Ahead, the sky exploded in the shattering, bursting, tracer-flecked patterns of heavy antiaircraft defenses. He concentrated on his flying for a moment, weaving in and out of the triple-A patterns, twice breaking hard and firing chaff as a missile streaked up to meet him. The second missile exploded somewhere behind his F/A-18 and rocked the aircraft. For a moment, Tombstone battled the controls, but then he fell into calm air and brought the Hornet level. He looked forward through his HUD . . .

. . . and then he saw it, seven miles ahead and a mile below, *Kreml,* pride of the Soviet fleet, vanguard of the flotilla that was to have been the fulfillment of Russia's envy of the massive, globe-spanning fleet of supercarriers possessed by her archrival. Tombstone had overflown that ship before, during the joint U.S.-USSR operations in the Indian Ocean two years earlier. Her lines were at once familiar and alien.

She . . . no, Tombstone thought, for a Russian ship was *he.* He was not as big as the *Jefferson.* A last-minute change in his design had transformed him from a planned nuclear supercarrier to a conventionally powered vessel, and he lacked *Jefferson*'s steam catapults, relying instead on a ski jump forward like the British carriers to boost launching aircraft skyward.

But he was still impressive . . . especially now, viewed from five thousand feet up, as a dozen gun mounts on his deck and superstructure flickered and winked, hurling shells into the sky.

Tombstone's Hornet bucked and shuddered. Antiaircraft fire rose like a wall in front of him, puff upon puff of white smoke, as missile contrails scratched their twisting ways across the sky, threading toward the American strike planes in threes, in fives, in whole volleys of surface-to-air destruction, as green and orange tracers painted the sky in glowing splatters and broken streams of light.

An Intruder, dropping toward the deck for its attack run, collided head-on with a SAM from the *Irkutsk*. The detonation blew the A-6 into fiery fragments, with no chance at all that either pilot or B/N could have survived. Seconds later, one of the Hornets twisted wildly right, pumping chaff, but a Soviet missile snapped in from beneath, shattering his left wing in a flash and a shower of smoking fragments. Tombstone saw the flash as the canopy blew clear and the ejection seat hurled the pilot clear of the falling wreck. His eyes followed the man down, searching for a sign of . . . yes! Good chute!

One by one, lean, deadly, winged pencils slipped from the surviving Intruders, spat flame, and cleaved sky toward the Soviet ships. Tombstone watched the tracks curving in . . . accelerating. There was a flash as one Harpoon was struck by CIWS fire well short of the target, but seconds later two of the big AGMs slammed into *Kreml*'s starboard beam just forward of the island. The shock waves from the concussions jittered outward across the sea, like ripples in a pond.

Damn it! The ship-killers were hitting, but they weren't enough to do the job. How were they going to kill this monster?

And two more Intruders had been hit, were going down. With a shock, Tombstone realized that there were only three Blue Rangers left.

"All Dragons, all Dragons!" he called. "Split up and jink! Don't give them a steady target!"

Like a blossoming flower, Intruders and Hornets scattered across the sky.

One A-6, positioned badly for a run on the *Kreml,* elected instead to target one of the towering, floating fortresses cruising beyond. Both missiles plunged into the Kirov-class cruiser, one on the superstructure near the bridge, the other plunging into the hull. Flames seared from gaping holes where the missiles had struck. Tombstone saw fragments, gun mounts, boat davits, pieces of radar antennae and funnel spinning wildly through the air, but gun and missile fire from the big ship continued almost unabated. Oil glittered like metallic water, staining the surface of the sea.

Were the handful of Intruders and Hornets from Narvik the only American aircraft that had made it? Tombstone searched the sky, dividing his attention between an eyeball inspection of the blue around his canopy and the crawling, static-blasted images on his displays. The Tomcats of Viper Squadron had been deployed to Evanskjaer. Where . . . no, there they were. Just coming through the Lofotens forty miles northeast. But what about the other Intruders?

"Dragon Leader, this is Dealer. Look what followed us in! Can we keep them?"

Tombstone glanced at his displays, then at a new line of aircraft thundering in from the north. There were six Death Dealer Intruders out of Andøya . . . and they were accompanied by twelve stubby-looking aircraft with wings that canted down sharply from their fuselages.

"Dragon Leader, this is Sea Strike," a new voice called. "Thought you Navy boys could use some help. How about lettin' us join the party?"

Harriers. Marine Harriers off the *Iwo Jima* and the *Nassau*. "You're just in time, Marines," Tombstone replied. "Come on in! There's plenty to go around!"

0912 hours Zulu (1012 hours Zone), 24 June
Soviet Red Banner Baltic Fleet
The Norwegian Sea

From miles away the damage to *Kreml* did not look serious, but aboard the Russian carrier itself it seemed as though Hell was opening from the skies. Admiral Ivanov stood on *Kreml*'s bridge, leaning against the instrument panel, trying to stand upright as the shudders of repeated explosions banged and thudded through the deck beneath his feet. Shattered glass was everywhere; the bridge windows had been blown out. Blood dripped down the aft bulkhead where the quartermaster had died moments before, his arm sliced away by a whirling, scalpel-edged splinter of glass.

Ivanov turned, and his eyes met those of Kamarov, the captain. The man's lean, Siberian-weathered face was bloody, the mouth set in a disapproving scowl. "We cannot stand much more of this, Admiral," Kamarov said. "*Kreml* cannot take such punishment!"

Numbly, Ivanov nodded. "I agree, Captain." He flinched as an American Intruder shrieked toward the carrier, howling out of the north. Flames blazed from the aircraft's shattered tail as CIWS weapons tracked it. Like a missile it hurtled low over the deck, then burst like a bomb in the sea a hundred meters astern.

"Another carrier!" Ivanov gasped. "Another American carrier!"

Kamarov's scowl deepened. "Another carrier? What carrier?"

Weakly, he waved an arm toward the north, where fresh contrails were painting themselves above the horizon. "These aircraft are not coming from the *Jefferson,* but from the north! From the beachhead! Another supercarrier must have arrived. *Eisenhower.* It must be the *Eisenhower!*"

It was clear to Ivanov. The fierceness of the American air strike was overwhelming, totally unexpected. Ivanov's advisors had insisted that the Americans would be unable to get more than a couple of squadrons aloft in the short time they had after discovering *Kreml*'s movement, that *Kreml*'s air search would detect the launch, that the enemy would be totally incapable of launching a coordinated attack on the Soviet carrier battle group, at least not before *Kreml*'s own air wing had crippled or destroyed the *Jefferson.*

Intelligence. His fist came down on the console in front of him. Intelligence. A perennial problem within the Soviet military system was the slowness with which intelligence from, say, spy satellites was disseminated to the field commanders who needed it. *Eisenhower* must have joined the Marine forces last night, but Moscow had not yet gotten around to passing on that critical piece of information to him!

It fit. The Red Banner Baltic Fleet was outnumbered now, and in danger of being destroyed. If *Kreml* and her escorts were destroyed, the Baltic and the approaches to Leningrad would be wide open, helpless to Western invasion. He needed to preserve his fleet . . . for the safety of the *Rodina.*

"Put us about, Kamarov," he snapped.

"Sir?"

"Bring us around. Heading southwest. We have no chance of reaching the enemy beachhead now. Signalman! Pass the word to the other vessels in the fleet!"

"Yes, Admiral!"

Ponderously, beleaguered by the pinprick attacks by enemy air, *Kreml* and his consorts began coming about. From the air, their wakes described enormous white semi-circles across the explosion-pocked blue of the sea as *Kreml, Tallinn, Irkutsk,* and a dozen lesser vessels came 180 degrees about and began heading back in the direction from which they'd come.

By chance the five ships of the *Jefferson* battle group lay directly in their path.

0914 hours Zulu (1014 hours Zone)
Hornet 300
Over the Norwegian Sea

"Damn it, men, the bastards are trying to get away!" Tombstone felt a wild, exuberant rush of emotion, a giddiness overwhelming his usual rational approach to flying.

"Dragon Leader, Dragon Leader!" a voice called. "This is Tower Keep."

Tower Keep. That was *Shiloh,* where Tarrant was coordinating the battle.

"I read you, Tower Keep. Go ahead!"

"Dragon, request a radar paint of Citadel. Can you comply, over?"

Tombstone put his Hornet into a sweeping turn. He was clear of the triple-A now, and the enemy missile defenses appeared to have been scattered by the arrival of more attack aircraft. Missiles continued to slide through the air, to burst against the clear blue sky. Smoke spilled from stricken ships plowing through oil-streaked seas.

Yes, he was in the open, unnoticed beyond the fury of the Intruder and Harrier attacks. He guided the F/A-18 into a position where he could paint the *Kreml* with the beam from his APG-65. "Roger, Camelot. How's this?"

"Hold it right there, Dragon Leader, and keep your head down. Fire in the hole!"

0914 hours Zulu (1014 hours Zone)
U.S.S. *Lawrence Kearny*
Vanguard of CBG-14

Commander James Tennyson had never expected surface combat to be like this. For the first time since World War II, major surface warships were slugging it out in sight of one another!

"Bridge, CIC!" a voice from the bridge speaker called. "We have a SARH lock! *Shiloh* IDs it as the Russkie carrier!"

Shiloh had to be using spotters to sort targets from junk in the ECM clutter that was filling the skies. "Then fire, dammit!" Tennyson barked. "Fire before I have to ram the bastards!"

The launch-alert klaxon rasped warning. Then, with a roar of white noise and a blinding glare, the first of *Kearny*'s Standard SM-1 MR missiles blasted away from the Mark 13 launcher on the forward deck, followed almost immediately

by its twin. As the missiles arced toward the north, the
H-shape of the launch rails swiveled and rose straight up.
Hatches opened beneath them, and two more Standard
missiles slid straight up and onto the rails, locking in place.
The launcher swiveled again, tracking an unseen point in the
sky . . . and the roar engulfed the bridge once more.

Kearny was still firing minutes later, when three incoming SS-N-19 cruise missiles launched from the *Irkutsk*
struck the frigate amidships and detonated with a shattering
roar.

0915 hours Zulu (1015 hours Zone)
Hornet 300
Over the Norwegian Sea

Tombstone saw the Standards streak in from the south,
homing on the reflected radar energy from his APG-65.
With a small shock of realization, it occurred to him that this
was like firing SARH-guided Sparrows at an enemy plane,
as he identified the *Soyuz* for the combat center aboard
Shiloh and, through her, the rest of CBG-14.

Only these ship-launched killers were each three times
heavier than a Sparrow and carried a hell of a lot more
punch. Whipping across the waves, they slammed into the
Soviet carrier. Violent flashes snapped from *Kreml*'s deck,
just forward of the island; close by the ski jump; port, near
one of the elevators. Tombstone saw hull plating and radar
antennas, tow tractors and the wing of a parked aircraft all
hurled into the air like chips in a gale.

Smoke boiled from *Kreml*'s flanks as repeated hits by
surface-to-surface and air-to-surface missiles took their toll.
Farther away, nearly ten miles distant, flashes of light
rippled along the superstructure of both Kirov cruisers, and
a Soviet destroyer, its bow nearly sheared away by the
explosion of a Harpoon, foundered and sank.

Tombstone could see the American ships in the distance
now, flecks of gray on the southern horizon. He saw pillars

of smoke there and felt a chill. Those were burning ships. How many had been hit . . . how many destroyed? Dozens of missile trails were crisscrossing in the sky between the two fleets, a battle of epic, of titanic proportions waged by radar and high-speed computers and long-range missiles flailing at one another across a range of only a few short miles.

The contest would not, *could* not last much longer.

CHAPTER 27
Thursday, 26 June

0917 hours Zulu (1017 hours Zone)
MiG 1010
Over the Norwegian Sea

Flying north low above the water, Terekhov noted the lone American Hornet, circling like a hawk beyond the reach and snap of Soviet antiaircraft fire. He was trembling inside, the adrenaline surge of seeing his missiles strike the American carrier warring with shock as he saw the pall of smoke rising from the *Kreml*.

Waterspouts towered on either side as missiles were deflected by *Kreml*'s chaff blooms or were shot down by point-defense Gatlings. But other missiles were getting through. Flash followed flash from the Soviet carrier, as fragments scattered across the surface of the sea, and flames licked roiling tatters of smoke rising from rents in the carrier's hull and deck. His instruments proved what he'd already guessed. The Hornet was a spotter, locking its radar onto the carrier for the missile barrage from the American ships. Pulling back on his stick, he rammed the throttle forward, piling on speed. His targeting pipper slid across his HUD, centering on the distant aircraft.

He would kill this American pilot . . . *now*.

A threat warning chirped, and Tombstone searched the sky. Someone had a radar lock on him, but where? . . .

There it was, a MiG-29 Fulcrum, a tiny shape rocketing toward him from the sea. The radar lock was like a challenge, a gauntlet thrown down, a demand for satisfaction.

The American battle group no longer needed his spotting. They had the target now, and missiles were continuing to slam into all of the Russian ships. Breaking contact with the *Kreml,* Tombstone turned toward the approaching MiG.

Launch! He saw the puff of smoke, the flare of ignition beneath the Fulcrum's wing. Pushing his throttle control forward, Tombstone took the enemy missile head-on, closing with it, until the air-to-air killer's white contrail seemed to be probing right into his canopy. Then he pulled the control stick over, breaking left in a savage, high-G maneuver and plunging toward the sea. Diving, loosing chaff, he twisted in his seat, keeping his eye on the contrail until certain that it had been decoyed and cleanly missed the Hornet.

"Altitude low," a soft and feminine voice warned him. The tone of the Hornet's computer was almost sexy and infuriatingly calm. "Altitude low . . ."

"Quiet, lady," he said. "I'm busy now!"

Water swept beneath the Hornet as he pulled out, scant yards above the surface. As the F/A-18 climbed, he realized that the one thing he missed in the Hornet was the reassuring chatter of a backseater. The computer voice was simply not the same.

Tombstone saw the MiG centered in his HUD, squarely under his target pipper.

He was close enough for a Sidewinder but decided to go

for a radar lock instead. The MiG was pulling east, toward the sun, and that could scramble a heat-seeker's lock.

The Russian was turning away. "Stay with him, Tombstone," he muttered to himself. Damn, why didn't they build Hornets with personalities that could talk like a real backseater? "Stay with him . . ."

0918 hours Zulu (1018 hours Zone)
MiG 1010
Over the Norwegian Sea

The American was good . . . too good. Terekhov had been breaking right to put the sun behind his MiG in case the American tried for an IR-homer launch, but his opponent had gone for a short-range radar lock instead, a hard maneuver to sustain when the relative angles between the two aircraft were changing so rapidly.

Worried now, knowing he was up against a skillful adversary, Terekhov held his right break, then put his nose over into a dive, falling through a thousand meters of clear, cold air toward the sea.

Damn! Somehow, the F/A-18 turned inside the turn, as Terekhov heard the continuing, piercing warble of an enemy missile lock on his aircraft.

Terekhov turned again, trying to break the enemy's radar lock with a split-S. Glancing back, he caught the flash of a rocket ignition. Launch!

Firing chaff, he pulled up, feeling the crushing pressure of mounting G-forces. The missile, a SARH-active Sparrow, leaped toward him as he jinked. At the last possible second, the missile streaked overhead. There was a flash and a hard *bang* as something struck Terekhov's fuselage.

He scanned his instruments. He was losing some fuel . . . not much. Good. The Sparrow's proximity fuse had set it off as it passed the MiG, but too far away to more than nick him.

The F/A-18 was still behind him and edging closer. Terekhov searched for some way to brush the persistent

American off his tail. He couldn't outmaneuver him, but . . .

Their brief engagement had carried them north of the *Kreml.* Ahead, less than two miles away, the stern of the Soviet carrier rose like the hard, gray cliff of a Norwegian fjord. Smoke hung above her flight deck, but streams of antiaircraft tracers continued to spark and sweep through the sky.

It was dangerous. The AK-630 CIWS on *Kreml's* stern might well target him. But if he could angle in low, sweeping in above the carrier's roundoff almost as though he were coming in for a landing, and if the American followed . . .

For a few precious seconds, as Terekhov passed over the *Kreml's* flight deck, the American would be hanging in the sky astern, nakedly exposed to Soviet CIWS fire. If a human controlled the Russian carrier's point defenses, rather than a computer, he would hold his fire until the MiG was clear, then tear the Hornet into scrap.

He opened his throttles wider, hurtling toward the *Kreml's* stern.

0919 hours Zulu (1019 hours Zone)
Hornet 300
Over the Norwegian Sea

The Fulcrum dove toward the *Kreml,* and Tombstone followed. Dragging the targeting diamond in his HUD across the fleeing MiG, Tombstone held his breath as he snapped the target-select switch on his HOTAS grip, and watched the HUD symbols flash to missile-lock configuration.

"*Got you! . . .*" He squeezed the trigger, and the Sidewinder streaked across a mile and a half of open sky, struck the Fulcrum in the starboard engine, and exploded.

0919 hours Zulu (1019 hours Zone)
MiG 1010
Over the Norwegian Sea

He felt the shock, felt the wild flutter of his aircraft as he
lost control. Threat indicators exploded to life across his
console, and he heard the insistent rasp of the engine-fire
warning.

Terekhov tried to pull up and found the stick dead in his
hand. Out of control! Out of control and plunging toward
the carrier's roundoff!

He was reaching for the ejection handle when the CIWS
cannon on the stern of the Soviet aircraft carrier opened fire,
sending 30-mm shells sleeting through the flaming wreckage of his MiG. Fuel mixed with flame and the wreckage
exploded, a fiery mass of debris hurtling at nearly the speed
of sound squarely toward the Russian aircraft carrier.
Transformed into a volley of deadly missiles, the fragments
smashed into *Kreml*'s stern, driving forward, tearing steel,
igniting fuel, ripping the CIWS turret free from its mount
and smashing it into the hangar spaces, rupturing hull plates.
Half of the Fulcrum struck the water and kept traveling,
smashing through both rudders and into the ponderously
turning blades of the massive, thirty-three-ton propellers.

Kreml seemed to stagger, then hesitated as though trying
to decide whether or not to keep going.

Fire gouted into the sky. . . .

0919 hours Zulu (1019 hours Zone)
Hornet 300
Over the Norwegian Sea

Tombstone flashed across the Soviet carrier's deck, almost
like a practice touch-and-go aboard the *Jefferson* . . . or a
bolter, where his tailhook missed the arresting cables and he

roared full-throttle past the island. It was worse than a night pass, though, for he was almost completely blind, engulfed in a shroud of smoke.

He sensed, rather than saw, the carrier's island flicker past on his right, and felt the thud of small chunks of metal striking his fuselage and wings. Grimly, he held the aircraft flat and straight as it burst through the ink-black smear of smoke and emerged in the clear air beyond.

It took a moment for the reality of what had just happened to penetrate. The Fulcrum had disintegrated, smashing into the carrier's stern, and he'd flown right through the explosion. Warning lights flickered on his console. His Hornet had been damaged . . . though apparently not badly.

He held the Hornet in a long, straight climb, gaining altitude and distance from the Soviet carrier. Each second he expected to be his last, as missile or CIWS round slammed into the aircraft . . . but the sky, for the moment, was miraculously free of hurtling bits of death. Other aircraft approached from north and east . . . Batman leading the Tomcats of VF-95, more Harriers from the Marine carriers in Vagsfjord.

But the Soviet battle fleet appeared to be finished. *Irkutsk* clearly in bad trouble and appeared to be making its way slowly toward the west. The other Kirov and a smaller Kresta II had come about again and were heading northwest, pursued by Harriers and Intruders. Boiling columns of smoke, like erupting volcanos, marked *Kreml* and the sinking destroyer. Other Soviet ships were scattering toward the west.

Continued fighting was useless with *Kreml,* heart and soul of the Russian carrier battle group, aflame and helplessly adrift.

Only gradually did Tombstone allow himself to realize, with a cool, inner flood of relief, that the battle was over . . . that they had won.

Victory . . .

It scarcely seemed credible.

Turning south and descending, Tombstone approached

the American fleet. The exultation of victory was soon tempered by the realization of just how badly CBG-14 had been hurt, by how dear a price had been paid. One of the frigates—*Kearny*, he thought—was gone, nothing showing of the ship but the sharp angle of her bow probing above the water. Oil blackened the sea around her, and Tombstone could see the bobbing specks of hundreds of heads, men swimming for their lives or clinging to life rafts, as a handful of boats moved about them. Helicopters drifted and hovered. One battle was over. Another—the fight to rescue the survivors of marine disaster—had begun.

Continuing south, Tombstone turned his attention to the motionless cliff of smoke that hung in the sky ahead. *Jefferson* had been hit, and hit bad. Even now, the battle could still be lost. With *Jefferson* hurt, the Russians might reorganize, might strike again.

From his vantage point high in the crystalline sky, Tombstone looked down and willed the great carrier to live.

1030 hours Zulu (1130 hours Zone)
U.S.S. *Thomas Jefferson*
The Norwegian Sea

Aboard *Jefferson,* her officers and crew had long since given up the fight with the Soviets to face a new and more implacable foe, the firestorm that was raging out of control in the forward third of the hangar deck, in the area called Hangar Bay One.

Large sliding doors had already divided the hangar bay into three sections, a process much like dogging watertight doors, to keep fire or flooding in one part of the ship from spreading. In Damage Control Central, one deck below the aft hangar bay, the Damage Control Officer watched the spreading pattern of damage as presented by the array of three-dimensional charts across one entire bulkhead, charts showing every compartment and passageway, every fuel or water line, fire main, power line, and telephone circuit on the ship.

Fires had broken out on the 0-3 level, above Bay One, where temperatures were soaring and all personnel were being evacuated. Cats Three and Four were gone, of course, and there'd been extensive damage to the superstructure, but the Bay One fire was the real bitch.

Fortunately, the carrier's fire-control systems were still intact. Water gushed from overhead pipes, not the drizzle of an office building's automatic fire-sprinkler system, but a torrent, a downpour designed to control fuel fires in the hangar spaces . . . or decontaminate the entire carrier in a gas or nuclear attack by flooding the deck with gushing, high-pressure fountains of sea water.

For years, critics of America's aircraft carrier program had contended that supercarriers were bad investments, gigantic, traveling airfields that were turned into gigantic bombs by enormous stores of jet fuel and munitions. The spectacular destruction of *Soyuz* a few days before might well have proven the critics right; the destruction of *Jefferson* in a fiery holocaust could spell the end for Navy carriers, much as the spectacular crashes of the dirigibles *Hindenburg* and *Shenandoah* had ended the era of lighter-than-air flight.

But aircraft carriers are remarkably strong and flexible instruments, virtually unsinkable with their thousands of watertight compartments, with fire-control and damage-control systems of unparalleled scope and control.

It took time. The steel bulkheads of the hangar deck were red hot in places, and part of the deckhead sagged danger-ously as support struts gave way. When critical phone lines burned through and went dead, the DCO had to coordinate the fight through sound-powered telephones and messen-gers, as he deployed armies of sweating, gasping men in cumbersome OBA gear, wielding foam and high-pressure hoses in the inky, smoke-choked furnace of *Jefferson's* belly.

But at last, as water and foam flooded ankle-deep across

the deck of Bay One, the fires were brought under control. Cautiously, fire doors were open, sending streams of air through the stifling chamber to clear the smoke and choking, poisonous fumes . . . and to search out and expose new sources of flame that might be fanned alight by the rush of air. The DC parties waded ahead, hosing down every surface, smothering the now-retreating flames with foam.

It was nearly 1400 hours when the DCO at last made his report to the bridge.

The *Jefferson* was going to live after all.

1530 hours Zulu (1630 hours Zone)
Soviet Aircraft Carrier *Kreml*
The Norway Maelstrom

Within the five-mile gap between the islands of Mosken and Moskenesøya, the tide was running high. Through that gap, each day with the tide the water of the Norwegian Sea surged southeast into the Vestfjord, and then, as the tide changed, swirled back toward the way it had come.

Exercising their artistic license, Edgar Allen Poe and Jules Verne had greatly exaggerated the force of the so-called "Norway Maelstrom." Melville had transformed it into a living thing when he'd had Ahab vow to chase the white whale "round the Norway Maelstrom, and round Perdition's flames." In fact, the current might run as fast as seven knots when the tide was in full flood. The whirlpool had been known to snag smaller vessels, the fishing smacks and trawlers and merchantmen that had plied seafaring Norway's rugged coastline for centuries, but nothing larger.

This time, the Maelstrom had captured bigger game.

Kreml drifted southeast with the current. Had his engines been functioning he would have had no trouble pulling free, but adrift, helpless, the wrecked carrier could do nothing but move with the current. North of the tiny island of Mosken, *Kreml*'s keel ground against sand and jagged rock with a shudder that ran through his length and breadth like a fever's chill. He was already torn and battered, and this final shock was enough to break his back. He lay there, solidly aground, as the fires continued to burn.

Later, American and Norwegian vessels approached him, taking off those of his crew still trapped aboard, fishing others from the deadly currents as they were swept toward the sea by the tide. It was later estimated that perhaps a thousand of his crew had managed to escape the carrier's doom, though an accurate count was never possible. Some, perhaps many, made it ashore but never bothered to report their survival to Soviet military officials.

They had already seen too much of war and had no wish to see more.

The smoke of *Kreml*'s burning blackened the skies over the Vestfjord for another three days.

1745 hours Zulu (1845 hours Zone)
H.M.S. *Ark Royal*
The Norwegian Sea

The *Ark Royal* arrived in the area late that afternoon, too late to participate in the battle, but in time to offer her services as lifeguard and comrade-at-arms. Hundreds of men were still in the water, and the *Ark Royal*'s fleet of helicopters went to work, searching for drifting men, Americans and Soviets, plucking them from the water, dropping rafts, shuttling survivors to the British carrier's deck.

The British carrier was more than a search and rescue vessel. With *Kearny* gone, with *Decatur* damaged by a hit by a Soviet surface-to-surface missile, with *Jefferson*'s ASW helos unable to take off from her horribly torn flight deck, CBG-14 had almost no antisubmarine assets left. The Soviet fleet had scattered, but no one knew if they'd given up the fight for good. Far to the north, the *Kiev* and *Moskva* battle groups were still at large, and south, past Cape Lindesnes, the rest of the Soviet Baltic Fleet was still at sea, a potent threat.

Everyone in what was now being called the Allied Strike Force—British and American, at sea and ashore with the Marines—was painfully aware that another good, hard thrust by the Soviets might well succeed where the *Kreml* battle group had failed.

But the Soviets, too, appeared to be simply . . . waiting, as though dazed by their losses and the sheer ferocity of the fight.

At 1800 hours GMT, the BBC announced to the world that the government in London had decided to join Norway and the United States in their lonely stand in the northern seas. The *Ark Royal* battle group, until then officially on maneuvers, was declared part of the Allied Strike Force, first of Great Britain's contribution to the effort to drive the Soviet aggressors from Scandinavian territory.

The union was already more fact than fiction. Nearly a hundred Americans were aboard the *Ark Royal,* crewmen from the *Esek Hopkins* filling out technical positions to ease the British carrier's shorthandedness.

As *Ark Royal* moved alongside the *Jefferson,* a signal gun began banging out at regular intervals, a salute to the American flag still fluttering from the battered carrier's masthead. It was, Commander DuPont thought as he watched from the *Ark Royal*'s bridge, a proud tribute to brave men, alive and dead . . . and to a ship that had withstood a storm.

The following day, the first hint of revolution reached the West from Moscow and Leningrad, and the world held its collective breath.

And the day after that came word that Vorobyev had been shot, that the marshals who had begun the war were under arrest, that the great, the explosive demonstration of ''people power'' had once again brought the long-suffering republics of the Soviet Union out of the long night of slavery. Already there was endless speculation about the cause of the popular rising. Was it merely a resurgence of democratic forces long suppressed . . . or had the loss of two aircraft carriers so broken the military's prestige at home that the militarists were forever discredited?

Whatever the causes, social or military, as *Jefferson* began limping toward England in company with the *Ark Royal,* the world began to breathe once more.

EPILOGUE

"Put a scratch on her, Captain Magruder," Brandt said with mock fierceness. The bandages over his forehead and one eye and the sling on one arm gave him a piratical look. "Just one scratch, and it's coming out of your paycheck!"

"Probably for the next thousand years," Commander Parker, the XO, added with a lopsided grin. "Just try not to remember how many billions of dollars this ship cost the American taxpayers!"

Tombstone grinned nervously. It wasn't as though *Jefferson* hadn't been scratched already. Her deck and the bridge itself still showed the signs of the terrible damage inflicted during the final struggle off the Lofoten Islands— the Battle of the Norwegian Sea, as the press had tagged it. The shattered bridge windows were still open to the sky, and the air was sharp with the lingering tang of smoke and jet fuel.

"I like the way you guys have of putting a man at ease, Captain," Tombstone said.

He'd already decided he was far happier landing F-14s on a moving carrier deck than he was moving the carrier itself. Still, his career track was now aimed dead-on at the command of a carrier like *Jefferson* someday. For the first time in a long time, he knew exactly what he wanted and how he was going to go about it.

He did wonder if Brandt knew what he was doing. The Navy liked to do things in tradition-hallowed ways; all

carrier skippers were former CAGs who had survived
Washington's political tangles. Captain Brandt had sent for
Tombstone that morning and asked if he would like to take
Jefferson into her anchorage.

It was at once thrilling . . . and as terrifying as a
dogfight above the cold waters of the Norwegian Sea.

They were coming into Scapa Flow now. West was the
knobbed elevation of Tor Ness, east the hilly sprawl of
South Ronaldsay. *Ark Royal* had already entered the anchorage, giving the American carrier the honor of coming in last
and being saluted by the British flagship.

Tombstone stood at the center of the bridge, behind the
pedestal supporting the alidade, a navigation instrument that
would help him determine when *Jefferson* had reached the
invisible point on the water where she was to drop anchor.
He had long since memorized the landmarks on shore—a
point of land off the port bow, a lighthouse to starboard—
from which he would take his bearings. Captain Brandt sat
in his leatherette bridge chair, apparently unconcerned.
Commander Parker stood behind the enlisted man at the
helm. The bridge was silent, except for the pounding of
Tombstone's heart. He'd worked a long time for this
moment, and there wasn't *really* any way that he could
screw it up.

He hoped.

Jefferson made her way slowly dead north into the
anchorage, her engines at two thirds ahead. As the carrier
came abeam of the *Ark Royal,* three quarters of a mile to
starboard, he gave the first order. "Render honors to
starboard."

"Aye, aye, sir," the signalman answered, then passed the
word through a telephone handset. Moments later, the bright
shrilling of a boatswain's pipe coming over the ship's 5-MC
could be heard through the gaping bridge windows. "Now
hear this! Now hear this! Present honors to starboard!"

Jefferson's crew—those not involved in the actual work
of running and anchoring the ship—manned the rail, standing at equally spaced intervals along the weather deck

railings facing the Royal Navy flagship. They wore dress whites and, from the bridge high above the flight deck, appeared to be little more than regimented dabs of white paint. The signal gun began banging out its salute, answered gun for gun by the *Ark Royal* across the water, in a ceremony already old on November 16, 1776, when the first salute had been rendered to the American flag.

As the shots continued to echo with stately pace, Tombstone bent over the alidade, pressing his eye against the instrument's rubber optic shield, aligning the cross hair with the lighthouse to starboard. He checked the bearing. Almost there . . .

"All engines, ahead one third."

"All engines, ahead one third, aye," the quartermaster at the bridge telegraph announced.

"Commence walking starboard anchor to water's edge."

Time passed. Tombstone tried to remain relaxed, to keep his fists from nervously flexing at his sides. Someone had once compared conning an aircraft carrier to steering Manhattan from a vantage point on the top floor of the Empire State Building.

"Forecastle reports anchor walked to water's edge, sir."

"Very well." Tombstone took another bearing, this time on the point of land. The target he was aiming for now lay three thousand yards ahead. The problem in anchoring a ship like the *Jefferson* was the vessel's sheer, mind-numbing size. One did not stop 96,000 tons on a dime.

"What's the depth?"

"Sixty-two feet, sir."

That put twenty-six feet beneath *Jefferson*'s keel, and the tides in the anchorage ran less than three feet. Good. It was a glorious, blue-skied morning with very little wind, for which Tombstone was profoundly grateful. Handling a steel mountain like *Jefferson* was hard enough without her making leeway in a stiff breeze.

Jefferson was slowing. He checked both referents again. So far, so good . . .

He glanced to starboard, beyond the *Ark Royal*. Some of the buildings of Scapa Flow's naval base gleamed in the sun. There were a number of eyes up there, no doubt; half of Britain's high command was probably on hand to watch *Jefferson*'s arrival.

Four hundred fifty yards to go. "All engines stop!"

"All stop, aye."

There was no apparent change. *Jefferson* continued to drift slowly ahead.

"All engines back, one third."

"All back, one third."

"All stop."

"All stop, aye!"

A long moment passed. It was impossible to be sure they were stopped. The nearest land was two miles away, and the surface of the water itself no sure indicator.

Captain Brandt slid off his chair and stooped to retrieve a canvas bag from a corner of the deck. Inside were several blocks of fresh-cut wood, scraps sent up that morning from the carpentry shop. He selected one, then turned to an open window on the starboard side. "You want this job, son," he said with a grin, "you need a damned good pitching arm!"

He hurled the chip into space. It fell a long, long way before landing on the water off the starboard side, far below the bridge. Elsewhere, *Jefferson*'s sailors, dismissed now from manning the rail, tossed chips of their own, until the water alongside the carrier was littered with drifting chunks of wood.

Tombstone joined the captain for a moment on the starboard wing of the bridge, watching the wood chips closely. It was a strange commentary on Navy technology, he thought, that a modern warship like the *Jefferson* used the same method as Columbus to determine whether or not the vessel had stopped completely. It created a sense of unity with the mariners who had sailed Earth's oceans since the time of Odysseus.

The chips showed no apparent motion, either forward or

back. "Looks like a dead stop, Captain," Tombstone said.

"If you say so, CAG. She's your ship."

"Yes, sir." The bastard's not going to give an inch on this, Tombstone thought. He turned to the talker. "Let go the starboard anchor!"

"Let go the starboard anchor, aye, sir!"

The thunder of the chain, the dull splash as thirty tons of Danforth anchor plunged into the water, sounded remote on the bridge. Sailors cheered forward, a heartening sound.

"Deck crew reports anchor up and down on the bottom, sir."

"Very well. All back, dead slow."

Ponderously, the carrier began backing down, digging in the anchor's flukes and laying out nearly five hundred feet of chain along the bottom link by massive link. With the anchor sunk in the mud of Scapa Flow and backed up by several tons of chain, the *Jefferson* was going nowhere while riding her hook.

"All stop," Tombstone ordered. "Pass stoppers!" The order directed the deck apes forward to lock down the chain. He checked his watch, then walked across the bridge to the ship's log, where he entered the time and the fact that *Jefferson* was safely anchored in Scapa Flow.

"An excellent job, CAG," the captain said behind him. "Couldn't have done it better myself."

Tombstone decided to bask in the warmth of what from Brandt was high praise indeed and ignore the weakness he felt in his knees.

"Now hear this, now hear this," the 5-MC blared from the deck. "Stand by to receive helo. That is, stand by to receive helo. Beware rotor blades."

Moving to port, Tombstone looked across the waters of Scapa Flow and saw the helicopter approaching the carrier. It was a Gazelle, probably a Royal Navy liaison aircraft. Slowly it passed over the edge of the deck, settling wheels to steel on one of the few areas of the deck undamaged by the battle. Deck crewmen darted from cover, heads stooped beneath the turning blades, and chocked the wheels.

Jefferson had seemed strangely naked and vulnerable during her painful crawl southwest from Norway, for most of her aircraft had remained ashore. Tombstone had ferried out to the carrier from Narvik aboard a Sea King, for there was no way to land anything other than helicopters on her deck. For a long time to come, *Jefferson* would be less than a fighting ship. Her main weapons, her aircraft, were gone.

At least, thank God, the war was really over. Soviet forces in Norway, Sweden, Finland, and Denmark were already surrendering en masse, as UN forces patrolled the streets of Moscow and the city—once again renamed, as it had been in '91—of St. Petersburg.

People descended from the Gazelle. Tombstone caught a glimpse of long, lovely legs in a skirt, a flash of blond hair. Hurriedly, he brought the binoculars hanging from his neck to his eyes.

Pamela.

And behind her . . .

"My God!"

Brandt laughed. "He was picked up by a Norwegian fishing trawler off Smøla, CAG. I just got the word this morning. Seems he's been hiding out in Bergen for the past three days! They flew him to Scapa Flow yesterday aboard a P-3 Orion."

Coyote, alive.

It was a miracle.

"But what are they *doing* here?"

"Well, as for Miss Drake, I gather she's been burning the wires between Bergen, London, and Washington, trying to find out if you were still alive. I guess Commander Grant decided to tag along when she wangled transport to come see you!"

Still not quite daring to believe, he turned to face Captain Brandt. "Uh . . . sir? Request permission to leave the bridge."

Brandt's face cracked with a wry grin. "Granted."

War forged new bonds. It also strengthened old ones. Tombstone turned and hurried from the bridge, anxious to meet his friends.

"Fasten your seatbelt! Carrier is a stimulating, fast-paced novel brimming with action and high drama."—Joe Weber, bestselling author of <u>DEFCON One</u> and <u>Storm Flight</u>

CARRIER

Keith Douglass

U.S. MARINES. PILOTS. NAVY SEALS. THE ULTIMATE MILITARY POWER PLAY.

In the bestselling tradition of Tom Clancy, Larry Bond, and Charles D. Taylor, this electrifying novel captures the vivid reality of international combat. The Carrier Battle Group Fourteen—a force including a supercarrier, amphibious unit, guided missile cruiser, and destroyer—is brought to life with stunning authenticity and action in a high-tech thriller as explosive as today's headlines.

__CARRIER   0-515-10593-7/$5.50
__CARRIER 2: VIPER STRIKE   0-515-10729-8/$5.99
__CARRIER 3: ARMAGEDDON MODE   0-515-10864-2/$4.99
__CARRIER 4: FLAME-OUT   0-515-10994-0/$5.99
__CARRIER 5: MAELSTROM   0-515-11080-9/$5.99
__CARRIER 6: COUNTDOWN   0-515-11309-3/$4.99

Payable in U.S. funds. No cash orders accepted. Postage & handling: $1.75 for one book, 75¢ for each additional. Maximum postage $5.50. Prices, postage and handling charges may change without notice. Visa, Amex, MasterCard call 1-800-788-6262, ext. 1, refer to ad # 384

Or, check above books   Bill my: ☐ Visa ☐ MasterCard ☐ Amex
and send this order form to: (expires)
The Berkley Publishing Group   Card#_____
390 Murray Hill Pkwy., Dept. B   ($15 minimum)
East Rutherford, NJ 07073   Signature_____
Please allow 6 weeks for delivery.   Or enclosed is my: ☐ check   ☐ money order

Name_____   Book Total $_____
Address_____   Postage & Handling $_____
City_____   Applicable Sales Tax $_____
                                     (NY, NJ, PA, CA, GST Can.)
State/ZIP_____   Total Amount Due $_____

"Berent is the real thing!"–Tom Clancy

Nationwide Bestselling Novels by

Mark Berent

Three-tour veteran of Vietnam, author Mark Berent has won the Silver Star and two distinguished Flying Crosses

__STORM FLIGHT 0-515-11432-4/$5.99

"Terrifying action and heroism."–Kirkus Reviews

In the fifth and final volume of this saga, a daring raid on a POW camp ignites a chain reaction that forces Berent's men to examine their own strengths, abilities, and courage....

__EAGLE STATION 0-515-11208-9/$5.99

"Berent is without peer in the battle zone!"–Publishers Weekly

The war brought them together. Brothers in combat who fought, flew, and survived the Tet Offensive of 1968. The bravest and the best— even in the worst of times. Now they face their greatest challenge...

Don't miss any of Mark Berent's exhilirating novels

__PHANTOM LEADER 0-515-10785-9/$5.99

"Berent's ability to put the reader inside the fighter pilot's head is simply breathtaking."–The Washington Post

__STEEL TIGER 0-515-10467-1/$5.99

"Berent knows his planes and men and battle." –W.E.B. Griffin

__ROLLING THUNDER 0-515-10190-7/$5.99

"Hits like a thunderclap."–W.E.B. Griffin

Payable in U.S. funds. No cash orders accepted. Postage & handling: $1.75 for one book, 75¢ for each additional. Maximum postage $5.50. Prices, postage and handling charges may change without notice. Visa, Amex, MasterCard call 1-800-788-6262, ext. 1, refer to ad # 408

Or, check above books   Bill my: ☐ Visa ☐ MasterCard ☐ Amex

and send this order form to: (expires)

The Berkley Publishing Group   Card#_____

390 Murray Hill Pkwy., Dept. B

East Rutherford, NJ 07073   Signature_____ ($15 minimum)

Please allow 6 weeks for delivery.   Or enclosed is my: ☐ check ☐ money order

Name_____   Book Total $_____

Address_____   Postage & Handling $_____

City_____   Applicable Sales Tax $_____
(NY, NJ, PA, CA, GST Can.)

State/ZIP_____   Total Amount Due $_____

NEW YORK TIMES BESTSELLING AUTHOR OF
TARGETS OF OPPORTUNITY

JOE WEBER

__HONORABLE ENEMIES 0-515-11522-3/$5.99

World War II was a distant memory–until someone bombed Pearl Harbor. Now CIA Agent Steve Wickham and FBI Agent Susan Nakamura must search out the attacker before U.S./Japanese relations disintegrate and history repeats itself–at war.

__DEFCON ONE 0-515-10419-1/$5.99

Glasnost has failed. Near economic collapse, Russia readies to begin World War III. One CIA operative trapped in the Kremlin alone knows Russia's horrific plan–only he can stop a full-scale holocaust.

__SHADOW FLIGHT 0-515-10660-7/$5.95

The search of an American B-2 Stealth bomber that "disappeared" from Edwards Air Force Base leads CIA Agent Steve Wickham to Cuba. His orders from the president are clear: recover the B-2 or destroy it–before the situation leads to war.

__RULES OF ENGAGEMENT 0-515-10990-8/$5.99

In a war dividing America, marine fighter pilot Brad Austin was caught in government red tape and trapped in a one-on-one air battle with a top Vietnamese fighter pilot. Then Austin decided to break the rules. . . .

__TARGETS OF OPPORTUNITY 0-515-11246-1/$5.99

The CIA has captured a Soviet-built MiG-17. Brad Austin is recruited as the pilot and given a new Russian identity. His mission–to take the MiG deep behind enemy lines and gun down North Vietnam's top pilots. If he wins, America wins. If he loses, he dies alone.

Payable in U.S. funds. No cash orders accepted. Postage & handling: $1.75 for one book, 75¢ for each additional. Maximum postage $5.50. Prices, postage and handling charges may change without notice. Visa, Amex, MasterCard call 1-800-788-6262, ext. 1, refer to ad # 428

Or, check above books and send this order form to: The Berkley Publishing Group 390 Murray Hill Pkwy., Dept. B East Rutherford, NJ 07073 Please allow 6 weeks for delivery.	Bill my: ☐ Visa ☐ MasterCard ☐ Amex _____ (expires) Card#_____ ($15 minimum) Signature_____ Or enclosed is my: ☐ check ☐ money order
Name_____	Book Total $_____
Address_____	Postage & Handling $_____
City_____	Applicable Sales Tax $_____ (NY, NJ, PA, CA, GST Can.)
State/ZIP_____	Total Amount Due $_____

THE <u>NEW YORK TIMES</u> BESTSELLING SERIES!

THE CORPS
W.E.B. Griffin

Author of the bestselling <u>Brotherhood of War</u> series.

Spanning the decades from the 1930's right up to their most recent stints as peacekeepers of the world, THE CORPS chronicles the toughest, most determined branch of the United States armed forces—the Marines. In the same gripping style that has made the Brotherhood of War series so powerful, THE CORPS digs deep into the hearts and souls of the tough-as-nails men who are America's greatest fighting force.

___I: SEMPER FI 0-515-08749-1/$6.99

___II: CALL TO ARMS 0-515-09349-1/$6.99

___III: COUNTERATTACK 0-515-10417-5/$6.99

___IV: BATTLEGROUND 0-515-10640-2/$6.99

___V: LINE OF FIRE 0-515-11013-2/$6.99

___VI: CLOSE COMBAT 0-515-11269-0/$6.99

Payable in U.S. funds. No cash orders accepted. Postage & handling: $1.75 for one book, 75¢ for each additional. Maximum postage $5.50. Prices, postage and handling charges may change without notice. Visa, Amex, MasterCard call 1-800-788-6262, ext. 1, refer to ad # 269a

Or, check above books
and send this order form to:
The Berkley Publishing Group
390 Murray Hill Pkwy., Dept. B
East Rutherford, NJ 07073
Please allow 6 weeks for delivery.

Bill my: ☐ Visa ☐ MasterCard ☐ Amex _____ (expires)

Card#_____
($15 minimum)

Signature_____

Or enclosed is my: ☐ check ☐ money order

Name_____

Address_____

City_____

State/ZIP_____

Book Total $_____

Postage & Handling $_____

Applicable Sales Tax $_____
(NY, NJ, PA, CA, GST Can.)

Total Amount Due $_____